SO-AHL-616

FALCONER'S LAW

by

Jason Manning

A SIGNET BOOK

SIGNET
Published by the Penguin Group
Penguin Books USA Inc., 375 Hudson Street,
New York, New York 10014, U.S.A.
Penguin Books Ltd, 27 Wrights Lane,
London W8 5TZ, England
Penguin Books Australia Ltd, Ringwood,
Victoria, Australia
Penguin Books Canada Ltd, 10 Alcorn Avenue,
Toronto, Ontario, Canada M4V 3B2
Penguin Books (N.Z.) Ltd, 182–190 Wairau Road,
Auckland 10, New Zealand

Penguin Books Ltd, Registered Offices:
Harmondsworth, Middlesex, England

First published by Signet, an imprint of Dutton Signet,
a division of Penguin Books USA Inc.

First Printing, February, 1996
10 9 8 7 6 5 4 3 2 1

Copyright © Jason Manning, 1996
All rights reserved

 REGISTERED TRADEMARK—MARCA REGISTRADA

Printed in the United States of America

Without limiting the rights under copyright reserved above, no part of this publication may be reproduced, stored in or introduced into a retrieval system, or transmitted, in any form, or by any means (electronic, mechanical, photocopying, recording, or otherwise), without the prior written permission of both the copyright owner and the above publisher of this book.

BOOKS ARE AVAILABLE AT QUANTITY DISCOUNTS WHEN USED TO PROMOTE PRODUCTS OR SERVICES. FOR INFORMATION PLEASE WRITE TO PREMIUM MARKETING DIVISION, PENGUIN BOOKS USA INC., 375 HUDSON STREET, NEW YORK, NEW YORK 10014.

If you purchased this book without a cover you should be aware that this book is stolen property. It was reported as "unsold and destroyed" to the publisher and neither the author nor the publisher has received any payment for this "stripped book."

To
My son, Connor—
this novel, and all else I do,
is done for you

Chapter 1

He came down from the mountains, from the wild granite crags of the high lonesome with their shoulders cloaked in deep virgin snow, where the eagle soared and the grizzly roamed, and where he ruled like a king in splendid isolation. The solitude of the wild, raw reaches at the timberline was his solace, and seldom in recent years had he strayed down into the valleys that the summer splashed with the rainbow colors of wildflowers, where the creeks, fat and sassy with snowmelt, pranced and plunged down their rocky courses. So seldom, in fact, had he come down from the rugged realm that among his peers, the mountain men, speculation on the subject of whether he was still "above snakes" had become a prevalent topic of conversation around the cookfires.

Eben Nall was the first white man to lay eyes on him in three years—a distinction of which Eben was blissfully ignorant, as he sat with his back to a lodgepole pine, feet warming near a smokeless fire, striving to put into words in his journal his feelings as he stood one day shy of experiencing his very first rendezvous. He was excited, but it was a bittersweet anticipation, because Eben feared that this rendezvous might well be the last of its kind. The fur trade was on the decline. The days of the mountain man were numbered. Eben was sorry he had missed so much of a unique era.

This was Eben Nall's first season as a free trapper. He found the life much to his liking, as he had known, somehow, that he would on the very day he left the family store near Kaskaskia and headed west in the company of his brother, Silas, fleeing the drudgery of life as a dry goods clerk. West they went, across the mighty Mississippi, across the trackless plains, to the Shining Mountains, which had haunted Eben's every waking hour and indeed even his dreams since his uncle had returned from participation in the famed Ashley expedition of '25 to regale his nephews with tales of high adventure on the frontier. Uncle John's topknot now dangled from a Blackfoot scalp pole, but this had failed to dampen Eben's ardor for the wild, free life of the mountain man. Still, he could not shake the feeling that he was too late. One season of poor trapping in the year 1837—could it really be over so soon?

This gloomy thought distracted him from his journal, and when he looked up to cast a morose gaze across the valley to the majestic peaks of the Wind River Range, he saw the lone rider, leading a heavy-laden packhorse, emerge from the stand of white-stemmed aspen across the way. It was only natural for Eben to sit up and take sharp notice. Rarely in the high country did one come across another human being.

"Rube?"

His partner, Rube Holly, was cleaning his rifle, sitting cross-legged on the other side of the fire, with his back to the valley. Rube's squaw, the Nez Perce woman called Luck, was frying up some beavertail in bear grease. That was Rube's favorite dish. Luck was Rube's favorite pastime. When first Eben had laid eyes on Luck he had judged her to be singularly unattractive, with a short stocky build and coarse features, but Rube thought highly of her, and after eight months alone in the wilderness without seeing another living soul, Eben thought she was looking a little less ugly. It was nice having her around; in addition to being a passable cook she was adept at cleaning plews. Of course, Rube liked having her around for something else. Scarcely a night passed that the two of them didn't play around under their buffalo robes. At first their amorous activities had embarrassed Eben, but he had gradually grown accustomed to it. A lot of things that once upon a time had bothered Eben Nall didn't anymore—things like being cold and wet and hungry and falling-down tired and risking life and limb just to collect the pelt of a rather large rodent.

"What is it, lad?" Rube didn't look at Eben—his attention was drawn to Luck, who was bending over the cookfire, and a boyish grin split his bearded, weathered face.

"Rider comin'."

That got Rube Holly's attention. He peeled his gaze off Luck's prodigious derriere and swept it over the valley, locking in on the horseman, whose shaggy dun mountain mustang was plodding through sodden marsh grass browned by the summer sun.

"It's not an Injun," said Eben. Then, deciding that perhaps he was being far too unequivocal for a tyro with just a single season under his belt, he added, "Is it?"

"Hell, no, it ain't no Injun," rasped Rube, whose voice, even on the best of days, sounded like an overworked and rusty gate hinge. "By thunder! It cain't be!"

Eben figured Rube had seen sixty winters if he'd seen a day. Rube himself wasn't exactly sure how old he was. But he was a graybeard, that much was certain. Older than dirt. Plagued by rheumatism and slightly stooped, he tended to walk with a jerky hitch. Nonetheless he could be as spry as a younker when the occasion required—under the blankets with his Nez Perce squaw, or in a scrape with hostiles. Now, to Eben's surprise, he bounced to his feet, stared a bit more at the distant rider, then danced a nimble little jig, his beaded moccasins scuffing up the pine needle carpet.

"Hot diggity!" he exclaimed to the mountaintops. "I told 'em he warn't dead. No, not that one!"

Eben could scarcely believe Rube was really able to identify the rider at such a great distance— a feat made more remarkable by the fact that Rube had only one good eye. The other was made of glass. Sometimes Rube used that glass eye to good effect, plucking it out for the purpose of spooking Indians, who were susceptible to being spooked by such things. Among the Indians, Rube's glass eye was big medicine, but it was of no use to him when it came to seeing. Yet Rube Holly could see things with one eye that Eben consistently overlooked with two.

"Who is it?" asked Eben.

"Why, that's none other than Hugh Falconer, boy, or I'll eat my hat."

"Falconer!"

Of course Eben knew the name. Mountain men were a rare breed, but even so there were a handful who ranked a cut above the rest. Colter, Bridger, Old Man Williams, Jedediah Smith, Beckwourth, Walker. And Hugh Falconer. A catalog of the legends of the fur trade would be incomplete without Falconer.

Eben had heard of Falconer even before he had taken one step west of the Father of the Waters, and now he tried to remember all the stories about this living legend that had reached his young and impressionable ears.

No one knew for certain where Hugh Falconer had come from originally—Falconer himself had never seen fit to enlighten a single soul on that particular point. Truth be known, Falconer never said much about anything. If he strung two words together he felt as though he had been speechifying like a damn fool politician. Perhaps the most widely accepted rumor on the subject of his origins was that he was the black sheep of Scottish nobility, forced to seek his fortune in America. If he spoke at all, they said, it was with the hint of a Highland brogue.

Whatever his roots, Falconer had been blessed with those attributes most essential to a mountain man's success. He was such a splendid marksman that critters just gave up the ghost and fell down dead when they saw him aim his rifle at them. This saved Falconer a great deal in the way of powder and shot—precious commodities singularly hard to come by in the high country. The only real shooting he had to do anymore was on the occasions that he ran afoul of hostile Indians— which didn't happen all that often, since most Indians had the good sense to keep their distance, as it was said that there was one dead red man for every bullet Falconer had fired in anger.

Not to say that Hugh Falconer was an inveterate Indian killer, like Liver-Eating Johnson. No, Falconer got along passably well with most tribes, except the Blackfeet, who made a virtue of not getting along with anybody. He respected the Indians and their ways. With Falconer it was live and let live. Long as you left him alone, you would prosper. But if you muddied up his water you'd live just long enough to regret your rash behavior. It was better, folks said, to die and shake hands with the devil in hell than to be on Falconer's bad side. When Falconer got mad he was worse than a wildcat after a turpentine bath.

Ever since coming to the mountains Falconer had been a loner, a free trapper who shunned ties with any of the fur companies. In the old days he would show up once a year, at summer rendezvous, to trade in his furs for a mountain man's necessities: powder and shot, tobacco, sugar, coffee, and a few books if any were attainable. That was one of the peculiar things about Hugh Falconer—unlike many of his peers, he was well-read, an educated cuss who could quote the Bible or the Bard at the drop of a hat. He always brought in packs of fine plews, and it was said that he seldom had to bother with steel traps. No, he just shot the beavers in one eye at such an angle that the bullet exited through the other eye, killing the critter outright while avoiding any damage to the plew.

But Falconer had failed to appear at the two most recent rendezvous, and so the speculation had begun, with everyone wondering what had befallen him, puzzling over it, since Falconer was about as indestructible as a mortal man could hope to be. Had Injuns done him in? No, Falconer was too wise in wilderness ways for that. Maybe a grizzly? No, Falconer wrestled grizzlies with his bare hands just to get some morning exercise. Maybe he'd packed his possibles and made tracks for greener pastures, though it was hard to believe that Hugh Falconer would turn his back on the mountains he knew so well and loved so ardently.

"We got any coffee left, lad?" asked Rube Holly.

"A little."

"Best give it to Luck to brew up. We want to be good hosts."

Journal forgotten, Eben did as he was told, then

rejoined Rube at the edge of the camp to monitor
Falconer's progress across the valley.

"Reckon we ought to let him know we're here?"
asked Eben.

Rube spared him a smirky look. "Boy, he knows
damn well we're here."

Eben couldn't see how that could be. Their
camp was well hidden in the trees, the campfire
produced no smoke, and they were downwind of
Falconer's position in the valley. This was both
the time and the place for caution—they had
crossed the sign of several Blackfoot war parties
the past few weeks.

Turned out, though, that Rube Holly was right.
In a quarter of an hour Falconer was coming up
the slope through the pines. Years later, Eben Nall
would think back to that moment when Hugh Falconer arrived in camp as the beginning of the
most extraordinary adventure of his life.

Chapter 2

July 3, 1837. Late yesterday Hugh Falconer arrived at our camp on a shaggy mustang and I do not know which looked wilder, the man or the horse. I had never seen a horse that looked vicious, but this one did. When I ventured too close it tried to bite the side of my face off. Falconer warned me to stay well clear of the animal unless I was weary of this life and ready to throw off the mortal coil. It was not a threat, but rather friendly advice. Apparently Falconer is the only human being the creature will tolerate.

I find it difficult to describe Hugh Falconer. He is a powerfully built man, standing six feet six in his moccasins, with a tawny beard and dark brown eyes that seem to pierce to the very core of the unfortunate soul impaled upon his gaze. He speaks softly and sparingly, and I do think I detect a faint brogue. Surprisingly for a man of his size, he moves with the grace of a panther. What is difficult to put into words is the aura that surrounds the man. He strikes me as someone who belongs to this country as no one else does, as though the mountains made

him in their own image. He belongs in the same
way that the grizzly belongs, and he would
seem completely out of place in any other environment. He is a man not so much in the wilderness as *of* it, as integral a part of it as
lightning is of a thunderstorm . . .

"We've danged near trapped out the beaver,"
Rube lamented as they sat around the campfire
with their backs to the quick-fallen night, supping
on beavertail and coffee. "It's gettin' harder 'n'
harder to find the brown gold, Hugh. I hate to say
it like the devil hates holy water, but by thunder I
think these shinin' times are just about thrown
cold."

Falconer, drinking coffee, offered a noncommit-
tal grunt by way of response. In the dancing yellow light of the fire his features seemed to Eben
Nall as though they had been carved out of the
hard granite crags of the Wind River Range
whence he had come. He wore fringed buckskin
leggins, and red leg gaiters held up "half breeds"
below the knees. Beneath his fringed coat was a
muslin shirt, once white, now gray with wood-
smoke and sweat stain. Shoulder bands of colorful
quillwork on the coat appeared to be of Shoshone
origin. There was quillwork on his possibles bag
as well. Rube had asked Falconer how Touches
the Moon was faring, and Falconer had answered,
"She's dead." Those two words were the sum
total of Falconer's offering on the subject. Eben
wondered if Touches the Moon had been the
source of that splendid quillwork.

Hugh Falconer's weapons consisted of a Green
River knife and a Sam Hawken Percussion .41 pis-
tol in his leather belt, as well as the .50 caliber
Hawken mountain rifle. Eben admired the latter

immensely. It put his old Harpers Ferry flintlock to shame for looks, not to mention reliability and range. Lucky indeed was the mountain man who possessed a Hawken. The Hawken brothers, in their St. Louis gun shop, could not manufacture enough of their famous product to even come close to satisfying demand. The Hawken could drop a bull buffalo in its tracks. Its accuracy at long range and its sturdiness were legendary.

As headgear Falconer wore a wolfskin cap, with the animal's head preserved and displayed in the front, like a visor, and riding low over Falconer's eyes. His beard was full, his light brown hair long to the shoulders, so it was hard to tell about his features. He appeared to be in his mid-thirties. Eben Nall had expected a much older man, considering all the things he was reputed to have done.

"Just about the only prime beaver left that I know of is up smack-dab in the middle of Blackfoot country," continued Rube. "Iffen I was alone, why, I'd risk it. But I got Luck and now this younker to think about."

"You ought not to let me being along stop you," said Eben. He didn't like to think that Rube Holly, or anyone else, for that matter, was mollycoddling him on account of his age or inexperience. "I can take care of myself. And I'm not afraid of any Blackfeet."

Rube grinned at him. "He don't know enough to be skeered of the Blackfoot, Hugh, but he's game."

"I see," said Falconer, with a glance at Eben so intense it made the young man uncomfortable.

"I just don't want anyone to think of me as a burden," muttered Eben. "That's all I mean."

"Yep, he's game, sure nuff," repeated Rube. "And it's good to have a younker along. My ol' bones don't take to wadin' around in them ice cold criks settin' traps and such. When he's a little more seasoned he'll do to ride the river with. Only wish he wouldn't keep his nose stuck in that diary of his so much. Some Injun's gonna sneak up on him one day and lift his hair iffen he ain't keerful."

"Diary?" said Falconer, an eyebrow raised.

Eben blushed furiously. "It's a journal." Only girls kept diaries. "I'm keeping a written record of my adventures on the frontier." Eben realized belatedly that Rube Holly was engaged in a little good-natured ribbing at his expense.

"I get to wonderin' sometimes what he puts in there about yours truly," said Rube. "But he won't let me read it."

"Sometimes a journal is a very private matter," said Falconer. "Especially when there's no one around to share your innermost thoughts. Besides, since when could you read a lick, Rube?"

Rube laughed. "True words, Hugh. True goddamn words."

Falconer brandished a clay pipe and proceeded to pack it with kinnickinnick, but Rube offered him a few pinches of honest-to-God tobacco. Falconer gratefully accepted. Eben figured Rube had to hold Falconer in mighty high esteem to share the last of his honeydew tobacco with the man. Rube prepared his own pipe and they fired the bowls with a brand extracted from the fire.

"Are your steps bent for the Green River, Hugh?" asked Rube. The Green River was the site of this year's rendezvous, as it had been the year before.

Falconer nodded. "I've got a few plews to sell."

Eben's gaze strayed to the packs that Falconer had removed from the sawbuck saddle strapped to the back of his second horse, and against which the mountain man was now leaning, and he wondered if those beaver really had been shot through the eyes.

"We fetched six dollars for a prime plew two years ago," said Rube, "and four last year. If they bring three this year I'll consider myself one lucky cuss. Hellfire, Hugh, 'fore long we'll have to pay just to get shed of the fur."

"They were shinin' times, Rube," said Falconer. "But you're right. They're about over now."

Rube stared morosely into the fire for a moment, puffing furiously on his pipe, and Eben thought that maybe he had been hoping against hope that Falconer would have some news that might contradict the notion that the fur trade was on its last legs.

"'Member that scrape we had with them Bloods down on the Stinking Water, Hugh?" asked the old-timer suddenly.

"I recollect."

Rube glanced over at Eben. "Reckon mebbe I done told you about it already. If so, stop me. I was trappin' with a few of the Rocky Mountain Fur Company boys, back in '32 it was. There was Bob Thompson and that pork eater name of Surrett and a couple others. That was the year the Blackfeet were really on their hind legs, and we was keepin' our eyes skinned, but a war party Injuned-up on us anyhow, and we was in a bad enough fix, our backsides to a river too deep to cross. The Injuns tried to rush us, but we shot 'em to hell, though Thompson got thrown cold in the process. Then them red varmints got smarts and set fire to the grass. The wind was just right for 'em, and that fire was comin' straight for us. I'll tell you, Eben, this child thought he was gone beaver for sure.

"But then ol' Hugh here shows up. He cuts a dead Injun pony open from stem to stern, puts a rope on the carcass, and rides a circle around our stronghold, draggin' the dead horse, which made as fine a firebreak as yore ever likely to see. Two Injuns tried to jump him, but he shot one through the heart and put his knife into the other right up to the 'Green River.' "

A year ago Eben would not have understood half of what Rube had said, but now he knew that "up to the 'Green River' " meant thrusting a knife into someone to the hilt, where the words "Green River" were stamped into the blade by the manufacturer of the most popular knife among mountain men. He knew, too, that "thrown cold" meant killed, that a Blackfoot on his hind legs was one on a rampage, and that a "pork eater" referred to a French trapper.

"That knocked the fight right out of them red rascals," continued Rube, "and we saw their tail feathers then. Yep, ol' Hugh saved our bacon that day, and that's the gospel truth. Don't never let nobody tell you otherwise."

"I just happened along," said Falconer, "and had nothing better to do."

Rube laughed, but his merriment was short-lived, as he resumed his moody contemplation of the imminent demise of a way of life he purely loved. He went back to staring into the dancing flames of the cookfire, and Eben could have sworn his one good eye was misting up.

"What are we gonna do with ourselves, Hugh?" asked Rube. "Mebbe I'll take to scoutin' for the army. They'll be along, you know, them yellowlegs. Settlers are movin' west, and the army will have to protect 'em from the Injuns. I hate to think of it, hoss, but one day that valley yonder'll have a town smack in the middle of it, full of noise and stink, and there'll be roads and cornfields and lumber mills and such. When that happens these mountains won't be a fit place to live."

"Nothing lasts," muttered Falconer, and somehow Eben knew he was thinking about the squaw named Touches the Moon when he said it.

"What about you?" Rube asked Falconer. "What are yore plans?"

"I'm thinking I want to see California."

"California! By thunder, Hugh, there ain't no good way to even get to California from here. There's the tallest mountains, the hottest deserts, and the meanest damned Injuns betwixt you and California. An even iffen you get there, them Spaniards will like as not clean yore plow."

"It's not Spanish anymore, Rube. Part of the Republic of Mexico now."

"Makes no difference."

"Still," said Falconer, "I'm giving some thought to going."

"Alone?"

"No. I'll want twenty or thirty good men, I reckon. Maybe I'll find some volunteers at rendezvous."

Eben Nall's heart skipped a beat, for as he spoke of volunteers Falconer's dark gaze scanned the young man's face.

"I'll go," blurted Eben. Rube gaped at him, and Eben hastily added, "Of course, I'll stick to my end of our bargain, Rube. You know that. I'm with you until we trade our plews."

"No offense, boy, but you're still wet behind the ears. Hugh said he wanted . . ."

"I know what he said." Eben did not want to hear Rube imply that he did not meet Falconer's qualifications for "a good man." He met Falconer's unfathomable gaze. "I'll go, if you'll have me, Mr. Falconer."

"We'll see." Falconer put out his pipe, unrolled his blanket, and stretched out his long frame. In a moment he was asleep, embracing the Hawken mountain rifle as though it were his lover.

"You're a damned fool, boy," whispered Rube.

"Maybe so. What about you, Rube? Will you go along?"

"Sounds like too much adventure for an old coon like me. Reckon me and Luck'll stay home. Now I'm gonna get some shut-eye. You take the first watch."

Eben tried to stay alert and pay attention to the night around him, but fanciful images of golden California persistently distracted him. Huddled in his woolen Point blanket by the dying campfire, he thought of wine as red and potent as the lips of beautiful Mexican women whose cinnamon skin was as soft and warm as the California sun . . .

Rube relieved him a few hours later, and Eben tried to sleep, but California dreams kept him awake until almost dawn. Many were the tales he had heard of California, but it had always seemed as far away, as unattainable, as the Orient.

Finally he dozed off, awakening in time to hear Rube Holly say, "Keep yore powder dry, Hugh," and he rose from his blankets as Falconer rode out of camp on his wild-eyed shaggy mustang, leading the sturdy packhorse.

"Why isn't he riding with us if he's going to rendezvous, same as us?" Eben asked.

"He didn't tell me and I didn't ask."

"Did he say anything else about . . . about California?"

"He said he thought it'd be right fine to have you ride along. Which goes to show he ain't half as smart as I gave him credit for."

Rube Holly was joshing, of course. Eben could see that. He saw something else, and it surprised him—Rube was looking at him as proudly as a father would at his son.

Chapter 3

July 4, 1837. Rendezvous! There never has been anything like it, and when it is gone for good there never will be again. Rube, Luck, and I arrived in the afternoon of Independence Day, but the trappers and traders who congregate here do not need an excuse to celebrate. Most of them have spent the year in solitude, or nearly so, and in a dangerous occupation besides. Now, for three weeks, they cut loose and howl. Rube, however, informs me that this fur fair is not at all like previous ones—it is subdued as a church social by comparison. There are fewer trappers with fewer plews to trade. And he was right about the price of fur. It has gone down to three dollars, and that for a prime plew.

A missionary, Dr. Gray, has arrived, on his way to the country of the Flatheads, and accompanying him are four white women, who are also missionaries. They cause quite a stir, as most of these men have not seen a white woman in a month of Sundays. Also present is Sir William Drummond Stuart. He fought at the Battle of Waterloo, serving as an officer in the renowned Horse Guards, and has brought along his helmet and cuirass, which, he says, will protect him from Indian arrows. Little does he know that every Indian in this country will be hankering after that armor, which makes him something of a marked man. He has also brought with him fine wines and brandy, hams and preserved meats, countless other delicacies, as well as a complete silver service. However, the others do not begrudge him these fineries, as he is the soul of generosity when it comes to sharing his bounty—everything except the silver service.

Traveling with Sir William is Alfred Miller, a very talented artist. I am impressed by his watercolor sketches. He seems to dash them off so effortlessly. I especially like the one of Joe Meek, clad in Sir William's armor, parading around camp in a futile attempt to impress the lady missionaries. There is another I like very much, of Jim Bridger, mounted on his horse, on high ground looking down at this rendezvous on the banks of the Green River.

Tonight the Delawares and the Shawnees performed a great war dance for the entertainment of Dr. Gray and the ladies. Some of the mountain men joined in, and much fun was had by all, except perhaps by Dr. Gray, who seemed taken aback by the savage fervor of the scene . . .

The skin lodges of the trappers and Indians extended for a mile along the banks of the river in the vicinity of Horse Creek, on the rim of a wide, grassy plain hemmed in by the forested foothills of the great gray granite peaks. Despite Rube Holly's glum observation that this rendezvous compared poorly to previous fur fairs, Eben Nall was impressed by the gathering. He calculated there were about two hundred mountain men and at least that many friendly Indians present.

Of the latter, the Flatheads, Snakes, Nez Perces, and Shoshones were represented, in addition to the Delawares and the Shawnees. The last two tribes had once been great nations in the eastern forests, and the Shawnees had proved worthy foes as they fought the whites for a quarter of a century to keep their homeland in what was now the states of Ohio and Kentucky. Their lands lost, their tribe decimated by war and epidemic, a handful of Shawnee men had wandered west to ply the trapper's trade. Like the Delawares, they had become dependable allies of the white man.

The first priority upon arrival at rendezvous was trading plews for possibles. The traders had brought their wagonloads of goods across the plains from St. Louis. "Mountain prices" were exorbitant, but few complained. The journey west was a hazardous one for the trader; he faced ruin if he lost his load to disaster, natural or otherwise. A pint of coffee beans cost two dollars, as did a pint of sugar. A plug of chewing tobacco ran two dollars as well, while a pint of alcohol was priced at four dollars. Other commodities included guns, powder and shot, traps, blankets, pots and pans, knives, flint, and cheap trinkets for the squaws. The trapper paid for what he needed with the "hairy bank notes" he had spent arduous months harvesting from the mountain ponds.

Eben wanted to replace his old Harpers Ferry flintlock with a better weapon. Last winter the stock had been shattered, and though it was mended passably well with a rawhide wrap, put on wet to shrink tight as it dried, Eben figured he would need a more reliable gun if he was going to join Hugh Falconer on the great California adventure. A Hawken Percussion was not available, so he settled for a Kentucky rifle, a Lancaster. He did not come out too badly on the deal, as he managed to trade the Harpers Ferry, along with powder and shot and a Nor'west blanket, to a Flathead Indian in exchange for an Appaloosa mare—steelcast gray with four white stockings and black spots on a white rump.

Proud of himself, Eben showed the horse to Rube, who checked the animal over and pronounced it sound.

"Ordinarily," said Rube, "I'd say you got yoreself a real bargain, lad. But that Injun wouldn't never have traded this mare lessen he figured on either stealin' it or winnin' it back."

A short time later the Flathead found Eben and, using broken English, challenged him to a horse race. Eben wasn't interested, but the Flathead insisted.

"Won't do to turn him down," remarked Rube.

Eben didn't much like his chances of winning a horse race. He was no master equestrian, not by a long shot. But he realized Rube Holly was right. If he backed down from the Indian's challenge, the whole camp would know by nightfall that he lacked backbone. Eben agreed to the contest. The winner would take the loser's horse. The Flathead gloated as he went away. Clearly he expected the Appaloosa mare to be back in his possession before very long.

The word was soon out—there would be a horse race. A day would not go by at rendezvous without at least one, and there was no shortage of trappers eager to make a wager. Rube Holly took a stroll and came back an hour later to inform Eben that the white trappers were betting on him almost to the man. Eben was aghast at the news.

"Rube, they shouldn't," he moaned. "I'm going to lose."

Rube Holly frowned. "You arter not talk that way, boy."

"You know I don't stand a chance. I'm not half the horseman that Indian is."

"You cain't never tell what might happen," said Rube, and he moved on to help Luck with the lean-to she was erecting.

Eben tried to walk off his misery, but whimsical fate bent his steps to the river's edge, where some Nez Perces were putting on an exhibition of horsemanship. They thundered hither and yon at full gallop, one standing on the back of his pony, another leaning over precariously to snatch a jug of whiskey placed on the ground. Two riding side by side switched horses several times in a hundred yards. The crowd congregated to watch this spectacle roared approval with each daring exploit. What made matters worse, from Eben's point of view, was the knowledge that the Nez Perces were likkered up. They were all so drunk they could scarcely stand on their own two feet, but they could still ride like the devil. Eben resigned himself to losing the gray Appaloosa. These people were born to ride—in his youth all he had ever ridden was a store counter.

"Eben!"

He turned to see his brother, Silas, pushing through the crowd.

"Silas!" They hugged each other, then held one another at arm's length.

"You've still got your hair!" laughed Silas.

"You sound surprised."

"I am. I figured the Injuns would make short work of you, brother."

"I can take care of myself," said Eben resentfully.

Silas threw back his head and laughed again.

They were brothers, but different as right from wrong. Both were slim and wiry, of medium height, but Silas was towheaded and devilishly handsome, while Eben's hair was a dull brown and his features rather plain. Folks who knew swore Silas Nall got his looks from his mother, who was pretty and vivacious and clever, while Eben closely resembled his father, the moody, stolid Elijah. Where Eben was reserved, Silas was outgoing. Caution was Eben's long suit, while Silas was the impulsive ne'er-do-well. As a child Silas had always had a knack for getting into trouble—and a knack for wiggling out from under it later. Eben envied him, because heads turned when Silas Nall came into view, while hardly anyone ever noticed his brother.

Coming west together, they had gone their separate ways the previous fall. Eben partnered up with Rube Holly, a free trapper, while Silas signed on with a brigade affiliated with the American Fur Company—a brigade bound for beaver country perilously close to Blackfoot territory. Eben, of course, had decided to play it safe with Rube, whose goal first and foremost was staying alive.

"Did you have Indian trouble, Silas?"

"It was the Injuns had the trouble. See?"

For the first time Eben noticed the pair of scalplocks dangling from his brother's belt.

"My God!" he exclaimed. "Why on earth do you *wear* them?"

"Why shouldn't I? I earned them. That's a pair of red heathens who learned the hard way not to mess with Silas Nall. I reckon I'm an honest-to-God mountain man now, huh?"

"If it takes killing an Indian to become a mountain man, I guess so."

"Don't talk down that long nose of yours like Pa

always done, little brother. Now listen. I hear you're in a horse race with a Flathead named Sixkiller."

"Sixkiller? Is that his name?"

"Yep. They say he's meaner than hell with the hide off. Now, all the trappers are betting on you, Eben. They're fools, 'cause they can't bring themselves to admit that a red savage can best a white man at anything."

"What do you mean, they're fools?"

"I mean you're bound to lose."

Eben knew it was so. Still, he couldn't help but be offended.

"Me, I'm betting my whole poke on Sixkiller," said Silas, pitching his voice low in a conspirator's whisper.

"Thanks a lot," said Eben dryly.

"Hell, don't get your hackles up, Eben. I'll cut you in. All you got to do is make sure you lose. Just in case, by some miracle, you get the upper hand."

"I can't do that."

"Why the hell not?"

"A lot of these men stand to lose big if I don't win."

"Who cares about them?"

"I've got to at least try. They're counting on me."

"I'm your brother, Eben. What about me?"

Adamant, Eben shook his head. "I won't do it, Silas. I can't."

Naked malice twisted Silas Nall's features—but only for an instant. His expression smoothed out, and he forced an oily smile.

"It doesn't matter anyway," he drawled. "You're going to lose. You always lose, little brother."

With that, Silas turned on his heel and walked away.

Chapter 4

Approximately a half mile from the camp's outskirts, two lances were driven into the ground, side by side. The contestants were to ride out, take one lance, and return with it to the starting point. The first one back with a lance was the winner. These were the only rules.

It seemed to Eben Nall as though the whole camp was gathered to watch his ignominious defeat at the hands of Sixkiller. Evidently the Flathead had as few doubts as Eben regarding the outcome. He strutted like a rooster, cheered on by a handful of his fellow tribesmen. Eben studiously ignored him. He tried to ignore the crowd, too. He couldn't bring himself to look any of them squarely in the eye. They were relying on him and he was going to let them down. After that, no one would rely on him again.

As he and Sixkiller were about to mount up, Rube Holly arrived with, to Eben's chagrin, none other than Hugh Falconer. Falconer was absolutely the last person Eben wanted to see. The man had thought enough of him to extend an invitation to join the California expedition—no doubt that would change after this race.

"I wanted to wish you luck," said Falconer. "And to warn you about Sixkiller. I know him well. He's not a bad sort, but he plays dirty."

"He'll have a trick or two up his sleeve, that's

sartin," agreed Rube Holly. "It's hell for leather
to the lances and back."

Sixkiller was astride his pony now, a
high-stepping black stallion. The Flathead had
stripped down to a loincloth. He rode bareback. A
braided quirt dangled from his wrist. The stallion
reared as soon as it felt the Indian's weight, gnash-
ing at its rawhide bit. Sixkiller clung like a tick to
the stallion's back and let out a whoop of exultation. Eben realized bleakly that if the Appaloosa
were to rear like that he would wind up eating
dirt, with a broken neck into the bargain. But the
mare just stood there, stock-still, as lively as a
statue carved from stone, and Eben found himself
wishing, in a somewhat contradictory vein, that
the creature would display at least a little energy.

"Think I ought to get shed of this apishamore,
Rube?" he asked, indicating the Indian saddle.

Rube shook his head emphatically. "A few
pounds won't matter to this cayuse. No, you stand
a better chance staying aboard with it."

"You've got a fine horse," said Falconer. "She
has a sweet mouth and a smooth stride. Just stay
low and keep an eye on Sixkiller."

All I'll see is the back of his head, thought Eben
glumly, but he did not give voice to his doubts.
Instead, he nodded, putting on a brave front.

Falconer and Rube Holly moved away as Sir
William Drummond Stuart stepped forward. He
had been chosen to fire the shot that would start
the contest. He was a sight to behold, wearing a
knee-length elkskin coat with more quill-and-
beadwork than Eben had ever seen on a single
garment, along with a scarlet vest, plaid trousers
tucked into mud-caked cavalry boots, and a red
beret sporting an eagle feather. He carried one of
a matched pair of silver-inlaid English dueling
pistols.

"To your marks, gentlemen," he said, standing before the contestants, with one hand behind his back, the pistol pointed at the azure sky.

Eben expected him to say something else, perhaps "get ready," but instead he triggered the pistol.

With a shriek that startled Eben more than the pistol's discharge did, Sixkiller savagely applied his quirt, and the black stallion leapt forward into a stretched-out gallop. Eben kicked the Appaloosa in the ribs. The mare almost exploded out from under him. It was all Eben could do to stay aboard. He fumbled with the reins, slowing the horse in the process. Realizing his mistake, he gave the mare her head. Belatedly he remembered Falconer's advice and bent low. Half-blinded by the mare's wind-whipped mane, he was astonished to see that he was actually gaining on Sixkiller. The ground was a dizzy blur sweeping past. The thunder of hooves was loud in his ears. Falconer was right! The Appaloosa's stride was smooth indeed—like flying on the wind. The sheer, exhilarating power of the splendid beast beneath him took Eben Nall's breath away. *I cannot lose this animal,* he thought. How dull life would be without her!

The ground rose gently, a long, tan, grassy slope. Eben could see the two lances at the crest of the rise, silhouetted against the cloudless summer sky. Halfway to the lances the Appaloosa had drawn even with the black stallion. Sixkiller threw a look of disbelief at Eben, who laughed out loud.

Then Sixkiller lashed out with the quirt.

The braided rawhide caught the Appaloosa across the nose. Eben's deliriously joyful laugh turned into a strangled cry of impotent rage. The mare snorted and missed her stride, stumbling. Eben's heart lodged in his throat as, for a terrifying instant, he thought he was going to be thrown. But the Appaloosa recovered, and lunged forward without his having to urge her on. Eben felt the animal's great lungs bellow, every muscle strain, and he could almost believe that the mare was bent on revenge, so violently did she strive to close with Sixkiller, who had surged ahead.

The Indian was first to reach the lances. Plucking one from the ground, he used it to strike the second down. Eben shouted an incoherent protest. Sixkiller's harsh laugh seared Eben's nerves as they passed, Eben nearing the crest, the Flathead on his way back to the starting point a half mile away.

Eben knew he could not dismount to retrieve the fallen lance and hope to win the race. A vision flashed before his eyes—the Nez Perce horseman leaning low off the side of his galloping pony to pluck the whiskey jug off the ground. A part of Eben's mind screamed that it was sheer lunacy for him to try a similar feat. But what did he have to lose? Better to break his fool neck now than to suffer humiliating defeat. Try it. *Try it!*

Letting go of the reins, Eben grabbed a handful of the Appaloosa's mane and slid sideways off the apishamore, straining to reach down as far as he could. Tall grass whipped painfully at his face. He tried to keep his right leg hooked tightly over the apishamore. But it was slipping! He grabbed desperately for the lance. He had it! Exultation as sweet and wild as the mountains washed over him. But it was short-lived. He couldn't get back up square on the apishamore. A cry of despair escaped him. It seemed to him that he dangled precariously on the side of the Appaloosa for a hellish eternity. Sixkiller's insolent laugh rang in his head. With one last herculean effort he tried to pull himself upright. The muscles in his arm and leg burned with the effort. But it worked. He was astride the mare again.

He was amazed to find that the Appaloosa had turned on her own accord and was in hot pursuit of Sixkiller back toward the camp. The mare seemed determined to win in spite of her rider. Pride in the magnificent beast swelled Eben Nall's heart.

Even so, Sixkiller's lead was such that Eben did not see how the Appaloosa, game as she was, could close the gap in time. But then the Flathead used his quirt once too often, lashing viciously at the stallion's flank. The stallion balked, crow-hopping and spinning at the same time. Sixkiller managed somehow to stay aboard but spent precious seconds regaining control, and by the time he had the stallion straightened out Eben was only a length behind.

Seeing that his opponent was gaining infuriated Sixkiller. He swung the lance, trying to strike Eben this time rather than the mare. He missed—barely. Eben felt the lance brush his wind-tousled hair. The Appaloosa surged forward, drawing nearly even with the black stallion. Again Sixkiller swung the lance. This time Eben was ready. He struck at Sixkiller's lance with his own, jarring the weapon loose from the Indian's grasp. With an angry shout, Sixkiller lashed out with the quirt. He did not even consider going back for the fallen lance. The rawhide gashed Eben's arm, ripping through the buckskin sleeve and slicing deeply into the flesh. Eben gasped at the searing pain. Sixkiller steered the stallion into Eben's mare. The horses collided. Sixkiller grabbed for Eben's lance. The stallion snapped at the Appaloosa. For an instant men and horses both were locked in combat. Just as a furious Eben Nall wrenched the lance away from Sixkiller, the mare's blunt teeth tore a bloody

wound in the stallion's neck. The stallion shrieked
and veered away with a stiff-legged hop that
caught Sixkiller by surprise. The Flathead had
been riding with his knees, leaving both hands
free to grapple with Eben for possession of the
lance. Now, before he could grab a handful of the
stallion's mane, he lost his seat and toppled into
the grass.

A roar rose from the crowd of mountain men
congregated at the starting point. The Appaloosa
mare covered the last hundred yards with great
leaping strides, carrying a shaken Eben Nall to
victory.

Belatedly, Eben thought to slow the mare. The
Appaloosa had the wind in her teeth, and Eben
had a vision of a dozen trappers being trampled
beneath the animal's thundering hooves. But
again the Appaloosa took the initiative; locking
her front legs, she came to a skidding halt as the
crowd of buckskinners closed in. Before Eben
knew what was happening, strong rough hands
bore him from the apishamore and pounded him
on the back and shoulders so roundly that but for
the press of bodies he would have been driven to
the ground. His knees were jelly.

Rube Holly bulled his way through the crowd
of men congratulating Eben. "Give the boy some
air, goldurnit!" roared Holly. "Get back! Stand
aside!" As he reached Eben's side, Rube beamed
like a proud father. "You whupped him, boy! By
thunder, you've got gumption!"

"Not me," gasped Eben. "It wasn't me. It was
the mare."

"She's one hell of a horse, that's sartin."

Shouts of alarm mingled with a savage, bloodcurdling cry. The crowd parted like the Red Sea.
Eben caught a glimpse of Sixkiller astride the galloping stallion, bearing down on him. He shoved

Rube Holly out of harm's way. Sixkiller launched himself from the stallion's back and carried Eben to the ground. The impact of the Indian's body knocked the wind out of Eben, leaving him too weak for an instant to defend himself. The quirt bit deeply into his shoulder. Realizing that Sixkiller was aiming for his face, Eben flailed away with his fists, one of which grazed the Indian's jaw. Sixkiller wasn't fazed. His features were twisted with cold fury. He raised the quirt to strike again . . .

Falconer kicked him in the guts.

The blow knocked Sixkiller sideways off Eben. The Indian rolled and came lithely to his feet, snatching a knife from the belt sheath of a mountain man before the latter could react to prevent the theft. The Flathead fell into a knife fighter's crouch, sunlight flashing off the blade. Falconer grimly drew his own belduque.

Scrambling to his feet, Eben Nall grabbed Falconer by the shoulder and spun him around.

"Damn it, I'll fight my own fights," he cried, enraged.

Then, realizing he had dared lay a hand on the legendary Hugh Falconer, he stepped back, horrified.

But Falconer was smiling.

"My apologies," he said. "You're absolutely right."

Twirling the Green River, he offered the knife, handle first, to Eben.

Eben hesitated. He didn't want to kill anybody or—as was more likely—get killed himself. Against all odds he had bested Sixkiller in the race; he had an even more infinitesimal chance of whipping the Indian in a knife fight.

His dilemma was of short duration. The man whose knife Sixkiller had appropriated jumped the Flathead warrior, striking the weapon from the Indian's grasp and then knocking him to the ground. Dazed, Sixkiller looked up into a circle of grim, bearded faces. It was Falconer who intervened, shouldering his way through to give Sixkiller a hand up.

"I don't want you to kill that boy, Sixkiller," said Falconer. "He's going to California with me. Fact is, I was hoping you'd come along, too."

Sixkiller was inscrutable. "I not kill."

"Look here," said Eben standing at Falconer's side. "I've got two horses now. Got no use for a third. You keep your stallion, Sixkiller."

Anger flared in the Indian's eyes again. "No," he snapped, turning brusquely away. "You keep." Pushing through the press of mountain men, he stalked away.

Bewildered, Eben turned to Falconer. "What did I say? I was only trying to patch things up."

"You managed to insult him," replied Falconer. "Sixkiller's a prideful man. You won the stallion fair and square. The last thing he wants is your charity."

"I wasn't thinking," sighed Eben.

"Your heart's in the right place, lad. You just need to learn a few more things about the way things work out here. For now, just watch out for Sixkiller. He might get a notion to cut that good heart of yours right out of your chest." With that, Falconer went his way, chuckling.

Eben Nall didn't think it was at all amusing.

Chapter 5

July 6, 1837. Since the race I believe I have become the most popular person in camp—except, perhaps, among the Indians, who wagered heavily on Sixkiller. More than a few Indians have challenged me to a contest, and many are the trappers who have begged me to accept, but I have steadfastly refused. Rube tells me I am a marked man now among the Indians. To defeat me in a race would be big medicine. He is of the opinion that I should take on all comers, as I am now the proud owner, he says, of two horses that are without a doubt the swiftest in the camp. But I am not interested in making any more enemies. Sixkiller is more than enough in that respect.

Were he not my brother I would swear I have another enemy in Silas. He lost everything betting against me and refuses now to even speak to me. I am sorry for his misfortune. Rube says I should be offended that Silas thought so little of me that he would ask me to intentionally lose the race. Perhaps I should be, but Silas is my brother, and in spite of his shortcomings I cannot remain angry at him. I am sure Silas will recover from his disappointment. We may see things with different eyes, but we are the same blood.

The word that Hugh Falconer is going to California has spread through the camp. It seems as though every mountain man present is eager to accompany him. They are confident of a fair share of adventure and glory in a brigade led by such a man. Part of it, too, is the sorry state of the fur trade. The traders have brought word that the market is truly on its last legs. As Rube is fond of saying, too damn many trappers, too damn many silk hats.

The trappers are living it up like there is no tomorrow. Perhaps, in a sense, they are right. There is much drinking, gambling, and carousing. Scarcely a day goes by that there is not at least one fight. Rube says a man or two will get killed before the rendezvous is over—said it so matter of factly that one might have thought he was referring to the weather. Likely the blood will be spilled over a squaw.

Speaking of squaws, Rube keeps after me to pick one. Says I could get a right fine woman for the stallion. I cannot bring myself to trade for a human being as one would for a blanket or a gun. It doesn't seem proper. There are plenty of eligible young Indian maidens to choose from, however. They are forever sashaying through camp dressed in their best buckskins. You can hear them coming a mile away, as every last one is decked out top to bottom with little bells and tin trinkets. I am given to understand that an Indian girl will generally prefer a white trapper to a man from her own tribe for a husband. The mountain man treats his woman much better. They say an Indian is kinder to his horse than he is to his wife. If a mountain man has two horses he will load his possibles on one horse, his squaw on the other, and save the walking for himself. In the same situation an Indian will load his possibles on his squaw, ride one horse, and lead the other, making her walk. Some of the young Indian women are very pretty, and I suppose I must be considered quite a catch, with the stallion and the Appaloosa mare, because at times they are thick as fleas in the vicinity of our lean-to, but I am not inclined to take a wife just now.

A Captain Bonneville arrived in camp today. Resigning from the army several years ago, he raised sufficient capital to finance an expedition to the frontier, and he established a trading post, which is located not far from Horse Creek. He was not well received by the trappers, and as a result his venture has not been at all profitable. Yet he remains in this country, and his true motives are a mystery. I have the distinct impression he came here for the express purpose of seeing Hugh Falconer . . .

"I have a confession to make, Hugh," said Bonneville.

They sat alone around a small, crackling fire in front of Falconer's lean-to, on the edge of camp. The river was nearby, murmuring pleasantly to the cool, star-crowned night. Crickets chorused from the marsh grass at the river's muddy verge. Bonneville had brought some sipping whiskey, genuine Tennessee sour mash, a far cry from the "panther piss" rotgut sold by the cup—at exorbitant prices—by the St. Louis traders.

"I'm no father confessor," said Falconer.

Bonneville smiled. "And I am no retired army officer."

"You're not?"

"Not retired. I am officially on leave of absence."

"Since '32? That's one hell of a leave of absence, Benjamin."

Bonneville nodded. He was a solidly built man of medium height, his square face framed by bushy black side-whiskers. "I was given permission to explore these mountains, to map them, for the United States government."

"What does the government want with these mountains?"

Bonneville laughed softly. "This *is* part of the United States of America, Hugh. I realize you and your kind think of this country as your own private domain, but even if it has been, for all practical purposes, it won't remain so for much longer. Civilization is coming, Hugh."

"Good God," said Falconer, disgusted. He began to pack his clay pipe with honest-to-God tobacco, which he had recently purchased, along with powder and shot, a new blanket, and a volume of Shakespeare's sonnets.

"It's inevitable. The one certainty in this world is that it is constantly changing. You mountain men don't realize it, but you're the pathfinders. You blaze the trail for others to follow. The settlers are already beginning to arrive. The merchants will follow. Then the army will come along, too, in order to protect the settlers and the merchants. Towns will spring up in these valleys. Roads will be carved out of the wilderness."

With a sigh Falconer gazed into the night. He

seemed to be sniffing at the air like a wily old bull elk. Bonneville wondered if he was checking to see if he could smell the stench of civilization.

"They'll dam up the streams, cut down the timber, turn over the grass with their middle-busters," growled Falconer.

"One of my reasons for coming out here was to report on the fur trade. There's no denying it, Hugh. The trade is dying."

"I know that," said Falconer gruffly, puffing vigorously on the pipe to develop a good, even burn in the bowl.

"Is that why you're going to California?"

"Word gets around."

"A couple of Iroquois trappers came to the fort yesterday. Everyone here knows of your plans. You're looking for twenty, thirty good men to go along with you. When I heard that, I thought it somewhat odd. You ride alone, Hugh. You always have."

"I worked with a brigade when I first came out here. Turned out to be a bad experience. Some of the men were damned fools. Picked a fight with the Absaroka Crow and nearly got us all killed. I relied on the booshway, and he let me down. I have not relied on anyone since."

"Then why not go to California alone?"

Falconer did not answer at once. He fed a few sticks into the fire. Bonneville took a sip of whiskey, and waited. He knew better than to press this man.

"I heard Jedediah Smith had some trouble with the Mexicans," was Falconer's eventual reply.

Benjamin Bonneville was acquainted with Jed Smith's previous foray to the Pacific coast. Smith had journeyed from the Great Salt Lake into the desert, seeking untrapped beaver country. What he found instead was sand and sagebrush, the threat of starvation and constant, agonizing thirst. He and his men lost most of their horses in the desert crossing, and they might never have been seen or heard from again but for the hospitality of friendly Mojave Indians. By then Smith had abandoned all hope of finding new trapping ground. He'd had no intention of going to California originally, yet the Mojaves convinced him that he and his party would stand a better chance of survival heading west than if they tried to retrace their steps across the desert. The Mojaves had long enjoyed a profitable trading relationship with the Spaniards, and then the Mexicans, and it was along one of their trade routes that Smith marched west. A few weeks later, he and his bedraggled brigade arrived in the mission country of southern California, only to be arrested and detained in San Diego by order of the governor-general.

The captains of American merchant ships anchored in San Diego harbor came to the rescue, convincing the authorities that Smith and his men were trappers, not spies. The mountain men were released upon their word that they would depart California immediately. But Smith broke his word, wintering in the valley of the San Joaquin, knowing he could not survive the snowbound passes of the Sierra in January.

The crossing proved difficult enough the following summer. Smith and his men failed in their first attempt, losing a number of horses on the treacherous high country trails. Smith took only two men with him on his second try, leaving the balance of the brigade encamped on the western slope of the Sierras. It was a close thing, a life-and-death struggle, but Smith finally reached Bear Lake. Gathering together eighteen brave men, he started back to rescue the eleven left stranded in California.

Inexplicably, the Mojaves were hostile now. They fell upon Smith's party, killing ten men. When Smith reached California the second time he was not only an illegal but also a fugitive, as he had broken his word to the authorities there. He was arrested again, and again a Yankee sea captain negotiated his release. Once more Smith gave his solemn promise to leave California and never return, and yet he broke his word this time, too. Locating his original brigade, he wintered in the Sacramento Valley before escaping north along the coast, making for the Columbia River. Bad luck dogged him—again he and his men ran afoul of hostile Indians. Warriors of the Kelawatset tribe ambushed and killed fifteen trappers. Only Smith and three others survived. They found safe haven at Fort Vancouver, a Hudson's Bay Company outpost. Though the Hudson's Bay men had long been bitter rivals of American fur trappers, they gave Smith enough in the way of provisions to make it back to the United States.

Bonneville nodded. "In two trips Jedediah Smith took twenty-nine men west. Twenty-six of them lost their lives. But they weren't killed by the Californios, I hasten to point out."

"Maybe the Indians just beat 'em to it," was Falconer's laconic observation.

"Shame about Jed Smith," mused Bonneville. "It was said he planned to make detailed maps of the country he had seen on those expeditions. Instead, he set off down the Santa Fe Trail, hoping to recoup some of the money he had lost. After three years of wandering around in the far west he was flat broke. The Comanches caught him out alone, searching for a water hole, and curled his toes."

"They say he got off only one shot, but managed to kill the chief of the Comanches with it."

"He would have performed a great service for his country had he completed those maps."

Falconer squinted suspiciously at Bonneville through the blue, aromatic pipe smoke.

"Just what are you after, Benjamin?"

"It's not so much what I am after, Hugh. It's what the United States is after."

"What might that be?" Falconer had a hunch he really didn't want to know the answer.

"California."

Falconer extended a hand. "Hand over that tongue oil, and then start talking."

Chapter 6

"As I mentioned before," said Bonneville, "I have not resigned my commission from the United States Army. In fact, it was Andy Jackson, the president himself, who talked several New York money men into financing my expedition."

"They don't expect a return on their investment, I take it, since your trading post has been a failure."

Bonneville made a dismissive gesture. "That's of little consequence to anyone. But I must correct you on one point, Hugh. Those gentlemen invested in the future of our young nation, and, yes, they fully expect a return on that investment. A return which cannot be calculated in hairy bank notes, but rather in acquiring for the United States what is rightfully hers. I mean California, of course."

Falconer's expression was one of wry amusement. "Now how do you figure the United States has a right to California, Benjamin?"

The query seemed to astonish Bonneville. "I would have thought it was obvious to everyone."

"I'm just slow, I reckon."

"Look here." Bonneville was deadly serious now. "Mexico is too weak to hold on to California. We must have Pacific ports. The truly fabulous wealth in this world lies across that great ocean, in the Orient. If we do not possess the west coast we will never be a great nation. We will never achieve our true potential as a power to be reckoned with in this world. If we do not seize California, the British or the Russians will."

Again Falconer fell silent, pulling on his tawny beard and gazing pensively into the fire. This time Bonneville could not check his impatience.

"You could do your country a great service, Hugh. Find a better route to California than the one Jed Smith used, and bring back accurate maps."

Falconer shook his head. "I'll tell you, Benjamin, I don't much care for all this talk about the Mexicans owning this and the United States owning that. I mean, I just don't think that way."

"What, may I ask, prompts you to go at all?"

Falconer pointed with his chin at the snow-capped peaks, ghostly silver in the starlight. "Used to think I never wanted to leave these mountains. But now I think I need to get away for a spell."

"Touches the Moon," said Bonneville softly. "My sincerest condolences. I know she meant a lot to you."

"More than I ever knew—until she was gone. Thought it over all winter. Figured I'd see what California looks like. I'd go alone if I thought one man could make the trip. But I don't think one man alone would stand much of a chance. So I'll take along twenty or thirty men—good men, men to ride the river with."

"Don't take Sir William," advised Bonneville dryly.

"Why not?"

"Oh, you didn't know? Sir William and I have a lot in common. He is no more retired from his army than I am from mine."

"You're pulling my leg."

"On the contrary. I'm serious. He still holds the king's commission. His job is to find out what us colonials are up to out here."

"I'll be damned."

"For a hundred years and more the British have reigned supreme on the high seas. They've had the cream of world trade right here." Bonneville held his cupped hands together. "Lately we've started to horn in on that monopoly. Those New England sea dogs of ours have been popping up all over the place and taking business away from the limeys. The last thing they want is for us to own any Pacific ports. That's why we'll have a fight on our hands for the Oregon Territory. And why they've got their sights set on California."

"You folks might be underestimating the Californios. I reckon they'll put up a fight."

"Certainly. But the question is, How much of a fight? Our sea captains have provided us with some information, primarily regarding coastal towns and harbor defenses and the like. But we need to know more, much more. How strong are the Mexicans in California? Will the native tribes rise up against them when the time comes? Do they have inland strongholds? How well do they patrol the western slopes of the Sierras? The mountain passes—are they guarded?"

"Sounds to me like you're planning on a war."

"Oh, war will come. Just a matter of time, Hugh."

Falconer surrendered the jug of sour mash, now nearly empty. Bonneville jostled it ruefully. Although Falconer had consumed plenty of the whiskey, he was stone-cold sober as he spoke.

"I think I've heard enough, Benjamin. Maybe you and your government can own the trees and the rivers and maybe even the mountains, but you can't own me, any more than you could own the wind."

"It's *our* government."

"I live by my own laws, and bow to no one."

"Be reasonable . . ."

"No. I got away from people so I didn't have to be reasonable. Sorry, Benjamin, but I'm not your man."

"Well, then." Benjamin shrugged in good-natured resignation. With an easy smile he returned the jug to Falconer. "Here, my friend. Finish it off, with my compliments. Let me wish you the best of luck on your expedition. I hope you find whatever it is you're looking for."

"I found what I was looking for, and lost it. I guess I'm just killing time now."

"Shoot straight's the word."

Falconer watched Bonneville walk away. He was suspicious. Bonneville had gone to great lengths in trying to win him over—and then given up too easily by halves. Falconer figured Bonneville had an alternative plan, something to fall back on. What could it be?

Responding to his brother's summons, Eben Nall entered the skin lodge and stopped dead in his tracks. By the lurid, flickering light of a small fire in a circle of stones beneath the lodge's smoke-hole he could see Silas and an Indian woman, naked on the buffalo robes, writing in a passionate embrace.

Thinking back on it later, Eben wondered why he was so embarrassed. After all the cavorting Rube and Luck had done in a hundred night camps he should have been inured to such a scene. Of course, Rube and his Nez Perce squaw had always found a modicum of privacy between their blankets.

Silas looked up and grinned at his slack-jawed brother. "Damn, Eben," he chuckled breathlessly, as he withdrew from the woman and sprawled on his back, his lank body glistening with sweat.

"I'm—I'm sorry," babbled Eben. "You sent word . . ."

"Sure, I asked you to come see me. Just didn't think you'd come so quick."

"I'll come back later." Eben turned to go.

Silas laughed and jumped to his feet. "No. Stay. It ain't nothin' I can't finish later."

Eben had never seen a completely naked woman before. He couldn't help staring. Propped up on her elbows, legs spread in lewd abandon, she invited him to look. She was young, with a firm body, pert dark-tipped breasts, flat belly, shapely legs. One thing marred the picture—an ugly scar deformed her nose.

"This here's Annie," said Silas. "Never could pronounce her Injun name. As you can see, Annie's a shameless hussy." He scooped up a blanket and threw it to her. "Cover yourself, before my kid brother rips a stitch."

The woman stood up and did as she was told, although she took her sweet time doing it, and Eben realized she was teasing him. Or maybe there was more to it than that. Maybe she was trying to seduce him. Eben knew what the cut nose meant. Rube Holly had spent all winter sharing everything he knew about Indians with his young protégé. And Rube knew a great deal.

Silas searched for and found a whiskey jug. Shaking it, he cursed a blue streak to find it empty. "Go find Portugee," he told the woman. "Get me more whiskey." When she held out a hand to him, he scowled darkly. "I ain't got no more damned money. Tell him I'll pay him tomorrow. My credit's good with Portugee."

Once again cutting her eyes at Eben, the woman dropped the blanket, donned a buckskin dress in a leisurely manner, and left the skin lodge.

"You got an eyeful, didn't you, brother?" asked Silas. He laughed, but this time it had a raw edge. "Trying to make me jealous."

"She's Arapaho, isn't she?"

"By God, ain't you the savvy mountain man. How'd you know?"

"The cutnose sign. Isn't that what Arapaho men do to those of their women who are unfaithful?"

Silas shrugged. "Why should I care about that?"

"I know you. You hate to lose."

"What's that supposed to mean?"

"Nothing." Eben could tell Silas was getting hot under the collar. He wanted to let the matter drop, but Silas was the type who never could resist picking at a scab.

"Listen here, brother. If you're trying to tell me I shouldn't trust her, I don't. If she wants to run off with another man, so be it. I don't care. There are plenty of squaws to be had. Even you could have one, if you wanted. But then you wouldn't know what to do with a woman, would you? Being a virgin still."

"Shut up, Silas."

"Just don't stand there and try to tell me about women." Smirking, Silas turned away. He pulled on some leggins, then knelt to stir up the fire.

"What did you want to see me about, anyway?" asked Eben.

"Hear tell you're going to California with Hugh Falconer."

"I'm not surprised you know Falconer's going over the mountains. But how did you know I was going with him?"

"Word gets around. It's true, ain't it? You are, aren't you?"

Eben nodded, wary.

"I want to go along with you," said Silas.

"What for?"

"What for? That's a stupid damned question. For one thing, California's got the best wine and the warmest women. And you know how much I fancy both of those."

Eben shook his head. "There's more to it than that."

"Sure there is. California is rich."

"I don't know about that. No one's sure how the beaver . . ."

"Don't mean beaver. I'm talking about gold and silver. Those people got so much gold and silver they don't know what to do with it all."

"I doubt if those stories are true."

"I'm telling you they are," snapped Silas. "I wasn't asking for your opinion, anyway."

"Well, as for going along, you'll have to ask Hugh Falconer."

Silas stood face-to-face with his brother. "I figured you'd put in a good word for me."

"It wouldn't help. Falconer's the kind to make up his own mind."

"You owe me that much, brother. I lost everything but the clothes on my back on account of you."

"On account of me?" That rubbed Eben the wrong way. Seldom had he stood up to his older brother—whenever he'd tried when they were children Silas had always made him pay—but this time his resentment boiled to the surface. "Maybe you shouldn't have bet against your own brother."

"You got lucky, that's all." Silas turned away. "Hell, Eben, I even lost my horse."

"You can have Sixkiller's stallion."

Silas Nall's eyes lit up. "I could win some races

with that critter. Yes, sir. I could be a rich man tomorrow with that black stallion."

"Fine," said Eben disgusted. "The stallion is yours, then."

Silas looped an arm around Eben's shoulders. "I'll pay you a fair price for him—once I've won a race or two."

Eben shrugged off his brother's arm. "Somehow I doubt that."

"I wonder where Annie is with that damned whiskey . . ."

Eben turned to go.

"Hey," said Silas. "Stay a spell. You might learn something." He leered.

Eben just stared, shaking his head.

"What about Falconer?" asked Silas.

"You ask him," said Eben on his way out of the skin lodge. "I reckon the stallion makes us even."

Chapter 7

July 13, 1837. The rendezvous is coming to a close. Many of the traders have turned their wagons around and headed east, loaded now with furs and hides. They must transport their hauls safely across the Great Plains. I wish them luck. I am told that every year one or two of them don't make it.

Most of the Indians have also left the camp. Generally they go empty-handed, having lost everything in games of chance, to which they have no resistance. The same can be said for some of the mountain men as well, though more often than not, I have noticed, it is the Indian who winds up holding the short end of the stick. I suppose it is the whiskey, which renders them fool-headed and easy prey.

All were agreed that next year's rendezvous should be held at this same location. But how many will come? Will there even be a market for beaver plews next year? Some of the traders told me they would not be back. The risks outweigh the profits. One predicted we would be lucky to get a dollar a plew next season. Such depressing forecasts have persuaded a number of trappers to call it quits. Some are going north, into Canada. They will have trouble with the Hudson's Bay people there. But trouble never gives these men pause. Canada, they say, is still wild, and a long way from becoming civilized. I feel sorry for these men, in a way. They did not fit in society, and so they came out here, but now society is closing in on them again, and they are looking for a place to escape to. Others are bending their steps south, to live and trade and hunt among the Mexicans. Thirty of us are going west, to California, with Hugh Falconer.

I am sorry to see the end of this great event, this rendezvous. Even though I am excited by the prospects of the California expedition, a melancholy intuition that an era is coming to a close plagues me. A grand, free way of life is vanishing before my eyes. The world will never see the likes of it again.

I was told to be ready to leave tomorrow, and the realization that I would soon be parting company with Rube Holly was added cause for melancholy. I had never completely grasped the depths of my feelings for the old man. He is a hard fellow to know—moody, irascible, crude at times, and occasionally eccentric. But no man could ask for a truer friend. Rube would lay down his life for me, and I for him, without a moment's hesitation. He is a surrogate father to me, and I am eternally grateful for all he has taught me. If I survive the journey to California it will be on account of the wiles and wisdom of Rube Holly, which he has so generously shared . . .

* * *

"You wouldn't last a fortnight without me to look after you," declared Rube Holly, "so I reckon I have to go along."

Eben couldn't believe his ears. He stared at Rube, who sat cross-legged on the other side of the campfire. A chunk of buffalo hump meat sizzled on a spit above the flames, and its aroma had made Eben almost delirious with hunger. Now, though, he forgot all about his empty stomach.

"You look downright addled, boy," growled Rube. "Pick yore jaw up off the ground, 'fore somebody trips over it."

"You mean it?" cried Eben. "You're going to California?"

"I said so, didn't I?"

Eben glanced beyond Rube, at Luck. The Nez Perce woman stood at the edge of the firelight. Her square, blunt-featured face was impassive. She seemed to hang on every word; although she pretended to know absolutely no English, Eben had long suspected otherwise. Now, watching her, he was sure of it.

"Rube, have you talked this over with Luck?"

"Now why would I do that? She'll go where I go."

"Listen," said Eben, leaning forward. "You ought to ask her."

"For what? Permission? By thunder, boy, I ain't asked nobody for permission to do nothin' since I was a young whippersnapper half your size, and I ain't about to start now."

"She's been a good and faithful mate to you, Rube. I'd hate to be the cause of discord between the two of you."

"Lookee, Eben. I ain't the sentimental kind, but I got to confess, since we been together . . . well, this past year . . . Hellfire! I kinda think of you as the son I never had. I just cain't sit by and let you go gallivantin' off to California, of all places, without me. You don't know half of what you need to know to survive out here, and if I don't teach you, who the hell is going to? Them other pilgrims in Falconer's brigade . . ." Rube Holly shook his head. "Cain't trust 'em. And Falconer, he'll be too busy to pull yore chestnuts out of the fire every time he turns around."

"I'm not *that* helpless, Rube," protested Eben, smiling. "You're just blowing smoke. You know as well as I do that Falconer has put together the finest damned brigade this country's ever likely to see."

This was the general consensus. For instance, there was Gus Jenkins, regarded as one of the finest booshways ever to lead a passel of mountain men into the high country. In terms of the esteem in which he was held by his peers, Jenkins did not stand too much in Hugh Falconer's shadow. He was brave, and wise in wilderness ways, but perhaps best known for being fair-minded to a fault.

One story in particular was inevitably recounted to prove this point. Jenkins and his brigade were trapping in the Beartooth range. Camped one evening beside a trail along a river, they were startled when a solitary Blackfoot warrior rode into their camp, accompanied by his wife and daughter, the horses of the women further burdened by travois laden with the family's belongings. It was only natural for the mountain men to snatch up their rifles with the intention of killing the warrior. The Blackfeet hated the white trappers who interloped on their land, and there was scarcely a mountain man alive who did not reciprocate in kind. The only points at issue were whether to kill the women outright too and how to divvy up the be-

longings. Or so the brigade thought—until Gus
Jenkins placed himself between the Blackfoot and
his own men. Jenkins proceeded to tell them that
even the fierce Blackfeet lived by certain rules, and
one of them was that an enemy could not be slain
in a Blackfoot camp. It was only right that the
reverse also apply—if the men wanted to curl this
warrior's toes they would have to go through Gus
Jenkins first.

The mountain men were flabbergasted, then
angry, then keenly disappointed. But nary a soul
was willing to try Gus Jenkins on for size. At least,
they said, they should partake of the Indian family's possibles. Might be some tobacco to be purloined. But Jenkins would not budge an inch from
his principles. He would not, he declared, abide a
brigade of thieves and murderers. Ashamed, the
other trappers relented, and the Blackfeet were
given safe escort out of the camp. Jenkins was no
Indian lover—a few months later he took three
scalps in a scrape with a Blackfoot war party. But
on this occasion he reminded his men—and in ret-
rospect they were grateful for the lesson—that the
laws of God took precedence over the laws of nature, especially the one about kill-or-be-killed.

Another man who had signed on to accompany
Hugh Falconer to California was Bearclaw Johnson. Next to a Blackfoot Indian, a mountain man
dreaded the grizzly bear most. The grizzly was
the true king of the Rockies. But Bearclaw wasn't
afraid of them. Tracking down and killing bears,
especially grizzlies, was more than a hobby for
Johnson—it was an obsession. No one knew why
he hated bears so. Seldom did he speak to anyone,
so it was difficult to know anything at all about
him. He was a loner, a big growling hulk of a
man, and some said he looked more like a grizzly
than a man, and all agreed a grizzly's disposition

could be far more pleasant at times. The only man Bearclaw seemed to have any respect for was Falconer.

It was said of Bearclaw that he liked nothing better than to beard a grizzly in its den. While with a brigade up on the Musselshell, Bearclaw was called upon to rid the valley of a grizzly that had killed two horses and a mule. Happy to oblige, Bearclaw, accompanied by two other brave souls, tracked the creature to a cave. Entering the cave, the men were unpleasantly surprised to discover not one but three full-grown bears in residence. Rifles spoke. One bear fell dead in its tracks. Bearclaw's companions ran for their lives; wise enough to know that a man cannot outrun a bear, they clambered up a steep slope above the cave entrance. The second grizzly, wounded, gave chase, but Bearclaw fell upon it with pistol and knife and, after a terrible struggle, killed it. The third grizzly, the biggest and meanest of the lot, dragged the injured and now weaponless Bearclaw back into its lair. Giving Johnson up for dead, the other two mountain men contrived to start a rock slide, which completely closed the mouth of the cave.

Winter came, and passed. The brigade was preparing to leave the valley the following spring when, to everyone's astonishment, Bearclaw Johnson reappeared. He had slain the third grizzly with his bare hands. Trapped in the cave, more dead than alive, he had survived on raw bear meat, and kept from freezing by wrapping himself in the bloody hides of the two grizzlies killed inside the cave. Farther back in the cave he had discovered a spring—a bare trickle of water. Using bones from the carcasses, he had laboriously dug himself out of his mountain tomb—an endeavor that took him months to accomplish.

There were others in Falconer's brigade worthy of note: Bordeaux, better known among his peers as French Pete, a famous Indian fighter, the product of the union of a voyageur and an Arikara princess; "Doc" Maguire, an Irish-born physician wanted on a murder charge in Great Britain, a man who liked strong drink and who kept his set of pearl-handled throwing knives as sharp as a surgeon's scalpel; Cotton Phillips, a runaway slave who was as talented as any Indian when it came to reading sign and the weather. This was a rough-hewn collection of free souls, grown half wild in the high country, square pegs in civilization's round holes. Only a man like Hugh Falconer could mold them into a brigade, where every man would have to rely on every other if any were going to survive.

"Finest set of misfits, scoundrels, and outcasts ever assembled," said Rube Holly, sardonically. "And how 'bout Falconer pickin' that feller Sixkiller to go along?"

Eben nodded ruefully. "Reckon I'll have to sleep with one eye open. But I'm not going to back out just because Sixkiller's part of the brigade."

"Oh, no, not you. Back out? That would be too smart a thing to do. You'd do well to slit that Injun's throat first night out. Iffen you don't, he'll like as not have yore head tied to his saddle."

"There won't be any of that. Falconer won't allow it. He called us all together this afternoon. Laid down the law. And nobody wants to answer to him. He knows what he's doing, Rube. If he wants Sixkiller along, then he must have a good reason."

"Why do you reckon he's takin' you?"

Eben lifted his leather-bound journal. "We'll be writing a page of history, and everybody knows it. So someone has to make a record."

"Well, I hope yore book has a happy ending for us all. It's the great unknown we're going to on the morrow."

"You're not coming just on my account," smiled Eben. "Admit it. You're dying to see California, too, like the rest of us."

"True enough," admitted Rube. "I just hope we don't all *have* to die just to see it."

Eben brushed the old mountain man's reservations aside. "We'll do fine. Wait and see. With Hugh Falconer leading us, what could go wrong?"

Chapter 8

At daybreak of the following day, Falconer and his brigade put the Green River behind them and embarked on their great adventure. There were thirty men in the group, including two Indians— Sixkiller and a Nez Perce named Blue Feather— and three women, all of them squaws, with Luck among them. Some of the trappers had signed on because they knew that ahead of them lay the last of the unexplored wilderness. Others conceived of the benefits that might accrue from the blazing of a new trade route to that land of untold riches known as California. Almost all of them were conscious of the fact that just to be a participant in Hugh Falconer's quest would be a feather in their cap, for the very scope and daring of the expedition guaranteed that it would be long remembered, the subject of conversation around countless campfires for many years to come.

It should have been a moment to remember for Eben Nall, a moment of great excitement and flavor. But he scarcely took note of the world around him, for he was deeply troubled.

Late last night he had been roughly awakened by a trapper bearing bad tidings. Silas had killed a man, the trader named Portugee, and then fled the camp on the black stallion, escaping certain retribution at the hands of Portugee's vengeful partners.

Immediately Eben had a hunch that the Arapaho woman named Annie, the one with the cut nose, was at the center of this storm of violence. He was right. Apparently Annie had shared Portugee's blankets. In a jealous rage Silas had confronted the trader. There were no witnesses to the killing—not even Annie, who had run for her life. But the evidence indicated that Portugee had put up one hell of a fight, and some even suggested that Silas might have slain the man in self-defense. Portugee had owned a well-deserved reputation for being violent and bad-tempered.

Eben cursed his brother for a fool. It was bad enough that Silas had allowed Annie to get under his skin—what had he expected when he sent a woman with a propensity for infidelity to a man like Portugee to barter for whiskey without money to pay for it? Naturally Portugee had thought of another medium of exchange. But for Silas to flee the scene had been a downright stupid thing to do. Had he stayed, most of the other mountain men would have accepted a claim of self-defense. It wouldn't have been the first killing over a woman at rendezvous, not by a long shot. But by running away Silas had wrapped himself in the black mantle of guilt—it must have been murder, reasoned the others, else why would he run?

"Doesn't necessarily make it murder," Eben told Rube Holly. "Might just mean he knew Portugee's partners would want his hide."

Rube shook his head. "You're within yore rights to take up for kin, boy, but that won't float, and you know it. A man don't run away from trouble, not if he's in the right, and any kind of a man."

There was no use in trying to defend Silas—Eben's heart really wasn't in it, so he gave it up as hopeless. You could not convincingly argue a point that you yourself did not believe. Whether

Portugee put up a fight or not, whether it was self-defense or not, it was still murder, because Portugee was dead for no good reason, and the blame came back squarely on Silas, since Silas had made the fatal mistake of caring whose blankets Annie shared. His mistake, because the cutnose sign was a warning he had not heeded. It was there to advertise the indisputable fact that this woman was an adulteress who would betray any man's trust. You could not attach even a sliver of blame to Annie. She had made no promises; she had not masqueraded behind false pretense. Eben had known Silas was lying when he'd said he didn't care. I know you, Eben remembered saying. You hate to lose. At that moment Eben had had a premonition. He wasn't really surprised that something like this had happened. Worst of all, it was not passion but possessiveness that had motivated Silas to strike out in a bloody rage—Eben was fairly sure his brother never had loved the Arapaho woman.

And so that morning, as he rode out of camp a member of Falconer's brigade, with everyone else in fine spirits, Eben felt no pride, no excitement, but rather was sick to his stomach with shame and disappointment.

That Hugh Falconer knew what he was doing was obvious to all concerned from the very beginning. Each man was required to have at least two horses in addition to the one he chose to ride— the extras were to be loaded with provisions. Rube Holly explained to Eben the significance of this.

"I've ridden with quite a few outfits in my day," said the old-timer, "and more often than not they come up short on possibles before the year is out. A mountain man just natcherly likes to travel light. He'll give precious little thought to tomorrow. I've seen men who'll eat till they're sick on a good day of huntin', and let most of the meat spoil—and a week later they're starvin'. Hugh's got it figured so's we shouldn't lack for anything on this trip. And if for some reason we get in a tight spot where our next meal's concerned, well, we've got all these extry ponies for emergency rations."

"I would never make steaks out of this mare," said Eben, indicating the Appaloosa beneath his saddle.

"Huh!" grunted Rube. "You just ain't been hungry enough, younker. I have been. Hell, I've been so hungry a time or two my partner started to look pretty tasty."

Eben had to laugh. "You've got no worries there. You'd be too tough and stringy to chew."

" 'Nother thing about these extry horses. A lot of men left rendezvous poor as a church mouse. Not these pilgrims, though. Hugh knows they've all got good sense iffen they still have the wherewithal to own three horses and lay in all these supplies. Means they didn't drink or gamble away all of their profits."

"Or maybe," said Eben, wryly, "they were all smart enough to bet on me beating Sixkiller in that race."

Four days out they reached the Bear River country. Here Falconer called a halt.

"We're going to linger a while," he told the others. "There is plenty of game in these parts, and I want every man in the brigade to have at least fifty pounds of dried and jerked meat before we head on. Hunt in pairs. I haven't seen much in the way of Indian sign for several days, but you know that doesn't mean anything. The Blackfeet have been plenty active since green-up, and so have the Snakes."

The valley of the Bear River had plenty of good grass and water, and lots of timber filled with game, as Falconer had said it would be. Eben, of course, paired up with Rube Holly. He was glad for the chance to try out his brand-new Kentucky rifle. Their first day out they bagged a deer and several wild turkeys. They put the turkeys in the pot and gave the deer to Luck for dressing out and transforming into strips of smoked and sundried venison. It was an auspicious beginning; with thirty men scouring the valley for prey the game was bound to become scarce in a hurry. Such indeed proved to be the case. Every day thereafter they were forced to venture farther and farther afield to find something besides tree squirrels to shoot at.

With all the shooting going on in the valley, Eben began to wonder when, not whether, the Indians would show up. Only question was, would they be friendly? Turned out they were. A small hunting party of Bannocks appeared on the fourth day of their sojourn on the banks of the Bear River. The Bannocks lived to the west, and Falconer engaged them in a daylong palaver, questioning them about every detail of the land that lay in the direction of the setting sun.

"Reckon they'll raise a fuss over our passing through their country?" Eben asked Rube Holly.

"It's true, you never know with them Bannocks. They're as changeable as the wind. Not like the Nez Perces, who've been friendly with white folk from the get go. Bannocks can be all smiles one day and trying their level best to lift yore hair the next. But I think they'll let us come on without too much squawlin'."

"On account of Falconer?"

"On account we got sixty packhorses loaded up with goods."

"You mean you think they'll try to steal our possibles?"

" 'Course they will. They're Injuns, ain't they? And not just our possibles but the ponies too. Lessen he's been converted by some Bible-thumper like that Reverend Gray, an Injun ain't never heard of the Ten Commandments, 'specially the ones about not stealin' and covetin'. In their book it's perfectly all right to steal. Not a thing in the world wrong with it. More like a game to them than anything else. I recalls spending dang near a whole season up on the Rosebud playin' who's got the horses with a band of pesky Absaroka Crows. They stole 'em from me four or five times, and I always stole 'em right back. Oh, we fired a few potshots at each other now and agin, but nobody got hurt. It was all in good sport, you understand."

The Bannocks left all smiles and handshakes, having smoked a pipe of peace with Falconer and accepted a few blankets and some brand-new knives as tokens of his gratitude for their information.

Eben wondered if the Indians had really left the valley. Maybe they would linger, lurking out of sight and hoping one of the "hairfaces" would grow careless. Before long, Eben's overwrought imagination had him seeing an Indian crouched behind every rock and tree trunk. Two days after the Bannocks' visit, he saw a lone rider back up in the trees. He and Rube had been out hunting all day, with no success. The sun had dropped behind the snow-clad peaks to the west, and a purple gloom permeated the forest. They were a long way from camp, and on their way back, when Eben happened to throw a glance over one shoulder. That was when he saw the horseman, sitting his motionless cayuse, watching them from about fifty yards away. Eben's heart jumped into his throat and lodged there, choking him. A cold chill shot down his spine into his scrotum. He brought up the Kentucky rifle and was drawing a bead when the rider called out.

"Don't shoot, Eben."

It was Silas!

Eben's brother steered the black stallion through the trees. Close enough to see the expression of disbelief on Eben's face, he smiled. Eben experienced a quick, hot surge of anger.

"What the hell are you doing here?"

"Looking for you, brother."

"You've got some nerve, after what happened."

Silas stayed aboard the stallion, scanning the darkening forest with fugitive eyes. His cheeks were hollow, his eyes sunk deep in gray sockets. He had the look of the hunted about him—a man who had not eaten or slept for days.

"I didn't do anything wrong," he said.

"Nothin' wrong?" echoed Rube Holly and snorted. "You squared off against Portugee on account of an Arapaho woman, and a cutnose to boot, pilgrim. Then you run like a rabbit."

"You better watch—" Silas bit down hard on the retort, forced the smile back in place on his haunted face. "Look, you got it all wrong. My quarrel with the trader wasn't over a woman. It was about the whiskey he sold me. Gospel truth, Eben, he tried to poison me. It was him trying to kill me for Annie. When I threatened to expose him, he tried to cut me open from groin to gullet. I was just defending myself. I swear."

Eben didn't believe it. He knew his brother too well. How many times had he seen Silas lie himself out of a tight spot? Silas was a master at devising barely plausible excuses for his malfeasance. Had been even as a child. But Eben said nothing now. He didn't have to. Rube took one look at Eben's face and saw, plain as mother's milk, that Eben thought Silas was speaking with a forked tongue.

"Whatever happened," said Rube, "you'd better light out, feller. Ain't a man in this brigade will buy that story now. Might have, had you stood your ground."

"How could I have done that? Portugee's partners were dead set on seeing me thrown cold. I'd have been gone beaver for sure, had I stuck."

"What do you want from us?" asked Eben, ambivalent.

"I think I finally shook those two off my trail two days ago. Followed your sign here. Waited until I got this chance to talk to you without anybody else knowing. I've got to go to California now, Eben. Don't you see? It ain't safe for me anywhere east of the Sierras."

"You can't come with us."

"You're not the booshway. All I want is a chance to tell Falconer my side of the story. He's a fair-minded man. Besides, I've got something to offer."

"And I guess you still want me to put in a good word for you. Well, I won't, Silas. I can't."

Silas had to work a little harder to keep his counterfeit smile intact, as cold fury swirled behind his eyes.

"Not asking," he said. "Just bring Falconer out to meet with me. I'll throw myself on his mercy."

"Hugh Falconer ain't got none of that," remarked Rube.

"I won't bring him," said Eben coldly. "You come into camp and talk to him—if you've got the guts."

"Let's go," said Silas, quick as always to accept

any challenge, and Eben immediately regretted having issued one. He didn't like his brother's chances. No telling what the brigade would do. There was only one kind of justice on the frontier—rough justice.

Chapter 9

July 25, 1837. My brother said he had something of value to offer in exchange for our letting him join the expedition. I shouldn't say "our," as it was Hugh Falconer's decision, as booshway. He did not have to, but yesterday he let us all vote on the matter. But I am getting ahead of myself.

Silas informed Falconer that indeed, as I had feared, the Bannocks had not left the valley. Eight of them had come into our camp to talk with Falconer—more than enough to cause mischief—and all eight were now camped at the north end of the valley. No one doubted what they were after: our horses, and our possibles too, if they could make away with them. Silas had stumbled upon their hidden camp quite by accident. With Portugee's partners after him, he said he was always on the move, never staying in one place too long. The Bannocks hadn't spotted him, but he had seen them, and he described them and their ponies so accurately that none could doubt that, at least this time, he was telling the truth.

Falconer gave Silas an opportunity to tell his story to the entire brigade. When he was done,

a majority voted to give my wayward brother
the benefit of the doubt, since what he had said
about the Bannocks was clearly true. I must
confess I abstained from voting, though if I had
been pressed to do so I would have voted
against Silas. Some of the men were of a mind
to ride north and confront the Indians. Falconer
had a better idea. Like as not, he said, the Bannocks kept a scout posted where he could watch
our camp, as the Indians were aware we were
here only temporarily and might leave the valley at any moment. He told us to get our packs
together that evening, which would lead that
Indian spy to believe we intended to pull out
in the morning. Under the cover of night, Falconer and six others slipped out of camp. I and
the others who remained behind were instructed not to act in any way out of the ordinary. As usual, our horses were allowed to
graze the meadows north of camp, with the cus-
tomary two herd guards.

This morning the Bannocks struck before sunrise. The valley was cloaked in a mist risen from
the river bottoms. The Indians ambushed the
two horse guards. From the first it was clear
they hoped to avoid any bloodshed. They fired
over the heads of the guards, who lit out for
camp. Then the Indians fled northward with
our ponies. Following Falconer's instructions,
every one of us gave chase, leaving only Luck
and the other squaws behind to watch the
camp.

Shortly after our hasty departure, four of the
Bannocks arrived in camp, having circled
around with some of our purloined horses.

Their intent was to make off with as much of our supplies as they could load onto the ponies. Imagine their surprise when they found themselves surrounded by Falconer and the six men who had accompanied him. The Indians were disarmed without a fight. Falconer was pleased with the catch. He identified one of the Indians as the son of a prominent Bannock chief. The warrior was surprised that Falconer knew his true identity—he had made no mention of his pedigree at the previous parlay—but he did not deny Falconer's claim.

The rest of us managed to pick up a few of the stolen horses, those that had strayed from the herd during the chase. All told, the thieving Bannocks made off with twenty-seven head. Falconer assured us we need not worry over the loss. Two days later a large contingent of Bannocks arrived. Some of us thought for sure we were going to have a big scrape. But Falconer wasn't concerned in the least. He ventured out alone to talk things over with the chief, the father of one of our prisoners. An exchange was agreed upon—our stolen ponies for the four warriors in our custody. The chief chastised his son for being so foolhardy as to even attempt to outwit Hugh Falconer. I was amazed to see that the Indians were generally amused by the incident. They had been bested by Falconer but harbored no grudge. As Rube Holly explained it to me, there was no shame attached to being outfoxed by a man of Hugh Falconer's caliber.

At Falconer's invitation the Bannocks shared our camp and our food that night. A rousing

good time was had by all, and we laughed and
joked about the horse-stealing incident. The Indians took their leave the next morning. Later
that day, we too put the Bear River behind us
and headed west, secure in the knowledge that
at least the Bannocks would not trouble us further . . .

Falconer led the brigade due west from the Bear
River camp, over a pine-strewn saddle. On the
other side of the mountain range that hemmed the
valley in that direction, the land quickly changed,
and everyone was in agreement that the change
was for the worse. In a single day's ride they left
behind the tall, verdant stands of fir and spruce
and pine, the snow-nurtured streams gamboling
down the slopes, the emerald meadows of lush
grass, and entered a realm of sand and stone and
salt flat. For days the men could glance longingly
over their shoulders and see the jagged purple line
of the Wasatch Range on the eastern horizon. Up
there, they knew, the gooseberries were ripe, the
wild roses were in bloom, and the deer emerged
in legions from the brush to drink daintily at
sweetwater springs and dancing creeks. Up there,
even in summer, water in a tin cup could acquire
a film of ice overnight.

Here, though, on the northern rim of the alka-
line desert that played host to a great salt lake,
there was withered sagebrush, a sun hammering
spikes of blistering heat into the heads and shoulders of travelers, a truculent wind that stirred up
a curtain of stinging dust. In July, most of the
creek beds were dry as bone. In the summer, if
the water came, it would be from flash floods, but
for a week they did not spy a single cloud in the
brass bowl of sky.

Still, somehow, creatures survived, even flourished, on the salt desert. Pronghorns, usually mustered in groups of two or three, grazed on the sagebrush. They proved difficult to hunt, being twice as fleet as horses on the short haul. An occasional coyote trailed the brigade. Horned larks by the thousands nested in the sagebrush, exploding into the air to fly in low, darting swarms. There had to be water, the men told one another, but where?

Falconer seemed to know. When the confidence of the other men began to falter, they had only to glance at him to recover. When almost every canteen was dry, he called a halt at midday on the rim of an arroyo, took ten men down to the bottom of the cut, and with their help dug a hole six feet in depth. The men started to despair, until they saw that at four feet the sand became damp. They dug with renewed vigor, but at six feet there was still no water. Falconer told them not to worry. In the morning they would have a drink. He was right. At daybreak they found two feet of muddy gray water in the bottom of the hole. Falconer ordered the water poured through strips of cloth before any of it was consumed; when the exercise was complete the cloth was stiff and caked with salt.

According to Indian legend, this great basin had once been an immense inland sea a thousand feet deep. By comparison, the great salt lake, all that remained of this ancient sea, was a mere puddle. Long ago the sea had been connected to the western ocean. A tremendous earthquake closed this outlet. Because of its inordinately high saline content, the sea eventually evaporated.

Skirting the salt lake, the brigade doggedly kept to its westering course. In time a range of distant mountains could be discerned straight ahead. The men cheered, so great was their relief. But another ten days of suffering was required to reach this high country, and the last three days were pure hell, as one of the water holes the Bannocks had told Falconer about turned out to be dust dry. After forty-eight hours without water, horses and men alike were on their last legs. One man was caught bleeding a packhorse, to slake his raging thirst with the animal's blood. Falconer flew into a towering rage. He threatened to cut the man's throat and let him drink his own blood. This was a side of Hugh Falconer that Eben had not seen before, and he questioned Rube Holly about it, since Rube seemed to know their booshway as well as anyone.

"He ain't no saint, that's for sartin," conceded the old-timer.

"Still, a man's life is of more value than a single horse."

"And I thought you were smart," chided Rube. "Our ponies are bottomed out. If Falconer let one man get away with that, what do you reckon the rest would do, if they were thirsty enough? Then, 'fore you know it, half our horses would be buzzard bait. If that happens, who's gonna carry our supplies? You want to load up with about a hunnerd pounds of gear and try walkin' to California, boy? How far you reckon you'd get?"

"I never thought of it that way," confessed Eben.

" 'Course you didn't. That's why Hugh Falconer's leadin' this crew of cutthroats and scoundrels, and not you. Don't you ever cross him, Eben. He'll skin you alive and not blink an eye. He may seem like a nice enough feller most of the time, but you don't want him riled at you."

On the third day without water Eben began to think they were all going to perish. Floating like a dream above the heat shimmer, the mountains seemed no closer than they had appeared to be two days earlier. Eben's tongue and throat were so swollen he could hardly swallow. His stomach was a knot of twisting agony—he could scarcely sit upright in his saddle, much less stand. His salt-rimmed eyes burned like the gates of hell. That morning, two horses dropped dead in their tracks. Falconer finally called a halt. Eben slipped off the stalwart Appaloosa and lay, weak as a kitten, in the strip of shade cast by the mare. He never knew if he passed out or just went to sleep, but when someone shook him awake he opened his eyes to see the sun higher in the sky and Hugh Falconer bending over him.

"I'll have to borrow that horse of yours," said Falconer.

His words gave Eben a small dose of strength, enough to get to his feet. He clutched the mare's reins tightly.

"I don't think so," he said, and the croaking travesty of his voice startled him.

Falconer's brown eyes darkened with anger, turning almost black. Eben's heart lurched in his chest. It was insane to stand up to this man. He would not have risked drinking his own blood for anything else in the world except the Appaloosa mare.

"I—I won't make it without the mare," he stammered, trying to explain his insubordination, putting into words a feeling that had only just crystallized into conscious thought, and then dead certitude, when he was faced with the prospect of losing the horse—the certainty that the Appaloosa, with her unfathomable stamina and indomitable spirit, was the key to his own survival.

Falconer heard the despair, the dread, in Eben's voice, and his anger subsided. "You will get her

back. And you will survive. We all will. But I'm
sending Gus Jenkins ahead to find water, and I
want him to have the best two horses in the brigade. Means I need the loan of your Appaloosa."

"We can't just sit here and wait for death," protested Eben.

"I know," said Falconer, suddenly the soul of
tolerance. "We'll move on during the night. But
Jenkins must ride day and night, if need be. The
life of every man here depends on it."

It almost broke Eben's heart to do it, but he
handed over the reins.

With Luck's help, Eben and Rube rigged some
shade using their rifles and the lean-to cover of
skins sewn together. Huddled beneath this shelter,
the three of them settled down to await day's end.
The salt flats were eerily silent. Not a man or
woman spoke. The horses stood still as statues,
their necks bowed. Falconer had ordered all saddles and packs removed. Every now and then one
of the ponies would blow, drooling yellow lather.
The flies came, crawling all over the men and
horses, seeking moisture. Eben was too exhausted
to swipe at them. Then the buzzards showed up,
and before long dozens were circling effortlessly
on the heat rising from the blistered flats.

Eben was beginning to drift off again when he
heard a scuffling sound, and opened his eyes to
see Silas crawling on hands and knees toward the
lean-to, a wolfish grin on his face.

"We're all gonna die," slurred Silas.

"Shut up."

"We're all gonna die in this godforsaken desert." He giggled.

"He's plumb out of his mind," observed Rube
Holly.

Silas got to his feet, stood bent over, arms dangling, body swaying to and fro. Pure malice tugged his features into a grotesque mask.

"I'm gonna kill you, old man. I'm gonna kill you and drink your blood . . ."

Eben lashed out with a foot and swept his brother's legs out from under him. Silas hit the ground hard and passed out.

"I'm sorry," Eben told his partner. "It's the heat and lack of water. Made him crazy."

"Probably drank his own piss. You gonna spend yore whole life makin' excuses for this feller?"

Eben didn't reply.

Rube stirred himself. "Well, come on. We cain't leave him out in the sun for what's left of his brains to bake. Help me drag him into the shade."

Time had ceased to be of any consequence to Eben, and he had no idea how much of it crawled by before a thought lodged itself in his skull.

"You think Jenkins will come back, Rube?"

His tongue was swollen, his lips cracked and bleeding, and he had trouble pronouncing the words. They sounded like a foreign language to his ears, but Rube Holly seemed to have no trouble comprehending.

"Long as there's breath left in his body he won't let us down."

"Why didn't Falconer go?"

"Reckon he wants to stick close, in case we need him. He's our booshway, boy. Wouldn't be right, him leavin' us behind. If there's water to be found up ahead, Jenkins will find it just as quick as Hugh could."

Eben lapsed into silent misery. The sun, or so it seemed to his fevered mind, was stuck in the sky at its zenith. Would this hellish day never end? But if it did end, they would have to start moving again—and Eben didn't think he could make another mile. Why trade one agony for another? Why not just lie here and count buzzards until he went to sleep one last time?

"Hey, boy."

Eben had been drifting away. His eyes were open, but everything was a colorless, and meaningless, blur. He tried to focus. The sun had sapped all the color out of the world. Rube Holly was standing in front of the shelter.

"Eben, Jenkins is back."

Somehow Eben mustered up enough energy to bestir himself. Crawling out into the merciless sunlight, he groaned as heat hammered between his shoulder blades.

"Look!" exclaimed Rube Holly. "He found water!"

The old-timer helped Eben to his feet. Eben had to narrow his eyes to slits—the brightness was like needles jammed into his temples from the inside. He could see Jenkins, on the Appaloosa mare, leading the other horse, bent slightly over in the saddle as he spoke to Hugh Falconer. Then he noticed that almost all the horses were moving, plodding closer to the mare and the other horse Jenkins had taken with him. They pressed near the mare, sniffing its muzzle, whickering softly.

"See?" asked Rube, so excited he was almost dancing a jig. "Them ponies know. Yore mare and that other cayuse have had themselves a drink. Yessir, Jenkins found water, and we're gonna see another sunrise after all."

Chapter 10

The brigade's desert ordeal wasn't over. For eleven more days they trudged across the parched plains. But every now and then they found good water, and eventually they reached the Humboldt. A river had never looked so wonderful to Eben Nall. Neither the men nor the horses could be restrained when they topped a dusty rise and spotted the stream, curling like a silver-blue ribbon through the dun-colored hills. A stampede followed, with snorting horses and hollering men. The men cavorted in the shallows all afternoon, or crawled up into the blessed shade cast by gray cottonwoods to sleep like the dead, while the horses preferred to stand shoulder-deep in the river, soaking up moisture through every pore.

Only Hugh Falconer did not indulge in the river's delights. Eben watched him as he rode up and down the river, then crossed to the other side and repeated the process. Was this man, wondered Eben, made of iron rather than flesh and blood? Did he ever succumb to weariness or thirst, or suffer from heat or cold? It did not seem as though the three-week desert crossing had affected him the way it would any mortal man.

Eben deduced that Falconer was exercising caution, seeking sign of anyone who had previously passed this way, but Eben thought it a fruitless enterprise. Nobody in their right mind would have come through here. He had a poignant sense of their being very much alone in this wild, strange immensity. Not even Indians, he decided, would attempt to eke out an existence in this god-forsaken country.

That evening, with the brigade gathered around the campfire, Falconer announced they would follow the river south until they reached a place called the Humboldt Sink, a vast marshland. At that point they would turn west again and, if his information was correct, reach the Sierras in less than twenty days.

"There is little time to waste," he said. "It's nearly mid-September now, by my calculations. If we don't get across the Sierras by the middle of October we will be in for some trouble."

"What kind of trouble?" someone asked.

"The Sierras rise fourteen thousand feet, if memory serves," announced Doc Maguire, jumping in unbidden. "It will be one hell of a bloody climb, because we shall be starting near sea level. If we get caught in a high pass by an early snow— well, you will all wish you were back down here, basking in the sun."

Falconer nodded as the others looked to him for confirmation.

"How come you know so all-fired much about them mountains, Maguire?" queried French Pete Bordeaux. "You've not been there before."

"No. But I was once a proud member of the esteemed Royal Geographic Society," said the Irishman, with a sardonic twist to his mouth. He was flicking one of his pearl-handled knives into the sand between his booted feet. "When I was charged—falsely, I might add—with murder most foul, they revoked my membership. It mattered not that I was innocent, or that I had not even had a fair trial. The Society's good name could not be sullied by scandal."

"Who you murder, you?" asked French Pete.

Maguire's gaze was as steely as twin stilettos. "You are deaf as well as ugly, French Pete. I told you, I was falsely accused of murdering the wife of a duke, a woman with whom I was having an affair at the time. I am convinced she was the victim of a jealous husband." Maguire's smile was cold—Eben took an immediate and powerful dislike for the man when he saw that smile. "Yes, gentlemen, I impaled her—but not with one of these." He held up the knife.

Some of the others laughed. Eben glanced at Falconer. The booshway's face might have been carved from stone, and Eben was left without a clue to what Falconer was thinking.

"We'll linger here for one day," said Falconer, and the men fell silent. "Leave the following morning. Sixkiller, Cotton—come with me."

The Flathead Indian and the runaway-slave-turned-mountain-man followed Falconer away from the campfire, into the starlit darkness.

"Reckon he'll send them two out tomorrow for a little scout downriver," mused Rube Holly. "Next to him they're the best at readin' sign."

"What is he worried about?" queried Eben. "There's probably not another living soul within a hundred miles of this spot."

"Think not?" Holly shrugged and fired up his evening pipe. "Who knows? We're the first white men ever to set foot in this country. This here's the great unknown, hoss. And that's what worries Falconer, I reckon. No tellin' what we'll run into. Whatever's out there, he don't want to be surprised by it."

Far off in the distance a coyote bayed at the moon, a singularly lonesome sound, shredded by the chilly night breeze—a sound that touched an icy finger of primitive dread between Eben Nall's shoulder blades and shook him with an involuntary shudder.

Early the next morning, before the rising of the sun, Sixkiller and Cotton Phillips set out southward, the Indian on one side of the river and the black man on the other. Eben Nall was certain they would find nothing out of the ordinary, and he gave no more thought to the matter, joining the others in enjoying to the fullest this brief respite on the banks of the Humboldt. He ate, slept, and swam in the shallows when the mood struck him, as did all the other men, and closed his mind to any futile speculations about what lay ahead. There would be tribulations, surely. But nothing, he decided, could be any worse than what they had endured in the desert crossing.

Only one thing intruded on his peace of mind—his brother. Silas had made every effort to avoid him since the ugly scene twelve days ago. Eben regretted the fact that Silas had been allowed to join the brigade. Intuition warned him that he would have cause to regret it even more in the near future. His feelings toward his brother burdened Eben with a degree of guilt, but he couldn't help those feelings. He had been dependent on Silas after they left home and ventured west into the great unknown together. His year in the mountains with Rube Holly had apparently cured him of this dependency. Now he tried to cope with the dilemma of kinship—how far was he obliged to go by blood bond in helping or defending Silas? He had a hunch that he would find out before this journey was over.

That afternoon Hugh Falconer searched out Doc Maguire and found the Irish doctor apart from the others, seated with his back propped up against the trunk of a cottonwood. Maguire was drawing in a sketchbook balanced on his knees.

"Didn't know you were an artist," said Falconer, sitting on his heels.

"A hobby."

"Thought you might like to tell me who you're working for."

"I don't understand."

"Is it Bonneville? Or the British?"

Maguire wore a carefully crafted blank stare. "I'm sure I don't . . ."

"Doc, don't you lie to me." Falconer's Scottish brogue thickened.

The Irishman dropped all pretense and smiled wryly. "Have you been rooting through my possibles, Hugh?"

Falconer shook his head. "You know better than that. But you're making a map."

"So I am. What harm is there in that?"

"Plenty."

"Even if your suspicions are well founded, what will you do? Leave me behind to die?"

Falconer let that pass. "Bonneville approached you back at the rendezvous, didn't he? You were one of the first men I picked to come with me, and he must have known about that."

"I have been meaning to ask, Hugh—why *did* you pick me? Doesn't my checkered past concern you?"

"I'd be making this trip alone if I refused to sign up anyone who fell short of sainthood."

"I didn't murder anyone."

"Until someone proves otherwise, I'm willing to take your word on that. But you could get us all killed with that map of yours."

"How so?"

"Do you know why Bonneville wants a map?"

"To establish a trade route to California."

Again Falconer shook his head. " 'He is come to open the purple testament of bleeding war.' "

Delighted, Maguire laughed. "Shakespeare! *Richard III*, is it not? By God, Hugh, you're full of surprises."

"I have a hobby, too. Bonneville is dead set on taking California away from Mexico. Any maps he can get his hands on will be used to that end."

Maguire nodded. "I suppose I had guessed as much."

"How did he enlist your aid? By telling you that if we didn't seize California the British would?"

"Something like that. To quote Shakespeare, he knew I've been 'eating the bitter bread of banishment.' For some reason, I harbor a tremendous amount of resentment toward anything British. Imagine that. They were going to send me to the gallows for a murder I did not commit, Hugh. They weren't the least bit interested in giving me a fair hearing. In fact, they didn't want to hear my side of it at all. I was just a bloody Irishman. What was my word against that of a duke? Well, I say to hell with that 'precious stone set in the silver sea. This blessed plot, this earth, this realm, this England.' "

Falconer nodded. It was just as he had surmised. "Destroy the map, Doc. Give me your word."

Maguire gave him a funny look. "You would *accept* my word?"

"Of course. Look, if the Mexicans find out we're making maps they'll peg us all as spies, and none of us will get out of California alive. It's going to be hard enough to convince them we're not working for the United States. They're suspicious, Doc, and I think they have a right to be."

"Very well, then. If you'll take my word, you can have it."

"Good enough." Falconer rose to go.

"Bonneville approached you, too, didn't he, Hugh?"

"He did. I turned him down. But I thought he gave up too easily. I figured he had something up his sleeve. Made sense he would try to recruit someone else in the brigade."

"Why are you going to California, anyway?"

"Why are you?"

Maguire shrugged.

"Why not go?" asked Falconer. "It's there."

"No. There's more to it than that, I think. We're all running away from something. What are you running away from?"

Falconer looked away, out into the heat haze in the middle distance, and pictured in his mind a lonely snow-covered grave way up above the timberline in the Wind River Range—the grave of a pretty Shoshone woman named Touches the Moon who had stolen his heart in spite of his every precaution.

"Memories," he said, and walked on.

Chapter 11

They seemed to materialize out of thin air. First a handful of them emerged from the stunted, wind-twisted shrubbery up ahead, to stand along the bank of the shallow river. They looked nothing like any Indians Eben Nall had ever seen; they were squat, stocky, wearing only loincloths and carrying spears and bows and arrows for weapons. Their faces and shoulders were daubed with dried clay, giving them a grotesque and fear-some appearance.

The brigade had been following the Humboldt River for days. Sixkiller and Cotton Phillips had returned from their initial scouting foray to report no evidence that this bleak immensity was inhab-ited, and no sign that might indicate otherwise had been seen since. The sudden appearance of the Indians was all the more startling for that reason.

At the head of the column, Hugh Falconer raised a hand to halt the brigade. The hammers of a dozen rifles being cocked made a sharp, lethal sound in the hot stillness of the river bottom. The mountain men didn't know what to expect from these fierce-looking natives, so they prepared for the worst.

"No shooting unless I give the word," said Falconer.

The five Indians cautiously approached.

"If they make trouble," murmured Eben, "at least we've got the numbers on our side."

Rube Holly glanced wryly at him. "Reckon so?"

One of the five spoke in a guttural dialect to his companions, and they stood their ground as he came on alone. Falconer dismounted to stand at the head of his horse. The Indian leader advanced warily. Resorting to sign language, Falconer tapped his chest, then extended his right hand, chest high, palm turned outward, index and second fingers pointing skyward, and raised the hand until it was in front of his face. In this way he signed ME FRIEND.

The Indian pointed at Falconer, then, with index finger crooked, brought his hand toward his face. Falconer nodded. Indicating the rest of the brigade, he described a counterclockwise circle with his right hand and then closed the hand into a fist and made as though he were pounding an invisible table with it.

"That Injun wants us to come with him," Rube told Eben. "Hugh says he'll go, but the rest of us will stay put." Watching the Indian's response, Rube grunted. "He says we all come. Says we're his prisoners." Rube crossed his wrists, imitating the sign the Indian had just made.

"Prisoners?" Eben laughed nervously. "He's sure of himself, isn't he?"

At that moment the Indian uttered a sound reminiscent of a coyote's bark.

On both flanks of the river were ten-foot cutbanks. At the signal, more Indians appeared to line the rims of the cutbanks. Eben's Appaloosa fiddle-footed, snorting in surprise. Several of the mountain men uttered grim curses. Though outnumbered three or four to one, they were ready for a scrape. Falconer turned and snapped, "The first man who shoots will answer to me."

No one fired.

Turning back to the Indian leader, Falconer signed WE GO.

FROM THE JOURNAL OF EBEN NALL

September 14, 1837. These Indians, known as Diggers, are a poor and primitive people. Their diet consists mainly of roots, insects, and small game. They live in varmint-infested huts made of sticks, and have no concept of personal hygiene, as far as I can tell. Men and women alike wear only the loincloth. The women do not seem the least bit embarrassed by their nudity, and why should they? They know no better. They nurse their infants and perform their bodily functions out in plain sight of everyone, with no sense of modesty.

Having had a little contact with the Mojaves and the Utes, some of them are acquainted with the sign language that serves as a universal tool of communication between the western tribes. But it is manifestly evident that they have never seen white men before, and if there have been any white men before us who made contact with these people no one in our company has heard tell of it.

We were escorted several miles downriver, flanked on both sides by columns of warriors, to their village, a miserable collection of approximately one hundred huts. I was struck by the absence of livestock. The Diggers are unacquainted with cattle and know nothing of horses. This explains much about their primitive existence. The introduction of the horse by the Spanish conquistadores to the great plains

dramatically altered the culture of the tribes re-
siding west of the Mississippi River. Thanks to
the horse, those tribes enjoyed an enhanced potential for trade and hunting and for the making
of war. Without the horse, the Diggers have remained isolated on this desert plain.

These people are so different from other Indians with whom we are acquainted that my colleagues do not know what to make of them. I
overheard someone suggest that they might be
cannibals, and that by following Falconer into
their village we were going to our deaths as
meek as sheep to the slaughter. They were of
the strong opinion that we ought to make a
fight of it. Of the four hundred or so inhabitants
of the village, perhaps a hundred were warriors, and a hundred warriors, no matter the
tribe, will never cause thirty mountain men to
break a sweat. But so great is the respect in
which these men hold Falconer that in this instance they went against their better judgment.

When we arrived at the village, the leader of
the warriors addressed his people, and although
none of us could make heads or tails of the
language, it was clear by his gestures that he
was regaling them with an embellished and no
doubt self-serving account of our "capture."
Some of those gestures were so belligerent that
I began to wonder if indeed Falconer had led us
to our doom. But Falconer appeared supremely
calm, and I took courage. Apparently he knew
all along that the leader of the party that had
surprised us was not the chief, and he turned
out to be right, as the chief later appeared. He
was a wrinkled old man who wore a deerskin

cape draped about his bony shoulders. To this man Falconer offered a few trinkets. Using sign language, he explained that we wished only to pass through their land in peace.

The chief had to have been a hundred years old if he was a day, and he was slow in comprehending, but Falconer persevered, and eventually the message was put across. The old man was beside himself with wonder at the brightly colored beads and tin bells that Falconer bestowed upon him. The leader of the warriors believed himself worthy of a gift too, and Falconer gave him a knife. Testing the blade, the Indian cut himself. Obviously he had never seen a metal blade before. He dropped the knife to nurse his wound, but was quick to pick it up again, as he realized what a fine weapon it would make.

Falconer's gifts changed the complexion of the whole situation. The old chief spoke to his people, and they swarmed forward with smiles and shouts. We were accosted by men, women, and children. They tugged at our clothes and hair. They put their hands on our horses and possibles. One of them latched onto my rifle with such determination that I could only dislodge him by planting a foot firmly in his chest and propelling him backward into the crowd. Rube Holly scared them off of him by plucking the glass eye from his head. Then one of our colleagues, flustered by this pestering onslaught, fired his rifle at the sky, just to buy some elbow room. The effect of the rifle's discharge upon the Diggers was a wonder to behold. All of them took to their heels, including the leader of the warriors. They scattered in all directions like quail. Much relieved, we all had a good laugh. These people no longer seemed to pose much of a threat. It was obvious that they had never seen a firearm, and just the sound of one being fired struck terror into their hearts.

That day we camped near the village. Motivated by greed, the Indians gradually overcame their fear, and bothered us like a cloud of mosquitoes all night. Falconer had his hands full trying to prevent bloodshed, as the Indians vexed us sorely . . .

A shout roused Eben Nall from exhausted sleep. He grabbed his rifle and was on his feet in a heartbeat. Blinking himself awake, he saw a Digger Indian running through the river shallows, holding a pair of moccasins. He was trying to reach the other side. Eben had no doubt he had stolen the moccasins, and he expected to hear a rifle shot that would signal a bloody end to the attempted theft. Instead, a heavy cast-iron frying pan cartwheeled through the air and struck the fleeing thief squarely between the shoulder blades. He flopped limply forward into the river. A roar of delight and approval rose up from the brigade's camp.

The hurler of the frying pan proved to be none other than Gus Jenkins, who waded out to retrieve his purloined footwear. Falconer was waiting for him as he sloshed back to dry land.

"Thanks for not shooting him, Gus," said Falconer, deadpan. "Where did you learn to throw iron like that?"

"My ma," replied Jenkins, pouring river water

out of the moccasins. "She was almighty good at it. Ask my pa if you don't believe me."

The unconscious Indian was floating facedown with the current, and Falconer had him fished out before he could drown. Meanwhile, everyone took a quick inventory of their belongings. Despite uncommon vigil, a few items turned up missing. Fortunately, the horse herd was intact. Falconer had taken the precaution of doubling the guard, and Eben had done a few hours of duty as a pony nurse himself.

All were in accord that the sooner they put the Diggers behind them the better. Forgoing their morning coffee and smoke, the mountain men broke camp in record time and made tracks south. Falconer put scouts on both flanks and had one man trail behind with orders to hasten forward and warn the others if the Diggers appeared to be pursuing the brigade.

The men kept their eyes peeled all day, expecting trouble. But not an Indian was seen. By evening, everyone was breathing a little easier—until it became apparent that Newell, the one-man rearguard, was overdue. Falconer called the brigade together.

"Something's happened to Joe Newell," he said. "I want two volunteers to go back and find him."

"You mean find what's left of him," growled French Pete Bordeaux. "Them Injuns, they done him in, old Joe."

"We should go back and clean their plows," was someone's truculent opinion.

"No," said Falconer. "We don't know what's happened."

Eben expected every man in the company to step forward and volunteer. After all, Newell was one of their own, and to let your partner down was to violate a cardinal tenet of the mountain

man code. But no one moved. Overcoming his initial astonishment, Eben concluded that the Digger
Indians had these men spooked. A man fears what
he does not know, and the Diggers were markedly
dissimilar from any of the Indians to which the
trappers were accustomed. Consulting his own
soul, Eben found himself more than a little
spooked, too. But he hitched his shoulders and
stepped forward just the same.

"I'll go."

Falconer nodded, a ghost of an approving smile
lurking beneath his tawny beard. "One more."

Sixkiller pushed through the crowd. "I go."

Eben stared at the Flathead Indian. His first
thought was that Sixkiller intended to wait until
they were well away from camp before seeking
long-nurtured revenge for the humiliation Eben
had heaped upon him back at rendezvous.

"You both realize you must go now, tonight.
We can't wait until morning to begin the search."

Sixkiller nodded. "Sky clear. Moon come soon.
We see."

"If you find no trace of him by daybreak, come
back. We will linger here until mid-morning before moving on."

As the brigade dispersed, Eben took the journal
from beneath his buckskin tunic and presented it
to Rube Holly, who, as usual, stood close by.

"I want you to hold on to this for me, Rube, in
case I don't make it back."

"Can I read it while yore gone?"

"Not until you throw dirt on my face, Rube
Holly."

Holly chuckled. "Hell, boy, yule outlive me.
'Course you're gonna make it."

But, try as he might, Rube Holly couldn't hide
the fact that he was a little worried, too.

Chapter 12

It wasn't difficult to follow the brigade's backtrail, even at night. The passage of almost a hundred horses in the soft ground along the river produced sign a blind man could have followed. As Sixkiller had pointed out, a full moon appeared an hour after sunset, casting its silver light upon the cooling face of the earth. It also cast deep black shadows around every bush, and Eben Nall tried to keep his imagination in check, because it had a disconcerting habit of fashioning a Digger Indian out of every shadow, leaving his nerves overwrought.

Sixkiller's presence didn't help much, either. Eben was careful not to turn his back on the Flathead Indian. *You'd do well to slit that Injun's throat first night out*, Rube Holly had said. *Iffen you don't he'll have yore head tied to his saddle.* Eben silently cursed old Rube's fondness for such graphic descriptions. He also cursed himself for being so all-fired foolish as to volunteer for this mission. What in the world was he trying to prove? That he could get himself killed just as easily as the next man? Braver men than he—men like Gus Jenkins and French Pete Bordeaux and Doc Maguire—had balked at this business. Braver men—and clearly smarter men, as well.

They rode for an hour, seeing nothing out of the ordinary, hearing little besides the splash and gurgle of the river in its rocky bed and the scurry of furtive night critters in the shinnery. A soothing breeze, redolent with the scent of sage, whispered in Eben's ears.

Eben knew instinctively that he could rely on the Appaloosa to warn him if something was amiss, and the mare did not let him down. The horse sniffed a disturbing scent on the night air and whickered softly, plunging her head down against the pull of the rein leather in Eben's grasp. Eben froze in the saddle, straining his eyes into the darkness, thinking that it must be Diggers the mare had sensed. The Indians were lurking in ambush. His heart pounded against his rib cage, like a man shaking the bars of his cell trying to get out. Perhaps if he fired off his Kentucky rifle the Diggers would scatter, as he had seen them do before. He slid the rifle out of its horn strap, but Sixkiller reached over and pushed the barrel down.

"The mare smells something she doesn't like," whispered Eben. "Might be those . . ."

Sixkiller shook his head. His eyes glittered like chips of black ice in the night. "No. Blood she smells. I know. She mine once."

Eben grimaced. He didn't cotton to the idea that Sixkiller knew the Appaloosa better than he did. But this was neither the time nor the place to make an issue of that.

The Flathead Indian slid off his pony and made a sharp gesture indicating he wanted Eben to do the same. Leading their horses, they moved cautiously forward, side by side. Directly ahead, a deadfall tangle of brush was wedged against a cutbank, lodged there by long-ago floodwaters and resembling in the moonlight a charnel house pile of broken skeletons.

At the foot of the deadfall they found Joe Newell—or what was left of him.

Eben Nall had seen one or two dead men in his
time. He had witnessed a hanging back in Ohio,
and another man had been shot down in the street
in front of the Nall dry goods store. He'd seen
a trapper cut to ribbons in a knife fight at the
rendezvous, wounds that had proved fatal. But
none of it had prepared him for what he witnessed now.

Newell resembled a bloody piece of raw meat.
There was no way of telling how many times he
had been struck by the spears and arrows and
clubs of the Diggers. Then his body had been
stripped clean, though Eben could not imagine
what the Indians could want with clothing that
must have been torn and soaked with blood beyond repair.

While Eben stared in gut-churning horror at the
mutilated remains, Sixkiller spared the body the
merest glance and then proceeded to examine the
sandy soil all around. Eben was too busy trying
to swallow bile and keep from puking to be aware
of what the Flathead warrior was up to, until a
guttural sound from Sixkiller's throat wrested his
attention from the grisly scene.

"Here," said Sixkiller, pointing to the ground.
"And here. Over there. Much blood. Big fight."

"Reckon Newell accounted for some of them?"

"Think maybe yes."

"Good." Eben had suddenly ceased to think of
the Diggers as human beings. They were savage
animals. As such, they were fair game.

"They pull him off horse, there," said Sixkiller,
pointing yonder. "He fight good, but they too
many. He trapped. No escape."

Eben nodded. Newell had indeed been cornered
against the cutbank and the deadfall, with no way

over either obstacle, especially with—how many?—Diggers nipping at his heels. He asked Sixkiller if he could calculate the odds Joe Newell had faced in the last moments of his life.

The Flathead shrugged. "Twenty, maybe. They take dead, and horse. Go that way." He pointed upriver, in the direction of the Digger village.

"Well, at least they're not after the brigade. We had better get back and tell Falconer what happened."

Sixkiller clutched at his sleeve. "They not far. They not move in dark. I smell fire."

"How close?"

"One mile. Maybe less."

Eben squinted suspiciously at Sixkiller. Could the Flathead really smell a campfire a mile away? Or was he hoping to lure Eben to a suitable place for recovering the Appaloosa mare—and at the same time doing away with the white man who had humiliated him?

"Forget it," said Eben. "Falconer sent us out here to find out what happened to Newell. Not to get ourselves killed."

Sixkiller glanced at Newell's remains with a cold and clinical detachment. "Him mountain man. You not mountain man?"

Eben knew what the Flathead was trying to do. A true mountain man did not leave a colleague's death unavenged if he could help it. What would the others in the brigade think if he told them how Newell had been butchered by a handful of Diggers and then confessed that he had not even tried to retrieve Newell's horse and possibles from the murderers, who were camped, unsuspecting, only a mile away? Eben swore softly. Sixkiller could sense how much the regard of the trappers meant to him. The Flathead warrior was cannily using Eben's pride to manipulate him.

"Why do you care?" hissed Eben. "You don't care that Joe Newell's lying there dead. He means nothing to you. Why do you want to pick a fight with those Diggers so bad?"

Sixkiller looked at him as though he were a doddering idiot. "Count coup. Many scalps make great warrior." He struck his chest with a fist.

"Whether you're a great warrior or not is of no consequence to me," said Eben indignantly, "and I'm certainly not going to be sacrificed on the altar of your glory."

Sixkiller's brows knit together. He did not understand Eben's last comment, but he got the gist of the response.

"You no different. You want scalps."

"I most certainly do not. I would never take a scalp."

"You want big name. You want be like Falconer. You kill many Indians, get big name."

Eben shook his head. "No," he said, his tone bitter with self-disgust. "But we'll go after them. Because you're right about one thing. It isn't right not to strike a blow for poor Newell. He'd do the same for us."

Sixkiller grunted. It was obvious by his expression that he believed Eben's real motive for going after the Diggers was, as he had discerned, to seek glory rather than vengeance.

"Come on," snapped Eben, turning abruptly to the Appaloosa. "If we're going to commit suicide, let's get it over with."

They rode another half mile along the river, single file, with Sixkiller in the lead, before dismounting to go the rest of the way on foot, leaving their ponies tied to heavy stones by their rein leather. Before moving on, Sixkiller stripped off his leggins and fringed deerskin shirt. Clad now only in loincloth and moccasins, he squatted at the river's edge, scooped mud up in both hands, and smeared it in horizontal bands across his forehead, chest, and thighs. When he turned to Eben he was grinning like a wolf about to close in for the kill. With a curt gesture, he took off upriver at a lope.

"Sweet Jesus," breathed Eben, as he fell in behind the Indian. He was thinking that if he had to die it would at least be better to die among friends. But now he would not even have that small consolation.

Before long they could see the yellow flicker of a campfire straight ahead. Sixkiller veered away from the river and scrambled with the agility of a monkey to the rim of a cutbank. Eben stayed right behind him. Another fifty yards along the rim, and then Sixkiller suddenly plopped to the ground, crawled to the edge of the cutbank on his belly, and peered down into the river bottom.

There they were, gathered around a cookfire, with four of their dead companions laid out to one side, and Newell's horse, butchered, laid out on the other. They were cooking choice cuts of horse meat over the fire, impaled on sticks or on the ends of spears. Two of them were quarreling over the possession of Newell's rifle. Eben was fairly confident that none of them would know how to load the gun. Considering what they had done to Newell with their traditional weapons, though, this was cold comfort.

"I count fourteen," whispered Eben. "Reckon that's all there are? Maybe there's a guard . . ."

Sixkiller shook his head.

"What do we do? We could shoot down into them, maybe kill a couple before they scatter." Even as he said it Eben didn't cotton to the idea. It meant trying to get back to their horses with a bunch of angry aborigines lurking in the night shadows. "Let's go back and get the horses," he suggested. "Then we can ride right through them and bring down a few and be long gone before they know what hit them."

"No. They kill horses."

"Well, then, what do you want to do?" rasped Eben, exasperated and wondering why he was such a fool to be here in the first place.

"I go around," said the Flathead. "When I shoot, you shoot."

"Wait a minute . . ."

But Sixkiller was already gone.

Eben muttered bitterly to himself. "Now that's downright stupid. There are fourteen of them and only two of us and *we* split up? I've got half a mind to haul my freight out of here."

But of course he knew down deep inside that he could not abandon a colleague—not even Six-killer—and not even if it meant certain death to stay.

Chapter 13

Eben Nall checked his Kentucky rifle's load and made sure there was a dab of powder in the flashpan. Then he rolled over on his back in the sparse grass at the crest of the cutbank and stared up at the stars. The moon was setting behind distant mountains, shading to an arctic blue the cloaks of ice and snow on the shoulders of the soaring crags. Clutching the rifle to his chest, Eben waited for Sixkiller's opening shot—a wait that proved almost unbearable. It gave him entirely too much time to contemplate all the things he had never experienced and now, it appeared, never would. And it gave him time to consider the fate that would befall his Appaloosa mare. He hated to think of her at the mercy of these savages.

When Sixkiller fired, Eben stopped thinking. Leaping to his feet, he brought the rifle to shoulder. Down below, confusion reigned in the camp of the Digger Indians. One of them was sprawled facedown; Sixkiller's bullet had hit him dead center between the shoulder blades. Caught by surprise, the Diggers did not know where the shot had come from. Some stood their ground, crouched, spears or clubs ready. Others were on the run. One seemed intent on clambering up the steep side of the cutbank, clawing at the fluted red hardpack. Halfway to the rim, he saw Eben above him for the first time—an instant before

Eben fired. The bullet struck the Indian above one eye and exited the back of the skull in a pink mist. The corpse flopped to the base of the cutbank.

Eben hastened to reload, fumbling with shot pouch and powder horn, his eyes and nostrils stinging from the powder smoke. Then, aware that several Diggers were about to dispatch spears or arrows in his direction, he threw himself to the ground. The spears and arrows hissed like snakes as they sailed harmlessly overhead. Rolling over on his side, Eben reloaded, his ears ringing with the guttural shouts of the Diggers and the rapid pounding of his pulse. He had his wits sufficiently about him to roll to his right a few yards before rising again, this time to one knee, so that when he reappeared it was not in the same spot.

Sixkiller was entering the camp now, charging out of the darkness and looking like the devil himself bounding through the gates of hell. Uttering a bloodcurdling scream, he fired his rifle point-blank into the belly of a Digger, then used the butt of the weapon to crack open another's skull. Dropping the empty rifle, he picked up a fallen spear, with which he parried the lance of a third Digger, before impaling his adversary on it. Mesmerized by the ferocious audacity of the Flathead warrior's attack, Eben saw the head of the spear emerge from the Digger's back, so powerful was Sixkiller's killing thrust.

Letting go of the spear, Sixkiller whirled with knife drawn, somehow evading the swinging club of another Digger. The knife flashed; the blade nearly decapitated the Digger. A scarlet geyser of blood arched skyward as the Digger toppled sideways into the campfire, creating a shower of burning embers.

In a matter of seconds Sixkiller, a whirling dervish of sudden death, had dispatched four of the

Diggers. But there were eight still alive, and only two of these had fled, while the others converged on the Flathead from all points. Eben fired a second time. The rifle jumped against his shoulder. Through a drift of acrid white powder smoke he saw one of the Diggers stumble and fall.

As he began to reload, Eben caught movement out of the corner of his eye. A Digger, armed with a war club, had gained the cutbank rim and was coming for him. This was one of the Indians Eben had thought was running away. Eben tried to club him to the ground with the butt of the rifle. The Digger ducked under and hit him hard. Eben fell backward, wrenched away as the Digger swung the club. The chiseled stone head of the club missed Eben's skull by a hair's breadth. Eben brought a leg up and knocked the Digger sideways, then scrambled in the opposite direction, tugging frantically at the pistol in his belt as he rose. The Digger recovered and came at him with club raised. Eben triggered the pistol, and the impact of the bullet lifted the Indian off his feet and hurled him backward. Sprawled on the ground at the lip of the cutbank, the Digger convulsed once and then lay forever still.

Breath rasping in his throat, Eben tucked the pistol back in his belt and retrieved the Kentucky rifle. It occurred to him then that until today he had never killed another human being. Now, in a matter of seconds, he had taken three lives. He found himself curiously ambivalent. He had trouble thinking of these primitive men as humans, especially after what had been done to poor Joe Newell. This was more like shooting at a pack of wolves. He knew, in an analytical way, that he was probably wrong in thinking like that. But now was not the time to debate the matter with himself.

Down below, the Diggers had converged on Sixkiller. Eben's heart sank. The Flathead warrior had gravely underestimated the fighting ability of these Indians, and now the sheer weight of numbers doomed him. Three of the Diggers bore him to the ground. Two others turned their attention to Eben. The awareness that he now stood alone against these savages rattled Eben. As the two Diggers loped toward the cutbank, Eben turned and fled into the night.

He ran as though the hounds of hell were nipping at his heels. How far to the horses? Four hundred yards? Seemed like four hundred miles. Time and again he threw fearful glances over his shoulder, expecting to see the Diggers closing on him.

But he never saw them.

Reaching the horses, he was completely winded. Bent over double, he dragged air into aching lungs. Then he remembered that he had never finished reloading the Kentucky rifle, and he hastened to correct this oversight, watching his backtrail as he worked, waiting for his pursuers to appear. They didn't, though, and he had cause to wonder if they had even given chase.

Climbing into the Appaloosa's saddle, Eben felt better about his chances. The mare would carry him to safety. But Eben could not bring himself to turn the horse and head south. His conscience nagged at him mercilessly. What if Sixkiller wasn't dead? The Flathead had still been fighting for his life when Eben had turned tail. Surely he was dead by now. That was likely, but it didn't ease Eben's guilt, not one bit. And it made no difference that it was Sixkiller back there. It really had nothing at all to do with Sixkiller. This was all about living with himself, and Eben knew this, just as he knew that he had to go back into the camp of the Diggers, even if it was certain death to do so, because he couldn't leave, no matter how sorely he wanted to, until he was sure Sixkiller was beyond help.

At that moment Eben wished he were more like his brother. No question what Silas Nall would do in this situation. Silas would look out for himself, which struck Eben as an eminently sensible thing to do, considering the circumstances. Too bad he wasn't made that way. He wouldn't be able to live with himself if he ran away without trying to help Sixkiller.

Leading Sixkiller's horse by its reins, Eben muttered a fervent prayer—and kicked the Appaloosa into a canter, heading upriver for the Digger's camp.

It didn't take long to get there, and Eben was glad of that, because Sixkiller was still alive. Somehow the Flathead had gotten back on his feet. He was still surrounded by the five Diggers, and all he had was a knife. A concerted rush and the Diggers would have him, but they seemed to be afraid of him, jabbing with their spears or taking swipes at him with their war clubs, and it was unclear whether the Flathead was keeping them at bay or vice versa.

Eben's arrival disrupted the standoff. As one of the Diggers hurled a spear at him, Eben fired the Kentucky rifle. The Digger crumpled, drilled through the chest. The spear missed Eben, but not by much. Eben resolutely steered the Appaloosa into the midst of the enemy. The Diggers scattered like quail. Sixkiller leaped onto the back of his pony, and Eben threw him the reins. A Digger spear struck the Flathead's horse in the neck; with a scream the animal went down. Eben cut loose with a curse. He hammered a Digger to the ground with the barrel of the flintlock rifle, as Sixkiller, with remarkable agility, jumped clear of the dying horse and bounded onto the back of the Appaloosa mare behind Eben. Eben needed only a tap of his heels to provoke the Appaloosa into a spirited gallop, and in an instant they were clear of the camp.

Eben could hardly believe he was still above snakes. His relief was so vast that he laughed like a madman as the mare thundered through the night, carrying him and Sixkiller to safety.

"You've done well," said Hugh Falconer, hunkered down across a campfire from Eben Nall. "Not many men would have gone back for Sixkiller."

"Not many men would have run off in the first place," replied Eben.

He had just finished telling Falconer about the entire escapade. Having considered trying to say that he had left the Diggers' camp in order to retrieve the horses, with every intention of returning for Sixkiller in a gallant charge, for some reason, when confronted by Falconer's piercing gaze, he had decided at the last moment to be brutally honest in recounting his actions. He'd been scared—scared clean down to the bone marrow—and to admit as much lifted a great burden from his shoulders.

"Don't know if that's true," allowed Falconer.

"You wouldn't have," said Eben with conviction.

Falconer busied himself packing his clay pipe. He glanced over at Rube Holly. "You must be right proud of this lad."

"Damn right I am."

"How is Sixkiller?" asked Eben.

It was not until arriving back in the brigade's camp that Eben had learned of Sixkiller's injury—

the result of a spear driven deep into his shoulder. The Flathead warrior had ridden for over an hour without betraying his pain. But in that time he lost so much blood that he passed out and fell off the Appaloosa as soon as they arrived at their destination, giving Eben his first clue that something was terribly wrong.

Because of Sixkiller's injury Falconer had chosen to remain in camp an extra day, posting a strong guard in case the Diggers had an appetite for more trouble. Eben had slept most of the day, while Rube kept the curious at bay. Naturally, every man in the company was dying to hear all the details of Eben's adventure. But Eben had told only Hugh Falconer his story.

"Sixkiller is as tough as an old buffalo hide," said Falconer. "He'll pull through. Of that I'm certain."

Remembering the night before, Eben shook his head in wonder. "I've never seen a man fight like that. Like he was possessed by demons."

"Fighting is Sixkiller's forte." Falconer mused in silence for a moment, puffing vigorously on the pipe. "He's not too happy about being alive, though," he added eventually.

"What?"

"You saved his life. Now's he beholden to you. That doesn't sit well with him."

Eben was nonplussed. "Well, I'm not going to ask him to kiss my feet every time I walk by. Truth is, I didn't even do it for him. Not really."

"I know. But Indians are funny in some ways. You're not his favorite person, by a long shot, on account of your taking that Appaloosa mare, and then the stallion, away from him the way you did."

"Then why did he volunteer to go along with me yesterday?"

"Because he figured that would be his best chance of collecting some scalps, I reckon. Had nothing to do with you, Eben. He owes you his life now, though, and he purely hates the thought."

"Huh!" Eben shook his head. "Seems like I just can't win."

"Look at it this way," said Falconer, with the trace of a smile moving beneath his full beard. "Sixkiller's an honorable man, in his own way. He won't rest easy until he gets the chance to repay you by saving your life."

"That's funny," said Eben, though he wasn't the least bit amused. "Now I've got a guardian angel who hates my guts."

"That's about the long and short of it," concurred Falconer. He stood to go.

"Hugh," said Rube. "We leavin' out of hyar come daybreak?"

"Reckon. It will be a hardship on Sixkiller, but by morning he'll be strong enough to make do."

"Good. I got me an itch 'tween the shoulder blades, hoss. Like we're bein' watched."

Falconer scanned the night, and nodded slowly. "I know that feeling."

"I don't think we're shed of them Injuns just yet."

Falconer walked away without saying anything.

Chapter 14

They got under way early, before sunrise, as the first gray threads of dawn began to weave through the disintegrating fabric of night. A travois had been fashioned to transport the wounded Sixkiller, but the Flathead refused to be carried in that manner. It was not befitting a warrior of his status.

Some of the men were openly unhappy with Falconer. They felt it only proper that Joe Newell's death be avenged. Which meant wiping the Digger Indians off the face of the earth. But Falconer would have none of that.

"We didn't come all this way to get into a full-scale war with the Diggers," he told Gus Jenkins.

"I agree. But others don't."

"They underestimate those people. As it stands, we'll be lucky to get out without a fight."

By mid-morning this had become apparent to everyone else in the brigade. They began to see small bands of Diggers, off in the distance, beyond the reach of their rifles, running single file and shadowing them.

"I suppose they have acquired a taste for horse meat," quipped Doc Maguire.

The presence of the Diggers quickly began to wear on the nerves of the mountain men. Some wanted to ride out and confront the Indians, or at least chase them off. Falconer warned them against it. He told them that by doing so they would play right into the hands of the enemy.

That afternoon a hundred Diggers were in evidence. The next morning that number had doubled. By nightfall it had doubled again. By now Falconer had concluded they would not get out of the Humboldt River valley without a fight.

They were near the Humboldt Sink, a vast swamp; here the river became deeper and wider. Falconer found ground to his liking for the night camp. A dry ravine shaped like a horseshoe would form the camp's perimeter on two sides, while the river protected their backs. The mountain men worked feverishly through the night to construct a breastworks of dead timber on the rim of the ravine and the fourth side of the camp. When morning dawned the Diggers discovered their prey dug in deep in a strong defensive position.

By Falconer's calculations there were now about five hundred Indians amassed on the dusty flats half a mile west of camp. The brigade, outnumbered twenty to one, realized that things looked pretty bleak for them. Falconer did not hold out much hope that this time the Diggers would turn and run at the sound of a rifle. In the scrape with Sixkiller and Eben Nall they had proved themselves tenacious fighters.

But the day dragged by without an attack. One concerted charge and they could overrun the brigade—so what were they waiting for?

Late that afternoon a deputation of six Indians approached the camp. In the lead was the warrior with whom the mountain men had first come into contact, the one who had audaciously claimed that Falconer and his men were his prisoners. Eben pointed this out to Rube Holly.

Rube nodded. "I may be old and have but one

good eye, boy, but I kin see who it is. This time he's got the numbers to make it stick."

"You don't think Falconer would even consider surrendering, do you?"

"Surrender? Hugh Falconer?" Rube snorted. "That word ain't even in his vocabulary."

"Well, if it's a fight, we don't stand much of a chance."

"You never know. Long as yore suckin' air you got hope."

Falconer boldly ventured beyond the breastworks to confer with the warrior in sign language. The parlay was of short duration. By the end of it the warrior was plainly agitated. But no attempt was made on Falconer's life. The Diggers were all too aware of the thirty rifles aimed at them.

"They say they want to make peace," Falconer told the others. "Say they want to come into our camp and shake hands and smoke a pipe and share a meal."

"They must think we're half-wits," said Gus Jenkins. "What did you tell them, Hugh?"

"That it didn't take five hundred warriors to make a peace. Told him they'd started it by murdering Joe Newell and that didn't strike me as a very friendly thing to do."

"What do you reckon they'll do now?"

Falconer drew a long breath. "I got a strong hunch they'll hit us before the sun goes down."

He was right.

They came an hour before sunset, after indulging in an hour of chanting brave-making songs. Then a single warrior ran forward to hurl taunts at the mountain men, shaking his spear over his head.

"They're wanting to know how far our rifles will reach," mused Falconer.

"Let's oblige the bastards," growled Bearclaw

Johnson, which were more words than Eben Nall had heard him utter since leaving the Green River. Bearclaw drew a bead. Falconer made no move to stop him, and Bearclaw dropped the Digger in his tracks at two hundred yards.

Immediately a second warrior ventured forth, stopping a hundred yards farther away. Bearclaw cleaned this one's plow as well. A third warrior rushed forward.

Doc Maguire laughed harshly. "If they keep coming at us one at a time, we'll do fine."

Bearclaw killed the third Digger at a range of almost five hundred yards. "Like shootin' fish in a barrel," he growled, making light of a shot that drew the admiration of all who witnessed it.

Eben Nall was watching the distant horde of Indians so intently that he was not at first aware of the presence of his brother at his side.

"Maybe that will discourage them," said Silas hopefully.

"Wouldn't bet on it," replied Eben, remembering his recent scrape with the Diggers. Glancing at Silas, he realized that his brother was white as a sheet. Silas was scared, and that surprised Eben. Silas had always claimed he wasn't scared of anything—said it so often that Eben had just accepted as gospel truth that his brother was braver than he.

As for himself, Eben felt remarkably calm in the face of what he deemed to be certain disaster. He was not so much scared as he was full of regret. He'd been looking forward to seeing California. Odd, he thought, that a few days ago he had been almost paralyzed with fear in his confrontation with the Diggers who had murdered Joe Newell. But now he wasn't. Perhaps this had something to do with being in the presence of Hugh Falconer and the other mountain men. Maybe the unflinching courage they displayed in the face of such daunting odds was contagious.

"Don't want there to be any hard feelings between us," said Silas. "I-I didn't mean what I said back there in the desert. Just lost my head, I guess."

"Forget it," said Eben. Such matters were of little consequence now.

"So we'll just let bygones be bygones, right?"

"Sure."

"If I get killed, and you survive, I want you to have all my possibles. Not that I have much to my name right now, but . . ."

Eben nodded.

"Guess the same goes for you?"

Eben hadn't given it much thought. "I'll want Rube to have the Appaloosa, Silas. Everything else is yours if you want it."

"That ain't very brotherly."

"So it's the mare you're after." Eben shook his head. "I should have known."

"You always thought you were better than me," sneered Silas.

"That's not true."

"Yeah, it is. Well, one day, little brother—one day you'll find out otherwise."

As Silas walked away Eben stared after him, perplexed. He had not known until today that Silas resented him, and he was at a loss as to why this should be so.

Rube Holly came running. "Here they go."

About half of the Diggers were charging across the dusty flats.

"Looks like Bearclaw Johnson's shooting discouraged some of them," observed Eben.

"There's still plenty of 'em to go around."

They rushed to their places at the breastworks. Luck joined them there. Rube did not even try to send her away. It would have been a pointless exercise, and, besides, there was no safe place for her to go.

Eben noticed that Sixkiller, though still suffering greatly from his wound, had taken up a rifle and placed himself nearby.

When the Diggers were five hundred yards away the mountain men began firing at will. For every shot a Digger fell. But the Indians kept coming, the hot, still air filled with their shouts. Every man got off three or four shots before the Diggers reached the ravine, thinning the Indian ranks considerably and leaving the flats strewn with the dead and dying. But there were plenty of them still standing, and now they began to hurl their spears and fire their arrows into the brigade's stronghold.

The effect was devastating. Several trappers fell. The horses, collected in the center of the stronghold, also suffered; a half dozen of them were struck, some fatally. A number of Diggers attempted to cross the ravine and clamber up to the breastworks. They were cut down at almost point-blank range. By now their numbers were no longer sufficient to press the issue, and they began to fall back, leaving the bottom of the ravine carpeted with brown-skinned bodies, the wounded writhing among the dead.

Falconer seized the initiative. He called upon the mountain men to mount up and follow him, leading the way out of camp at a gallop, around the head of the ravine and in hot pursuit of the fleeing Diggers. Many of the Indians were unarmed, having thrown their spears and expended all their arrows. Some carried war clubs, but clubs were no match for flintlocks. The trappers knew how to fire accurately and reload quickly on the back of a running horse. The retreat of the Diggers soon became a rout, as dozens fell beneath the guns of the mountain men. Their panic was infectious. Those Indians who had not chosen to participate in the attack turned and ran.

Two trappers were dead, five more wounded. At least a hundred Diggers had been slain outright, with that number and then some wounded. Many of the latter would perish where they lay during the night. Eben found his opinion of these people changed drastically. Before, he had considered them savages, little better than wild animals. Now, having watched so many die so bravely, he felt somewhat differently about them.

Falconer presided over the hasty burial of the two dead trappers, then led the brigade south under cover of darkness. When morning broke there was no sign of the Diggers. But they could see a black cloud hovering over the battlefield miles away—hundreds of buzzards, come to feast on their bloody handiwork.

Later that day they turned west, making for the distant mountains—the Sierras, beyond which lay golden California.

Chapter 15

October 8, 1837. After nine days crossing desert flatland, we finally reached the foothills of the mountains, which have been tormenting us for so long now, floating like apparitions above the ever-present shimmer of the heat haze.

We have not lately suffered from a lack of water. On several occasions, always in the afternoon, the clouds would gather, building quickly into towering thunderheads, before bursting open to spill their contents upon the thirsty desert. These storms were preceded by very strong winds, which whipped the dust and sand into a stinging fury. The rain, when it came, was very cold and driving. Though of short duration, these rains deposited sufficient water in the rock pools and buffalo wallows to supply our needs.

Game, however, was almost nonexistent. Falconer dispatched several hunting parties, which forayed far afield, but to no avail. In those nine days we managed to kill only a handful of scrawny rabbits and a couple of rattlesnakes. The latter, I must admit, weren't half bad. You must make sure the venom sacs have been removed, of course, but skinned and sliced and cooked on a sharp stick over a hot fire, snake meat is surprisingly palatable.

The rains caused the desert to bloom. Groundsel, snakeweed, and thistle blossomed. The last is used as a medicinal by the Indians. One variety produces a sap that, when dried into a gum, is a powerful cathartic. A decoction of another plant, the broomrape, is commonly used as a treatment for sores, or so I am informed by none other than Doc Maguire, who has more than a passing interest in the healing properties of plants on the frontier. A number of these plants are poisonous to livestock, so care was taken to keep our horses away from them. Without doubt the most imposing vegetation in this part of the country is the joshua tree. There are very large stands of them, and they host a startling variety of birds. But the most abundant and omnipresent of all plants in this country is the sagebrush. This is a very hardy plant, resembling a miniature oak tree, and grows in deep sand or among rocks. Each night we build our campfires with sage. A hole two feet deep and just as wide is dug into the ground. Sagebrush is chopped up and burned in it until the hole is filled to the brim with glowing red coals. There is little smoke produced, and such a fire will provide warmth all night to those who huddle around it. The horses don't care for sage, but almost always where sage grows, so also grows bunchgrass, more nutritious than almost any other grass for livestock.

But for the lack of fresh meat we fared well in the crossing, and all were at a loss to explain the shortage of game, just as everyone was glad

Falconer had made us lay in a stock of dried meat along the Bear River. The only creature larger than a rabbit that we saw during those nine days was a coyote, which seemed bent on accompanying us across the plains. It stayed with us night and day. At first several of the men tried to hunt it down and kill it, supposing that even coyote steaks beat leather-tough jerky. But the coyote managed to elude them all. During the day, while we were on the move, the creature could be seen off to one side of the column or the other, keeping a parallel course. Whenever anyone unlimbered a rifle, the coyote vanished. Eventually we all agreed it would be better to live and let live where our coyote companion was concerned. At night it would sing for us. A coyote's "music" isn't easy to describe. It has many different voices, which seem to echo, so that several coyotes in concert can sound like a hundred. Sometimes our coyote would be answered by one or two others, way off in the distance. Theirs is a distinctly lonesome sound, yet oddly comforting at the same time.

I think only Rube Holly refused to indulge in a fond regard for our strange coyote friend. "He is the Ishmaelite of the desert, boy," says Rube. "The consort of rattlesnakes and turkey vultures. He is a bushwhacker and a tyrant and a prankster. When first I come out here, a greenhorn like you, a coyote latched onto me and damn near stole everything I owned, which warn't much, I can tell you. The devil even dragged my saddle off one night and chewed big holes in the leather—for the salt, I reckon. I set many a trap for the cunning varmint, and finally thought I had him, but he chewed clean through his trapped leg and got away."

When we reached the foothills of the Sierras, the coyote left us. I, for one, missed him.

Our spirits rose when we reached the foothills. The great mountains soared into the sky before us, a towering, jagged barrier of granite, capped with snowfields, the highest peaks wreathed in cloud. These mountains are particularly imposing, as they rise up in great red ramparts thousands of feet above the desert plain. The hills are well timbered with oak and pine. They are steep and broken, rising steeper and higher, increasing in height like stairs until they reach the Sierra. They are cut by deep, wild ravines, clogged with boulders and dead timber and thorny chaparral. Numerous streams, born in the high snows, tumble down through the gulches. Among the trees can be found an occasional meadow, lush and green. These shady glens are inviting to us all, as we have been two long months in the desert. The air is sweet, filled with the resinous aroma of pine, cedar, and wild bay. For mountain men this is heaven, and our inclination is to linger here and recover from our previous ordeals. Yet, as Falconer tells us, to tarry would be a foolish, perhaps fatal, mistake. Soon the snows will come to the high reaches, and the passes will be blocked for the winter, and if we are caught here on the eastern slope, between the desert and the divide, we would suffer immensely before spring arrived.

The question remains, How do we cross these forbidding mountains? No notch or pass is immediately evident. Falconer has decided to leave the brigade encamped upon one of these lush meadows and reconnoiter ahead. He has asked Bearclaw Johnson and me to accompany him. Imagine my astonishment at this unexpected invitation! I can't think why he would want me, of all people, to come along ...

It was rough going for both men and horses, a stiff climb, but Eben's Appaloosa mare proved equal to the task, as he had known she would be. She seemed every bit as strong and surefooted as Falconer's wild-eyed mountain mustang. Bearclaw's pony, though, had some trouble. Part of it was Johnson's bulk. Bearclaw weighed two hundred and fifty pounds if he weighed an ounce. Not that he was fat. It was all grit and gristle. But he was a load, and his horse slowed them down some.

Falconer was convinced that a way across the mountain existed somewhere nearby, based on what the Bannocks had told him, but at first they had no luck in finding even so much as a promising trail. The high palisades towered above them to dizzy heights, apparently unconquerable.

It got much colder as they climbed higher, and that afternoon the clouds gathered, as usual, piling up against the crags. Before long a slashing rain struck at them, saturating their clothing. The chill searched their bones. The wind howled in their ears. In a matter of minutes Eben was perfectly miserable.

They camped for the night not far below the timberline, where junipers, stunted and warped by the weather, grew somehow among red stone needles that rose like a predator's fangs from the base of a shale slope, twenty to thirty feet tall. At some point in time boulders the size of cabins had become detached from the parapet cliffs above and rolled down to the needles, crushing some of the trees. Beneath and between these jumbled boulders the mountain men found dry wood and a modicum of shelter from the storm. Building a small fire, they heated a pot of water, into which they placed strips of jerked venison. This softened the jerky and left a hot, flavorable soup, which all of them drank greedily. After eating, Bearclaw Johnson rolled up in a buffalo robe and in moments was snoring loudly. He had not, as far as Eben knew, spoken a word all day.

"He's not too sociable," said Falconer, as though he could read Eben's mind, "but he knows how to survive in the high country, no matter what."

"I was just thinking," said Eben, "that this country sure has a mean streak. It must bleed something out of a man if he succeeds in adapting to it."

Falconer nodded. "That's reasonable. For everything a man gains he must lose something else. The way life is, I reckon."

"These are the most unfriendly mountains I've ever seen. They were tailor-made for suffering."

"There's a reason for everything. A reason the grass grows. A reason the rivers run. A reason for the snow to fall. That's how God planned it. I guess He had a reason to put some mean-spirited mountains here."

"Yes, but is there a reason for us being here?"

"My mother," said Falconer, with a wistful smile, "used to tell me we were put on this earth to suffer. It's God's plan. I reckon that's why a man is never satisfied with what he's got. Always wants to know what's on the other side of the mountain, and he'll play hell getting across that mountain, too, but he'll do it, only to find he's not going to be satisfied with what he sees on the other side either."

"That makes our existence seem kind of futile."

"Not really. Because sooner or later we're supposed to pluck the scales from our eyes and see life for what it is."

"What's that?"

"A lesson. Life is supposed to teach us that our only satisfaction lies beyond the grave—not in this life, but in the next. Of course, we don't always learn that lesson."

Eben was silent for a moment, mulling it over. "What you're saying is that California won't turn out to be that paradise on earth we've all heard so much about."

"That's right."

"Then why do we bother?"

"We have a foolish nature."

"Then what's the use in having dreams?"

"Dreams are meant to humble us, because they never turn out just right. I had a dream once, of living alone in the high country with Touches the Moon until the day I died. I'd leave the world alone if it would leave me alone. I had a few years of living my dream, which is more than a lot of men can say, and I thought I was fairly well satisfied. Thought I had everything I could possibly ever need. But then Touches the Moon died, and I was reminded that nothing ever stays the same. You see, the dream was supposed to last forever."

"If what you're saying is true, I might as well have stayed a store clerk back in Ohio."

"No. That's not what I'm saying at all. If you don't chase your dreams, you'll never learn your lesson."

"Well," said Eben, "I'm still not sure I understand why you're so dead set on getting to California, if you know it won't turn out to be what you're looking for."

Falconer smiled as he rolled up in his blankets. "I never said I'd learned my lesson."

Chapter 16

Eben Nall found it hard to sleep that night. This had nothing to do with the storm, or the cold, but rather with the conversation he'd had with Hugh Falconer. Though disturbing in some of its aspects, the talk was a comfort to Eben. Falconer, the living legend, had become more human in Eben's eyes as a result of their parlay. And it occurred to Eben that Falconer had seen fit to share his innermost thoughts with him. Eben suspected that this was an honor bestowed upon very few men, even while he was mystified that Falconer would choose him, of all people, to confide in.

As a rule, mountain men were a profane and rowdy bunch, and Eben was somewhat surprised to learn that Falconer had a deeply ingrained religious streak. For this had been Falconer's point: nothing in this life would ever truly satisfy a person—such fulfillment could be had in the next life. Nonetheless, Eben found his desire to experience the wonders of California undimmed. For some reason he felt certain he would find answers there—answers to questions regarding what he was supposed to do with his life. Of course, first they had to find a way across the forbidding Sierras—no easy task.

Finally Eben drifted off to sleep.

Falconer woke him at dawn. The storm had passed. The sky was a beautiful robin's egg blue, and dawn light painted the high snows in shades of pink and indigo. But it was bitterly cold. Falconer had the fire blazing and coffee brewing; Eben managed to pour some into a tin cup even though he was shivering violently. The coffee was hot enough to burn his tongue, yet, oddly, he could scarcely feel the heat of the cup on his frozen hands.

"We'd better get over these hills in a hurry," he said. "I'd hate to be stuck here when winter comes in earnest."

"I think we ought to split up," said Falconer. "Cover more ground that way. You go north. I'll head south. We'll meet back here no later than tomorrow morning."

Eben looked around for Bearclaw Johnson and noticed for the first time that the man was gone.

"He lit out about an hour ago," said Falconer, with a sigh. "When he woke up he said he smelled bear. He has spells like this sometimes. When it happens there is nothing you can do to stop him. He forgets about everything else and goes off to hunt grizzly."

"Hadn't we better look for him?"

"When he's over it, he'll find us. If you do run across him, just let him be. He's not in his right mind."

Nursing the coffee, Eben spent some time in somber deliberation of his immediate future. The prospect of exploring these strange mountains on his own was daunting enough without having a loco Bearclaw Johnson to look out for. But he said nothing to Falconer, merely trying to conceal his anxiety.

A half hour later Eben was on the trail. He climbed higher, across gray and barren screes of shale, through the last of the wind-sculptured junipers. A chill wind fluted around the peaks and, striking him, seemed to bore holes right through him, holes out of which his energy seeped. Above loomed majestic peaks, and in their presence Eben was reminded of the helpless inconsequence of man. Still, the cautions that were so much a part of his nature ebbed away, and thoughts of the risky endeavor in which he now found himself were intoxicating. It struck him again that Hugh Falconer had seen something inside him—something he himself had not been aware of—that had prompted the legendary booshway to burden him with awesome responsibility. The success of the expedition, and quite possibly even the lives of the men in the brigade, rested at least in part on his shoulders at this moment. They had to find a passage through the Sierras, or there would be hell to pay, and of all the savvy frontiersmen to choose from, Falconer had elected to bring him along.

About midday he reached the crest of a rocky shoulder and heard for the first time the gushing roar of a waterfall. Far below, in a deep gorge strewn with boulders, a river foamed as it careened wildly along its rocky course. Descending from the shoulder, Eben tried to keep to the rim of the gorge, but the going was too treacherous for even the surefooted Appaloosa, and after a couple of hair-raising close calls, he urged the mare back up onto the mountain's flank. He realized that the river gorge snaked through the peaks in such a way that from the lowlands to the east it went undetected.

Finally he reached a point from which he could see the falls, cascading in three stages into the gorge below, falling at least a thousand feet in all. A swirling mist rose from the depths of the gorge, accompanied by perpetual thunder. It was a magnificent scene, but Eben was more interested in what lay beyond the falls: it appeared that a narrow canyon gave access to the heart of the Sierra range.

Riding on, he found a game trail that skirted the head of the falls, providing several dizzy glimpses of a chasm filled with indigo shadows and the sound and fury of the cascades. This led him into the mountain trench. He had gone but a mile when the afternoon clouds gathered quickly overhead to blot out the sun, their gray-black bellies pregnant with rain. The wind picked up; trapped in the canyon, it swirled madly and tore at his clothing with invisible claws. Then the heavy mists of rain closed in, and the tattered shreds of the broken thunderheads crept down into the trench to blind him. The Appaloosa slipped and slid on the slick rocks of the trail. Thoroughly miserable, Eben retreated within himself, seeking to escape the surface misery. He left progress entirely to the Appaloosa; his faith in her was complete.

By late afternoon the coldness in him was a burning ache. At day's end it had become a numb sensation in his arms and legs. The trench widened. The river widened too and became less violent, and Eben sought refuge in a stand of pines. Nightfall trapped him there—but better there, he decided, than on the perilous game trail above the gorge. There was nothing for it—he would wait here until morning light and pray throughout the long, cold, wet, hungry, miserable night that by daybreak the storm would have passed. Then he would take one quick look at the valley before starting back. No chance of reaching the needles, where he was due to meet Falconer, by the appointed time. But he had to know if the valley was going to pan out. Anticipation prevented him from getting a wink of sleep. Sitting on a carpet of wet pine needles, wrapped in a thoroughly saturated Point blanket, in the lee of the Appaloosa mare, he suffered through an interminable night. Finally the rain ceased. The bitter cold wracked his aching bones with merciless persistence. Dawn crept over the peaks and down into the valley. His heart sank as he watched a thick cottony mist rise from the white-water river. But when the sun reached the skyline, its golden rays seemed to shred the mist, and Eben rejoiced at the sight of pristine blue sky.

Ahead of him lay the panorama of the valley, with its wooded flanks and its high mountain meadows sparkling like emerald facets with the morning dew. By the angle of the sun he could tell that the valley cut east to west, through the Sierras. Was he the very first white man to ever see this valley? Probably. Would there be a pass at the other end, along the divide? No telling. That was a chance they would have to take, unless Falconer had discovered a more promising route.

Wincing as he rose from beneath the mare, Eben wiped the saddle with his blanket before mounting up. A solitary timber wolf appeared across the river, stopped short in surprise at the sight of him, barked once before melting back into the purple shadows of the forest. Eben turned the Appaloosa around and headed back.

He was surprised to find Falconer waiting for him at the needles, well past the appointed hour.

"I had no luck," said Falconer. "What about you?"

Eben told him about the promising valley he had discovered, but he stressed that he did not know if it would take them all the way through the Sierras.

"We'll have to risk it," decided Falconer, studying the sky, which was once again filling up with angry clouds. "We don't have much time before the first snow falls."

"What about Bearclaw? Any sign of him?"

"Not a trace. And we don't have the time to search for him. He'll find us, if he's able."

They reached the brigade late that night. They were on their way before the next sunrise, and the long climb to Eben's hidden valley began.

FROM THE JOURNAL OF EBEN NALL

October 21, 1837. I have been too busy trying to stay alive to attend to this journal with any kind of regularity. The crossing of the Sierra Nevadas was a difficult one. On our second day in the mountains the snow began to fall, and it fell in abundance every day thereafter. The drifts became so deep that we lost several horses to them, and I believe we were lucky not to lose any men. The snow piled up so thick in the pine forests that at times we could not make passage through the trees at all, and had to seek a way around them, which often entailed ascending a steep and treacherous precipice.

Even without the snow the passage would have been an arduous undertaking. The valley that I had stumbled upon proved to be a short one, and its western outlet was a saddle of granite boulders wedged between a pair of lofty peaks. Trying to find a way through or over these boulders was no easy task, and we lost two more horses in the attempt. One of them was carrying Rufus Fuller when it slipped and fell. Both man and horse suffered a broken leg. The horse was put out of its misery. Although Fuller had multiple fractures and was in tremendous pain, we could not do him the same favor, even though he begged us to do so. He knew, as we all did, that he would be crippled for the rest of his life and probably would never walk again. Doc Maguire did the best he could trying to set the broken bones, but the damage was severe, as nine hundred pounds of horse had rolled over the leg. Our only medicine was a jug of whiskey. A travois was built, but more often than not we had to rely on four strong volunteers to carry Fuller, as the terrain was too rough for riding.

On the western side of the saddle we discovered a modest stream, which we followed into yet another high valley. We hopscotched from one valley to the next for two weeks. All the while the snow fell and the frozen winds pierced us to the bone. It was so cold at times that a mist of ice particles could be seen floating in the air. On the rare occasion that the sun broke through the clouds, its light made this mist sparkle like a rainbow of diamonds. We had to take care not to lay bare hand to metal, as one would freeze fast to the other. It was so cold that I saw trees split apart, as though they had been struck by invisible lightning. We had several cases of frostbite. Sometimes an icy hail fell from the sky, piercing like needles. Our blankets and beards were white with frost, and at night spittle would freeze on one's lips.

To contribute to our anguish there was precious little game to hunt. This was a keenly felt disappointment; after many hungry days in the sagebrush country we had all anticipated good hunting in the mountains. But the early snow had apparently driven most of the game to lower elevations. Our provisions were nearly exhausted, and all of us were haunted by the fear of becoming snowbound prisoners in this high country. I have heard stories of men in such situations resorting to cannibalism to survive, but of course in our case we had the horses.

After the first week in the Sierras some of the men petitioned Falconer to let them kill one or two of the ponies so that the company could have some fresh meat. The two horses lost to broken legs had been consumed earlier, and I must confess that horse meat becomes quite palatable after weeks of dried venison. The plan was that all the men would draw sticks, and the two who drew the shortest sticks would each surrender one of his horses to the communal cooking pot. It testifies to the desperate nature of our predicament that Falconer approved the scheme. I was resolved to give up one of my packhorses if I chanced to draw a short stick. The Appaloosa mare, of course, was completely out of the question. But, as luck would have it, I did not have to.

We saw no sign of Bearclaw Johnson, and it became the consensus that a grizzly had finally got the better of him. Johnson was the fourth man the brigade had lost—the other three had fallen victim to the Digger Indians. Those are not bad numbers, I suppose, considering what this company has endured since leaving the Green River valley three months ago.

After a fortnight in the Sierras mutiny reared its ugly head. Prompted by their fear of being trapped by the snows, several men began to campaign for our turning back. I hate to admit it, but one of those men was my brother, Silas. I had not thought it possible that he could have embarrassed me any more than he already had, but I was wrong. Falconer dismissed their demands out of hand, at which point, according to what Silas told me, the conspirators planned to desert the brigade and go on their own stick. This would have violated the promise every last man had given Falconer in the beginning. Each of us had given our solemn word to stick with the brigade until we got to California. Personally, I was willing to bid farewell to Silas and let him go his own way. But Falconer would not permit it to happen. He let it be known that he would hunt down and kill any deserter. That struck me as a bit severe, but Rube defended our booshway, explaining that if Falconer were to let a few men break the rules now he would catch pure hell trying to keep the rest of the company in line the next time we got into a little trouble.

After Falconer's warning, I heard no more about desertion from Silas or any of his fellow malcontents. No one wanted Falconer on his trail. Our booshway strikes me as a very decent fellow, but there is a dark side to him, and I do not doubt he would track a deserter down and slit his throat without blinking an eye. Hugh Falconer is not a man to cross.

I for one never for a moment doubted we would survive this new ordeal and make it to the western slope of the Sierras, and today, the twenty-first day of October, we have before us the splendid panorama of fabled California stretching as far as the eye can see, a beautiful tapestry of forested hills and tawny plains, all caressed with sunlight and warm breezes.

We have made it, and all our troubles lie behind us . . .

Chapter 17

In the foothills on the western slopes of the Sierra Nevada, Hugh Falconer searched for and found an ideal spot for a camp, where there was plenty of timber, several spring-fed creeks, and meadows of golden wild oats upon which the horses could feast. It was his intention to encamp the brigade in this spot for several days. One reason was obvious: the condition of the horses, gaunt and exhausted after the mountain passage, during which, because of the heavy snows, good graze had been almost nonexistent.

There was another reason, and that night Falconer addressed all the men to explain.

"I realize all of you are eager to see what this country has to offer," he said, "but for now most of you will stay put right here. Tomorrow I will send out three hunting parties, two men in each. The rest of you are not to stray more than a mile from this camp."

This announcement triggered some disgruntled muttering. Falconer watched and listened for a moment, trying to gauge by their initial reactions the degree of difficulty he would have enforcing the order. He didn't blame them for being upset. These men had been through hell to get this far, and now that they were here he was keeping them on a short rope. Which was why he was about to do what he seldom did—explain himself. He figured he owed them that much.

"I want all of you to keep this in mind: we are no longer in the United States. This isn't our country. It's part and parcel of the Republic of Mexico. Most of you know what happened to Jedediah Smith and his men when they came through here some years back. Since then, nothing has happened between the United States and Mexico that would lead me to believe we would get a more pleasant reception than Smith got. We have to walk soft and keep our eyes open. What we don't want is to start a damned war."

"I ain't never much cared who claims to own what," was one mountain man's resentful response. "I'm accustomed to goin' where I please, when I please, and doin' what I please, the devil take the cost."

Falconer suppressed a smile. This was precisely the sentiment he had expressed to Benjamin Bonneville months ago, back at the rendezvous, when Bonneville had tried to recruit him as, in essence, a scout and spy for a California-coveting United States of America. But no one saw the twitch of his lips beneath his tawny beard. His dark brown eyes were stern.

"This time you'll do things my way," he replied curtly. "If there's anybody here who doesn't cotton to that, he had better say so now, and we'll settle right here."

He took the time to look each one of them squarely in the eye. No one spoke up.

"When we find the first settlement, Gus Jenkins and I will go in alone," continued Falconer. "I'm taking Gus because he speaks a little of the lingo. I want the people to know we mean them no harm."

"What if the two of you don't come back?" asked Eben.

"Then I suggest you all find a way to get back across those mountains. If you can't do that, head north. If Gus and I are arrested, I don't want anybody trying to cut us loose either."

Eben scanned the faces of the other mountain men seated or standing around him. Their expressions confirmed what he suspected—none of them could easily turn their backs on Falconer and Jenkins if this worst-case scenario became reality.

The next morning, Eben and Rube Holly saddled their best horses at daybreak. They were one of the three hunting parties Falconer was sending out. Falconer came by to see them off. He was staying close to camp, and Eben understood why; Falconer wanted to make sure none of the others surrendered to their desires and wandered off to explore this strange new world.

"I reckon you two know you're hunting for more than fresh meat."

Rube grinned. "You ain't got to spell it out for us, Hugh. Iffen we see any sign of other folks we'll let you know." He tapped his false eye—an act that made Eben cringe every time he did it. "We'll keep our three eyes peeled."

They headed due west out of camp. The morning was clear and fresh. A sultry breeze riffled the tall grass. The sun and the wind and the warmth fueled Eben's high spirits. He was beguiled by the pristine beauty surrounding him. Indeed, it seemed like a paradise on earth, especially after the ordeals of their desert crossing and mountain passage. There was no evidence that anyone had ever passed this way before; the land appeared as unsullied by human hands as it must have at the moment of God's creation.

They had gone but a handful of miles from the

camp when they spotted several deer at the edge of a bosquet of oaks. Spying the pair of horsemen, the deer plunged back into the shadowy depths of the trees. Eben and Rube turned into the bosquet; dismounting, they tethered their horses, primed their rifles, and ventured deeper into the woods, spreading out but keeping each other in view.

Rube was the first to spot a target and shoot. The crash of his rifle was shockingly loud in the sylvan setting. His aim was true, and a moment later he and Eben stood over a ten-point buck, shot through the heart.

"By thunder there'll be some good eatin' to-night!" crowed Rube. "Don't know 'bout you, boy, but I'm right tired of feelin' my belly button rubbin' up agin my spine."

Eben nodded, and had to spit, he was salivating so at the thought of hot venison steaks.

"You go on and git one, too," urged Rube. "I'll bring up the horses."

Eben went on alone. A hundred yards farther on he heard a telltale rustle and caught a fleeting glimpse of a deer running through the trees. Stalking the animal, he found himself on a slope that grew ever more steep. To his left rose the rocky spine of a ridge—and there, briefly silhouetted against the sky, stood his prey! Eben brought the Kentucky rifle to his shoulder and squeezed the trigger. He had the deer dead to rights. But when the powder smoke cleared there was no sign of the creature. Eben's heart plummeted. How could he have missed such an easy shot? Reloading, he scrambled to the top of the ridge, found spots of blood on the stone where the deer had been standing. So he hadn't missed, after all! At least that was something. But now he had to track the wounded animal down.

Below him was a ravine, filled with boulders

and thicket. Eben doubted he would ever be able to locate the deer if it was down there, but he proceeded to try. A year in the high country with Rube Holly had wrought a marked improvement in his vision; he spotted traces of bright red blood, on the face of a rock here, on waist-high blades of grass there. He spent an hour struggling over, under, and through the tangle, pausing often to listen hopefully for some sound that would provide him with a clue to his prey's whereabouts. No luck.

Then, when he was on the verge of giving up, the ravine widened and cleared, becoming a small valley squeezed between steep, rock-strewn hills perhaps four hundred feet from rim to rim. And just as Eben broke free of the thicket, he saw the deer, a hundred feet straight ahead, tottering through the tall grass. He raised the rifle, intending to put the suffering creature down, but before he could fire the deer collapsed.

Eben broke into a loping run. When he reached the deer, he was glad to see the animal was already dead. The bullet had struck well behind the heart—in essence, it had been a gut shot, and Eben silently cursed himself for being such a poor hand with a rifle. He did not like to see any animal suffer, especially when that suffering was the result of his own incompetence. Rube Holly had poked fun at him for his qualms when they had first begun to trap beaver. It had seemed to Eben that setting their Number 10 traps in such a way that the caught beaver drowned was a distinctly inhumane procedure. Fishing a hundred-odd dead beavers from the ice-cold shallows of mountain ponds had not served to harden Eben's heart to any perceptible degree.

Eben took a good long look around and tried to calculate how far he had strayed from the bosquet where the hunt had commenced. At least a half mile. Now he was confronted by the daunting prospect of having to carry the deer back. Even if Rube Holly was tracking him, it would be next to impossible to negotiate the horses through the ravine, clogged as it was with boulders and rampant brush. Passing through that stretch had worn Eben to a frazzle. He wiped sweat from his furrowed brow. But nothing, he told himself, was ever gained by postponing unpleasant business.

Laying down the Kentucky rifle, he bent to gather up the deer's forelegs and pulled them over one shoulder, then reached back to collect the hind legs and hauled them over the other shoulder. Doubled over, the deer balanced on his back, he managed to retrieve his rifle from the ground. A groan escaped him as he straightened. The kill was a young buck, probably weighing in at less than two hundred pounds, but it felt ten times that heavy to Eben.

"One step at a time," he muttered without enthusiasm.

As he took that first step he heard a loud *crack!* and something whipped through the tall grass in front of him. An instant later he heard the gunshot.

Somebody was shooting at him!

His first reaction, quite irrational, was anger. What damn fool would take a shot at him? His first thought was that it had to be someone from the brigade, maybe a member of one of the other hunting parties. It was a perfectly ridiculous notion, but Eben was working under the false assumption that the only human beings within one hundred miles of this particular spot were the mountain men who had accompanied him across the Sierras.

His gaze swung to the top of the hill to the

west. There, silhouetted against the bright midday sky, was a man on foot. The man wore a wide-brimmed hat—and that was about all Eben could discern of his garb. Then the sun that lanced into Eben's eyes also flashed off the barrel of the man's rifle.

The man spoke, yelling down at him. A chill traveled along Eben's spine, because whatever lingo the man was speaking, it sure wasn't the King's English.

Two more men appeared on the hill, to either side of the first man, and Eben threw a desperate glance in the direction of the thicket, a hundred feet away. That tangle of brush and vine and thorn he had been cursing a few minutes ago was now as inviting as the Garden of Eden. A hundred feet. So close, and yet so far. He could drop the deer and make a run for it. He was a swift runner. How long would it take to cover that little bit of ground? Four or five seconds?

The man was yelling again. A furtive glance told Eben that the trio were proceeding down the hill toward him, spread well apart, their rifles leveled. Eben's feverish brain kept racing. What kind of marksmen were they? Had the man meant to fire a shot across his bow? Or had he aimed at Eben and missed? On the verge of bolting for the thicket, Eben felt his deeply ingrained caution rear up and grab him by the throat, throttling the life out of his reckless inclinations. His feet suddenly became rooted to the ground, and he dared not even drop the deer for fear that any movement on his part might prompt one of the men to shoot.

He studied them as they drew near, and he didn't like what he saw. Mexicans, obviously. A scrofulous lot, dirty and bearded. They were giving him the once-over, too, looking at him as though they had never in their lives seen anything

like him. The one in the middle—the man who
had fired the shot—made a sharp sideways motion with his rifle, an old flintlock musket. Eben
understood perfectly well what that meant, and
he let his Kentucky rifle slip from his grasp.

One of the other Mexicans pounced forward to
snatch up the rifle. As he admired the weapon,
one of his companions made an abrupt attempt to
wrestle it away from him. Eben had a brief hope
that while the Mexicans quarreled and scuffled
over the rifle's possession he might be able to
make a break for the thicket. But the third Mexican, the one who had fired at him, kept his eyes
and his rifle fixed on him.

"Look," said Eben, hands raised, "you can keep
the rifle. And the deer, too. Just let me go."

He realized as soon as he spoke how silly the
offer really was. Of course they had every intention of keeping both the rifle and the deer he had
slain—and they didn't need to make a deal with
him to do it.

The Mexican snapped something at him, and
Eben had a hunch he was being told to shut up.
Then the man shouted crossly at his two companions. By the tone of voice Eben could tell it was a
command—or maybe a command coupled with a
threat. Whatever it was, it worked. The two men
stopped scuffling over the rifle. The man who had
tried to confiscate the rifle from the one who had
picked it up had failed in his endeavor; now he
spun around and put the tip of his knife to Eben's
throat. He did not appear to be in a very good
frame of mind. Somehow Eben managed to stand
his ground—surprising himself as well as his cap-
tors with his composure.

"*Muy valiente,*" sneered the man with the knife,
his face close to Eben's. Eben winced at his fetid
breath.

"*El cuchillo*," barked the leader. "*El pistola*."

The man with the knife plucked Eben's knife and pistol from his belt, one at a time, keeping his blade pressed against Eben's throat and depositing Eben's weapons in his own belt. Then he asked the leader a question. Eben had a good idea what he was asking.

They had his weapons, they had the deer he had slain—now all that was left was to decide what to do about him.

Grinning, the leader answered the query by drawing a finger across his throat.

Chapter 18

An inner voice, manufactured out of sheer terror, shrilled in Eben's head.

I'm going to die!

He had come all this way, endured so much to get here, and now he was going to die, right here, right now, and that was as certain as the turning of the earth.

And then another voice, grim and calm. *Yes, you are going to die, so you should die fighting.* That way, at least, when Hugh Falconer stood on this very spot and read the sign as other men might read a book, he would know that Eben Nall had not gone quietly.

The man with the knife was still looking at the leader—all of this had passed through Eben's mind before the leader was through with his throat-cutting gesture. Eben's left hand, clenched into a fist, came surging up to plow into the man's face and his right arm swept down to strike the knife away from his throat. The blade grazed Eben's collarbone. He hardly felt the wound. Grappling with the stunned Mexican, he managed to swing the man's body between him and the leader just as the latter's rifle discharged. At such close range the impact of the bullet, squarely in the chest, hurled the knife-wielding Mexican into Eben. Eben lost his balance and fell, with the dead weight of the Mexican on top of him. The leader

yanked a pistol free of his belt, screaming something at Eben, his ugly face twisted with rage.

A rifle spoke.

Eben's body jerked involuntarily, in anticipation
of the bullet.

But neither Mexican had fired. Eben watched,
dumbfounded, as the leader toppled sideways, an
expression of disbelief frozen on his face.
Sprawled in the tall grass, his body arched in one
terrible spasm. A guttural sound welled up in his
throat and then ceased abruptly, and his body
went limp as life deserted it.

It took a few seconds for what had happened
to register in Eben's numbed brain.

Rube. It had to be Rube . . .

The last Mexican turned and ran, heading for
the top of the hill. Eben felt the ground tremble
beneath him. He shoved the dead man aside and
rolled up on one knee—then fell back down,
throwing up his arms to shield his head as a horse
thundered by so close he could feel the wind of
its passage. Two more horses galloped by, almost
on top of him. Shaken, Eben looked after them.
Three horsemen, riding the last Mexican down.
They closed on him just as he reached the top of
the hill. There he turned at bay, realizing the riders were upon him, and determined to face death.
Several pistols, one in each rider's hand, spat
flame and smoke. The Mexican crumpled, riddled
with bullets.

Eben did not see what the three riders did
next—another horse appeared above him, and he
looked up to identify the rider, but the sun
seemed to be perched on the horseman's shoulder,
and it momentarily blinded Eben. He glimpsed a
concho-studded saddle complete with *mochilla* and
tapaderos, a leg encased in black pants with con-
chos along the outer seam. Big-roweled spurs jan-

gled their music as the man dismounted, to sit lithely on his heels in front of Eben, reins in one hand, rifle in the other. Eben thought, *There's the rifle that killed the leader.*

"*Buenos tardes, amigo. Como esta usted?*"

Eben just stared, in the grip of an uncomprehending stupor.

The man smiled. He was young, about Eben's age. The fierce sweep of a black mustache that reached from one jawbone to the other gave his demeanor a rakish cast. His brown eyes were so dark they glittered like polished obsidian. He wore a short scarlet jacket embroidered with bold black swirls on the cuffs and lapels. A sombrero hung by a rawhide cheek strap down his back.

"Yankee?" he asked.

"What?"

He pointed at Eben. "Yankee?"

"Yes. American."

The man nodded. "English, I speak a little." He seemed quite proud of the fact. "You hurt?"

"No."

"*Bueno. Muerte*, almost."

"What?"

The man's brows knit together, then came unraveled. "Dead," he said, and smiled—a token smile, devoid of feeling.

"Yes," said Eben. "Almost dead." He began to shake, and couldn't stop.

The man stood and glanced at the crest of the hill. Eben looked that way too, just as the three horsemen reappeared from the opposite slope. Two of them were each leading a pair of saddle horses. The third was leading a man by a rope. The rope was tight around the man's chest and shoulders, pinning his arms to his sides. As they got closer Eben realized the prisoner was not a man at all, but rather a boy, maybe fourteen or fifteen years old. Lank black hair hung down over his forehead, behind which flashed scared eyes. The three horsemen were laughing and joking. Eben didn't have to know the language to know that much. Their carefree attitude troubled him. After all, they had just finished killing two men. Regardless of whether those men deserved killing, it was nothing to take so lightly. But apparently killing was old hat to these men.

When the trio of horsemen reached the spot where Eben stood with the Mexican in the scarlet jacket, the rider who had the boy in tow gathered up the rope, reeling in his prisoner as one would a fish hooked on a line. Some words passed between the rider and the Mexican standing with Eben. Then the horseman planted a booted foot between the boy's shoulder blades and gave him a hard shove. The boy sprawled in the grass at the foot of the Mexican in the scarlet *chaqueta*.

"*Como se llama*," said the latter.

"Arturo."

"*Ladron*," said the man in the scarlet jacket, using the tone of one who is correcting a child.

"No!" The boy shook his head emphatically. He cast desperate eyes in Eben's direction and spoke rapid-fire, and though Eben could not decipher a word of it, he could tell the boy was making an earnest plea.

The man in the scarlet jacket smiled another one of those meaningless smiles and shook his head. "He say he no want to kill you," he told Eben.

"He didn't try. I never saw him."

The man in the scarlet jacket looked at him with such impassivity that Eben had no clue what was going through his mind.

Then the man turned abruptly, slipping his rifle into a hard leather boot tied to the side of his saddle. When he turned back around, he had a pistol drawn. He put the pistol to the boy's temple. The boy fell to his knees with an anguished cry.

"Good God," said Eben, horrified.

His words were punctuated by the crack of the pistol.

The boy's lifeless body was flung violently sideways to the ground. His assassin belted the pistol and smiled at Eben. The smile turned Eben's blood cold.

"We go," said the man.

One of the horsemen leaned in his saddle to offer Eben the reins of one of the ponies he was leading. Eben dragged his gaze away from the corpse of the boy to the proffered reins and then to the face of the horseman. Outraged, he felt his anger thaw the paralysis that had gripped him. He surmised that the boy had been holding the horses of the three men who had waylaid him. That had been Arturo's only crime. Yet he had been executed. Shot down in cold blood, without even the chance to make his peace with God. It was the most brutal act Eben Nall had ever witnessed.

"You bastards," he muttered, then turned on the man garbed in the scarlet jacket, the one who was proud that he could speak a little English, and repeated himself, louder this time and with more feeling.

The boy's executioner froze, one foot fitted into a stirrup, one hand on the horn of his high-cantle saddle. He looked at Eben without a trace of emotion. Yet Eben sensed that he understood. *This one is the most dangerous man I have ever met*, thought Eben, *because his eyes tell you nothing. They give no warning. It is impossible to know what he is thinking, or what he will do next.*

"We go," repeated the man, and mounted up.

"I don't go," said Eben hotly. "I'm staying right here. I've got—"

He caught himself on the verge of telling them he had friends nearby. Would it be wise to tell them about the brigade? Who were these men, anyway? Where did they come from? All he knew about them was that they had saved his life, but he didn't take it personally, feeling certain somehow that they had been hunting the three men and the boy and had not slain them because they had attacked him. And the fact that they had saved his life was cold comfort to Eben; they were cut from the same cloth as the three who had ambushed him. They had gunned down two of the robbers and laughed about the deed. They had executed a defenseless boy. And now they were going to leave the bodies to the buzzards. Eben didn't feel at all like a man who had just been rescued.

The one in the scarlet jacket sat his horse, watching Eben, and Eben could tell he really had no choice in the matter. They wanted him to go with them, and that was precisely what he was going to do, willingly or otherwise.

Eben scanned the skyline, wondering what had become of Rube Holly. He had a feeling the old-timer was close by. Or maybe it was simply wishful thinking. Resigned to his fate, he retrieved his Kentucky rifle—moving slowly and with circumspection, careful not to make any sudden moves that might be construed as threatening. He didn't want to give these men another corpse to joke about. Mounting the horse that was offered him, he nodded at the man wearing the scarlet jacket, who spun his pony around and raked those big-roweled spurs to provoke the animal into a gallop. Eben and the others followed.

Chapter 19

It was called Hacienda Gavilan.

Eben Nall had never seen anything like the place in all his born days. Having ridden for hours across wild, beautiful country seemingly untouched by human hands, he reached the crest of a hill and looked down upon an amber plain stretching to a distant blue line of ridges, and there it was, hard by a sparkling river that wound its serpentine way across the plain. Speckling the plain were cattle—hundreds, maybe thousands, of head—but Eben paid them little attention compared to the time he spent gazing in rapt fascination at the hacienda itself.

The main house was a square two-story structure, built around a courtyard large enough to hold a hundred horses with room to spare. Its adobe walls, Eben would learn, were three feet thick, impervious to bullets or arrows or fire—impervious to anything, in fact, except the blast of a sizable cannon. In essence it was a fortress, the heavy shutters on its narrow windows crosshatched with gun ports, while its doors were made of solid mountain-mahogany timbers, reinforced with strap iron. The lower level's windows also sported grills of iron elaborately wrought. Four massive chimneys, one on each side of the house, pierced a roof of red clay tiles.

Around the main house were dozens of other

buildings and a number of pole corrals. Encircling all of this was a mudbrick wall. In places the wall stood ten feet high, in other places half that. A great arch marked the main entrance into the compound, access that could be denied by a pair of gates fashioned from squared timbers more than a foot in thickness. Above the gate, secured to the arch, was a set of cow horns spanning nearly ten feet. Eben found it hard to envision the cow that had once worn such headgear.

As Eben and his escort approached the gate, a solitary rider exploded out of the compound on a stretched-out bay horse. He did not check his pony until almost upon them; then he pulled rein so hard the horse sat down on its haunches. The man was dressed in the same manner as Eben's four companions; he was clad in terra-cotta buckskin *chaqueta,* white muslin shirt, and a bright blue neckerchief, and he wore heavy cowhide leggings over his trousers. A sombrero hung down his back by its chin strap. Big spurs jingled against his boot heels. A gaily colored serape was draped over the back of his saddle. He spoke to the man in the scarlet jacket a moment, and his bright, inquisitive eyes kept flicking over to Eben. His unkempt black locks and angular brown features gave him a wild look. Then, abruptly, he spun the responsive pony around and thundered back to the hacienda, shouting to the collection of men, women, and children now gathered in the vicinity of the gate.

As they passed through the gate, Eben studied the crowd assembled there with every bit as much curiosity as they examined him. The women were clad in calico dresses and blue cotton rebozos. The children wore white muslin shirts and trousers or dresses, if they wore anything at all, and every one of them was barefoot. The men fell into two distinctly different categories. There were those clad in a style akin to that affected by Eben's companions, while the rest wore white shirts and trousers and straw hats, sometimes with a serape draped over a shoulder.

As they crossed the hardpack to the main house, Eben tried to take in everything around him. Over there was a blacksmith at his forge. Stripes of sunlight coming through the pole roof of the *ramada* lay across sweat-glistening shoulders rippling with muscles as the smitty wielded a heavy mallet to shape a piece of red-hot iron clasped in the jaws of a pair of tongs. Over here, an old woman sat in a ribbon of blue shade beside a doorway. Her face was creased with countless seams, as brown as old leather. She deftly rolled a cornhusk cigarette with one hand while her eyes followed Eben riding by. Next to her lay an old white bulldog, stirring itself only to nip at pestering flies. Over there, children played stickball, screaming in delight; they froze in place as Eben passed, falling silent. Then they leaped into action again. Beyond the big house stood a structure that Eben recognized as a small church when the bells in its squat tower suddenly began to chime, competing with the rhythmic ringing of the blacksmith's mallet. Up on pole parapets located at strategic points along the wall, men stood gazing watchfully out across the plain. Between the wall and the river—a stretch where the wall was low enough to see over from the vantage point of a horse's back—men in white labored in irrigated fields where corn, beans, and potatoes flourished. Over in a pole corral, young men were busting broncos in a swirl of dun-colored dust.

Eben realized this was much more than just a ranch. It was a self-sufficient community, an outpost of civilization in the wilderness. At first

glance he estimated at least a hundred residents.
It was all wondrous and intriguingly foreign to
him, and for a moment he forgot that he was, in
effect, the captive of a band of cold-blooded
killers.

As they neared the big house, Eben saw a man
emerge from a door on the second floor, stepping
out onto a balcony of wrought iron. He was tall
and square-shouldered, with black hair streaked
at the temples with silver and brushed straight
back, curling long at the shoulders, forming a widow's peak in front. Long side-whiskers framed a
strong, chiseled face. He wore a white ruffled shirt
and yellow doeskin trousers. A scarlet kerchief
fluttered at his throat. There was no doubt in
Eben's mind that this man was the lord and master of all he surveyed—the aura of power and maj-
esty invested in him was apparent to anyone with
eyes to see.

As Eben's four companions checked their horses
below the balcony, all of them doffed their sombreros out of respect for the man above them.
Eben was bareheaded, but had he owned a hat
he would have followed suit—it seemed a natural
thing to do in this man's presence.

"*Buenos tardes, Patrón*," said the man in the scarlet jacket.

"Remo, *quien esta hombre*?"

As he spoke, the man on the balcony pointed
to Eben. It was natural to assume he was asking
for the identity of the stranger, so Eben took it
upon himself to speak up.

"My name is Eben Nall," he said. "I'm an
American."

The man on the balcony cocked an eyebrow.
"Indeed. My name is Don Carlos Chagres. An
American, eh? What, may I ask, are you doing
in California?"

"I was hunting. Minding my own business, when three men attacked me. They were going to cut my throat, and then these men showed up and shot them down."

"I see." Chagres glanced at the man in the scarlet jacket. *"Es verdad,* Remo?"

"Si, Patrón."

"Who were these men?"

"They were the thieves who have been stealing our horses and cattle. The ones you ordered us to find."

"Good." Chagres turned his attention back to Eben, switching to English, which he spoke with impressive fluency. "I am very happy that my *vaqueros* arrived in time to save your life, Señor Nall."

"This man," said Eben, pointing to Remo, "killed a boy in cold blood. The boy could not have been more than fifteen years old. He was unarmed and had done nothing wrong."

Chagres raised his brows at Remo. "Did you kill an innocent boy in cold blood, Remo?"

"He was one of them, *Patrón.* Those were your orders."

"He was a thief, like the others, Señor Nall."

"He had no chance. He begged for mercy."

"Obviously, then, he was not yet a man. Perhaps my *vaqueros* should have set him free. Then he could have stolen our livestock for several more years, until he was old enough to kill."

Eben glanced at Remo. Remo was watching him, his eyes as blank as a doll's stare, a hint of a smile on his lips, and Eben realized that while Remo was indisputably a cold-blooded killer, he was no more so that Don Carlos Chagres. *Maybe,* thought Eben, *I should just let the matter drop and be thankful for my life.*

"I'm grateful to your men for saving me," Eben

told Chagres. "It is just that the boy's death . . . bothers me. In my country, every man has a right to a fair trial before he is judged."

"Ah, but this is not your country, is it? Which brings us back to you, Señor. What are you doing so far from home?"

Eben didn't know what to say. He was reluctant to tell Chagres about the brigade, not knowing how the man would respond to the news. What if he dispatched Remo and a host of *vaqueros* to deal with his companions in the same way they had dealt with the thieves? No doubt the brigade would give a better accounting of itself than the cutthroats had done. But Falconer had said in no uncertain terms that he did not want to start a war, and Eben wasn't about to start one.

But, with the truth unavailable to him, Eben was at a loss to explain his presence. *If only I could lie like Silas,* he thought. Eben was sure his brother, if placed in this situation, would have deftly fabricated some entirely plausible falsehood without missing a beat. By his silence Eben knew he appeared to be hiding something. Chagres obviously thought so.

"I am a poor host," said Don Carlos. "You must be very tired after your ordeal. Come, you are welcome in my house." Switching to Spanish, he said, "Remo, show our guest in."

As Chagres left the second-floor balcony, Remo gestured for Eben to precede him. Eben approached the door, his heart heavy, for it seemed to him that he was entering a den of lions. And he was no Daniel.

Creaking on its iron hinges, the heavy door swung ponderously open as he drew near. A fat woman wearing a dough-encrusted apron around her prodigious waist smiled pleasantly at him. Remo followed him in. Eben found himself standing in a wide, tile-floored hall. Straight ahead was another door, open to the courtyard around which the house had been built. To left and right were double doors of dark, heavy oak, leading to other rooms. Remo showed him through the doors to the left. The room beyond was very long, furnished with age-blackened pieces of furniture. Dusty channels of sunlight angled through the narrow windows lining one wall. Moody portraits in ornate, gilded frames stared down at them. Eben's attention was drawn to one of a man clad in the armor of a conquistador. Seeing the armor reminded Eben of the eccentric Britisher, Sir William Drummond Stuart, whom he had met at the Green River rendezvous. But Stuart and the rendezvous and everything else comfortingly familiar to Eben Nall were a world away from here, and for the first time Eben truly regretted having accompanied Hugh Falconer on this foolish venture.

The door at the other end of the room opened. Eben braced himself, expecting to be confronted at close quarters by the intimidating Don Carlos Chagres.

Instead, a young woman entered the room.

One look at her took Eben Nall's breath away.

Chapter 20

Eben knew it wasn't polite to stare. But he just couldn't help himself.

The young woman was beautiful—the most beautiful woman in the world. Eben was as certain of this as he was that the sun rose in the east and set in the west, even though he was no authority on women, not by a long shot, having seen relatively few of the softer sex, especially of the young and attractive variety, during his short lifetime. The Kaskaskia region of Ohio had still been wilderness when Eben was born, with more men than women in the sparse population, and since coming to the mountains the only women he had seen were Indian, with the exception of Reverend Gray's lady missionaries. Now, gazing at this woman, he realized just how plain those lady missionaries had been.

The vision standing before him was petite—only a few inches over five feet in height and weighing maybe a hundred pounds soaking wet. Eben could have enveloped her narrow waist with his two big hands. But she was shapely, and the dress of pale yellow organdy she wore accentuated every curvy attribute. Her hands and feet were tiny, her skin as white and smooth as polished alabaster. Her hair was long and black and shiny, her eyes limpid hazel pools, and her lips were red and moist like rose blossoms after a spring rain.

As she approached Eben from across the room, she seemed to be examining him with an intense curiosity, taking his measure, and he assumed it was because she had never seen the likes of him before. Eben became suddenly and uncomfortably aware of the sorry appearance he presented. His buckskins were black with grime under the arm-pits, between the shoulder blades, and in the crotch. And, as she drew near, and the faint, pleasing scent of flowers reached him, he dismally assumed that he stunk to high heaven. He had last bathed in the Humboldt River. That had been a month ago.

"*Buenos tardes, Señor*," she said, smiling warmly, her eyes roaming over his face, and Eben raised a self-conscious hand to feel the beard stubble on his cheeks. "Or, I should say, Good afternoon."

Eben swallowed hard, trying to dislodge the large lump in his throat. "Ma'am," he mumbled in reply.

Again he wished he possessed another of his brother's gifts—a fleeting but nonetheless fervent wish. Silas was never at a loss for words, especially when it came to charming the ladies.

"Welcome to Hacienda Gavilan. I hope your stay with us will be a pleasant one."

Her voice was lilting, soft, musical. Her accent, in his opinion, was quite fetching.

"So do I, ma'am."

"Please, call me Sombra."

"Sombra. That's a—a very pretty name."

Her smile deepened. She was delighted with the clumsy compliment. Eben felt his cheeks get hot, and he was mortified. He was blushing! Good thing he was unshaven. He wondered if he had been too forward, and he glanced at Remo, who stood beside him.

Remo was trying to maintain that stoic mask of his. But Eben was surprised to see the careful facade begin to crack. The *vaquero* was watching him with jealousy a lurid glimmer in his dark eyes.

Eben turned back to Sombra. "Are you the wife of Don Carlos, by chance?"

Sombra's smile began to fall apart. She struggled to keep it in place, but Eben caught a glimpse of a strange expression as it flicked across her face. Was that fear he saw? Fear, or loathing. Whatever it was, clearly he had touched a nerve. He began to stumble through an apology, but she stopped him with a hand upraised.

"I am his daughter," she said stiffly.

Eben glanced again at Remo. So this man was in love with the boss's daughter! Eben wondered if Don Carlos was aware of Remo's feelings for Sombra. If he didn't know, what would his reaction be if he found out?

His powerful dislike for Remo emboldened Eben. "Don Carlos is lucky," he told Sombra, "to have such a lovely daughter." And he bowed slightly from the waist. He felt absurd doing it, but he was compelled to throw caution to the wind just for the satisfaction of provoking Remo. It was a foolish thing to do, but Sombra's presence encouraged an odd recklessness lurking in his heart.

"Lucky," said Sombra, uncertain.

"Fortunate."

"Yes. Fortunate." Her tone of voice was unmistakably sarcastic, leaving Eben befuddled. There was more here—much more, lying beneath the surface—than met the eye. But before Eben could give the matter further deliberation, Don Carlos Chagres entered the room.

"Ah," said the *patrón*, "I see you have met my daughter." He put an arm around her tiny waist and pulled her close to his side. Eben thought her smile was more than a little strained.

"I've had the honor, sir."

Chagres cocked an eyebrow. "You are well mannered for an American. But then, perhaps I am not being fair. You see, our only contact with your people are our business transactions with your Yankee sea captains and their crews. As a rule, I have found these men to be somewhat— how do you say it?—rough around the edges."

"You speak English very well, sir. So does your daughter."

"I have taught her the best I can. She is my only child. My sole heir. This will all belong to her when I am gone. She must know your language to conduct the affairs of this hacienda. Most of our commerce is with British and American traders."

"But this place must be a long way from the sea," said Eben.

"True. But we are not all that far from the San Joaquin, which is navigable a fair distance from the coast." Releasing Sombra, Chagres stepped back and gestured at the furnishings. "I beg your forgiveness. Please, sit down. You look very tired. You have had a difficult day, haven't you? Would you care for a drink? Some wine, perhaps? Madeira?"

Eben didn't know what Madeira was, but he thought it would be rude to decline. "Anything will be fine."

"Sombra, pour our American guest a glass."

She moved obediently to a sideboard and poured the wine from a crystal decanter into a glass, which she then handed to Eben, who now sat in a chair. Eben realized that two years had passed since he had enjoyed the comforts of resting his bones on honest-to-God furniture. And just as long since he had drunk from a glass. The Madeira was quite different from the raw whiskey available in the mountains.

"Tell me, Señor Nall," said Chagres, standing before him. "Where are you bound?"

Eben did not want to fail to give an answer for the second time. "Nowhere in particular. I just wanted to see what California looked like."

"You did not come by sea. You look like no sailor I have ever known. Do you mean to tell me you came across the Sierras?"

"That's right." Eben didn't think there was much point in denying it. Chagres would scarcely believe he had dropped out of the sky.

"Alone?"

There was no help for it now. Eben could not answer. Chagres had backed him into that same corner. Then he realized that by not speaking he was, in fact, answering the question.

"So, have you been sent to spy on us, Señor Nall?" Chagres said it with a smile, his tone light, almost joking. But Eben knew it was no joke.

"No, sir. Honest, I just wanted to see California."

Chagres let him off the hook. "And what do you think of it?"

Eben glanced at Sombra, who was sitting primly on a horsehair sofa behind Chagres. Finishing off the Madeira, he rose from the chair.

"Am I to consider myself a prisoner here, sir?"

"A prisoner? But of course not. You are our guest."

"Well, I've never been one for wearing out my welcome. If you don't mind, I'll just be on my way."

"It grows late, young man. Please, feel free to stay the night with us. In the morning you may go or stay, as you wish. You have my solemn word—I will not ask any more questions of you. At least none that make you uncomfortable, or that you feel you cannot answer. It is only that we do not see many Americans in these parts. Naturally, we are curious."

Eben decided his wisest course of action would be immediate departure. But he made the mistake of looking once more at Sombra—and he changed his mind on the spot.

Even though it meant lingering in the lion's den.

Never in his life had Eben Nall sat down to such a meal as the supper laid on that night at Hacienda Gavilan. Thick beefsteaks, potatoes, roasted ears of corn, bread, marmalade, strawberries swimming in cream for dessert, hot coffee and brandy for after dinner. Just laying eyes on such a feast reminded Eben how famished he was, and had been for weeks, and he had to make a special effort to remember his table manners. The last thing he wanted to do was behave like a barbarian in front of Sombra.

There were just the three of them—him, Don Carlos, and the girl—and they sat together at one end of a long polished table in the dining room. Chagres sat at the head of the table, with his daughter on one side and Eben on the other. The portly woman who had met Eben at the door that afternoon served them.

"I hope you find your room agreeable," said Chagres, as they began to dine.

"Yes, sir."

The serving woman had shown him upstairs to a guest room two hours earlier. A big four-poster bed had beckoned to the bone-weary Eben, but he had pulled a chair up to the window and gazed out across the compound at the golden plain and beyond, to the snowcapped mountains, a good long day's ride east. Many unanswered—and perhaps unanswerable—questions assailed him. Would he truly be free to leave in the morning? Where were Rube and Hugh Falconer and the rest of the brigade? Did they have any idea what had befallen him? Bearclaw Johnson had disappeared in the mountains and the brigade had moved on without any attempt to locate the missing man. What if the same happened here? Eben felt very much alone.

Later, the serving woman brought him some clean clothes—dark trousers, a white linen shirt, a pair of black half boots that fit just right. Eben didn't want to change, but he figured he would be a poor guest if he sat down to supper in his grimy buckskins. The clothes fit him well, but they felt awfully strange on his skin. Eben had not worn such attire since his last day behind the counter at his father's store, almost two years ago.

"You have quite a place here, sir," added Eben. "I've never seen such a fine home."

Chagres glanced about the room, satisfaction stamped deeply on his face. "I am fond of it. It was built one hundred and seventy years ago, by the Jesuits. A mission, you see."

"A hundred and seventy years!"

"Yes. Back when the French and the English were fighting each other for possession of the other side of this continent. Your United States would not exist for another hundred years. Forty years ago the priests were murdered by Indians. For some time the mission stood abandoned. Then it was granted to me, this place and all the land you can see from the top of the bell tower."

"That's a lot of land for one man to own."

"I do not own just the land, my young friend, but everything and everyone on it. You might liken it to feudal days in Europe. I am the lord and master of all that I survey. Every head of stock, every ear of corn, every drop of water in the creeks, every blade of grass on the plains—it all belongs to me."

"The people, too?"

"But of course. They are obliged to do my will. In return, I gladly accept the responsibility of seeing to their every need. I feed them in times of famine. I clothe them, I arbitrate their disputes. I care for them when they are sick. My word is law among them."

"Sounds kind of like the plantations down South I heard about when I was a boy," said Eben. "That's a pretty big responsibility."

"And one I take very seriously. This is the reason why those *ladrons*—those thieves—who accosted you had to die."

"I don't think I follow . . ."

"They were stealing my cattle and horses. And when they steal from me they steal from everyone else who lives here."

Eben took a moment to digest this novel concept of one man lord and master, lawgiver and judge, over many. In the mountains there was no law, or so they said back east. In Eben's opinion that wasn't exactly true; there was the law of nature—the strong prevail over the weak—and every mountain man was essentially a law unto himself. He answered to no one but himself, his own conscience. But this—this was quite different from anything Eben had experienced. Don Carlos Chagres ruled all. This was his kingdom. He possessed everything that lived on it, down to that old woman smoking cornhusk cigarettes in front of her *choza*, and the old white bulldog who was her companion. That meant Eben too was subject to the whims of Don Carlos. His life rested in the hands of the *haciendero*.

After the meal, the serving woman brought a bottle of brandy and a humidor of hammered silver that contained cigars. Eben declined the latter while accepting a glass of the former. Chagres indulged in both. He took great care in lighting the cigar so that it burned evenly. Sombra excused herself, giving Eben one final, speculative glance as she left the dining room. Eben's thoughts dwelled on her long after she was gone. Her fragrance lingered.

"My daughter is a gentle soul," said Chagres. "She is not much older than the boy Remo killed. They used to play together."

Eben was stunned. "You knew Arturo?"

"Oh, yes. I knew them all. They used to live here. The men worked for me. I provided for them, as I do for all the others. But they were not content with what I gave them and began to take what did not belong to them. For many months they have been killing my cattle and selling their hides. The horses they rode carry my brand. My daughter would say that a few horses and some cattle are of no consequence when measured against the lives of men. But she is wrong. Were I to let them continue, others would perceive my weakness, and soon we would have more predators, and all would be lost. With blood and sweat I have built an empire for my daughter. I fear she will lose it all when I am gone unless she hardens her heart."

"If you don't mind my asking, where is her mother?"

"Her mother died, after a long illness, several years ago. God rest her gentle soul. I have tried to raise Sombra the best I can alone. It is not easy. Consuela here"—he gestured at the serving woman—"has been a surrogate mother to Sombra."

True to his word, Chagres asked no questions of Eben. When the *patrón* was finished with his postprandial brandy and cigar, he announced his intention to retire for the evening. Eben returned to his room. Somewhere beyond the walls of the house he heard men singing a ballad to the accompaniment of guitars. In the distance an infant cried, and a dog barked. The hacienda, this remote outpost of civilization, was a peaceful setting, mused Eben, and he had been treated very well. Still, he was ill at ease and made certain his rifle was primed and loaded before turning in.

Stripping down to the buff, Eben slipped his lanky frame under the covers. The crisp, clean linen sheets and goosedown mattress were pure heaven. It had been an eventful day; exhausted, Eben drifted off to sleep.

The creak of a floorboard jerked him awake. The door to the room opened onto an inner balcony overlooking the courtyard. The door was ajar, and a shadow moved between it and the bed.

Eben's first, panicked thought was that Remo had come to kill him. Remo—the killer with the lifeless eyes—had been haunting his dreams. The image of the boy, Arturo, on his knees, Remo's pistol to his head, had plagued Eben even in his sleep. And now Remo had come for him, jealous of the way Sombra had looked at him . . .

Eben lunged for the Kentucky rifle leaning against the wall by the bed.

As Sombra hurried forward, she passed through a stream of moonlight at the window, and he saw her clearly, clad in a long white nightgown, her raven hair cascading over her shoulders.

"No! Please!" she whispered. "It is only I."

Sitting up in bed, Eben remembered his nakedness and frantically clutched the covers to his chest.

"Good Lord," he breathed, "you've got to get out of here." He could just imagine what Chagres would do if he found his daughter here.

"You must help me." Standing by the bed, framed against the moonlight, Sombra's body, every firm, alluring curve, was clear to him through the thin fabric of the gown.

"Help you?" he echoed, dumbfounded.

"Take me away from here when you go. Please! I have no one else to turn to. My father—he is a wicked man. I cannot remain here any longer. Please, take me with you." She leaned closer and her hands touched his bare shoulders, and that heady fragrance swept over him as her warm breath caressed his face. "I would do anything . . ."

Chapter 21

Eben Nall took Sombra firmly by the shoulders and pushed her away from the bed.

"You have got to get out of here, miss," he whispered. "If your father ..."

Realizing that the counterpane had fallen down into his lap, Eben snatched it back up to shoulder level. Sombra covered her face with her hands and quietly sobbed.

"My father is an evil man."

"If this has something to do with the boy Remo killed ..."

She lowered her hands. Tears glistened on her pale cheeks. "You do not understand. My father ... he ... I am too ashamed to speak of it."

Eben's heart went out to her. Sombra was genuinely distraught, and clearly desperate as well, to turn to a total stranger for help. Whatever her trouble, what could she expect of him? What did she think he could do? He was no Hugh Falconer. Eben doubted if even a man like Falconer could take on Don Carlos and his men alone and hope to survive. But Eben could not bring himself to turn her away. Not when she was crying like that.

"Listen, miss, if you'll just turn around I'd ... well, I'd like to get some clothes on, if you don't mind."

With a glimmer of hope in her eyes, Sombra did as he asked. Eben slipped out of bed on the other side and donned his borrowed clothes in record time. Then he went around the bed, took her ever so gently by the arm, and guided her to the chair over by the window. He sat her down and hunkered down in front of her.

"I honestly don't know what I can do," he said, "but if there is any way in the world to help you, I will."

Her smile was tenuous. "I knew you were a good and brave man, Señor Nall."

"Well, I don't know about that . . ."

"My father comes to my bed."

She blurted it out, and the expression on her face told Eben she had never spoken of this to anyone else. Shame burned in her cheeks.

Eben was stunned. Surely he hadn't heard right!

"Es verdad," she breathed, looking away. "It is true. I wish it were not. Several times this thing has happened. It makes me sick to my stomach just to think of it."

"Good God. How long has this been going on?"

"For a year, maybe a little more."

"And you've told no one else?"

"Who could I tell?" she asked, in despair.

"That feller Remo, maybe. I think he'd probably do just about anything for you, if you asked him."

The look of disgust on her face somehow cheered Eben. Obviously she did not hold Remo in very high regard.

"Remo would never turn against my father. Not even for me. And I never would ask him, anyway."

"So you know he has feelings for you."

"He does not really care for me. He wants to marry me so that the hacienda would be his one day."

"I see."

"Consuela knows. She would help me if she

could. But what can she do?" Leaning urgently forward, she clutched his hand in both of hers. "Please. Help me escape. I cannot bear it any longer."

"You're not free to come and go as you please?"

"I am a prisoner here. When I ride, two *vaqueros* must always be with me. This is my father's law. He says it is for my protection. But he knows I would keep riding and never return of my own free will, if once he let me pass through the gates alone."

Eben thought it over. If they could steal some horses and slip away under cover of night, by dawn they could be well on their way back to the brigade, their lead too great for . . .

What was he thinking? He could not in good conscience place the entire brigade in jeopardy like that. Chagres could probably put a hundred men into the field, every last one of them sworn to die in the service of his *patrón*.

On the other hand, knowing what he did, he could not simply go his way and leave Sombra to her fate.

He heaved a deep sigh. "I didn't tell your father the truth, miss. I'm not alone. I came to California with some friends. When I leave tomorrow I will talk to Hugh Falconer. He's our booshway . . . our leader. If anyone can think of a way to get you out of this, it will be Falconer."

She squeezed his hand tighter, panic flaring in her eyes. "No. *You must not leave me here.*"

"I won't be leaving you here, at least not for good. Miss, listen to me. I give you my solemn word, I'll help you somehow. Even if I have to come back alone. I'll come back."

She studied his earnest face for a moment, Then that trembling, sad, brave smile reappeared. "I believe you."

He stood, helped her to her feet. "I'll get you out. Take you wherever you want to go."

"I have nowhere to go."

"No other family?"

She shook her head. "No place in California would be safe. My father is a very powerful man. No one who lives here would dare stand against him."

"Well, then, where . . . ?"

"I will go with you."

"Back to the mountains? That's a pretty rough trip, miss."

But why, he thought, would that matter to her? After what she had suffered here, escape would be worth any price, wouldn't it?

"Please. My name is Sombra."

Hands resting light as feathers on his broad shoulders, she stood on tiptoes and her lips, soft and wet with tears, brushed his cheek.

Then she was gone, as silently as she had come.

Stunned, Eben stood there a while, staring at the door that she had closed so softly behind her. Finally he sank into the chair and touched his cheek in wonder, breathed deep to capture the trace of sweet fragrance yet lingering in the air.

A little before dawn he dozed off, sitting up in the chair. A commotion outside roused him from his restless sleep. Dawn light pearled the sky. The sun had yet to rise above the Sierras' formidable high reaches.

Looking out the window, Eben's heart leaped with joy.

Hugh Falconer, Rube Holly, and Sixkiller—the Flathead warrior leading Eben's Appaloosa mare—were coming through the hacienda's main gate.

Eben Nall was so happy to see Falconer and the others—even Sixkiller—that he had a powerful urge to run down to the front door and greet them with open arms. Then he thought better of it. Maybe he ought to just sit tight and see what happened.

Between the time that Falconer and Rube Holly entered the house—Sixkiller stayed outside to watch the horses, glowering at the curious Californios who hovered around him—and Remo came up to the room to fetch him, Eben tried to exercise a little self-discipline and stay seated in the chair by the window. But he couldn't; instead he paced the floor for a good thirty minutes. When Remo knocked, he threw the door open.

"Come," said the *vaquero*.

For some reason unbeknownst to him, Eben decided to play disingenuous. "What's going on?"

Remo's lips curled. It was a smirk, not a smile. "You lied."

"Oh, well, I didn't lie, exactly," replied Eben, feeling much bolder now that Hugh Falconer was around. "I just didn't tell the whole truth."

"Your *companeros* have come looking for you." Remo nodded sideways, indicating that he wanted Eben to precede him.

Falconer and Rube were standing with Don Carlos in the big room adjacent to the entry hall, where Eben had first laid eyes on Sombra. Relief washed over Rube Holly's craggy features when he saw Eben.

"Hoss, we thought you was gone beaver."

"Almost was."

"Yeah, I know. Even Sixkiller was worried. Was you to go and git yoreself kilt before he has a chance to save yore life and square things between the two of you, why it would be a black stain upon his honor."

"I'm fine," said Eben, "thanks to Don Carlos and his men."

Until now he had carefully avoided looking at Chagres, but now he did so. Just as he had expected, powerful dislike for the man surged through him—so powerful he could taste bile. He tried to keep his features impassive, taking a page from Remo's book. It wasn't easy, knowing what he knew about the son of a bitch.

"I tracked you best I could," said Rube, "but that ravine slowed me down some. When I heard the shootin' I come runnin'. But this feller"—the old-timer motioned at Remo—"this feller and his three pardners got to you first. When I seen they warn't gonna curl yore toes, I figured I ought to git back to Hugh and tell him what happened."

"Don't fret about it, Rube." Eben could tell Holly was bothered some by what had transpired.

"I was skeered you might have thought I let you down," confessed Rube.

Eben smiled, put a hand on the old codger's bony shoulder. "Not a chance. I knew you were around. Remo just beat you to it." He turned to Chagres. "I apologize, Don Carlos. I couldn't tell you . . ."

"I've explained all that," said Falconer. "You were acting under my orders not to divulge the existence of the brigade."

"I admire loyalty," said Chagres. "Señor Falconer assures me you mean to make no trouble for us, and I believe him. It is apparent to me that he is a man of honor. I have suggested he go straight to Monterey to see the governor-general, and explain everything to him. I know Don Luis. He is a reasonable man."

"Don Carlos," said Falconer, "has kindly offered to accompany us to Monterey and intercede with the governor-general on our behalf."

But what of Sombra? Eben desperately wanted a moment alone with Hugh Falconer to tell him about the girl. Somehow he had to get her away from Hacienda Gavilan. One thing was certain: he wasn't about to leave her behind.

"I have other business I need to attend to in Monterey," said Chagres. "I have needed to make the journey for some time now. Besides, I promised my daughter she could buy some new dresses in the shops there."

"Sombra is coming with us?" blurted Eben.

All four of the others gave him a funny look. Eben wanted to kick himself for being such a loose-tongued fool.

Fantastic plans whirled through his mind. Surely it would be easier to slip away with Sombra once they reached Monterey. Maybe they could book passage on a merchant ship. Don Carlos would never catch them then. But how could he pay for such a passage? He was as poor as a church mouse.

Of course, there was always the Appaloosa ...

Could he give up the mare to help Sombra?

Yes, he decided. He could, though it would pain him to do so.

"Sombra will accompany us," said Chagres. The gaze he fixed on Eben Nall was piercing, speculative, and Eben realized that by his careless words he had made the task of helping Sombra escape her father more problematical. Chagres would be watching him now, suspecting something. And, of course, there would be Remo to contend with. Eben did not doubt for a moment that Remo would kill him rather than let him take Sombra away.

"We will leave tomorrow morning," continued Don Carlos, "if that is acceptable to you, Señor Falconer."

"We'll ride and bring back the brigade," replied Falconer.

Eben felt a hard cold knot twist his guts. He would be expected to ride with Falconer, which meant leaving Sombra here, at least one more night, at the mercy of Chagres. What would she think if she saw him ride away? He could derive some consolation from knowing that Don Carlos would surely tell her about the arrangements for the journey to Monterey. But Eben desperately wracked his brain for a plausible ruse that might buy him one minute alone, now, with Sombra, so he could reassure her that he was not deserting her, wasn't going back on his word, not to worry.

He didn't get the chance. A few minutes later he and Falconer and Rube and Sixkiller were mounting up to leave the hacienda. Eben was frantic.

Then the serving woman, Consuela, came out of the house with his buckskins. They had been scrubbed and mended and neatly folded. As he leaned in the saddle to take the buckskins from her, knowing that he was taking a big chance, he whispered so that only Consuela could hear.

"Tell Sombra I'll keep my promise."

He rode on with the others, wondering if the woman had understood even a word, wondering too where Sombra was at this moment, and praying that if she was watching she would not give up hope.

Chapter 22

They were still within sight of the hacienda when Eben Nall urged the Appaloosa to a slightly faster gait, which brought him alongside Falconer's shaggy, half-wild mountain mustang.

"Mr. Falconer, I need to talk to you."

"Later."

"But I've got something real important to tell you."

Falconer's eyes stabbed at him like a pair of daggers. "I know you're up to your eyebrows in something, Eben. We'll talk it over—later."

There was a definite note of finality in Falconer's voice that made it clear to Eben that this was the booshway's last word on the subject. Dejected, Eben climbed rein leather to slow the Appaloosa, allowing Falconer to go on ahead, while Rube Holly came alongside.

"Rube, I . . ."

The old-timer held up a gnarled hand. "Don't go tellin' me yore troubles, boy."

"But Rube . . ." Thoroughly frustrated, Eben stopped the mare in her tracks.

Trying hard to suppress a smile, Rube Holly shook his head and rode on after Falconer.

Sixkiller came alongside, stopped his horse, and looked with impeccable stoicism at Eben.

"Just forget it," muttered Eben and angrily heeled the Appaloosa into a canter.

They rode most of the day, stopping briefly twice to loosen their saddle cinches so the horses could blow, always at a stream running clear and sweet like wine over tree-shaded, smooth gray stones, from which men and mounts could drink their fill. Both times Eben teetered on the brink of confronting Falconer and demanding that the man listen to him. But Falconer seemed to be wrapped up in deep thoughts and never gave Eben an opening.

As they were remounting after the second stop, Rube Holly swung by and gave Eben a word of advice.

"I kin tell sumpin's got yore insides tied up in a knot, boy. But whatever you do, don't go and rile Hugh Falconer, hear?"

They reached the brigade about sundown. All the men gathered round to welcome Eben back and to tell him how glad they were he was still among the living. They wanted to hear about his adventures, but Eben wasn't in the mood. Rube Holly took up the slack for him. He knew most of it anyway. What he had not seen with his own eye, the ground—which he could read like other men read a book—had told him all he needed to know to make the picture complete.

Eben managed to slip away as night fell and found a spot near a creek where he could sit in lush grass and listen to the music of the stream tripping past, with his back to the trunk of a stately old oak tree. Crickets chorused in the tule, and unseen night birds chirruped in the boughs above his head. The stars twinkled in a lambent purple sky. Eben was heartsick. He was so far removed from Sombra Chagres! And she—she was still a prisoner in Hacienda Gavilan, subject to the sick whims of her father. Eben was of half a mind to slip away from camp in the middle of

the night and ride back to save her—or at least
die trying . . .

"I'll listen now to what you have to say."

Eben jumped to his feet and whirled to find
Hugh Falconer standing there.

"I didn't hear you come up."

"You've got a lot of loud thoughts rattling
around in your head."

Eben knew that wasn't it. Falconer was a big
man, but light on his feet. Moving soundlessly
was second nature to him.

Falconer hunkered down on his heels. The clay
pipe materialized; he packed it with tobacco and
then, leaving it unlighted, chewed on the tip. That
gave Eben some time to sort out what he wanted
to say. It was funny, though. Eben had been dying
to tell Falconer about Sombra, and now that the
moment was upon him he didn't know exactly
where to start.

"I reckon what you want to tell me has something to do with that girl Sombra," surmised
Falconer.

"How did you know?"

"When Don Carlos said he was taking his
daughter to Monterey along with him, well, you
should have seen your face."

"I was that obvious?"

"It was as plain as the ears on a mule."

"She asked me to help her run away."

Falconer contemplated this revelation for a moment, chewing the unlit pipe. "What did you
tell her?"

"I promised to help in any way I could."

"How come?"

"She has no one else to turn to."

" 'What a woman says should be written in
wind and running water.' One of the Roman
poets—I forget which."

"That's not fair. You've not even met her. How do you know what she's like? How can you judge her?"

"You're right. I've not had much experience with women."

"What about Touches the Moon? She must have been a good person, for you to love her the way you did."

Falconer's eyes glittered like chips of black ice in the darkness. "True enough," he conceded gruffly. "And we'll say no more about Touches the Moon."

"Sorry. It's just that, well, Sombra is desperate. She's about at the end of her rope. Her father has been . . . he's . . ." Eben didn't know how to put it.

"Incest?"

"Not willingly, on her part."

Falconer pondered some more. "I knew there had to be a reason I didn't cotton to that man."

"Then can I count on you to help us?"

"No."

Eben was stunned. "But why not?"

Falconer sighed. "I have a responsibility to the men in this brigade. I won't get them all killed on account of your girl." He fastened a steely gaze on Eben. "And you won't either."

"I gave her my solemn word."

"So you've said. You also gave me your word, back on the Green River. Swore you would live by my rules as long as you rode with the brigade."

Eben had no retort for that. What Falconer said was true. It was time to make a decision. He had to choose—Sombra or the brigade?

"Then maybe I ought not to be a part of the brigade any longer, Mr. Falconer."

Falconer looked off into the night. "Since I know how much taking part in this expedition meant to you, I reckon you must be in love with this girl."

"In love?" Eben was shocked. "Why, no, at least I don't think I am. I mean I haven't . . ."

"Sometimes love Indians up on you, so as you don't notice it coming until it's too late to defend yourself. Happened that way with me. I used to visit the Shoshone village where Touches the Moon lived, once or twice a year. I knew who she was all along, but I never really paid her much attention, or gave her much thought, or at least I didn't think so, until I found out that a Snake raiding party had hit the village and stolen some horses and a few young women. Touches the Moon was one of those women. That's when it hit me. Her being gone really bothered me."

"What did you do?"

"I rode with the Shoshones to get their horses and womenfolk back, of course. One of the Snakes had taken a strong liking to Touches the Moon, and he wasn't about to let her live if he couldn't have her. When the tide of battle turned against him and his, he was all set to split her skull open with his war club."

"And you saved her life."

Falconer smiled wistfully. "You've got a splendid imagination, Eben. That is the way it would happen in the storybooks, I guess. But no, I tried, got an arrow in my side for my trouble. It was her brother, Tall Bear, who killed the Snake rascal before he could kill her. Touches the Moon nursed me back to health. And when I went back up into the mountains she went with me."

"I'm right honored you see fit to talk to me about her," said Eben gratefully. "I know you don't like to make mention of her."

"Just said we wouldn't, didn't I? Well, it still cuts pretty deep. They say time heals such

wounds, but I believe there are some wounds that
never heal."

"I don't know if I love Sombra or not," confessed Eben. "I haven't had time to think about it.
I really don't know much about her, to be honest."

"How did you feel when you first saw her?"

"Like I'd been kicked in the chest by a knob-
head. I couldn't catch my breath."

Falconer nodded. "What I thought. There's that
need in a man. Burns strong and steady and can
turn him away from his instincts. It's a constant
battle to keep that need at bay, keep it from taking
charge over his soul, because if he lets that happen
he can't put things in the proper perspective anymore. That's what happened to your brother, I
think, over that Arapaho cutnose woman."

"No. Silas just doesn't like to lose."

"Isn't that cut-and-dried. If he lost his plews or
his horse or his rifle would he commit murder
because of it? Sure, he might fight to get his possibles back, because he needs all those things to
make a living in the high country. But would he
throw caution and common sense to the four
winds and kill in cold blood and risk a hard
mountain justice? No, it's that burning need a man
has to deal with, makes him feel like he isn't a
whole man, or a real honest-to-God man, anyway,
if he doesn't have a woman, or the woman
leaves him."

"I haven't thought much beyond helping Sombra escape her father," said Eben. "She didn't
come to me for help because she has any feelings
for me. And even if she did, and we managed to
get away from Don Carlos, what could I give her?
She's accustomed to living in pretty high style,
wouldn't you say? How could I provide for her?
I have little or nothing to offer."

"You're getting way ahead of yourself. But I

know how you're feeling. Way I felt about Touches the Moon. I lived alone, way up at the timberline, and years could go by without me seeing another living soul unless I saddled my horse and rode down and made a real effort to find somebody to talk to. Touches the Moon had spent her whole life surrounded by friends and family in her village. And she got plenty lonesome, there at the beginning. I wasn't sure the feelings she had for me were deep enough that she could overcome that loneliness. Turned out they were. If a woman truly loves you, you'll have no cause to worry. A woman's need is just as strong as the man's. You can be poor as dust, but if she knows you need her, she'll probably stick."

"All I know for sure is that I've got to help her," sighed Eben.

"I realize that. But I'll ask you one favor. It's a big one, too. Do nothing until we reach Monterey."

"Don't figure there will be any chance on the road anyway."

"I mean don't even talk to her, or look at her, if you can help it. You're sitting on a powder keg, Eben. The wrong word, even the wrong look at the wrong time, could blow you to kingdom come—and you might take the brigade with you."

"Won't be easy," admitted Eben.

"Do it anyway." Falconer stood up. "When we get to Monterey I'll do what I can to help you. Who knows. Maybe you've found what the Almighty intended for you when he turned your steps toward California."

"What about you, Mr. Falconer? Have you found what you're looking for?"

"Not yet." Falconer smiled. "But I have a feeling I'm getting closer."

"I'll do what you ask. You can rely on me."

"Why, I've always known as much."

Falconer walked away into the night shadows, silent as he had come, leaving Eben Nall with a heart full of pride.

Chapter 23

November 1, 1837. Yesterday we left Hacienda Gavilan, bound for the town of Monterey, which is located on the coast. I understand it will take us six or seven days to reach our destination.

We must be the most unusual caravan ever to have passed this way. Don Carlos and Sombra travel in a well-appointed coach with Consuela, the serving woman. The coach is pulled by a handsome team of four matching grays. It is driven by a taciturn man named Gaviota. He is a most strange-looking fellow, tall, cadaverous, pale, lantern-jawed. He wears the plain white shirt and trousers of the California field worker, the peon. On his person, according to Don Carlos, he carries three throwing knives, in the use of which he has no peer, or so says the *patrón*. His sole purpose in life is to protect Don Carlos. Odd, that I did not see him before, at the hacienda. No doubt he was always lurking in the shadows, near at hand.

Gaviota's renown with the knives prompted Doc Maguire to challenge him to a contest at our first night camp. The Irishman prides himself on his handling of those pearl-handled daggers he carries, and he cannot bear the thought that there is someone who might be better with the blade than he. I have seen him beat almost every man in the brigade during this expedition. All of us were eagerly anticipating the match he guaranteed he could arrange with Gaviota. But Gaviota would have nothing to do with him. In fact, he said not a word to Maguire, simply turning his back to the Irishman and walking away. That ignited Maguire's notorious temper. It is one thing to decline a friendly contest, quite another to do it in such a rude manner. But Don Carlos forestalled violence by explaining that Gaviota cannot speak. He has no tongue. Don Carlos says that once there were some very dangerous and desperate men who were trying to kill him. They captured Gaviota and tried by brutal means to make him divulge his master's whereabouts. Since Gaviota refused to tell them what they wanted to know, they cut out his tongue. They would have done worse, except that Gaviota managed somehow to free himself, and proceeded to kill all of his tormentors. Hearing this story, Doc Maguire found his temper quickly cooled.

In addition to Gaviota, Don Carlos travels with eight of his *vaqueros*. Remo is one of them. It was Gus Jenkins who asked Chagres if he always traveled with such a well-armed escort. Don Carlos said that he did, that in addition to a pestilence of highwaymen in California, he has a number of very powerful enemies who would like nothing better than to see him dead. He would not elaborate further. I wonder who

these powerful men are. The enemy of my
enemy is my friend.

The brigade completed our strange caravan.
In contrast to the elegant coach and the flam-
boyantly clad *vaqueros*, we looked like a scruffy
band of bearded scoundrels indeed in our old
buckskins and homespun.

I had given my word to Hugh Falconer that
I would treat Sombra as though she did not
exist until we arrived in Monterey. This was an
awfully hard promise to keep. So far I have
succeeded. I owe Falconer, and the rest of the
brigade, that much. It occurs to me that Falconer has depended on me a lot since we left
the Green River. He depended on me when he
sent Sixkiller and me to search for the missing
Joe Newell. And he did so again when we were
seeking a way through the Sierras. Now a third
time. I cannot let him down.

The brigade rode behind the *vaqueros* and the
coach bearing Don Carlos and Sombra, so I did
not often have occasion to even see her, except
for a brief glimpse when we stopped at midday
and in the evening. The first time, yesterday
noon, as she stepped out of the coach to stretch
cramped limbs, she looked back toward the brigade and began to search every face. I knew
she was looking for me. I quickly looked away,
feigning intense interest in the far horizon.

Last night I could not escape so easily. The
brigade camped apart from the Californios, but
she came strolling past our fires, exchanging
pleasantries with a man here and another there.
Remo followed in her wake, watching my companions like a hawk for any sign of disrespect,

I suppose. But my companions were quite respectful, demonstrating that years in the mountains had not transformed them into the complete barbarians Remo clearly expected them to be.

I was petrified when I saw her coming toward me, and as she drew closer I launched into an impromptu discussion with Rube Holly, who, fortunately for me, was sitting right beside me. I babbled about the likelihood of our finding beaver in California. Rube was caught off guard, but, sensing my desperation, and deducing its cause, he played along, for which I am eternally grateful. Of course later he gave me a few good-natured prods. "I kin see you ain't learnt nothin' at all," he said, with a smirk. "Any wet-behind-the-ears greenhorn fresh off the farm could take one look at this hyar country and know there ain't no beaver to speak of, leastways not around these parts." I saw Sombra out of the corner of my eye but pretended to be completely unaware of her presence, and she walked on. I felt perfectly wretched then and looked after her. It was then that I noticed Hugh Falconer. He was watching me and gave a curt nod, and, if I am not mistaken, there was sympathy for my plight in his eyes.

Today we made good progress, more than thirty miles by my reckoning, and pitched camp early on the banks of a broad, yet shallow, river. I went off down the bank a ways, to be alone with my misery, which is always the best course for a miserable man. Sitting by the river, skimming rocks in the soft golden glow of a California twilight, I heard something rustling in the shinnery and reached for my rifle, thinking it must be either a bandit or a deer. In either case, I was resolved to shoot. But it was Consuela. Thinking she must be wanting her own privacy, I prepared to take my leave. But she caught my arm and stopped me.

"Señor Nall," she said, "I have a message for you."

"You speak English!" I exclaimed, delighted and relieved. "Thank the good Lord."

"Yes. I speak it, a little."

"Did you tell Sombra what I said when I left the hacienda?"

"Yes. She want me to say to you . . ."

I grimaced. "I know, I've been unforgivably rude. But I had no choice. Falconer asked me . . ."

"She knows."

I gaped at her, slow to comprehend. "She knows what? That I had no choice? But, how could she know that?"

"Señor Falconer, he tell her. There was a moment today, when we stopped to eat, that the *patrón* was away from the coach, talking to the *vaqueros*. That is when Señor Falconer spoke to her."

My relief was so great I could not say a word. Consuela squeezed my arm.

"Do not worry. She has faith in you." Then, with a sly wink, she added, "And I think she like you, Señor Nall."

She likes me! Those magic words are still ringing in my ears even as I write this, by the flickering light of a dying campfire.

On my way back to camp I was all set to find Falconer and kiss his feet, so great was my gratitude. But the moment I laid eyes on him I knew that any show of emotion from me was the last thing he wanted. So I said nothing to him, though I know I owe him a debt I may never be able to repay.

Seven days after leaving Hacienda Gavilan, they reached their destination. Coming in on a road that passed through sand hills covered with scrub and then down to the coast between a pair of ridges thick with pine, they saw the town, nestled between the slopes and the blue waters of a deep harbor where a few sailing ships lay calmly at anchor, all canvas furled. The flag of the Republic of Mexico fluttered in the constant sea breeze above a fort on the bluff commanding the entrance to the harbor.

The houses of Monterey were built on a gentle slope of land two miles from the southern extremity of the bay. The northern shore of the bay, twenty miles distant at its farthest point, described a great arc to the west, so that from nowhere in the immediate vicinity of the town could the Pacific Ocean be seen. Another bay lay beyond piney hills to the west of town. This was a less protected anchorage than the harbor the mountain men could see as they approached the town.

A road circled the western bay from the south, passing the Carmel Mission and Point Lobos, a promontory much favored by seals and sea lions. It continued northward to Monterey and then made its way around the eastern edge of Monterey Bay to San Francisco, two days' ride to the north.

Monterey was the seat of the provincial government of California, and the governor-general resided in a mansion of yellow sandstone in the center of town, across a large plaza from the customs house, presidio, and a church. Nearby was a hotel and several restaurants, and the streets radiating out from the plaza like spokes on a wheel were lined with shops where, thanks to the merchant ships that regularly dropped their anchors in the bay after sailing the seven seas, an astonishingly wide variety of goods from all over the world could be had.

At the edge of town a halt was called to allow Falconer and Chagres to confer. Falconer then returned to the brigade and gathered the men around.

"I'm riding in with Don Carlos," he announced. "With any luck, I'll be able to see the governor-general today. Eben Nall and Doc Maguire will come with me. The rest of you will camp here for the night."

The mountain men weren't shy about letting their disappointment at this arrangement be known. They'd been looking forward to exploring the town and seeing what delights it held in store for them—especially in the way of good whiskey and young señoritas.

"It's best this way," said Falconer. "Everyone who wants to will have a chance to visit Monterey. But we won't ride in all at once. Don't want to make these folks nervous. Gus Jenkins will be in charge until I get back."

Accompanying Chagres and his entourage took Falconer, Eben, and Maguire through a residential area where small, neat adobe and sandstone houses, most of them whitewashed, sheltered behind high walls with wooden or wrought iron gates. Flocks of blackbirds perched on the tile roofs or wheeled en masse in the azure sky. Cobblestone sidewalks hugged the walls on either side of wide streets of yellow dust. Eben marveled at how clean and tranquil the sleepy little town seemed to be.

The business district, however, bustled with activity. Wagons, carts, horsemen, and pedestrians clogged the streets and the great plaza. The shops were doing a brisk trade. Sailors and traders—English, Russian, and American—mingled with the Californios in their colorful serapes and sombreros. A squadron of lancers in green-and-black uniforms clattered by. Eben was glad to see that he and his two companions did not elicit an inordinate amount of curiosity. He figured the residents of such a thriving port and center of commerce had to be accustomed to the presence of foreigners.

Chagres ordered Gaviota to stop the coach in the plaza, near the governor-general's mansion. Don Carlos emerged from the coach to stand alongside Falconer's horse. Falconer's half-wild mountain mustang gave the *haciendero* the evil eye, and Eben wondered, with some relish, if it was going to take a chunk out of the man's hide, but Falconer kept the beast in check.

"I will go with you to seek an audience with Don Luis," said Chagres. "Perhaps I can be of some assistance in that regard, Señor Falconer."

"You're very kind, Don Carlos."

Chagres made a dismissive gesture. "It is nothing." He turned to Remo and spoke to the *vaquero* in Spanish. Remo nodded and, dismounting, took Gaviota's place atop the coach, while Gaviota took charge of Remo's horse.

"I maintain a residence here in town," Don Carlos explained to Falconer, "so I am sending my daughter on ahead. It has been a long journey for her, and she is weary."

Remo stirred up the grays, and the coach rocked on its broad leather thoroughbraces as it began to roll, flanked by the other *vaqueros*. Eben watched it go with a heavy heart, hoping for one last glimpse of Sombra, but he was disappointed.

Dismounting, Falconer handed his reins to Eben. "The two of you stick close," he said, "while I find out what kind of reception we're going to get."

He and Chagres started for a gate in the wall surrounding the governor-general's house. A solitary Mexican soldier stood at attention beside the gate. Don Carlos spoke to the soldier, and they were allowed to pass through, leaving Eben, Maguire, and Gaviota to stand in the warm California sunshine bathing the plaza.

"I think I'm going to like this place," said Maguire, watching a pair of señoritas sashay by. They wore lace-frilled dresses and flower-bedecked bonnets and twirled gaily colored parasols. Eben thought they would have looked right at home in any sizable American town. The latest fashions apparently knew no boundaries, other than class.

"Yes, indeed," continued the Irishman, smiling broadly. "A man can get into all sorts of trouble in this little hamlet."

"It's trouble we're trying to steer clear of," reminded Eben, and then it struck him that he was certainly one to talk. After all, wasn't he planning to help the daughter of Don Carlos Chagres run away from home?

"Oh, I don't mean bad trouble, lad," said Maguire. "I mean the *good* kind of trouble."

Eben shrugged. He wasn't really listening. Sombra Chagres monopolized his thoughts.

In time, though, he would have cause to think back on Maguire's words that day and wish he had paid closer attention.

Chapter 24

Hugh Falconer remained inside the governor-general's house for such a long time that Eben began to fret. What if the whole brigade was rounded up and locked away in the local jail? He would have a hard time helping Sombra if he was behind bars. Turning to Maguire, he asked the Irishman what he thought might happen.

Maguire's shrug was indifferent. "Whatever a whimsical Fate decrees, I am ready. I learned long ago to expect the unexpected."

"If they try to arrest us, will Falconer fight?"

"Will he fight?" Maguire chuckled. "When you push Hugh Falconer too far you learn the true meaning of the word 'trouble.' He is the fighting-est fool I've ever had the pleasure of seeing in action."

"Those Mexican lancers look pretty tough."

"True, lad. Worthy opponents for a mountain man. We'd give them a reason to remember us. Of course, we'd lose the fight. They have the advantage of numbers. But the longer the odds, the better. All a mountain man asks for is to die game."

Eben thought back to Joe Newell, dying alone on the Humboldt, surrounded by Digger Indians. Had Newell died with a satisfied smile on his face or with one last terrified scream stillborn on his tongue? Of one thing Eben was certain. He did not want to die right now. Not until he knew what the future held for him and Sombra. Of course, he mused, a man could always find some reason not to die.

A little while later Don Carlos emerged from the governor-general's house—without Falconer. That gave Eben a bad feeling in the pit of his stomach, until Chagres informed them that all was well.

"Don Luis has generously granted Señor Falconer an audience," said the *haciendero*.

Eben thought he detected a trace of sarcasm in the man's tone of voice, but he couldn't be sure.

"I have done all that I can do," continued Chagres. "Now I must go and attend to my own business. *Vaya con Dios*, my friends."

He mounted Remo's horse and rode away, with Gaviota trotting alongside.

"I don't like that chap," muttered Maguire.

"Neither do I," said Eben.

"He reminds me of all those high and mighty English noblemen, looking down their long noses at you."

You don't know the half of it, thought Eben. But he wasn't about to share Sombra's terrible secret with anyone else.

A half hour crawled by before Falconer came out of the governor-general's house.

"Well," he said, "as long as we mind our manners and obey their laws we're welcome to come and go as we please. Doc, ride back to the brigade and tell Gus Jenkins he can send half the brigade into town today. The other half will wait until tomorrow. I want every man who visits Monterey to be back in camp by midnight."

Maguire was clearly dismayed by this condition. "What's wrong, Hugh? Don't you trust us?"

Eben thought he saw a strange and unfathomable expression skim across Hugh Falconer's chiseled features.

"In some things, yes. In others, no."

Maguire turned to his horse.

"Doc."

"Yeah?"

"The man who gets out of hand and puts the brigade at risk will pay a steep price."

Maguire nodded solemnly, mounted up, and left them.

"Well, then, Eben," said Falconer. "You still bound and determined?"

"Yes, sir. More than ever."

Falconer nodded, slowly scanned the plaza. Eben thought, *This is it. The parting of the ways. He is going to cut me loose now.* Eben suddenly realized, now that the time had come to go on alone, how much the brigade meant to him.

"I spoke to Don Luis about our little problem," said Falconer.

Eben's jaw dropped. He had not thought Falconer capable of such a colossal blunder, such a monumental error in judgment. Falconer accurately read his expression and smiled.

"Don't worry. May not look like it, but I know what I'm doing. I could tell right away that Chagres and the governor-general aren't exactly friends. Oh, they're civil enough to each other, when they have to be. But they are both very powerful and ambitious men. I have a hunch Don Carlos is to the governor-general what Brutus was to Caesar."

"I don't think I . . ."

"You'd know what I mean, had you been in there. I think Don Carlos wants to live in that big yellow house."

"Chagres said he had powerful enemies."

"Ambitious men do. Don Carlos had to step on

a lot of people to climb as high as he has. But he's not quite king of the mountain yet. So, when he left, I stuck both our necks out and told Don Luis about Sombra."

"What did he say? Did he believe you?"

"He was shocked. But not too surprised. He's a decent enough fellow, but very willing to believe the worst about Don Carlos."

"Can he help us?"

"No."

Eben's hopes had been soaring high; now they were dashed to pieces on the hard and bitter rock of disappointment.

"But he gave me the names of two people who might be able to help," continued Falconer. "One's a Connecticut sea captain named Shagrue. His ship, the *Halcyon*, is anchored in the bay. It's a merchantman. Don Luis says Shagrue is about as close to being a pirate as you can get without hanging for it. He might be willing to take you and Sombra around the Cape and back to the United States. For a price."

"I have no means to pay passage," said Eben, glancing disconsolately at the Appaloosa mare. "I was thinking I might sell the mare . . ."

"We'll worry about that when the time comes. First, let's find Shagrue and palaver."

"Who is the second person the governor-general spoke of?"

"A priest. He lives in a mission down the coast. Don Luis seemed to think the padre has good reason to dislike Chagres. He didn't tell me why, though."

"I don't honestly see what good a priest would do us," confessed Eben.

"You might be surprised. But we'll look up Captain Shagrue first. Don Luis says he spends a lot of time at a cantina not far from here."

"We?"

Falconer nodded. "Thought I'd give you a hand."

"Too big a risk. I can't ask you to get involved."

"You didn't ask. I volunteered."

"But why? What about the brigade?"

"When it comes to taking Sombra you'll be on your own. Until then, don't look a gift horse in the mouth."

In Eben's opinion, Falconer was breaking his own law and putting the brigade in jeopardy. But he didn't argue.

They mounted up and left the plaza, riding down a street lined with businesses. It was obvious to Eben that the governor-general had given Falconer detailed directions, as Falconer led the way down a narrow side street flanked by adobe walls. This brought them to the cantina. The interior of the place was dark and cool and had a stale smell. The floor was hard-packed dirt. The walls were peeling and fly-specked. Clearly this was an establishment that did not try to cater to Monterey's upper class.

The appearance of the current patrons bore this out. Several Californios with the look of laborers played coon can at one of the rickety tables. A pair of Russian sailors were drinking *aguardiente* at the bar and seemed to be well on the way to inebriation. A woman sat at a table in the corner, drinking straight out of a wicker-encased jug. She was barefoot and wore a plain brown dress and sweat-stained *camisa*. When she saw Eben and Falconer she got up and walked over to them. Slipping an arm around Eben, she rubbed against him, and he felt her soft, unfettered breasts through the thin blouse, and she said something with a salacious smile that Eben figured would have made him blush had he understood even a word of it.

"Thanks anyway," he said, "but no."

The man behind the bar spoke sharply to the woman, who shrugged her indifference and returned to the table and the jug.

"My friends," said the man, smiling broadly beneath the black sweep of his long mustache. "American, no? What can I do for you?"

"We're looking for Captain Shagrue," said Falconer. "We were told he often comes here."

"Nothing to drink?"

Falconer glanced over at the Russian sailors. "Two of whatever they're drinking."

The man behind the bar beamed, produced two glasses, poured the *aguardiente*. Falconer downed his in one gulp. It seemed to have no more effect on him than plain water. Encouraged, Eben tried his—and nearly choked to death as the liquor seared the lining of his throat.

Removing a small leather pouch from his belt, Falconer opened it and took out a twenty-dollar gold piece. "Take American money, don't you?"

"I take any kind of money," assured the man. "Captain Shagrue, yes, I know of him."

Falconer handed him the coin. "Is he here?"

The man called across the room to the woman. All Eben could get out of what he said was that the woman's name was Maria. She rose and went out the back door. With the door open, Eben could hear a commotion, the sound of many excited voices shouting all at once.

"A cockfight," explained the man behind the bar. "Feel free to try your luck."

"I'm not a gambling man," said Falconer.

The man pocketed the gold piece and moved away.

"Pretty expensive drinks," murmured Eben. "Especially since they taste like coal oil."

"I had to pay for cooperation too."

"How am I ever going to repay you?"

Falconer didn't answer, turning as Maria reappeared with a man they assumed was the sea captain they had come to see.

Shagrue was a tall man, paunchy in the middle, his lantern-jawed face framed by bushy sidewhiskers linked by a wiry mustache that partially concealed his thin-lipped mouth. Tiny red veins stood out on his cheeks and on the tip of a nose that had been broken at least once. His small gray eyes were narrowed into a perpetual squint. He had an arm draped over Maria's shoulder, which put his hand near her breast—an opportunity that Shagrue did not squander. Maria didn't seem to mind. She steered Shagrue toward the bar and went back to her table in the shadows.

"You looking for me?" Shagrue asked Falconer.

"We were told you might be able to help us."

"Might be. Who told you that?"

"The governor-general."

"Help you how?"

"Where are you bound when you sail from here, Captain?"

"Bound for home, New Haven."

"Can you take on two passengers?"

"The two of you?"

Falconer gestured at Eben. "Him. And a young woman."

"Young woman? I don't abide women aboard my ship. They make trouble with a crew on a long voyage."

"You would be well paid."

"Who is this young woman?" asked Shagrue. He could sense there was a catch.

"The daughter of Don Carlos Chagres."

Shagrue tried to blink the surprise out of his eyes. Then he chuckled. "You say the governor-general sent you to me?"

Falconer nodded.

"And Chagres? I'll wager he doesn't know his daughter plans to take a little trip, does he?"

"No."

"And if he does find out, you won't be going anywhere," said Shagrue, jabbing a finger in Eben's direction. "Except six feet under. Am I right?"

"You're right," said Eben.

"Well, well, well." Shagrue leaned against the bar. "This is a dangerous little piece of commerce you're talking about, gentlemen."

"But at least it's commerce," said Falconer.

Shagrue grinned, displaying crooked yellow teeth. "True. And I never let danger interfere with business."

"So you'll do it?"

"It will cost you."

"How much?"

"How much do you have?"

Falconer opened the pouch and poured its contents on the bar. When he saw the gold pieces Shagrue's eyes gleamed with avarice.

"That will do nicely," he said and reached for the gold.

Falconer's hand clamped down on the sea captain's arm, stopping the grab just shy of the money.

"Half now," said Falconer. "Half when you take on your two passengers."

"Fair enough."

Falconer put half of the gold pieces back in the pouch, leaving the rest on the bar. "When can you sail?"

"I'm refitting the *Halcyon* and awaiting cargo due in from San Joaquin tomorrow or the next day. Let's say five days. Maybe six. But I won't have them board in the harbor. Too many eyes, if you get my meaning."

"What do you suggest?"

"I'll pick them up down the coast a ways. Find a place to your liking and then come back here and let me know."

Falconer put out a hand. Shagrue shook it. Surprise registered on his face when Falconer tightened his grip instead of releasing the captain's hand.

"This young man is a good friend of mine, Captain Shagrue," said Falconer. "I want him to reach New Haven safe and sound. I'll have your word that he will."

"You have my word," said Shagrue. His expression made it manifest that he understood the consequences of breaking his promise and that he took those consequences seriously.

Falconer let go. "Good. We'll be seeing you. Come on, Eben."

Out in the narrow street, Eben shook his head dubiously. "I don't know about this."

Falconer swung aboard his mountain mustang. "It's your best bet to get away from Don Carlos. Once he finds out Sombra is gone, there will be no place in California where you could hide for long."

"I don't think I trust Shagrue. And if his crew is anything like him . . ."

"Don't sell yourself short. You can handle Shagrue. I know it, and so should you."

Eben climbed into his saddle. "I'll want you to have the Appaloosa, Mr. Falconer. In fact, I wouldn't want anyone else to have her, except maybe Rube."

"Done. And I'd say I've got the better of the bargain. Now I think we should take a ride down the coast and find a good place for your rendezvous with the *Halcyon*."

Chapter 25

November 11, 1837. Tonight is the night. I am going to try to rescue Sombra Chagres from her father.

What are the odds of success? I do not even want to think about them. Any number of things could go wrong. It is quite possible that I will die in the attempt. If I fail and fall into the hands of Don Carlos and his *vaqueros*, my death is certain. In the event of my death, to anyone who may read this journal I state that if I do perish it is with but one regret, that Sombra will remain the unwilling subject of her father's perverted attentions. This endeavor must be undertaken, regardless of the risks.

After meeting with Captain Shagrue, Falconer and I traveled down the coast, looking for a suitable place for the rendezvous with the New Haven brigantine *Halcyon*. The road took us past the Carmel Mission, where we met Padre Pico, the priest who the governor-general thought would be willing to help me.

The priest greeted us warmly. He is a plump, middle-aged man whose warm heart and pleasant disposition are mirrored in a round, smiling face and twinkling eyes. He is of the Order of the Jesuits and has dedicated his entire life to the service of the people of California. When I told him what Don Carlos Chagres was doing to his daughter, he was shocked but not surprised. "Don Carlos is the most Godless man I have ever had the misfortune to meet," declared the priest.

He knew Sombra and her father well, for before acquiring the old mission that was transformed into Hacienda Gavilan, Don Carlos resided in Monterey. Padre Pico told us that Sombra's mother was a pious and gentle woman, adored by all who were acquainted with her. She died of a disease contracted while ministering to the poor. Padre Pico says he loved her dearly and feels likewise about her daughter. While he was not aware of what Don Carlos was doing to Sombra, he knows the man well enough to assert that he is capable of such depravity. His rise to a position of wealth and influence in California has been accomplished through the ruination of many lives. Don Carlos has also been instrumental in undermining the power of the Church. He is, says Padre Pico, an enemy of God.

The story of the California missions is one of amazing courage and perseverance. A handful of priests braved untold dangers to bring civilization and Christ to the Indian tribes of the region. Many paid with their lives. According to Padre Pico, the most heroic of them all was Junipero Serra, who founded the Mission of San Diego in 1769 and, in the thirteen years that followed, established nine more. These missions accumulated considerable wealth and held sway over thousands of natives.

Their power eventually excited the jealousy of the government. During the years of the Spanish possession, the padres had been granted unlimited privileges by the viceroys. Each mission came to own hundreds of thousands of acres, with tens of thousands head of livestock, and the Indians were their loyal subjects. Nearly all the commerce of this bountiful land rested, therefore, in the hands of the priests. They became adept at managing the economy.

The situation changed once Mexico threw off the yoke of Spain and established itself as an independent republic. The missions of California became public property, and the padres, once sovereigns of their own domains, were left with only spiritual power over the Indians. The government appropriated the lands and herds of the missions. Some of the land was parceled out to the Indians, four hundred *varas* square per family, in return for which they were expected to pay revenues to the government.

Without the guidance and encouragement of the priests, says Padre Pico, few of the Indians flourished as farmers. Many returned to their nomadic lifestyles. When soldiers tried to force them back to their abandoned farms, bloodshed was often the result. Several missions were closed, including the one that has become the private kingdom of Don Carlos Chagres.

Apparently, Don Carlos wants to do away with the missions altogether. Padre Pico is certain that if Chagres becomes governor-general, which is his greatest ambition, he would almost certainly de-

cree that all the remaining missions be sold at
auction. The proceeds of these sales would go
in large measure directly into the coffers of the
government. No doubt the missions would be
converted into more haciendas, more feudal domains like Gavilan, and Padre Pico is firmly convinced that the people fared better when they
were "ruled" by the priests. Personally, I think
they would fare better without any rulers at all,
but of course I did not voice my opinion on
that score.

Padre Pico gave me his blessing upon hearing
of my plan to help Sombra escape. He told of
a secluded cabin a half mile down the coast
from the mission. Overlooking the ocean, it
would be as good a place as any for the rendezvous with Captain Shagrue. It is abandoned,
and few know of it. Padre Pico said he would
make certain it was stocked with provisions, in
case Sombra and I had to remain there for any
length of time. He offered to be of service in
any other way I saw fit.

That night I returned with Hugh Falconer to
the brigade's camp, on the outskirts of Monterey. Half the company had spent the evening
carousing in town, and they were coming back
in twos and threes. I told Rube Holly all about
Sombra and what I intended to do. I expected
him to lecture me on the subject of women and
what men should and should not do with regard to them—something to the effect that
women were nice, but they damned sure
weren't worth getting killed over. He often says
such things, even though I believe he would
give his life for Luck's benefit. But he said noth-

ing of the kind. I suppose he must have seen the look of determination on my face. And he actually offered to assist me in the venture. I declined the offer. I am unwilling to put anyone else's life on the line.

We said our good-byes quickly, for the parting was a painful experience for both of us. I then bade farewell to Hugh Falconer. He gave me the pouch containing the rest of the gold pieces, and I was prepared to hand over the Appaloosa mare right then and there and take one of my packhorses into Monterey. But he told me to ride the mare, as she was clearly good luck for me, and said he would get the horse from Padre Pico after I had sailed on the *Halcyon.* I asked him to make sure my brother got all my things—the two packhorses and all that they carried. I had considered giving everything to Rube Holly, but Rube had told me to give it to Silas instead. I did not tell anyone else, not even Silas, that I was leaving the brigade for good, and before the sun had risen on a new day I had slipped away from the camp.

My heart was heavy. Among men who have engaged in such adventure and survived such an ordeal as we had done these past months, a bond is forged. Leaving the brigade was even more difficult for me than saying good-bye to my home and family back in Ohio had been. There were things I wanted to say to Falconer in particular, but could not find the words. Perhaps one day he will read this journal and know that I am grateful to him for instilling in me an awareness of my strengths and promise as a man. I am beholden to him for giving me the opportunity to prove to myself that I am capable of taking charge of my own destiny. Without this newfound confidence in myself I could not have embarked on such an enterprise as this. That confidence, I think, is what I came west to find, and, thanks to Hugh Falconer, I have found it.

I asked around town for directions to the Chagres house. The residence was a large, two-story dwelling surrounded by a high wall, perched on a slope overlooking Monterey. There were several other houses on the street, spaced well apart, with stands of pine trees between them. But I could find no good place on the street for engaging in what might become a very long vigil, so I rode to the end of the street and turned the Appaloosa up the hill to its crest, circling back to a point directly above and behind the Chagres house.

Leaving the mare on the backside of the hill, I found a place where I could see all of the house through the trees. Not knowing what else to do for the moment, I settled down to watch and wait.

A few hours later I saw Consuela, the serving woman, walking down the road from the house with a basket swinging on her arm. I did not follow her, for fear that Sombra might leave the house while I was away from my post. An hour later Consuela returned, the basket filled with food. I deduced that she had visited the market at the bottom of the hill.

Later that day several *vaqueros* left the house, riding down into Monterey. Still I saw no sign of Sombra. The sun sank below the horizon, and still I waited, with faltering hope, until quite late into the night, before going over the hill, unsaddling the mare, and rolling up in my blankets, to try and get some sleep.

A heavy fog, cold and damp, had rolled in from the sea by sunrise, but it was of short duration. Again I saw Consuela leave the house. This time I went after her, on foot, and waited until she had reached the market before approaching her. She seemed genuinely pleased to see me, and she gave me every assurance that Sombra was holding up well and wondering when we would be together again. I told Consuela that preparations had been made, but confessed to being at a loss as to how I could spirit Sombra away if she never left the house. Consuela said that since tomorrow was Sunday, they would be attending an evening mass. Don Carlos would not go—he never did—but Consuela surmised that the *patrón* would send either Gaviota or Remo, his two most trusted men, to accompany his daughter. I asked Consuela to tell Sombra to be ready to go with me then, as we might not have another opportunity. I had no idea what I was going to do, but I tried to maintain an air of confidence.

Returning to my lonely camp on the backside of the hill, I built a small fire and brewed some coffee to go with the strip of dried venison that was the sum total of my supper. I had a poor appetite but forced myself to eat nonetheless. Wracking my brain for some scheme that would have at least a modest chance of success to recommend it, I could come up with nothing besides a headache. How was I to get Sombra away under the watchful eye of Remo or Don Carlos's mute bodyguard? I could think of no

way, short of killing whichever one of them
Don Carlos assigned to protect her on the morrow. That was a last resort, if for no other reason than I thought it more likely I would be the
one who was killed.

I found myself wishing Hugh Falconer were
here—now there was a man who always
seemed to know the right thing to do no matter
what happened. No problem was a Gordian
knot for him. But Falconer had already done
more than enough to help me. I could not ask
him to do more. Besides, I had a feeling he
would have been disappointed in me if I failed
to deal with this situation myself.

Recalling that Padre Pico had offered his services, I decided to ride to the Carmel Mission
and consult with him. He greeted me like the
prodigal son, insisting that I stay and eat with
him. While we ate I told him my problem. "I
am afraid," I said, in conclusion, "that this will
be my one and only chance to take her away."

"We can do nothing in the church, during the
mass," he said.

I said of course not, which left making a
move while they were traveling from the house
to the church, or vice versa. Padre Pico tugged
vigorously on an earlobe as he pondered the
situation. Then a light seemed to blaze in his
eyes, and he smiled at me.

"We can do this thing," he said, with complete confidence. "I will help you."

"But how?"

He put a hand on my arm. "You must trust
me. There is a way. But I warn you, it is not
without risk."

I laughed at that. "Then it wouldn't be worth doing, would it?" I was so pleased that Padre Pico had devised some scheme to rescue Sombra that danger was of little consequence to me. "But I do not want to place you in harm's way, Father."

"My duty is to thwart Satan and all his works. And I am persuaded that Don Carlos is the devil's accomplice. Meet me outside the church during the mass. We will strike as they are returning home."

Trusting in him, I nodded and took my leave, declining his invitation to stay the night at the mission. I preferred the cold ground on the hill behind the Chagres house, if only because I would be closer to Sombra.

On the road back to Monterey I had the distinct impression that I was being followed. Circling back, I saw no one. Putting it down to an overactive imagination, I rode on.

Today seemed to last a lifetime. Finally, as the sun slipped down the western slope of the sky, I saw Sombra emerge from the house and climb into the coach that had conveyed her and her father here from Hacienda Gavilan. Consuela was with her. Gaviota rode on top of the coach. As the team of matched grays, under his expert guidance, pulled the coach out of the gate, I was relieved to see that no *vaqueros* were accompanying them.

I had changed into the clothes I had been given at the hacienda, hoping this would allow me to blend in to the environment of the town better than the buckskins. The Appaloosa was saddled and ready. I rode down through the pines to the road and followed the coach at a safe distance.

Chapter 26

Eben Nall was standing at the mouth of an alley that ran behind the church when he saw Padre Pico. The shadows of night were fast gathering. The priest quartered across the plaza toward the church, moving as quickly as his short legs would allow. Eben left the alley and walked up the street that flanked the south side of the *iglesia*. Pico saw him, waved, and hurried forward.

"Sombra is inside," said Eben. "Along with Consuela. She works for Don Carlos, but she's on Sombra's side in this. Last time I looked, Gaviota was standing on the front steps of the church. He's Don Carlos's bodyguard."

"I know who he is. He is still there." There was a plain brown robe draped over Padre Pico's arm. This he offered to Eben. "Here. Put this on."

"This is a priest's robe, Father."

"Of course it is."

"I don't think I ought to be wearing a . . ."

Padre Pico waved his doubts aside. "Does this man Gaviota know you?"

"Yes, he would recognize me."

"Then you must wear the robe. Do not worry. Under the circumstances I don't think God will be offended."

Eben stepped back into the alley and donned the robe, putting it on over his other clothes and pulling the cowl over his head. He frowned at his booted feet. "I don't guess you brought any sandals along, did you, Father?"

"No. But it will soon be dark. Perhaps he will not notice."

"What do you have in mind?"

Padre Pico glanced at the Appaloosa mare, standing alertly, ground-hitched, in the alley behind Eben.

"Where is the Chagres coach?"

"On the other side of the street, a little further down." Eben took him to the mouth of the alley and pointed it out to him.

"Muy bien." Padre Pico rubbed his hands together. Excitement was a gleam in his eye. He seemed to relish the adventure. Eben thought it might be wise to remind him who they were dealing with.

"Father, you say you know who Gaviota is. He's a killer. Not a man to be trifled with."

"Then tell me, my son, how were you going to get Sombra Chagres away from him?"

Eben grimaced. "I guess I was going to try to kill him."

Padre Pico sternly wagged a finger. "There must be no bloodshed. Were you to take this man's life, you would be no better than he. No, there is another way."

"I'm dying to hear it," said Eben, and pondered his careless choice of words.

Padre Pico told him. When he was finished, Eben shrugged.

"Might work," he allowed. "But you'll be taking an awfully big chance, Father."

"Even such a man as Gaviota cares about his soul. He would not harm a priest."

"Maybe not. But what about Don Carlos? He doesn't like the Church to begin with. This might make trouble not just for you but for your mission as well."

Padre Pico put a hand on Eben's arm and smiled. "It is seldom easy to do the right thing. Life on this earth is a tribulation. The reward for doing God's work is in heaven. Do not fear. I will deal with Don Carlos Chagres when the time comes."

"Well," said Eben, dubious, "you don't switch horses in midstream. I guess we have no choice but to go ahead."

Thirty minutes later Sombra and Consuela emerged from the church in a stream of worshippers. Gaviota awaited them on the steps and followed them around to the street that ran along the side of the *iglesia*. Consuela could tell that Sombra's nerves were frayed. The servant woman took her hand and gave it a reassuring squeeze. When they arrived at the coach, Gaviota opened the door for them. Sombra gave the darkened street an anxious glance. Then, with a sigh of resignation, she got into the coach. Consuela got in after her. Gaviota shut the door and climbed up into the box.

"Where is he?" whispered Sombra, distraught.

"Have faith, my dear. That young man will not betray your trust."

Gaviota stirred up the team, and the coach lurched forward. By the time it reached the end of the street the horses had fallen into a brisk, swinging gait. Gaviota worked the leathers with nimble fingers of steel to turn the coach into an intersecting street. At that moment Padre Pico appeared out of the shadows of a deeply recessed doorway at the corner—stepping directly into the path of the coach. The grays snorted and balked, startled by his sudden appearance; the offside leader tried to rear in its traces. Crying out, Padre

Pico fell beneath the hooves of the horses. Gaviota climbed the reins, and the coach came to a jolting stop. Leaping from the top of the coach, Gaviota rushed to the front of the team.

Eben stepped out of the shadows of the doorway and stole to the rear of the coach, then slipped around to the door and opened it gently. The look on Sombra's face when he swept back the cowl warmed his soul. He held out a hand to her.

"Go, child!" whispered Consuela urgently.

Sombra took his hand, spared Consuela one last, saddened glance—and then Eben had her out of the coach, and back into the shadows.

By now Gaviota had Padre Pico on his feet.

"I am unhurt," said the priest. *"Gracias. Vaya con Dios."*

He continued on across the street with unhurried dignity.

Gaviota watched him for a moment, before returning to the top of the coach, where he took up the leathers and whipped the team into motion again.

"I'll be," breathed Eben. "It worked. It actually worked."

Sombra wasn't watching the coach turn the corner out of sight. She was gazing up at him in a very disconcerting way, tightly gripping his hand in hers, as though she would never let go.

Eben cleared his throat with some difficulty. "Come on. We had better get out of Monterey, quick."

He looked around for Padre Pico, but the priest was gone.

They crossed the street and turned into the alley where the Appaloosa waited. Shedding the robe, Eben had Sombra put it on, then helped her up into the saddle and mounted behind her. Filled

with elation, he put his arms around her to gather
the reins and with a tap of his heels prompted the
mare into a walk that, once they were away from
the plaza and the middle of town, turned into a
canter and then, as they reached the outskirts of
town, a gallop.

Padre Pico beat them back to the Carmel Mission, and Eben wondered how on earth the priest
had managed that, but he didn't ask. There were
more pressing questions on his mind, chief among
them the location of the seaside hideaway where
he and Sombra were supposed to wait for Captain
Shagrue and the *Halcyon*. The tireless priest took
them there immediately. As it was located several
miles up the coast, Padre Pico rode a white donkey. The donkey wasn't much for speed, and Eben
nervously checked their back trail at least a hundred times during the trip. He figured all of Monterey knew what had happened by now.

Padre Pico had said he knew Gaviota; did Gaviota know the priest? If so, had he been able to
identify him in the street? Eben decided it really
didn't matter in the long run. A priest was involved in Sombra's disappearance, and sooner or
later the trail would lead Don Carlos to the Carmel Mission. Hopefully it would be later—after
the *Halcyon* had sailed.

Eben wondered what story Don Carlos would
tell to explain his daughter's bizarre departure.
Surely he would claim she had been abducted
against her will. All of California would be on the
lookout for her. Eben hoped this hideaway Padre
Pico had arranged for them was sufficiently
remote.

He wasn't disappointed. The little cabin, nestled
in a stand of cedars, stood near the base of a steep,
rocky bluff. It overlooked a lonely stretch of

horseshoe-shaped beach between two bluffs where the surf crashed against huge boulders. There was no other dwelling anywhere near, said Padre Pico, and the nearest road was a mile inland.

The cabin itself consisted of only one room, with a hard-packed dirt floor and a mudstick chimney. The roof had been constructed with cedar shakes, and the walls were gray clapboard, warped and weathered. The only furnishings were a split-log table and bench and a narrow rope slat bed with a strawtick mattress rolled up at one end. Padre Pico had supplied some beans and flour and a little coffee, along with a pot and a skillet. For water the priest directed them to a creek that ran through a draw about two hundred paces to the south, near the point. Kindling was stacked high near the fireplace. Not to worry, the priest assured them, about the smoke from a fire. The constant breeze off the ocean would quickly dissipate any smoke that escaped the chimney.

With a promise to come check on them in a day or two if possible, Padre Pico blessed them both and took his leave.

Suddenly alone with Sombra, Eben contracted a bad case of nerves. She stood in the doorway for some time, looking out at the moonlight on the breakers, listening to the sullen roar of the surf. Finally he could stand the silence no longer.

"You're not sorry, are you?"

She turned, forcing a smile. "No. But I am afraid of what my father might do."

"He'll never lay hands on you again. Not as long as I am alive."

"That is what I am afraid of. What he will do to you if he finds us."

"He won't."

"You are very brave, Señor Nall."

"You told me to call you Sombra. I will, but only if you call me Eben." He glanced around the cabin, its interior illuminated by the flickering, mustard-yellow light of a coal oil lamp. "I apologize for the accommodations."

Now the smile was genuine. "I do not mind at all. For the first time in years I feel ... free."

"Do you really want to leave California, Sombra? I know it's the only home you've ever known."

"If I do not leave I will never truly be free. Yes, Eben, I will go where you go."

Eben told her all about the arrangements with Captain Shagrue, watching her closely as he spoke. But the prospect of a long sea voyage did not appear to be in the least daunting to her.

"I have no money with which to pay for my passage," she said. "I own nothing now but these clothes I am wearing."

"You've given up a lot, Sombra."

"I do not regret it. But how can I repay you?"

"You don't have to. I'm ... glad to help."

The way she was looking at him made Eben squirm inside.

"I'd better go unsaddle the mare and fetch some water," he mumbled and fled the cabin, bucket in hand.

When he returned, toting his saddle and a bucket sloshing with creek water, she was starting a fire. She stated her intentions of cooking some beans and tortillas. He busied himself cleaning his Kentucky rifle and flintlock pistol. They ate the meal in silence, Eben wishing he knew how to make small talk. But he dared not even attempt to do so, knowing he would likely just make a fool of himself.

"You look pretty worn out," he said when they

were done eating. "You can sleep in the bed. I'll take the floor."

"The floor?"

"Shoot, I've been sleeping on the ground so long I wouldn't know what to do in a . . . well, I mean . . ." He blushed.

"You did not sleep on the floor in the hacienda."

Thinking back to her nocturnal visit to his bedroom at Hacienda Gavilan put even more color in Eben Nall's cheeks. He cleared his throat and proceeded to unroll his blankets—on the other side of the table from the bed. Sombra cleared the table and lay down on the mattress. Realizing she had no cover, Eben carried one of his blankets over to her. She sat up to accept the blanket and, as she did, took his hand in hers.

"*Buenos noches*, Eben," she said, with a tender smile that stole his breath away. "And thank you, from the bottom of my heart."

Mumbling goodnight, Eben went back to his blankets, put out the lamp, and plunged the cabin into pitch blackness. In spite of his weariness he still had trouble going to sleep, and for a long time he lay there quite still and listened to the sound of Sombra's breathing.

Chapter 27

"Riders coming," said Gus Jenkins as he shook Hugh Falconer awake.

Falconer rolled out of his blankets, lithe and instantly alert. The rest of the brigade was stirring. Dawn was a gray promise of night's demise. Luck and the other squaws were disturbing the embers of the campfires, while the men looked to their rifles. This was a mountain man's second nature. They had no idea who the riders were or what they wanted, but they would not be caught with their guard down.

"Can't tell yet who it is," admitted Jenkins, standing alongside Falconer and squinting at the distant black specks moving across the amber background of the sun-ripened wild oats that carpeted the valley floor.

Falconer couldn't either, for the moment—but he had a real good idea. He had not told anyone else about Eben Nall. Some of the men had wondered where their young companion was and what he was up to, but Falconer had kept his lips sealed, and Rube Holly had done the same. Now Falconer had second thoughts. Had he been right to keep the truth from the brigade? All along he had figured there was an excellent chance that Don Carlos Chagres would pay them a visit after his daughter disappeared. Didn't the others have a right to know that there could be big trouble in store for them?

Guilt was part of the reason why he had kept silent. After all, he'd kept everyone else on a short rope, spouting a long can't-do list, while acting as the willing accomplice in Eben Nall's dangerous scheme to rescue Sombra Chagres. Wasn't very consistent. He realized that and wasn't even sure why he had gone to such lengths to help Eben. Paying for Eben's and Sombra's passage on Captain Shagrue's brigantine was really the least of it.

As the riders neared, Falconer could see he was right—it was Don Carlos, with Remo and seven *vaqueros*, and three more men clad in the distinctive green-and-black uniform of the Mexican soldier.

The presence of Don Carlos meant Eben Nall had succeeded in his venture.

"I don't like the looks of this," muttered Jenkins suspiciously. "But at least we've got them outnumbered."

Falconer glanced at Jenkins. "Gus, go around to every man here and tell them I don't want them to start anything."

"What if those fellers yonder start something?"

"The men have a right to defend themselves."

Gus nodded. Clear enough what Falconer meant. The men could shoot only if they were shot at. He lingered to gaze inquisitively at the oncoming riders. "I wonder if this has something to do with the Nall brothers and Doc Maguire."

"What do you mean?"

"Well, all I'm saying is, everything's fine and dandy between us and the Californios. Then Eben Nall disappears a couple days ago. And Silas Nall and Doc Maguire didn't come back from Monterey last night like they were supposed to. I noticed they were absent this morning."

Falconer grimaced. Just what he needed, something else to worry about.

As Jenkins moved off to deliver Falconer's caveat to the other mountain men, Falconer took up his Hawken rifle and went forward to meet Don Carlos at the edge of camp.

"We have come to search your camp," said Chagres curtly as he checked his high-stepping stallion.

"What are you looking for?"

The *haciendero's* demeanor was a portrait of cold rage. "For Eben Nall and my daughter."

"Neither one is here."

"I will see for myself."

Falconer's smile was bleak as a high country winter.

"You implying that I'm a liar, Don Carlos?" He spoke softly, but every man present could detect the iron menace beneath the words.

"I am Lieutenant Ramirez," said one of the soldiers. "Sombra Chagres has been kidnapped. Don Carlos has reason to believe one of your men, señor, is responsible."

"If Eben Nall ran off with your daughter, Don Carlos, I reckon she went of her own free will."

"And you, of course, know nothing about it," rasped Chagres.

Falconer didn't answer. One thing he would not do, even for Eben Nall, even for a good and just cause like the rescue of Sombra Chagres, was speak a lie.

"You are the leader of these men," said Ramirez. "As such, I presume you take responsibility for their actions."

"I do, long as they're part of the brigade."

"Then you will come with us, Señor Falconer."

"Am I under arrest?"

"Is it necessary to place you under arrest, señor?"

Some of the mountain men standing about the camp, rifles in hand, had edged closer, and they were near enough to hear this exchange. A clatter of hammers being pulled back punctuated the lieutenant's query.

Falconer whirled. "No shooting, damn it."

"Don't let 'em take you, Hugh," growled Rube Holly.

"We'll make a fight of it right here," suggested French Pete Bordeaux.

"No," snapped Falconer. "I'm going with them."

Gus Jenkins stepped forward. Face-to-face with Falconer, he cast a distrustful glance at Don Carlos.

"Don't go with them, Hugh," muttered Jenkins. "That feller there means to have somebody's hide, and that somebody could turn out to be you."

"Give me your word you'll keep all the men in camp until I get back."

Jenkins pursed his lips and let go a soft whistle. "Might not be easy, that. In case you haven't noticed, these men have become mighty loyal to you in the past few months."

"No, it won't be easy. You're the only one who could pull it off."

"And what if you don't come back, Hugh?"

Leaning forward, Falconer pitched his voice so that only Jenkins could hear.

"Then hightail it out of California, Gus, and don't look back."

"Leave you here on your own stick? These boys won't buy that bill of goods."

"I've been on my own stick all my life," replied Falconer. "I can look out for myself. I don't need you or anybody else to take care of me. You hear?"

"Yeah. I hear you."

Falconer turned back to Ramirez. "I will come with you, Lieutenant."

Ramirez nodded. *"Muy bien. Gracias."*

"I want to search this camp," Chagres told Ramirez.

Ramirez scanned the brigade's camp. "Your daughter is not here, Don Carlos. With all due respect, I am not willing to start a shooting war to prove the obvious."

"I will not tolerate insolence, even from you, Lieutenant."

"You may report me to the governor-general, señor," replied Ramirez, cool and unruffled. "But the one thing you may *not* do is search this camp. Not while I am present."

Falconer was beginning to take a liking to Lieutenant Ramirez. The man was fair-minded, hard as nails, and he kept his head in a crisis.

Chagres was another matter entirely. It was obvious that neither Eben Nall nor Sombra was here. Yet Don Carlos insisted on pressing the issue. Was he mad? With the odds clearly stacked against him, he still wanted to provoke a fight. Falconer watched warily as Chagres teetered precariously on the edge of defying Ramirez—and twenty-five mountain men aching for a good bloodletting before breakfast. One word, and his *vaqueros* would start the ball rolling. They would ride into the teeth of hell for their *patrón*. Their loyalty was that unequivocal. They would not back down, under any circumstances.

In the end, Don Carlos thought better of it. Falconer fetched his horse and moments later was riding toward Monterey with the Californios, leaving a worried bunch of mountain men behind.

*   *   *

Lieutenant Ramirez informed Falconer that the governor-general wished to see him. Don Luis was not presently in his residence, but rather across the square in the building that housed the offices of state, the old presidio. Falconer was escorted to a room off an entrance hall. The only furnishings were a table and a chair. The single window boasted a grill of ornate wrought iron bolted to the outside. Bars by any other name, mused Falconer.

Not that he felt like a prisoner—just yet. He had been allowed to keep his weapons. But when he opened the door to the hall, the guard standing outside turned and looked at him with an expression he couldn't fathom. It definitely wasn't an invitation to step out into the hall, and Falconer realized the small courtesy they had shown him in allowing him to keep his pistol and Hawken mountain rifle when you considered he was smack-dab in the middle of a town that hosted probably two hundred soldiers. Falconer closed the door and went back to the table and sat down to wait.

It was a long wait, but Falconer had more patience than most men. He refused to let himself speculate on what might happen. That was a good way to get your nerves tied up in knots. After a time he took clay pipe and tobacco from his shoulder-slung possibles bag. Someone had built a fire in the room's hearth this morning—although the days were still warm enough as long as the sun was shining, the nights and mornings were quite cool, particularly inside the thick adobe brick walls of this old building. Falconer stirred up the embers and lit the pipe with the glowing end of a stick.

He smoked the pipe down and waited some

more. Several times he heard men running in the hall beyond the door and voices shouting, steeped in urgency. Eben Nall, it seemed, had stirred up a hornets' nest.

Finally the door swung open, and a grim Don Luis entered. The governor-general was accompanied by Chagres and Lieutenant Ramirez.

"Señor Falconer," said Don Luis gravely, "it is good to see you again. I only wish we were meeting under more pleasant circumstances."

"I'm afraid there isn't much I can tell you about Miss Chagres."

"Not to detract from the seriousness of Sombra's abduction, but we have another matter entirely to discuss."

Falconer said nothing. The look on the governor-general's face forewarned him. Whatever Don Luis was about to tell him, it wasn't going to be good news.

With a deep sigh, Don Luis said, "A woman was murdered last night."

"Who?"

The governor-general turned to Ramirez. "Lieutenant?"

"She was a prostitute, Señor Falconer," said Ramirez. "I have only just now learned the details of her death. They are . . . not pleasant."

"What's it got to do with me?"

"One of your men killed her."

Falconer was stunned. But he betrayed no emotion. This was a habit he had acquired through surviving many a tight spot with hostile Indians in the high country. It had proven to his advantage in such situations to keep what he was thinking a secret.

"Who is the man?" he asked.

"He calls himself Maguire."

Doc Maguire! Gus Jenkins had told him that

Maguire and Silas Nall had failed to return to camp last night . . .

"When did this happen?"

"Last night. In a room behind a cantina not far from here. She was stabbed, more than once. She cried out before she died. Señor Maguire tried to flee. But several men captured him. He seriously wounded one of them before he was disarmed and subdued."

A furious anger raged inside Falconer's soul. But none of the others could see it flaring behind the mountain man's stoic mask. Again he did not respond. What was there to say? Doc Maguire had been caught red-handed. Falconer felt betrayed. He had trusted Doc Maguire. But he was angry with himself too, for giving that trust. *I never learned my lesson*, he thought bitterly. Once before, long ago, he had put his trust in other men who had ultimately betrayed him. He had lived to regret it, but only barely.

He wasn't too sure that he or any other member of the brigade would survive this betrayal.

Chapter 28

"Señor Falconer," said the governor-general, "it will prove impossible to keep this crime a secret from the people for very long. Soon all of Monterey—indeed, all of California—will know of it. Do you understand what I am trying to say?"

"I think I do."

"Personally, I do not hold you to account for the barbaric act of this man, Maguire. But I am afraid the people will not be so . . . discerning."

Falconer nodded. "We'll have to leave California immediately. Won't be easy, getting back over those mountains so late in the year. We may have to . . ."

Don Carlos stepped forward, no longer able to contain himself. Fury crawled across his features.

"You cannot permit them to leave," he told Don Luis in Spanish.

The tone of voice Chagres employed rankled the governor-general. "You presume to tell me what I can and cannot do?"

"I am telling you that this man"—Don Carlos stabbed an accusing finger at Falconer—"and probably all of his followers, are parties to the kidnapping of my daughter."

"Since this obviously has something to do with me," said Falconer coldly, "I'd be obliged if you spoke English."

"Of course," said the governor-general. "That is

only fair. Don Carlos objects to letting you depart in peace, Señor Falconer. He believes you have knowledge pertaining to the whereabouts of Sombra Chagres."

Falconer had a real good idea where Sombra and Eben were at this very moment—the cabin by the sea that Padre Pico had spoken of the day he and Eben had visited the Carmel Mission.

"From what I hear, your daughter had a good reason for running away, Don Carlos," he said.

Chagres looked to be on the verge of lunging across the table at the mountain man.

"I ought to kill you where you stand," rasped the *haciendero.*

"You could sure try."

"Gentlemen, please," said the governor-general.

Chagres glowered at Don Luis. "Are you going to do something about this, or do I have to take matters into my own hands?"

Realizing that his fate lay in the hands of the governor-general, Falconer watched Don Luis closely. Clearly Chagres had power—enough influence, at least, to make the governor-general consider the warning carefully.

"I am sorry, Señor Falconer," said Don Luis, "but for the time being I must insist that you and your men remain in California. At least until the matter of Sombra's . . . disappearance . . . is cleared up."

"Seems like that's just asking for trouble, if the people get worked up about this killing."

The governor-general shrugged helplessly. "I will have Lieutenant Ramirez place your men under . . . under our protection."

"That's just a nice way of saying we'll all be under arrest."

"I would not describe it as 'arrest.' "

Falconer noticed for the first time that his hands

were clenched into fists, and he tried to relax. It wasn't easy. He had never cottoned to folks telling him he could not come and go as he pleased. And he knew full well the buckskinners in his brigade would not meekly surrender themselves into custody.

"I don't think that's a very good idea," he said. "My men won't give up their weapons without a fight. It's just not in them to do it."

"Then they will all die," said Chagres with relish.

"Don Carlos, please," said the governor-general.

"Maybe they will," replied Falconer, fixing Chagres with a bold and piercing stare. "That won't bother them. To go down fighting is the way those men want to go."

"Perhaps if you talked to them," suggested Don Luis. "Tried to reason with them."

Falconer felt sorry for the governor-general. The man was trying to be reasonable and trying to prevent more bloodshed. But he was caught between the rock of an intractable Don Carlos and the hard place of a bunch of mountain men who would not bow to any authority they did not choose to recognize—and who most assuredly would not go like lambs to the slaughter.

"I can't," he said, with genuine regret, because everything he had done since arriving in California had been to keep the peace, and now it appeared to have all been for naught. "In this case, they wouldn't listen to me."

"But you are their leader."

Falconer nodded. "But they still wouldn't listen, believe me."

Flustered, Don Luis glanced at Ramirez. The young lieutenant was carefully impassive. He knew his place and would do his duty. His place was not to make suggestions or make his personal feelings known, and his duty was to do the bidding of the governor-general, without question, without hesitation, and whether he agreed with it or not.

The governor-general walked to the window, hands clasped tightly behind his back, shoulders bowed with the weight of his troubles, his brows knit in a worried frown.

"Don't do it," said Falconer. "You have me. I won't make any trouble for you. Let my men go. I can promise you they will leave California immediately."

"You and your men should never have come here," snapped Chagres. "We opened our homes to you, gave you our friendship and our trust. And this is how we have been repaid. A woman murdered. My daughter abducted."

"Your daughter was not kidnapped," said Falconer, slowly but surely losing his grip on his temper. "She left you of her own free will because you were . . ."

With a snarl like a wild animal's, Don Carlos launched himself at Falconer. Falconer's Hawken lay on the table. A pistol and knife were stuck in his belt. But he did not reach for a weapon. He was ready, willing, and able to take Chagres apart with his bare hands.

But Lieutenant Ramirez intervened. He knew better than to lay a hand on Don Carlos; he merely placed his body in Chagres's path. Don Carlos drew up short. There was something about Ramirez—perhaps it was his stance or his stoic expression—that made it clear to Don Carlos, and everyone else in the room, that it would be far simpler to get through a mountain of solid rock than the young lieutenant.

"Don Carlos," said the governor-general severely, "you are only making matters worse. I must ask you to leave."

Chagres stared at Don Luis as though he could not believe his ears. But this time the governor-general was not making a request. He was telling Chagres what to do, and in no uncertain terms. He had drawn a line, finally, and now it was up to Chagres to decide whether he dared cross it.

Don Carlos turned to Falconer. "I will get my daughter back," he said. "And every man who was involved in her abduction will die. I promise you that."

He left the room.

"Lieutenant," said Don Luis, with a heavy heart, "take as many men as you think you will require and bring Señor Falconer's men to Monterey."

"You're making a mistake," warned Falconer.

Don Luis ignored him. "Bring them, Lieutenant. One way or the other."

"I will surprise them at dawn tomorrow," said Ramirez. He executed a snappy salute and also left the room.

"I am sorry, Señor Falconer," said the governor-general. "But I believe this is best for all concerned. I wish to prevent more bloodshed."

"You're going about it the wrong way."

"Your men will be protected by the army. If I do not do this thing, Don Carlos will ride against them with all his *vaqueros*. Many men would die."

"But who is going to protect your army from my men, Don Luis?"

Don Luis smiled. "I hope we can work together to keep the peace."

"Am I under arrest?"

"Not in so many words. But I would prefer that you remain here until your men arrive. Then I will find a safe place for all of you to stay."

"Stay until when?"

"That I cannot say."

"I want to see Maguire."

"Of course. He is being held here, in this building. I will have him brought up."

"What about Silas Nall?"

"I do not know this man."

Falconer nodded. Don Luis went to the door and spoke to the guard standing outside.

"Señor Maguire will be here in a few moments," he said, returning to the table and sinking with a heavy sigh into the chair. "This is a very bad business. Forgive me for saying so, but I wish you had never come to California."

"What's done is done. What will happen to Maguire?"

"He will have a fair trial, I can assure you. Considering the evidence against him, I have little doubt he will be found guilty and condemned to death."

Falconer went to the window. He was standing there when two soldiers led Doc Maguire into the room. Only then did Falconer turn. Maguire wore heavy shackles on his wrists and ankles. His clothes were torn, his face battered and bruised. When he saw Falconer his swollen lips curled into a crooked grin.

"Thank Christ you're here, Hugh. Now at least there's somebody who will listen to my side of the story."

"I'm listening."

"It was self-defense. I swear on my mother's grave, it was, Hugh. The wench was trying to rob me. I woke up and caught her red-handed, and that's when she tried to stick a knife between my ribs."

"You will have an opportunity to tell your story

in court," said Don Luis. By his tone it was apparent he did not believe a word Maguire was saying.

"In court? Hugh, you're not going to let them kill me, are you? We're supposed to stick together, through thick or thin, right?"

"Not much I can do, Doc."

Maguire held up his hands and rattled the chains that held his wrists together. "This is sure no way for a mountain man to live."

Falconer stepped closer to the Irishman. "You killed that woman in England, didn't you, Doc?"

Maguire's crooked grin faded just a bit. On the verge of sticking to the old lie, he glimpsed something in Falconer's dark gaze and changed his mind.

"Yes," he said softly. "Yes, I surely did. She told me our affair was over. She was through with me. As though I were just some servant she could use and then dispose of. It rubbed me the wrong way, you know? But this time it was self-defense, Hugh. You've got to believe me."

"You gave me your word. I put my trust in you. Now the life of every man in the brigade is at risk."

"I'm bloody sorry . . ."

"I'm just as much to blame as you."

"No, Hugh, don't blame yourself. You're a damn fine booshway. It's been an honor and a privilege to ride with you. I'm the one. I broke the flamin' rules . . ."

"I broke my own rule. Never trust anybody."

"There's an old Irish saying, 'Put your trust in God, my boys, but keep your powder dry.'"

"You broke your word to me, Doc."

"All I'm asking for is justice."

"'Though justice be thy plea, consider this, that in the course of justice none of us shall see salvation.'"

"Shakespeare." Maguire chuckled. "I swear, Hugh Falconer, you're a strange one . . ."

Falconer drove the knife into Maguire, all the way up to the "Green River," just below the sternum, then tilted it so that the blade pierced the Irishman's heart.

A look of surprise frozen on his face, Maguire gasped and fell dead.

"*Madre de Dios!*" exclaimed Don Luis, standing up so fast that he knocked the chair over.

Recovering quickly, the soldiers pounced on Falconer, driving him back against the table. He did not resist, dropping the bloody knife.

Staring in horror at Maguire's corpse, the governor-general struggled to keep his dinner down. When he was sure he would not humiliate himself by puking, he collected himself and started for the door, as dignified as possible, carefully stepping around the dead man.

"Put him in irons," said Don Luis.

Chapter 29

From a hill a quarter of a mile away, Gus Jenkins and Rube Holly watched the detachment of soldiers approach the trees where the brigade had been camped up until only a few hours earlier.

"How many you reckon, Gus?" asked Rube. "My eye ain't as sharp as it used to be. Hell, I'll prob'ly be seein' better out of the glass one than I will the real one 'fore too much longer."

"Must be fifty of them," replied Jenkins grimly.

"Reckon they kin read sign?"

"We'll find out in a few minutes."

The soldiers were roaming through the woods. Rube Holly figured they hadn't come on a social call. He slid an approving glance sideways at Gus Jenkins, belly down in the tall grass beside him. Behind the hill were ten men, including Sixkiller and French Pete Bordeaux. The rest of the brigade was miles away by now, thanks to a bad feeling Jenkins had experienced this morning around daybreak.

"Think we'd better pull up stakes," he had told Rube. "Hugh would be back by now if he was coming back."

"You mean we're gonna ride into Monterey and fetch him back?" Rube Holly was getting on in years, but that didn't mean he didn't hanker after a little excitement every now and then.

"I mean nothing of the kind. We just move camp."

"What fer?"

"Because I'd feel better if we did," said Jenkins, a little testy. "How's that for a reason?"

Rube Holly had just shrugged, being somewhat mystified.

Now he could see why Gus Jenkins had a reputation for being one of the best booshways in the business. He had good instincts and was wise enough to listen to them. Those Californios yonder were looking for trouble. It sure didn't take fifty of them to drop by and say howdy. Without Gus Jenkins and his sixth sense for danger there would be some leadslinging right now.

"What do you reckon happened to Hugh?" asked Holly.

"I'd say they've got him locked up—if he's still above snakes."

Rube scowled. "If those bastards have done for him there'll be pure hell to pay."

"Hugh's orders were clear. My job is to get the brigade as far from here as possible."

"We're just gonna run out and leave Hugh to float his stick alone? Is that what you're sayin', Gus?"

"That's what he wanted."

"Well, I'd purely like to see how you get the rest of the boys to go along with that."

Jenkins grimaced. It would not be easy to sell that bill of goods to the brigade. He knew as much.

"Doesn't look like I'll have to," he muttered, as the soldiers, back in a nice neat column of twos, began to ride toward their vantage point.

"Guess that answers my question," observed Rube Holly wryly. "They kin read sign."

Jenkins sighed. Clearly those soldiers had been

dispatched to capture or kill the brigade. There could be no other reason for such a force. Which meant some shooting was inevitable, regardless of Hugh Falconer's best efforts to prevent such a thing from happening.

"Come on," he said, and crawled off the rim of the hill before rising to trot down the slope and join the others. Rube Holly was right on his heels.

"Fifty soldiers," said Jenkins, mounting his horse. "Coming straight for us."

French Pete Bordeaux glanced at the men to either side of him. Then, grinning broadly, he drew his rifle from its horn strap.

"Only fifty? That's just five for each of us, my friends."

"Let's try to discourage them before we start killing them," said Jenkins. By his tone of voice it was clear he did not expect the soldiers to be easily discouraged.

He led the way to the top of the hill, checked his horse, and motioned for the others to spread out. The column of soldiers was only a few hundred yards away now. When he saw the mountain men arrayed along the spine of the hill, their backs to the morning sun, the officer in front of the column raised an arm, signaling the column to halt.

"Just turn around and go home," muttered Gus Jenkins under his breath.

The officer rode forward, flanked by two men, a sergeant-major and a standard-bearer.

" 'Pears they want to parlay," said Rube Holly.

"Keep the rest of the men here," said Jenkins. "And for God's sake, no shooting."

As he rode down the hill, Jenkins mused that he and Hugh Falconer had been saying "no shooting," or some variation thereof, till they were blue in the face. And all to no avail, in the end.

He didn't get too close—just close enough to

talk to the officer without having to shout. Now he recognized the man. It was Ramirez, the level-headed lieutenant who had accompanied Don Carlos Chagres and the *vaqueros* to the brigade's camp yesterday morning.

"Where is Falconer?" asked Jenkins.

"I am the bearer of bad news, I am afraid," said Ramirez. He seemed genuinely sorry. "Señor Falconer is under arrest."

"Under arrest? For what? What's the charge against him?"

"Murder."

"I don't believe it. Hugh Falconer would never kill a man that didn't need killing."

"He murdered one of your own. A man named Maguire. Maguire, in turn, had been arrested for the murder of a young woman in Monterey."

This was a lot for Gus Jenkins to absorb in a single dose. "I wouldn't necessarily call it murder, Lieutenant, what Falconer did. You see, he's our booshway. That makes him the brigade's judge, jury, and executioner. Doc Maguire broke Falconer's law. So he had to pay. Hugh just saved you folks the trouble, sounds like to me."

Ramirez nodded. "I understand. But, in the process, he broke our law. And he must be punished."

Jenkins grimly twisted in the saddle and scanned the top of the hill bristling with mountain men.

"Lieutenant," he said, "for the sake of peace, turn Hugh Falconer loose and let us ride out of here."

"I cannot. I am sorry. I have my orders. The governor-general has instructed me to bring all of you back to Monterey. This is for your own protection. The abduction of Sombra Chagres and the murder of the other woman has the people up in arms. You will be in the army's custody."

Jenkins shook his head. "Won't float with the others."

"I must carry out my orders."

"I reckon you'll allow me to rejoin my men."

"Of course."

"Good luck, Lieutenant."

"*Buena suerte, Señor.*"

Jenkins jerked his horse around and rode back to the top of the hill.

"Get ready, boys," he said. "All hell's fixing to break loose."

"Ain't they purty," said one of the mountain men with Gus Jenkins on the hill. Then he hawked and spat.

The soldiers were switching from column formation to a single line, with the left-hand troops turning to the left and the right-hand to the right, parting ways where Lieutenant Ramirez sat his horse, flanked by the sergeant-major and the standard-bearer. When all the men were in line, Ramirez shouted a curt order and they turned their horses as one to face the hill. Then the lieutenant drew his saber. Sunlight flashed off fifty blades as the cavalrymen followed suit, holding the weapons at shoulder rest.

"The fools," said French Pete contemptuously. "They bring knives to a gunfight."

Gus Jenkins was not amused. In his opinion, French Pete and the others gravely underestimated Ramirez and his troops. The lieutenant seemed to be a very capable commander, and the men he led today were obviously well trained.

"Dismount, boys," said Jenkins.

He swung down just as Ramirez swept the saber forward, and the whole Mexican line surged

forward on galloping horses. Jenkins braced his
rifle across the bow of his saddle and drew a bead
on the lieutenant. Made sense to chop the head
off the snake. Kill the brave ones first; they led
the others. But Jenkins couldn't pull the trigger.
His heart wasn't in this business in the first place,
and he particularly did not want to be the one to
drop Ramirez. So he switched to the burly
sergeant-major riding beside Ramirez, fired, and
saw his target somersault backward off his horse.
No doubt just as brave a man as the lieutenant, mused
Jenkins bleakly as he reloaded. *But at least I did
not know his name.*

More rifles spoke along the crest of the hill.
More soldiers toppled from their horses. But the
rest of the cavalrymen kept coming. As the middle
of the line charged straight up the grassy slope,
the two ends began to swing around to enclose
the knot of mountain men on the rim. All the
buckskinners got off a second shot, and eight
more soldiers were plucked from their saddles,
dead or wounded. Those remaining closed in, and
the fight became hand to hand.

Jenkins managed to reload a third time.
Crouched, he fired at a soldier looming over him
with saber raised. The soldier slipped sideways
off his horse, shot through the chest. Another one
tried to ride Jenkins down. Jenkins blocked this
one's saber stroke by using the empty rifle like a
club. The soldier's horse carried him past. Jenkins
pulled a pistol from his belt and shot the man in
the back.

Turning to see French Pete fall beneath the
bloodied blades of two soldiers, Jenkins dispensed
with his empty guns, whipped his Green River
hunting knife from its sheath, and took off running, an Indian war whoop on his lips. He
launched himself at one of French Pete's killers

and carried him bodily out of the saddle. Before they hit the ground Jenkins had ripped the man open from sternum to crotch. As he rose, a saber slashed his arm to the bone. The impact knocked him off his feet. Jenkins rolled to escape the flashing hooves of the soldier's horse. The soldier aimed a pistol at his head. The pistol spat orange flame and Jenkins winced. But the bullet merely plucked at the shoulder of his deerskin shirt, barely grazing the skin beneath. An instant later the soldier plunged to the ground. As his horse galloped away riderless, Sixkiller appeared out of the powder smoke haze and, with a savage cry, fell upon the dying man to lift his scalp.

Jenkins got to his feet, clutching his wounded arm, dizzy from shock and the loss of blood. Disoriented, he needed a moment to realize that the soldiers were no longer swarming the hill.

Rube Holly appeared beside him. "It's Cotton Phillips and Bluefeather and the rest of the boys!" crowed the old-timer. "They come back to save our bacon."

Peering north, Jenkins saw that it was so. The rest of the brigade was coming on at a mad gallop. To the southwest, the remnants of the detachment were making a run for distant Monterey.

Holly applied a kerchief to Jenkins's arm as a tourniquet, hoping to staunch the flow of blood. As he worked, Jenkins bleakly surveyed the battleground. It amazed him that so much carnage could be wrought in such a brief span of time. How long had the fight lasted? Two minutes? Maybe three?

Only he, Rube Holly, Sixkiller, and one other mountain man were left standing. Twenty-eight soldiers lay dead or dying. Several horses had also been slain.

Jenkins searched for, and was dismayed to find,

Lieutenant Ramirez among the casualties. The officer had been gutshot during the melee on the hilltop. He lay, gazing calmly at the blue California sky. Jenkins knelt beside him, and in a glance knew there was nothing he could do to save this man.

"I'm right sorry it had to come to this," said Jenkins.

"Will you hear my confession, señor?"

Jenkins was taken aback. "But I'm no priest . . ." The plea in the lieutenant's eyes cut his protest short. "Sure I will."

But Ramirez did not have time to unburden his soul. He convulsed, and a trickle of blood leaked from the corner of his mouth. Then his eyes took on the glaze of death. Jenkins gently closed them and said a silent prayer, hoping that it would suffice.

Chapter 30

Since he could not be certain that the soldiers were gone for good, or if they would return with reinforcements and a vengeance, Gus Jenkins did not linger long on the field of battle. Taking their dead with them, the brigade rode north, leaving the bodies of the Californios where they lay. Jenkins figured such brave men deserved a decent burial, but most of the other mountain men were not of like mind. Besides, there was no time to waste in digging graves. Jenkins could only hope the Californios would retrieve their dead before the buzzards came to feast on the remains.

His wound made the ride a nightmare of agony for Jenkins, but he carried on, stoic and without complaint. They stayed in their saddles most of the day, stopping only when night had thrown its dark cloak across the land. By then Jenkins was only half conscious. They had to lift him gently off his horse and lay him out on some blankets spread over the cold ground. Rube Holly cauterized the wound with gunpowder set ablaze. Jenkins passed out. He missed the burial of the six dead trappers. Cotton Phillips broke out his well-worn Bible, but he didn't read from it; the ex-slave spoke the passages from memory.

Jenkins came to the following morning, feeling like he might live after all. Rube Holly quipped that he was just about the only man in the brigade who had gotten any sleep. Everybody else had kept their eyes peeled and rifles handy, expecting pursuit and another attack. But there did not appear to be any pursuit. The Nez Perce, Bluefeather, had ridden out on a scouting foray before daybreak. He returned a little while later to report seeing no sign of any soldiers.

Cotton Phillips apologized to Jenkins for disobeying his orders and bringing the rest of the brigade back in time for the fight: The men, he explained, had just not catered to the idea of leaving their ten companions behind while they ran like scared rabbits. They had been of one mind on turning around, and Cotton confessed that he had not tried very hard to talk them out of it.

Jenkins called the men to gather round, and counted heads. There were seventeen men left in the brigade—but only sixteen were present and accounted for. Sixkiller, the Flathead warrior, had gone missing.

"Who was the last to see Sixkiller?" he asked.

The Flathead had last been seen late the previous day, during the long ride. Nobody could recall having noticed him splitting off from the group, but apparently that was exactly what he had done.

"Damned red scoundrel prob'ly went back to harvest some more scalps," opined Rube Holly. "Get that rascal's blood up and he's likely to take on the whole danged Republic of Mexico."

"I say we join him," said someone else. "Ain't fair that he gets to have all the fun."

Jenkins shook his head. It was certain death for all of them if they stayed, but not one among these men seemed especially eager to keep running. The fact that six of their friends had lost their lives yesterday had not dampened their enthusiasm for trouble.

"Hugh Falconer's been arrested by the authorities in Monterey," said Jenkins. "His orders were for us to hightail it out of California if that happened."

The others muttered unhappily among themselves. Jenkins listened and watched and judged the collective mood.

"I reckon it will be a cold day in hell before I can convince you boys to abide by our booshway's orders," he sighed.

"You hit that one right on the mark," said Rube Holly.

"I don't cotton to bein' run out of no place with my tail 'twixt my legs," growled another mountain man.

"And I won't leave Falconer to rot in some hole with iron on his leg," declared a third.

Several others vocalized their agreement with this sentiment.

"Okay," said Jenkins. "But we can't do him any good by getting ourselves thrown cold. We have to figure out what to do. Can't just ride into Monterey bold as brass and start shooting up the place. They'd make short work of us if we were to be so foolheaded."

"Iffen you got any ideas," said Holly, "we're all ears."

"I say two or three of us try to sneak in, dressed up like the locals, and see if we can't cut Falconer loose."

Every man present eagerly spoke up to volunteer.

"Does anybody else besides me speak some Spanish?" asked Jenkins.

A man named Taggart stepped forward. "I went down to Santa Fe with Becknell in '21," he said. "Made the trip a few times after that. I was wet behind the ears back then, but I picked up a little of the lingo, and some of it stuck."

"Good. You and I will go."

"You said two or three," reminded Rube. "How 'bout if I go along too?"

"No. I want you to take over while I'm gone."

"Me?" Rube was aghast. "Hellfire, Gus, I couldn't lead a thirsty horse to water. You know that."

"You'll do fine. Taggart and I will go in. With any luck, we'll be able to pass ourselves off as locals."

"And what do the rest of us do in the meantime?" asked Holly. "Twiddle our thumbs and sing songs?"

"Just keep out of sight. Once we get Hugh out, we'll make a run for it."

"Been meanin' to ask you 'bout that," said Holly, squinty-eyed. "I reckon it's been snowin' dang near ever' day up in them mountain passes since we come across the Sierra. We'd have to sprout wings and fly to get back over them mountains now."

Jenkins nodded. "Figure we'll have to go around them, Rube. North or south. Jedediah Smith went north, into the Hudson Bay's country."

That was the end of the meeting. Jenkins and Taggart got ready to depart immediately for Monterey. Rube Holly pulled Jenkins aside just before they rode out.

"I ain't too sure yule ever make it to Monterey, Gus," said the old-timer. "You're in purty bad shape with that arm . . ."

"I'll make it."

"Say you do. How you aim to git Hugh away from them Mescans?"

Jenkins shrugged. "To be honest, I have no idea. We'll cross that river when we come to it."

"Well, just keep yore powder dry when you

cross that river, hoss, 'cause I got a powerful feelin' yule need it on the other side.''

As they got close to Monterey it became readily
apparent to Jenkins and Taggart that all hell had
broken loose. The fight on the hill had stirred up
a hornets' nest. Details of soldiers galloped up and
down the roads leading into town. Off in the distance they could hear Monterey's church bells
ringing, as the inhabitants were called to congregate and be warned of the crisis caused by the
American mountain men. Leading the spare horse
intended for Hugh Falconer, Jenkins finally gave
it up and led the way deep into a bosquet of old
oaks. There he dismounted.

"We'll be better off waiting until dark," he
told Taggart.

Privately, Jenkins held out little hope for the
success of their mission. Too bad they couldn't
wait a week or two, laying low until the furor
subsided. By then the locals would have figured
the mountain men were long gone—assuming the
brigade could stay hidden that long. But they
couldn't wait. Waiting might prove unhealthy for
Falconer. No, they had to go in. Even though the
odds were stacked against their coming out in
one piece.

Of course, Jenkins wasn't going to share his
grim assessment of their chances with Taggart.
Glancing at his companion, he could tell by Taggart's expression that Taggart had made his own
calculations—and didn't care for the outcome.

Still, neither man gave a moment's thought to
turning back and leaving Falconer to meet whatever fate the Californios had in store for him.

Only after night had fallen did they venture out
of the trees. There was a road near at hand. They
gave it a try, turning their horses toward Monte-

rey, which Jenkins reckoned was maybe two miles to the west. But a few minutes later they heard the thunder of many horses behind them and veered off the road, dismounting to lead their ponies down into a ravine. Thirty soldiers riding hell-bent for leather passed within spitting distance of them. Jenkins thanked the good Lord for moonless nights.

A little farther on they spied a small adobe *choza* just off the road. Mustard-yellow candlelight gleamed in its windows. Stirrup to stirrup, the two mountain men sat their horses and watched the house for a spell. A man came out carrying a bucket. He went down to a nearby creek to fetch some water. Two little children stood in the doorway and called after him. Neither the man nor the children saw the two horsemen a hundred yards away.

"Kinda hate to do it," admitted Taggart. He knew what Jenkins was thinking—he was thinking the same thing. They wouldn't get far in Monterey looking the way they did. Their buckskins were dead giveaways.

"Well, he's got some mules yonder in the pen, and that cart might come in handy."

Taggart nodded. "Let's go ahead then."

When they went through the door, rifles leveled, the man and his family—wife, older son, two little children—were sitting down to a modest dinner of frijoles and tortillas. The wife screamed at the sight of the two strangers. The older boy stood up, fists clenched, lips tight-pressed, but froze as Taggart's rifle swung toward him. The man went for a cane knife over near the mudstick fireplace. Jenkins got in his way.

"No one will come to harm," said Jenkins in Spanish, keeping his voice as calm as possible. "Unless you do something stupid, friend."

The man went back to the table, put a comforting arm around his wife's trembling shoulders.

"We are a poor family, mister. We have nothing worth stealing."

"We didn't come here to steal, or to hurt anybody. We just want the loan of your cart and your mules. We'll try to return them to you when we are finished with them."

The man didn't believe him. "Go and take them. Take anything you want. Just do not hurt my wife and children."

Jenkins glanced at Taggart. What he was about to do was distasteful to him. But the situation did not lend itself to any other option.

"I'm going to have to borrow your son, too."

The wife wailed her protest, certain she would never see her son again—certain that these American barbarians would kill him.

"Please, no," said the man. "Take me instead."

Jenkins shook his head. "Sorry. Your son will have to come with us. He will be released unharmed—as long as you don't make trouble for us."

"I will make no trouble for you, mister. I swear to God."

"Let me make it plain. No one will leave this house until the sun comes up. In the morning, your son will be home, safe and sound—as long as you do what I say."

"No!" cried the distraught mother. "Do not let them take Jesus, husband."

"Hush, Mother," said Jesus. "I will go with them." His eyes were steady as they met Jenkins's gaze.

Jenkins nodded approvingly. "You're a brave young man."

"Let's go," said Taggart. "Quickly."

Jesus bent to kiss his mother's tearstained cheek, then preceded Taggart out into the night.

"My friend and I," said Jenkins, "will need some different clothes. Anything you can spare."

"Yes, yes. I will get them," said the man.

When Jenkins got outside, the borrowed clothes draped over an arm, the mules were already hitched to the two-wheeled cart. He and Taggart stripped down and donned their new attire—the white shirts and trousers of the common laborer, a couple of old serapes. They bundled up their buckskins and hid them beneath the hay strewn in the bed of the cart.

"What about the horses?" asked Taggart.

"We're only a mile from town. We'll have to hope we can get back here. Bringing them with us would draw too much attention. Take them down to the creek."

Taggart led the horses away. When he returned, Jenkins and Jesus were up in the cart, with the leathers in the boy's hands. Jenkins figured Jesus knew how to handle a brace of knobheads as well or better than he did. Taggart climbed into the cart and settled down in the hay. Jesus coerced the mules into motion, and a moment later they were back on the road, heading into Monterey.

Chapter 31

November 13, 1837. This is our second day in the cabin by the sea. Padre Pico was right. It is secluded. I have not seen a soul since we arrived. This morning I went out to scout up and down the coast, looking for sign. There was none that I could find. How nice it would be, I thought, if Sombra and I could have this stretch of coast to ourselves forever. I think I know now how Hugh Falconer must have felt, alone in the high country with his Shoshone bride, Touches the Moon.

It probably would have been wiser to stay in the cabin, out of sight, but Sombra wanted to go down to the sea. The sun was shining, the day warm, the gentle surf beckoning. I found out how impossible it was for me to say no to her. So, down to the beach we ventured. I sat in the sand with my rifle across my knees and watched her as she walked barefoot in the waves as they broke, foaming, on the white sand. Seagulls winged over our heads. Way out to sea, barely visible on the horizon, was a sailing ship, southward bound. It wasn't the *Halcyon*, of course—Captain Shagrue had said he would arrive tomorrow, sending a boat to pick us up. I did not relish the thought of setting sail with the captain and his crew, and I had a hunch Sombra wasn't looking forward to it either. I couldn't blame her. California was her home, the only home she had ever known. Though we hadn't left yet, she already missed it. She said not a word to me on the subject, but I could tell, just the same.

That afternoon, much to my surprise, Padre Pico showed up, riding his white donkey. One look at his face and I could see that something was terribly wrong.

"Señor Falconer has been placed under arrest."

I couldn't believe I had heard him right. How could this have happened? Padre Pico told me all he knew. How Doc Maguire had murdered a woman night before last—the night he and I had helped Sombra escape from Gaviota outside the church. The soldiers had gone out to the brigade's camp with Don Carlos Chagres and his *vaqueros* the following morning—yesterday—looking for Sombra. Falconer had agreed to return to Monterey with them, to see the governor-general. Only then was he informed of the murder. He had asked to see Maguire. In the presence of the governor-general he had killed the Irishman. Now he was charged with murder.

"An eye for an eye, Father," I said. Padre Pico did not say how he knew all this, and I did not ask. There wasn't any doubt in my mind that it was all true.

"He was wrong to take a life," said the priest,

shaking his head morosely. "But you do not appear to be surprised by his actions."

I wasn't, really. Doc Maguire had given his word to Falconer that he would abide by Falconer's rules. And Falconer's foremost rule was that no member of the brigade should do anything that put the rest of the company at risk. Of course, in my case, Falconer himself had bent, if not broken, that very rule, by helping me arrange Sombra's escape from her father. I could only surmise that he had done so for Sombra's benefit.

I tried to explain it to Padre Pico, defending Falconer's actions. As booshway, it was Falconer's duty to act as judge, jury—and, if need be, executioner. He took his responsibilities seriously. This was the code of the mountain man. We all tried to live by it. I couldn't help but believe that Doc Maguire had known Falconer would kill him if given the chance, thereby seeing that mountain justice was done.

Padre Pico was no less perplexed when I was done. "But Maguire would have paid for his crime. Señor Falconer did not have to kill him."

"Maguire would have paid for murdering the woman, yes. But not for betraying the brigade."

A man can get into all sorts of trouble here.

Those had been Doc Maguire's exact words, spoken as he and I waited for Falconer outside the governor-general's house. I remembered, then, how he had looked at those two señoritas as they sashayed by us. If I had only been paying more attention! I might have been able to warn Falconer. But would that have done any good? Probably not. Falconer had Maguire's word, and he would have expected the Irishman to keep it. He would not have forbidden Maguire to visit Monterey just on my hunch that Doc was up to no good.

Try as I might, I could not make Padre Pico see my side of it. It all made perfect sense to me, but he refused to accept the notion that Hugh Falconer had in fact done what was expected of him.

Of course, Sombra's disappearance and the murder of the woman had Monterey in an uproar, but it was nothing compared to the panic in the streets that resulted from a big fight this morning between a detachment of soldiers and the brigade, now led, I assumed, by Gus Jenkins. Padre Pico had heard that thirty soldiers had perished in an ambush set by my friends. I assured him that the first shot would not have been fired by any man in the brigade, especially if Jenkins was in command. Now there was a man who would go to any lengths to stay out of a fight. That is not to say that Gus Jenkins is a coward. Nothing could be further from the truth. I've heard that when a fight is inevitable few men can best Jenkins when it comes to what we call cut'n'shoot.

Regardless of who had started what, one thing was beyond dispute: all hell had broken loose, and Padre Pico had come to warn me, because there was no way of knowing what might happen next. It was possible, said the priest, that Captain Shagrue would back out of our arrangement. Don Carlos had already had every ship anchored in the bay searched from stem to stern, and that might have given

Shagrue a bad case of cold feet. I had to agree; Shagrue had a handful of Falconer's gold pieces, and with Falconer in jail facing a murder charge, it would be just like that drunken old Yankee pirate to forget all about picking us up on his way south.

Having delivered the bad news, Padre Pico started back to the mission, assuring me that if there was anything he could do for us to let him know. But we would have to be extremely cautious now, if we came anywhere near the mission, as yesterday some of the *vaqueros* who ride for Don Carlos had come calling, on orders from their *patrón* to search for Sombra. They had been permitted to look as long as they wanted, and had departed, apparently satisfied that the object of their search had not sought sanctuary within the mission walls. But there was no guarantee they wouldn't return. Clearly, Don Carlos was going to leave no stone unturned.

After the priest's departure I sat for what must have been hours at the table, brooding over the turn of events. Everything had fallen to pieces. Sombra and I were trapped in the eye of the storm, and if Shagrue did not carry through with his part of the bargain there seemed to me to be no way out. My first thought was that we ought to make a run for it. Tonight we could ride north, giving Monterey a wide berth. Perhaps the Appaloosa could carry us both to freedom. She had never failed me before. Like Falconer had said, she was good luck.

Jedediah Smith had escaped an inhospitable

California by going far enough north to reach the country of the Hudson's Bay Company. But just how far was that country? I had no idea. And what would our chances be? I did have an idea on that—slim and none. Probably only slightly better than our chances if we chose to remain hidden here until the storm blew over.

But there was a problem with trying to escape to the north. It would be akin to turning my back on Hugh Falconer. No matter that he had repeatedly told us to look out for ourselves if some ill fate befell him. I realized I could no more leave Falconer to rot in some California jail, or face a firing squad or a hangman's noose, than I could fly to the moon.

Now all I had to do was explain this to Sombra . . .

She cut him short.

"You cannot desert your friend in his time of need," she told Eben. "You would not be the man I fell in love with if you did."

"What?"

"Yes, I am in love with you, Eben Nall. Are you not in love with me, as well?"

"Uh . . . yes, I am." There. He'd said it.

"I knew you must be, to have done the things you have done for my sake."

"Any man would have done the same."

"That is not true."

"You understand, there's a real good chance I won't come back. Likely I'll get my fool head shot off. But . . . well, I've got to try, Sombra. I've got to try to save him. He would do the same for me. I know he would."

The thought of his getting killed plainly upset

Sombra, but she bravely held herself together. "Then you must do what you have to. I will wait here, and pray to God to keep you safe."

Eben nodded. "I'll leave at sundown." The decision was made, but he felt strangely disconsolate. Their brief idyll here, in the cabin by the sea, was over, and he realized now it had been only an illusion.

He proceeded to clean and load his weapons. Sombra built a small fire in the fireplace, then sat on the floor, hugging her knees, rocking slightly, and watching the flames crackle and dance. There was something forlorn about the way she sat there. Eben felt guilty for leaving her—probably for good. But what could he do? The fact that he had to go, and she expected him to, didn't make the leaving any easier. He wanted to go to her, put his arm around her, hold her tightly. But he didn't. Knowing that if he did it would just make their parting an even more difficult proposition.

Night came, all too soon. It was time to go. His weapons were cleaned, loaded, and primed. The Appaloosa mare was saddled and waiting outside. Eben had put on his buckskins. He had the priest's robe with him, intending to put it on over the buckskins as he neared Monterey. He had no definite plan for getting Falconer out of jail—he didn't even know where the jail was—but he figured the cassock would increase his chances, a little. A man in buckskins was gone beaver for sure in Monterey tonight. The soldiers—and probably the people too—would kill him first and ask questions later.

Sombra had scarcely stirred for hours. Still she sat before the slowly expiring fire.

"Guess I'd better be going," he said lamely.

"My prayers go with you."

That was it? Eben's feelings were bruised. He

shrugged and turned to the door, knowing he shouldn't blame her for feeling betrayed and abandoned and without hope. He had come along and she had believed she was getting away from her father, but it had all been illusion, that sense of newfound freedom from despair, and he was going to leave her now to her own devices, getting himself killed, and eventually she would be at her father's mercy again. It was inevitable.

As he reached for the door latch, she got up and flew to him, throwing her arms around him, resting her head against his chest, and heard his racing heart. Eben cupped her chin in his hand and lifted her head so he could see her face, streaked with quiet tears.

"I will come back," he said. "I promise I will."

She nodded and tried to smile, but they both knew that was one promise it might not be within his power to keep.

He pushed her gently away and opened the door.

Sombra cried out in terror.

Gaviota stood there in the windswept darkness.

Chapter 32

Eben pushed Sombra away with the sweep of an arm. Stepping back himself, he brought the Kentucky rifle up. But Gaviota was quick. He grabbed the barrel of the rifle and twisted the weapon out of Eben's grasp. In the scuffle Eben lost his balance and fell backward. Gaviota glanced at the rifle, now in his grasp. Eben expected him to use it. But the Californio tossed the weapon aside with obvious disdain.

"Don't hurt him, Gaviota," said Sombra. "I will go back with you. Just don't hurt him."

His features inscrutable, Gaviota looked at her.

Eben assumed that Padre Pico had unwittingly led Gaviota to the cabin. That meant Gaviota had recognized the priest three nights ago, and Don Carlos had sent him to Carmel Mission, to watch Pico and wait, in the hope that sooner or later the priest would lead him to where Sombra was hiding.

"You're not going anywhere with him," Eben told her grimly.

Leaping to his feet, he yanked the flintlock pistol from his belt.

Gaviota moved quick as thought, striking Eben's arm such a numbing blow that the pistol slipped from his useless fingers. Grabbing Eben by the front of his hunting shirt, Gaviota hurled the young mountain man over the split-log table

effortlessly. Eben hit the hard-packed earth of the
cabin floor so hard it knocked the wind out of
him. The overturned table falling on top of him
didn't help matters either. Despair was a quick
black cancer in Eben's soul. Gaviota was an in-
credibly strong man, a natural killer, and Eben
realized he had no chance against him.

But he had to try.

He kicked the table away and again got to his
feet, his breathing ragged and labored, his arm
still numb and pressed against his side, the copper
taste of blood in his mouth. His rifle was gone,
and the pistol too—Gaviota would not let him get
near them. All he had left was his hunting knife.
He drew it from its sheath.

Gaviota smiled.

The Californio reached behind him, and when
his hand reappeared it held a knife—a short,
straight blade, a ribbed handle, a steel ball at the
end to balance the knife for throwing. By drawing
his own knife Eben had played into Gaviota's
hands.

"Sombra," said Eben. "Run. Now."

"No."

She flew to him, trying to shield him with her
body, assuming Gaviota would want no harm to
come to her. Don Carlos would want his daughter
back safe and sound. Gaviota's contented smile
faded as he saw what Sombra was trying to do.
But Eben could not bring himself to hide behind
a woman—even if it was the only way to survive.

He pried her loose and pushed her away.

"Get back, Sombra. I'll handle this."

Gaviota took one step toward Eben.

Then he whirled to face the open door as Sixkiller exploded into the cabin with a war whoop
that sent chills shooting down Eben Nall's spine.

A knife flashed in the warrior's hand. He

plowed into Gaviota and bore him to the ground. Locked in a death struggle, the two men rolled across the floor, fetching up against the over-turned table. As Sixkiller plunged his blade into Gaviota's neck, the Californio's knife slid between the warrior's ribs and pierced his heart. Sixkiller died instantly. Pinned to the floor by the Indian's weight, Gaviota convulsed, groping at the knife in his throat, his mouth gaping in a silent scream. Then he, too, was dead.

For a long time Eben stood there, staring at the two corpses in death's embrace at his feet, illumi-nated by the dancing yellow light of the coal oil lamp whose flame guttered in the sea wind whis-pering plaintively through the doorway. Finally he bestirred himself, picking Sixkiller up and car-rying him across the cabin to lay him out on the strawtick mattress covering the rope slat bed.

"Who is he?" asked Sombra.

"I saved his life once," replied Eben flatly. "He figured he owed me the same favor."

"Your friend."

"No. My enemy." Looking up at her, Eben could see she did not understand.

"But how did they find us?"

"Gaviota followed Padre Pico, I guess. Sixkiller must have followed Gaviota." With one last look at the warrior, he went to Sombra. "Come on. I'm taking you to the mission. Padre Pico will look out for you until I return from Monterey."

Eben stopped just shy of town in a thick stand of trees. Dismounting, he tethered the mare, then donned the priest's cassock over his buckskins. Almost as an afterthought he shed his moccasins and rolled up his leggings so that they did not extend below the hem of the robe. As for his rifle, he experimented with carrying it concealed beneath the cassock, but it was no use. He would leave it behind, then, and rely on the pistol and knife in his belt.

Going barefoot wasn't easy—it seemed that he managed somehow to step on every sharply pointed stone in the road. By the time he reached the outskirts of town his feet hurt like hell. But he would just have to endure. This disguise was his best hope of getting anywhere near the place they were holding Hugh Falconer.

Padre Pico had told him that most prisoners were kept in the old presidio, across the plaza from the governor-general's house. So Eben headed straight for the center of town. It was late, and he was counting on the majority of Monterey's inhabitants being asleep in their beds. The residential areas through which he passed were quiet enough, but as he neared the plaza he began to see people in the streets. He kept his cowl-covered head down. When a pair of soldiers emerged suddenly from an alley and almost collided with him he had a bad moment. They were off duty; they reeked of strong spirits. One of them spoke to Eben in Spanish. Eben made the sign of the cross and hurried on by. The soldiers laughed and went the other way, none too steady on their feet. *Thank God they were drunk*, thought Eben.

Reaching the plaza, he slipped back into the shadows of a doorway and bleakly surveyed the stern facade of the presidio across the way. The building, two stories high, had been built around a courtyard. Once a fortress, it had no exterior windows that Eben could see from his vantage point; all the windows must open on the courtyard. The only way in seemed to be an archway where a pair of sentries stood their posts at an iron gate.

Eben tried to fend off mounting despair. How could he get inside? He couldn't speak a word of Spanish. Even if he could, what would he say to persuade those guards to let him pass at this hour? It all seemed quite hopeless.

A woman walked by and saw him. Her *camisa* was pulled down off both shoulders and revealed a lot of cleavage. Eben belatedly recognized her. It was Maria, the woman from the cantina where he and Hugh Falconer had met with Captain Shagrue of the brig *Halcyon*. Her lips were as red as the petals of the blossom in her raven hair. His presence startled her, and she spoke, crossly, in rapid-fire Spanish. Eben ducked his head quickly, hoping she would not remember him from the cantina. He made the sign of the cross again as he brushed by her and walked quickly away. Throwing a furtive look over his shoulder, Eben saw her standing there, staring after him. He cursed under his breath. Had she recognized him? Even if she hadn't, there was something about him that made her suspicious. He set a course for the church where Sombra had attended mass last Sunday. When he glanced behind him again, the prostitute had vanished.

He turned down a street, negotiated the alley behind the church, and, crossing another street, reached the back corner of the presidio. The sound of hooves on cobblestone alerted him, and he ducked into the shadows of another alley. A *carreta*, pulled by a pair of mules, its great wooden wheels creaking loudly in the stillness of the night, appeared at the end of the street. A Californio was driving, and he stopped the cart a hundred feet from where Eben was hiding. Two men got out of the back of the cart. They were dressed like poor laborers.

But they were carrying rifles.

Eben took a closer look—and recognized them. Jenkins and Taggart!

They approached the presidio on foot, the young Californio in tow. As they neared the alley Eben stepped out of the shadows.

"Jesus!" gasped Taggart, swinging his rifle around to aim it at Eben.

Grinning, Eben swept back the cowl that hid his features. "Not even close," he said.

"Eben!" exclaimed Gus Jenkins. He grabbed Eben by the arm and dragged him into the alley. Taggart and the Californio followed. "What the blue blazes are you doing here?"

"If I had to guess, I'd say I'm here for the same reason you are, Gus."

"Where did you get that robe?"

"It's a long story."

"Well, then, you can tell me all about it later— if we manage to live through the night." Jenkins scanned the outer wall of the presidio looming over them and shook his head dolefully. "This looks like it's gonna be a tough nut to crack."

"Only one way in, I think," said Eben. "And there are two guards . . ."

"How were you planning to get in?"

"To be honest, I really didn't have what you could call a plan. How about you?"

"Same here." Jenkins was eyeing the priest's robe. "But I just got an idea. A pair of guards, you say?"

Eben nodded.

"Mind if I borrow that robe?"

Chapter 33

Eben Nall didn't think the idea Jenkins had come up with would work, but he kept his mouth shut as he shed the cassock and gave it to Jenkins to put on. Truth was, he didn't have a better idea.

"You watch this boy," Taggart told him, gesturing at the young Californio. "He's a smart one. Keeps his eyes open and doesn't say much. Just waiting for us to get a little careless. If he gets away he'll wake up the whole town in nothing flat, and then we're gone beaver for sure."

Drawing his pistol, Eben told Taggart not to worry.

That was good enough for Taggart. Like the other men in the brigade, he had learned to trust Eben Nall. At first, back at the Green River rendezvous, he had harbored some serious reservations about this untested young man who was only one year removed from an Ohio dry goods counter. Eben had obviously benefited some from Rube Holly's tutelage, but that wasn't enough to suit Taggart and the other veterans of high country living. Now, though, all doubts had been erased. Eben Nall was tried and true. He had proven himself against the Digger Indians, and again in the Sierras.

Eben was smart enough to understand what Taggart's trust signified, and he was proud to be entrusted with such an important task as watching

the young man, but he didn't cotton to being left
behind while his colleagues tried to infiltrate the
presidio. If they got into trouble there wasn't
going to be a hell of a lot he could to help them
out. But he had to admit it made sense—both Jenkins and Taggart could speak the language.

Jenkins and Taggart left the alley and started
toward the plaza. The latter stopped just shy of
turning the corner, while the former, clad in the
priest's robe, made the turn without hesitation
and walked right up to the gate.

"Padre," said one of the sentries, as Jenkins
drew near, "don't you know it is not safe to be
on the streets so late at night?"

"No one is safe," said the second guard, "as
long as those American barbarians are roaming
free."

With a quick look Jenkins saw two things: the
padlock on a heavy chain holding the two sections
of the gate together, and the big skeleton key dangling from a long rawhide thong secured to the
belt of one of the soldiers.

"God's work is never done," he said—and
prayed his Spanish was good enough to pass muster and fool these men.

"What brings you here, Padre?" asked the
first sentry.

"I have come to see one of the prisoners."

"Come back in the morning. No one can enter
at this hour."

Jenkins had concealed his pistol in one of the
sleeves of the cassock. Now, very close to the sentry, he drew the weapon from its place of concealment and laid the barrel across the man's skull.
The soldier crumpled, out cold. Before the second
guard could bring his rifle to bear or shout an
alarm, Jenkins had the pistol planted in his belly.

"Are you ready to meet your Maker, my son?"

The soldier froze and allowed Jenkins to relieve him of his rifle.

Without taking his eye off the soldier, Jenkins pursed his lips and whistled. The sound, thought the guard, was uncannily like the soft cry of a nightbird.

At the signal, Taggart loped around the corner of the building. He slung the unconscious sentry over a shoulder and followed Jenkins, who marched the second guard around the corner and down the alley where Eben was watching over the young Californio.

Tossing the rifle to Eben, Jenkins ordered the soldier to strip, while Taggart removed the unconscious man's uniform. In minutes both Jenkins and Taggart were wearing the uniforms. Not perfect fits, but they would have to do.

"Watch 'em close, Eben," said Jenkins. "We'll be back before you know it."

"What if you get caught?"

"If we get caught you'll hear one big ruckus," said Taggart. "Then you'd better run like the hounds of hell are nipping at your heels."

"Good luck."

Jenkins and Taggart hurried back to the gate. Apparently no one had noticed the momentary absence of the sentries. The skeleton key worked in the gate's padlock.

"Stay here," said Jenkins.

Taggart nodded. If the gate appeared too long unguarded someone was bound to pass by and notice. He watched Jenkins proceed through the archway into the deeper shadows of the courtyard, then turned to survey the plaza carefully. He saw no one. So far, so good.

There did not appear to be anyone in the courtyard, but Jenkins kept close to the walls. This brought him to a window through which streamed a broad ribbon of lamplight. He took a quick peek. The room was obviously part of a barracks, with narrow bunks lining the walls. Four soldiers were playing cards at a table in the middle of the room. Others slept in their bunks. Jenkins got down on his hands and knees and crawled under the window.

Going on, he came to an open door. A single soldier sat at a table in a small stone room. Beyond him was a wall of heavy strap iron, with an inset door. It looked like a jail to Jenkins. He slipped inside and eased around behind the unawares soldier, who was engrossed in a leather-bound book. Jenkins did not fail to notice the pistol in the man's belt, and, as he edged closer, silent as a ghost, the ring of keys riding on the man's hip.

Catfooting up behind the soldier, Jenkins pressed the barrel of the rifle against the base of his skull.

"Move and you die," he said quietly.

The soldier's body went rigid—but he didn't move.

Jenkins appropriated his pistol.

"I've come for the American. Is he here?"

The soldier nodded.

Jenkins thought, *This is too easy. Something is going to happen, and I'm not going to like it . . .*

He stepped back as the soldier stood up, his hands above his hand, and went around the table to the strap-iron door. This he unlocked with one of the keys on the ring. Jenkins kept the rifle barrel nestled against the soldier's spine as they walked down a dark, narrow corridor of stone. They came to a flight of sagging stone steps leading down. A lantern burned low on an iron spike driven into the wall at the top of the steps.

"Take the lantern and keep moving," said Jenkins.

The soldier took the lantern. He gave Jenkins a

look that warned the mountain man that he was
over his initial fright and was beginning to
scheme. Jenkins realized that one shot would
bring the whole garrison down on him. The soldier knew this, too. But was he willing to give his
life to raise the alarm?

"Don't make me kill you," said Jenkins.

For the moment, at least, the soldier was dis-
suaded. He started down the steps. Jenkins pulled
back a little and followed. At the bottom of the
steps was a long underground chamber with
strap-iron cells lining both sides.

The area was dimly illuminated by lanterns at
either end. Some of the cells were occupied—Jenkins could hear the snores of several men, and he
could smell the men too—but it was hard to tell
who was in what cell in this dank gloom.

"Where is the American? Falconer?" asked
Jenkins.

The soldier pointed to the far end of the chamber—then swung the lantern he was holding, trying to strike Jenkins in the face with it. The
mountain man had extraordinary reflexes. He
ducked under the lantern and drove the stock of
the rifle into the soldier's midsection. The soldier
grunted and jackknifed, dropping the lantern. Jenkins laid the rifle barrel alongside the man's head,
just hard enough to knock him out, not hard
enough to kill him.

Relieving the unconscious man of the ring of
keys, Jenkins started down the passageway between the cells.

"Hugh? Hugh Falconer?"

A man appeared at the door of one of the cells,
groping at Jenkins with clawing hands through
the strap iron.

"Let me out," said the man, his voice rumbling
like distant thunder. Crazy eyes blazed out of a

dirty, bearded face. It wasn't Falconer, but a local, and by the looks of him he had been incarcerated down here for quite a spell.

"Sorry," said Jenkins, in Spanish. "I cannot."

"Let me out, or I will yell, and the soldiers will come."

Jenkins found a key that unlocked the cell door. The man took one step across the threshold and ran into a rock-hard fist. The eyes in his head rolled, and he toppled backward, unconscious. Jenkins closed and locked the cell door, ruefully flexing his aching hand.

He found Falconer down at the end of the cellblock, just as the soldier had said. A lantern was hanging on a nearby wall, and he could get a pretty good look at Falconer. He didn't like what he saw. Falconer sat at the edge of a narrow iron bunk, his head hanging. When he raised his head to look at Jenkins, his eyes were sunk deep in their sockets.

Jenkins knew right away what was wrong. To be locked in a cage was a fate worse than death for a man like Hugh Falconer, who had spent the better part of his life roaming free in the high country. Falconer had been in the cell for only a day and a half, but that was plenty long enough. Being closed in like this ate at his insides like a cancer.

"Come on, Hugh," said Jenkins. "Let's get the hell out of California. What do you say?"

At the sound of Jenkins' voice Falconer seemed to come to life. He stood up stiffly. "Amen to that."

Leaving the cellblock, they went back up the steps and into the courtyard. As they were nearing the barracks, a door creaked open and a man stepped out directly in their path. He took one look at Jenkins and Falconer, blinked in disbelief, then his eyes got wide. Falconer wasted no time. He plowed into the soldier, driving him back into the door frame, slamming a forearm into his face. Catching the dazed man as he slumped forward, drooling blood, Falconer hurled him through the doorway where he collided with a second soldier rushing out. Both men went down.

"Run for it, Gus."

Jenkins tossed Falconer the rifle as he drew his pistol from its place of concealment beneath the soldier's uniform. They sprinted for the gate. Taggart had it open for them. The shouts and curses of the soldiers pursued them, and, as they reached the gate, several guns spoke. Bullets burned the air around them. One ricocheted off the gate in a shower of sparks. Falconer whirled and fired. Taggart got off a shot too. Neither man wasted time hanging around to see if they had hit anything. Falconer bolted around the corner of the presidio, hot on the heels of Gus Jenkins. Taggart followed, as soon as he had padlocked the gate and hurled the skeleton key out into the plaza.

Jenkins was surprised to see the *carreta* rolling toward him as he churned around the corner. The young Californio was steering the mules, and Eben Nall stood beside him.

"Good work, Eben," said Jenkins, as he piled into the back of the cart with Falconer and Taggart. "What about the guards?"

"They're both sleeping like babies now," replied Eben.

"Turn this thing around," Jenkins told the young driver in curt Spanish. "Let's see how fast those mules can move."

The young man complied, knowing the soldiers would make no distinction between him and the Americans until it was too late.

There was no pursuit. Locking the gate had

been quick thinking on Taggart's part. The soldiers wasted precious minutes locating a key and getting through the gate. By then the mountain men were long gone.

On the way back to the *choza* where the young man lived with his family, Jenkins told Falconer about the fight between the brigade and the detachment of soldiers commanded by Lieutenant Ramirez.

Falconer just shook his head at the news. Things had come unraveled so fast and so completely that he had a tough time believing it was real. He didn't waste time trying to second-guess himself, wondering what he might have done differently. Hindsight was a luxury he had no time for now. Almost half the brigade was dead, and the rest of them were, for all intents and purposes, trapped in California, where everyone was the enemy.

Jenkins had a real good idea what thoughts were racing through his booshway's mind. "Which way are we going to go, Hugh? I don't know if we'll be able to make it back across the Sierras."

"No. We'll have to go north."

"Of course, the soldiers will figure that out too."

Falconer nodded. Maybe so. The countryside would be crawling with army patrols. They were going to have one hell of a time trying to reach the Oregon country.

When they reached the *choza*, Taggart ran down to the creek to fetch the horses. While he was absent on that errand, and Jenkins was in the house convincing the people there that it would be unwise for them to step one foot outside until sunrise, Falconer turned to Eben.

"Where is Sombra?"

"With Padre Pico at the mission."

"I'd be right surprised if Captain Shagrue holds

up his end of the bargain now, with everything that has happened."

"I know."

Falconer scanned the night, thinking. "There's no help for it. You two had better come along with us. Probably your only chance—and a damned poor one at that."

Eben had already come to the same conclusion. He was glad Falconer had made the offer, since he hadn't planned to ask, feeling that he had made enough trouble for the brigade already.

When Jenkins and Taggart returned, Falconer told them he was going to ride with Eben. "Get back to the brigade, Gus. Ride due east."

"East? But I thought . . ."

"We'll turn north when we can do it without leaving much sign. Hopefully, we'll fool them into thinking we're going to try the mountains. Eben and I will catch up with you. Stay on an eastern course until we do."

Jenkins nodded and swung into the saddle.

"Gus," said Falconer.

"Yeah?"

"Thanks. Thanks to all of you. I wouldn't have lasted long in that iron cage."

Jenkins tried to make light of what he had done. "Now aren't you glad we don't obey orders very well?"

He and Taggart rode on, leading the two mules, which they planned to cut loose a few miles from the *choza,* not wanting that brave young Californio to go galloping back into Monterey anytime soon.

Falconer climbed on his horse and gave Eben a hand up behind him.

"Gaviota's dead," said Eben. "Sixkiller too."

"Tell me later."

Falconer kicked the horse into a gallop.

Chapter 34

When they came through the door, Silas Nall
was sleeping.

He groped instinctively for the pistol he thought
was there at his side. But it wasn't there anymore.
At that moment Silas got the first inkling that he
had been betrayed. But he was too groggy—how
much *aguardiente* had he consumed the night before?—to think clearly.

It was dark in the *choza*. The gray suggestion of
dawn crept through the doorway, against which
the dark shapes of the men who had come for
him were silhouetted. Rough hands grabbed him.
Obviously this was no social call. Silas tried to
fight back. He landed a fist in somebody's face,
heard a muttered curse in Spanish, and felt fleeting satisfaction. Fleeting, because fists hammered
back at him, paying him back in kind and then
some. He fell to hands and knees on the hard-
packed dirt of the floor, the copper taste of blood
bitter on his tongue. A booted foot struck him in
the guts, knocking the wind and all the fight out
of him. A wave of nausea washed over him and
he vomited. He clawed at the leg of one of the
men standing over him. Someone up there
laughed, an ugly and discomfiting sound, and
kicked him again. Silas rolled over on his side and
curled up into a fetal position and lay there with

his arms covering his face, lay there in his puke, shivering uncontrollably.

A candle was lit, and then he saw they were not soldiers, as he had first believed. The two men looming over him were *vaqueros*, and he recognized them. They rode for that son of a bitch Don Carlos Chagres.

Speak of the devil. Chagres appeared in the doorway. He had the prostitute, Maria, with him, holding her by the arm, and he pushed her roughly inside. She faded back into a corner of the room and cowered there, frightened eyes wide and glistening behind a veil of raven-black hair that had fallen down over her face.

"Stand him up," said Chagres.

The *vaqueros* grabbed Silas and hauled him to his feet. He was naked, covered with dirt and vomit. Don Carlos looked him over with disdain and shook his head, his patrician features a mask of derision.

"Why do the people fear these men so?" he asked. It was a rhetorical question. "They are little better than animals." He spoke in English, for Silas's benefit.

"I didn't do anything," said Silas, still wheezing from the kicks. "Swear to God, I'm innocent."

"Really? Then why have you been hiding here, in the house of a prostitute, for four days?"

"Doc Maguire killed that woman. But I had nothing to do with it."

"But you were there, were you not?"

"Wasn't with him. You got to understand. I was ... I was nearby. But I wasn't with him when he killed her."

"So why did you not return to the brigade?"

"The brigade? Are you crazy? Do you know what Falconer did to Maguire? He'd do the exact same thing to me."

"But you were not involved—you said so yourself. Why would you have anything to fear from Falconer?"

"You don't know him. He's one mean son of a bitch, Falconer is."

"How did you know he killed Maguire?"

Silas nodded at the woman. "She told me."

Chagres smiled coldly at the prostitute. "She also betrayed you."

Slow to comprehend, Silas stared at Maria.

"It is true," said Don Carlos. "You see, I offered a generous reward for any information that might lead me to the capture of the Americans who kidnapped my daughter, Sombra."

"Had nothing to do with that, either."

"No? Are you not the brother of Eben Nall?"

"Yes, but . . . you mean Eben . . . ?"

Don Carlos nodded. "I am certain of it."

"I'll be damned," breathed Silas. "I never would have thought he had the backbone to do something like that. Not my little brother."

"Your little brother is as good as dead."

"You got to believe me when I tell you . . ."

Don Carlos held up an imperious hand, cutting short Silas's protest.

"You may still be of use to me. That is why I will pay this woman her thirty pieces of silver."

Chagres threw a handful of coins—gold, not silver—on the floor. Maria fell upon them as a vulture would fall upon carrion.

"You conniving bitch," snarled Silas, as it came clear to him what Maria had done. "If I get out of this alive I'll pay you a little visit."

Having gathered up all the coins, Maria stood, spat in his face, and kicked him, hard, between the legs.

Doubled over, Silas would have fallen but for the two *vaqueros* who had him by both arms. Another wave of nausea—this time he could only dry-heave. The *vaqueros* laughed as Maria loosed a string of venomous invective. Silas straightened up as much as he could, trying to act like the searing pain in his groin was of no consequence to him and like he wasn't really afraid for his life . . .

"Yeah," he gasped, manufacturing a little bravado, "and I'm getting pretty damned tired of you, too."

"Get him out of here," snapped Don Carlos.

"Hey," said Silas, as the two *vaqueros* hustled him out the door. "What about my clothes?"

No one bothered to answer him. Another *vaquero* sat his horse out in the street. This one had his *reata* ready, and tossed a loop over Silas, nice as you please. Before Silas knew what was happening, his arms were pinned to his sides as the loop tightened around his chest.

Don Carlos and the other two *vaqueros* climbed into their saddles. Chagres led the way. The *vaquero* at the easy end of the *reata* spurred his horse into a canter to follow his *patrón*. Silas tried to run, but in short order stumbled and fell. The *vaquero* did not slow his horse. He knew Silas had fallen, but he didn't care, and Silas was dragged. Somehow he managed to keep from crying out in pain as great swaths of skin were scraped off his body by the hardpack. The horseman took a corner, and Silas began to roll. He got his knees planted and lurched to his feet. Obviously the *vaquero* was willing to drag him halfway across California. The pair of *vaqueros* bringing up the rear were laughing at him. It was all such great sport.

Monterey was waking to a new day. The curious procession of Don Carlos, his men, and their prisoner drew a lot of interest. The *vaqueros* readily answered shouted questions regarding the identity of their prisoner. Upon hearing that Silas was one of the mountain men, many of the people hurled taunts and insults at him, and a few found rocks to throw at him.

When they reached the Chagres's house, Silas was a bruised and bloodied mess. Several times he had fallen and been dragged. The *vaquero* with the *reata* tossed his rope over a stout limb of one of the big oaks that shaded the house, and a moment later Silas found himself dangling several feet off the ground, twisting slowly.

They left him hanging there for hours. The rope was so tight around his chest that Silas began to have some trouble breathing. In a panic, he shouted for help. A *vaquero* appeared—the same one who had dragged him through the streets— and laid Silas's back and shoulders open with a rawhide quirt. From then on Silas suffered in silence.

The sun had passed its zenith when they came to take him down. He sank to the ground, too weak to stand. The *vaqueros* took pleasure in kicking him until he got up. One of them threw a shirt and a pair of trousers at him. Silas donned the clothes, wincing in pain. Every bone, muscle, and joint in his tortured body screamed in pain. Scarcely a square inch of his flesh was not cut, bruised, or abraded.

The *vaqueros* escorted him inside. They sat him down in a chair at the end of a long polished table in a dim, cool room. At the other end of the room, Don Carlos stood near a big stone hearth, gazing at the fire inside, a glass of Madeira in one hand, a cigar smoldering in the other. Silas stared longingly at the glass. He would have killed for a drink of water. He hadn't been this dry since the desert crossing months back.

Two *vaqueros* took up positions behind his chair. Minutes crawled by in silence. Don Carlos appeared to be lost in thought, unaware of their presence in the room. Silas tried not to wonder what they had in store for him. Sooner or later they would kill him—of this he had little doubt. He had been in some tight spots before and always managed to lie, cheat, or steal his way out of them. But this time he had no confidence in himself. *Damn you, Eben*, he thought. *This is all your fault.* Eben had made off with this man's daughter, and now this man was going to make him, Silas, pay for it. It wasn't fair.

You may still be of some use to me. Wasn't that what Chagres had said this morning? Maybe there was a chance, after all.

"I'll do anything you want, Don Carlos," he said. "Just tell me what it is, and I'll do it."

One of the *vaqueros* hit him a backhanded blow to the side of the face. Silas didn't see it coming. He collapsed sideways out of the chair and didn't think he had the strength left to get back up again. But when the *vaquero* began to kick him, he found the strength.

"That is enough," said Chagres.

The *vaquero* stepped away from Silas. Gasping, Silas hauled himself up into the chair.

"Do you wish to live, señor?" asked Don Carlos.

"God, yes."

"Even without honor? Some men, they would say life is not worth living without honor. But you are not such a man, are you?"

"No."

"No, I thought not. You will betray your friends for me, just to stay alive. That is what I ask of you."

Silas blinked. "The brigade?"

"Yes. Falconer and every last one of his men will die. I will do what the governor-general and his soldiers have been unable to do. And the people, señor, the people will cheer me. I will be their salvation."

"They'll . . . they'll kill me if I do."

"But I will kill you if you do not."

Silas thought it over. So long as he drew breath he had a chance. There had to be a way out of this. But if he said no they would probably kill him on the spot. So he had to pretend to go along.

"Okay," he said. "I'll do what you want."

"You would betray your own brother?"

"Eben's not with the brigade anymore."

"Oh, but I think you are wrong. I think he helped Falconer escape from the presidio. Now they are all trying to escape. And my daughter is with them. She must be. But, señor, they will not escape me. You will help me find them."

"Sure," said Silas. "Sure I will."

"But first you will come with me."

"Where are we going?"

Don Carlos smiled. "I am going to show you what happens to men who cross me."

Chapter 35

At some point during the ride back to Monterey from the Carmel Mission, Silas Nall decided he was trapped in a living nightmare from which there would be no awakening.

The weather played its part. A bank of angry gray-black clouds had rolled in off the sea late that afternoon, hastening the night. Now the wind was howling like all the lost souls in Dante's Inferno, and jagged bolts of lightning struck the earth, and the crack of thunder was so loud that Silas could feel it reverberate in his spine. It was, Silas decided, as though God was lashing out at the world and all its wickedness.

It had been twenty years since Silas had given God much more than a passing thought. When he was a child, he and his brother had been forced by their mother to attend Sunday services. Church had been a little white building of warped clapboard in Kakaskia, rather poorly constructed, with rows of rough-hewn benches that always managed to put splinters into the backs of your legs. The preacher had been a fearsome character named Goodwin. Goodwin preached fire and brimstone, everlasting hell and damnation, excoriating his congregation of lowly sinners with such passionate furor that his eyes seemed to shoot flames. Silas could vividly remember being terrified by Reverend Goodwin and his sermons, in which the fate of all those souls who by their wicked ways infuriated a stern and unforgiving Almighty was described in harrowingly graphic detail.

Goodwin would have been pleased to know that he caused a young Silas Nall to have bad dreams. When Silas was old enough to have a say in whether he attended church or not, he was very much relieved to avoid the place like the plague. The way the Reverend Goodwin told it, heaven was mighty empty and would remain that way, since precious few were the people who could earn the right to go there, so pervasive was the evil in human nature. Silas had decided it wasn't really worth suffering a lifetime of fear and torment just to please a God that mere mortal man simply could not ever please no matter how hard he tried. According to Goodwin, a man or woman passed through the pearly gates, if he or she got there at all, solely as a consequence of the good Lord's mercy, since every effort made to please God would never be sufficient, and Silas had not once been provided with any convincing evidence that God was endowed with any mercy. So for twenty years he had let God alone, hoping God would return the favor.

Tonight, though, Silas experienced that old terror, familiar from his childhood Sundays squirming on the splintery bench of the Kaskaskia church, or grimacing at the lancing pain in his knee joints as he knelt for interminable prayers on the hard puncheon floor. God was here, in California, this storm-swept night, and he was madder than hell.

Because Don Carlos Chagres had killed a priest.

They had arrived at the Carmel Mission just as the storm struck, unleashing its fury on a cowering earth, darkening the day. Don Carlos, three *vaqueros*, and a reluctant Silas Nall were welcomed into the ancient walls of the mission, and Chagres demanded to see Padre Pico. The meeting took place in a windowless chamber poorly lighted by guttering candles. Silas could tell right away that Don Carlos despised the priest. Hate was stamped on his face, a hate so strong it filled the room and made Silas uneasy. Surely Padre Pico could sense that hate too. But the priest did not appear in the least concerned. He must think, decided Silas, that God will protect him. But a merciless God was not going to shield him from the wrath of Don Carlos Chagres—of that Silas was certain.

"Gaviota is dead," said Don Carlos. Silas thought at first that he was accusing Padre Pico of the deed.

"I will pray for his soul," said the priest serenely.

"He had no soul. Pray for your own. It was you who helped Eben Nall kidnap my daughter outside the church in Monterey, wasn't it?"

"I helped Eben Nall free your daughter," corrected Padre Pico.

"It was you who helped hide them since that time."

Padre Pico nodded. "But what does this have to do with Gaviota?"

"I suspected you from the beginning. So I had Gaviota watch you. You never knew he was nearby, did you? No, you would not. Gaviota was like a ghost. You would not see him if he did not want you to. And then, last night, he followed you somewhere, to the place that Eben Nall was keeping Sombra against her will. He did not report back to me this morning. He would not have failed to do so were he still alive. Somehow Eben Nall killed him."

Standing against a wall, trying to be as inconspicuous as humanly possible, Silas shook his head. What the hell had gotten into his brother, anyway? Making off with this man's daughter. Rescuing Hugh Falconer from the Monterey presidio. And, if Don Carlos was correct in his deductions, getting the better of a killer like Gaviota? That didn't sound at all like the Eben Nall Silas knew. The Eben to whom caution and common sense were second nature. The Eben who, as a child, was too scared to get into fights. Silas had been in a dozen scrapes on Eben's behalf. He had always liked to fight, liked it because he was quick and strong and didn't mind getting hurt. Eben, on the other hand, had always seemed to be frightened by the sight of his own blood, something Silas could never understand. The only thing Silas hadn't liked about fighting was losing, and that had happened very seldom.

I knew no fear back then, thought Silas. *So what has happened to me now? And what has happened to my brother? Eben has done things these past few days I wouldn't have had the guts to try. Must be that woman. The one called Sombra. Women have a knack for making men do stupid things.*

Silas remembered Annie, the Arapaho cutnose over whom he had fought and slain the trader Portugee. If he hadn't been so stupid about Annie he wouldn't have had to join Falconer's brigade just to escape Portugee's vengeful partners, and he wouldn't be here in this godforsaken California, a short hair away from dying.

"I do not know anything about that," said Padre Pico. "But I do know that Eben Nall was not holding your daughter against her will, as you imply, Don Carlos. She went with him of her own free will, to get away from you. She begged him to help her escape. What you have done to your own daughter!" Padre Pico shook his head sorrowfully. "I suppose God can even forgive you for that. But you must get down on your knees and ask His forgiveness."

"On my knees?" Don Carlos laughed harshly. "Me?"

"As I thought. You are too proud, too vain, and too ambitious. You think you are above the law. Not just the laws of men, but the laws of God as well."

Don Carlos grabbed the front of the priest's cassock with both hands. "Where is my daughter?"

"They are gone," said Padre Pico, still serene in voice and demeanor.

"With the other Americans."

"No doubt that is the case. Sombra knows she must leave California if she is to be beyond your grasp."

"I will have my daughter back, priest, and I will do with her as I wish, and neither you nor anyone else—nor God—can prevent me."

Padre Pico was shocked. "You condemn your soul to everlasting damnation with those words, Don Carlos."

"All the Americans will die." Chagres glanced across the room at Silas, who actually cringed against the wall, for by now he had divined that the *haciendero* was truly a madman. "Except for this one, if he does my bidding."

He's lying, thought Silas. *He will kill me too.*

"I must tell you," said Padre Pico, "that before they left this morning, I married your daughter to Eben Nall."

Don Carlos looked like he had been struck by invisible fists. Pale, stricken, he took an unsteady backward step, letting go of the priest as though the cassock scorched his hands.

"Now," continued Padre Pico, with some smug satisfaction showing, "Eben Nall will be within his rights, by both the laws of man and the laws of God, to protect his wife from you, Don Carlos."

With a roar Don Carlos charged the priest, driving him backward against the wall, slamming his head against the stones again and again and again . . .

Silas and the two *vaqueros* watched in horror as scarlet smears of blood appeared on the stones where the back of the priest's head repeatedly struck the wall.

Above the *haciendero*'s maddened, incoherent snarls of blind rage, Silas heard Padre Pico murmur a final prayer.

Then the life went out of him. Don Carlos let go of him and stepped away. The priest fell in a lifeless heap at his feet.

For a moment no one moved. Silas scarcely breathed. Chagres slowly collected himself. He stepped disdainfully over the priest's corpse and approached Silas. It was all Silas could do to stay upright. His knees had turned into jelly.

"So you see," said Don Carlos, with a smile, "what happens to those who dare cross me."

Now, riding back to Monterey with Chagres and the *vaqueros*, through the storm-swept night, Silas Nall watched God's angry sky, expecting at any moment a bolt of lightning that would strike them all dead. A merciless God had seen everything. He was sure of it. Don Carlos Chagres would burn in hell. *And so will I*, thought Silas, with resigned certitude. *I did not kill the priest. I was an innocent bystander, present against my will. But God will have none of my excuses.*

Chapter 36

November 16, 1837. It has been three days since Jenkins and Taggart managed to free Hugh Falconer from the Monterey presidio. This is the first chance I've had to sit down and write in my journal since that time. We have been constantly on the move, and it is all I can do to keep my eyes open at this moment.

I am now a married man. When Falconer and I reached the Carmel Mission, where I had left Sombra in the ever vigilant care of Padre Pico, I had not, of course, given serious thought to marriage. I had told Sombra that I loved her, and she had said she loved me, but I would not have dared ask for her hand. What could I, who owned little more than the clothes on my back and a few horses, with no prospects to speak of, offer the daughter of one of the wealthiest men in California, a girl who was accustomed since birth to the very best of everything? Yes, she had indicated that material things were of no consequence to her, but that was entirely beside the point. A man naturally wants to provide his wife with the security of a home and a prosperous future. I could not put a roof over

Sombra's head, and, as for a future, it did not seem as though I had one. It isn't likely I will even get out of California alive. If I do, I have no clear notion of what I will do next, or even where I will go.

It was Padre Pico who suggested Sombra and I marry. He would do the honors. Having talked at length to Sombra while I was away in Monterey trying to help Falconer, he was certain that her feelings for me ran deep and true. While she slept in another room, he urged me to ask her to be my wife. I balked at the idea. This hardly seemed the time or the place. But he told me that in fact it was the perfect time. As her husband, I would have the right to take her anywhere I wished. I would also have the right to protect her from danger, and to kill, if necessary, to do so.

"That would make little or no difference to Don Carlos," I told him.

"No, but it would mean something to everyone else. Do you not love her, my son?"

"Yes, I do."

"Do you not wish to be with her always?"

"Well, yes . . ."

Beaming, the priest threw up his hands. "There you are, then. What are you waiting for? Go and ask her."

I turned to Falconer, thinking he might save me by agreeing that this was not a good time for getting hitched, or "squawed up," as they say in the mountains. But he just shrugged and told me I might as well take the plunge.

To make a long story short, I woke Sombra and asked her, though I have no idea whence I summoned the courage. I knew I was dreaming when she instantly said yes. Then she began to cry. I was mortified! What had I done? Was she weeping because she could foresee a future filled with poverty and hardship? Had she agreed to marry me only because she had no other options? But she assured me that the tears she cried were tears of happiness.

Right from the start it was manifest she had made a particularly poor choice for a husband, as I could not even produce a ring to place upon her finger as a symbol of my everlasting devotion. Otherwise the ceremony was quick and painless. Hugh Falconer stood as my best man. And when it was all said and done a strange feeling possessed me. I was proud that Sombra had consented to be my wife. I knew a profound fulfillment, as well as an abiding commitment to her happiness, which I knew at that moment would always take precedence over all other considerations. Everything I would do from that moment on—every breath I took until the last—would be with her foremost in my mind.

We did not tarry long at the mission, saying our good-byes to Padre Pico. Though I scarcely knew the man, I missed him terribly as soon as we rode away. I was also concerned for his safety. That he was a priest, I feared, would not shield him from the terrible wrath of Don Carlos Chagres.

I did not know how we would ever rejoin the brigade, but Falconer seemed confident. We rode most of the night, stopping for only an hour prior to sunrise, to rest the horses. Falconer stretched out on the hard ground, reins tied to his wrist, and fell instantly to sleep. I envied him the ability to do that. I put a blanket around Sombra's shivering shoulders and held her close as I sat with my back against a tree and anxiously watched the night slowly expire. Here we were, in the midst of our enemies, hundreds of miles from safety, with danger and, possibly, death waiting at every turn. How could Falconer sleep at a time like this?

At daybreak we were again on the move. I realized then that Falconer had made a beeline for the brigade's old camp just west of Monterey. From there we followed the sign north, past the place where Jenkins and the others had fought the soldiers. The trail took us farther north. By late afternoon we had come upon another abandoned campsite. Here, two horsemen had ridden south by west, in the direction of the town. Jenkins and Taggart, surmised Falconer, heading for Monterey twenty-four hours ago. They had returned late last night, and the brigade had started east. We were maybe six or seven hours behind them. The trail was one a blind man could follow; after all, the turn east was designed to fool pursuers into believing the brigade was going to try to cross the Sierras. They might then dash off to cover the passes, about which they knew more than we, in hopes of cutting us off. By then we would be far to the north.

Certain that we would soon rejoin our companions, and much relieved by the prospect, I turned my thoughts to what I would do if by some miracle we got out of California alive. The fur trade was on its last legs. There would be little profit to be had in harvesting brown gold from now on. A few trappers would keep at it, because they were loath to surrender that way of life. But it would be a struggle for those die-hards to even keep themselves supplied with powder and shot.

I love the mountains and the wild, free life of the trapper, but I knew it would not suit Sombra. Returning to Ohio was another option, though the thought of becoming a store clerk again turned my stomach. Becoming a farmer was an option almost as dismal. By the end of the day I was no closer to an answer than when I had started.

For a second night we kept moving until a few hours before daybreak. I figured we had to be real close to catching the brigade now and was surprised when Falconer called a halt.

"They're not far," he said, when I asked him about it. "A few miles east of us. But it will be safer coming up on them in daylight. They'll be quick on the trigger."

"You'll get no argument from me," I said. "I'm bone-tired. I don't think I could stand that saddle another mile."

Sombra went to sleep as soon as she hit the ground. We built no fire, though the night had turned quite cold. We had no provisions ei-ther—I had left the cabin by the sea in such haste that taking some of the supplies Padre Pico had so thoughtfully provided hadn't even occurred to me. But we dared not fire a shot to bag a deer or wild turkey, not knowing if a detachment of soldiers—or Don Carlos and his *vaqueros*—was just over the next hill.

"You've done yourself right proud," said Falconer, sitting cross-legged at the base of a tree, a rifle that had once been the property of a presidio guard resting across his knees. "She's a brave girl, and strong. Not a complaint out of her."

"She's better than I deserve," I replied. "I've been wondering what I can do to take good care of her. What are you going to do, if we get out of this?"

"If?" Falconer smiled. "O ye of little faith."

"You said yourself we had a damned poor chance. Those were your exact words."

"Were they? Well, I feel better about things the farther I get from the iron cage. In answer to your question, I really don't know."

"Me either. The fur trade is finished, and I don't think I'd make a very good farmer. I just don't see what I can do."

"You're overlooking the obvious."

"I am? What?"

"That mare of yours. She's the damnedest horse I've ever seen. Folks are going to need a lot of good horses out here. West of the Mississippi is not what I'd call walking country."

That was all Falconer said on the subject, but the more I thought about it the better I liked the idea. I fell asleep—Falconer said he would stand watch tonight—feeling pretty good about the future for the first time in a coon's age.

The next day we caught up with the brigade. It would be an understatement to say that the men were happy to see Hugh Falconer. Now they too could feel a lot better about the future. There was something about having Falconer at your side—you began to think anything was possible, no matter how steep the odds. It was the legend behind the man, I suppose. He had done many extraordinary things in his lifetime. I remembered the day I had first seen Falconer, coming down from the high lonesome. Rube Holly had regaled me with all the stories about him as we watched him make his way across the valley toward the camp. Sure, I knew some of it must be pure fancy. But I was convinced that much of what they said about the man was true.

Jenkins reported that they had seen nary a sign of the soldiers, and the men were beginning to think the Californios had exercised some common sense and decided to let the brigade go in peace. Falconer sought to disabuse them of this notion, knowing that overconfidence in our situation could prove fatal. And even if, he said, the soldiers were no longer after them, we could rest assured that Don Carlos Chagres would pursue us to the gates of hell.

It was clear that the men were all curious about Sombra and what she was doing with me. Falconer proceeded to tell them the whole story.

"So that's the long and short of it," said Falconer, in conclusion. "Except for one thing. Eben and Sombra got married a couple days ago."

Eben breathlessly watched the faces of his colleagues, having wondered what their reaction to Falconer's revelations might be.

Rube Holly was the first to step forward. "I'm tinkled pink to make yore acquaintance, Mrs. Nall," he told Sombra. "But I got to say, with all us handsome devils to choose from, how come you went and picked this hyar unpleasant-lookin' feller to get hitched to? Ask me, he's purt near ugly as a mud fence."

The others laughed. Much relieved, Eben joined them.

To spare Sombra, Falconer had omitted a few details from his narrative, telling the men only that Don Carlos Chagres had been mistreating Sombra cruelly. Now Taggart stepped forward to take Rube Holly's place.

"Don't you go worryin' your pretty head, ma'am," said the mountain man earnestly. "If your father wants to get his hands on you again it'll be over our dead bodies."

The others nodded and murmured assent. Eben smiled. He recalled expressing that very sentiment to Sombra not too long ago. Sombra tried to smile too, but her heart wasn't in it. She knew her father very well, and she was afraid of exactly that— more dead bodies.

"One thing," said Falconer grimly. "Before we move on, you boys ought to give some careful thought to this. I broke my own law by helping Eben. I did it knowing full well that I was putting everybody's neck on the chopping block. I don't think Don Carlos will give up trying to get his daughter back, no matter what."

"What are you trying to say, Hugh?" asked Gus Jenkins.

"I'm saying I killed Doc Maguire for doing pretty much the same thing I did."

For one fantastic moment Jenkins thought Falconer was going to order his own execution.

"Let me put it to you boys this way," said Eben.

"If you don't want Sombra and me along, we'll understand and go our own way, with no hard feelings."

"The three of us will go," corrected Falconer.

"Wagh!" exclaimed Rube Holly. "You reckon it would make a hair's difference to that feller Don Carlos if you three was with us or not? Way I see it, he'd try to put us all under ground, anyroad."

"Yeah," growled another. "And just let him try."

"You ain't goin' nowhere without us, Eben," declared Taggart.

All the other mountain men were in complete accord. Eben was so overwhelmed he dared not speak.

"As for you," Jenkins told Falconer, "there's a big difference between what you did and what Doc did, Hugh. He took a life. You did what you had to do to save one." He glanced at Sombra.

"We got a lot better chance of gettin' out of here with you than without you," added Rube Holly.

Falconer was silent a moment, a strange expression on his face. Eben could tell he was deeply moved. *I think he's found what he came all this way to find,* mused Eben, with a sudden, dazzling burst of insight into the man.

Finally Falconer nodded curtly and turned to his horse.

"Then let's ride, boys," he said. "We're burning daylight."

Chapter 37

Eben Nall closed his journal, tucked it away in his possibles bag, and rubbed his aching eyes.

It had surely been a long day. After rejoining the brigade, Falconer had led them west until they came upon a sizable stream. Here he had everyone except Gus Jenkins and the three squaws dismount. While Jenkins and his men took all the horses and continued east, Falconer and the rest waded upstream. He invited Sombra to remain mounted, but she would have none of it. They stayed in the creek all day. It was slow going, and especially difficult for Sombra, who was entirely unaccustomed to this kind of exertion. But she stuck to it without a word of complaint, doing her level best not to slow the others down. As his companions cast approving looks in her direction, Eben felt a sense of pride in her.

Falconer hoped that, if they were being chased, their pursuers would follow the horses east. It would take a tracker with sharp eyes and a lot to experience to tell that most of the horses were not carrying riders. Gus and the three squaws would split up an hour before dark, each with several riderless ponies in tow, and go off in all directions, to meet up at a prearranged point about sundown, then ride north to find the rest of the brigade as far as they had managed to walk upstream. Falconer hoped by this subterfuge to confuse their pursuers and, at the very least, slow them down.

Jenkins and the squaws rejoined the brigade several hours after nightfall. Falconer had everyone mount up and, keeping their horses in the creek, ride another few miles before stopping for the night. No fires were permitted, and no shooting game. A few fish had been harvested from the creek. These, and what little remained of the company's jerked venison, were the only food available. The Nez Perce warrior, Bluefeather, was fashioning a bow and a few arrows. They would be finished, he said, tomorrow.

Eben's thought turned to his brother, Silas. Falconer had informed him that Silas had gone missing along with Doc Maguire. Apparently he had not been involved in the murder of the prostitute. But what had become of him was anybody's guess. Eben figured Silas was probably laying low in Monterey, aware that in California it had suddenly become open season on all American buckskinners.

It bothered Eben some to leave Silas behind like this. But there was nothing he could do about it. His foremost responsibility now was to Sombra. He had to take her to safety, beyond the reach of her father. Were it not for her, he would have felt obliged to return to Monterey and try to find Silas. His guilt was mitigated somewhat by the sure and certain knowledge that, were their situations reversed, Silas would have no qualms about leaving him to his own devices.

Brotherly love had nothing to do with it. During the journey to California, Eben had learned to dislike Silas with a passion. His brother was a selfish, conniving, untrustworthy person, loyal only to himself. Still, he was Eben's brother, and that fact, unfortunate though it had proved to be, was enough to nibble at the edges of his conscience.

The camp was asleep. Apart from the guards Falconer had posted, the rest of the brigade were asleep in their blankets. Everyone was plumb worn out. A dozen different snores made a rumbling chorus to compete with the crickets in the marsh grass down along the banks of the creek. Eben stretched out alongside Sombra and fell immediately to sleep.

He woke before dawn, vaguely troubled, momentarily disoriented, and realized he had been dreaming. Don Carlos had been there in his dream, standing on a windswept skyline with a bloody red sun ablaze behind him and a struggling Sombra in his grasp. The *haciendero* was laughing, and the laughter seemed to linger, a faint echo, in Eben's head, even though he was awake. Remo was there too, his features inscrutable as he put a pistol to the head of a man kneeling on the ground. Eben had been able to see only the back of the victim's head in his dream. But he knew the identity of the man about to die . . .

Sombra was gone.

In his panic Eben leaped to his feet. His first instinct was to rouse the sleeping camp with a shout of alarm. But perhaps she had merely gone down to the creek for a drink. He looked for her there, but found Taggart instead.

"She's upstream a ways, by those trees yonder," said Taggart, rifle cradled in his arms, answering Eben's question before Eben could even speak. "Said she wanted to freshen up, so I wandered on over here to give her a little privacy. Don't worry, hoss. She promised not to go far."

"Thanks." Eben ran to the clump of trees, where the creek bent. He found the dress she had been wearing since the mass almost a week ago. Now it was draped over a low-lying limb. It was pretty tattered, after all they had been through. When he got the chance he would kill a deer and have Luck make her a buckskin dress. He figured she would look pretty good in buckskin.

As he turned he saw her emerging from the creek. He looked quickly away, embarrassed.

"Sorry," he mumbled. "Didn't mean to intrude."

"Don't you want me?" She stood before him, her willowy body glistening in the starlight.

"Yes." He tried not to choke on the lump in his throat.

"We *are* married."

"Yes, but, well, this doesn't strike me as the time or the place."

She curled her arms around his neck and pressed her body against his. "Make love to me, Eben. Here. Now. Please. Who knows what might happen to us tomorrow?"

Eben glanced nervously around. What if Taggart or one of the other guards, prowling the perimeter of the camp, saw them like this? He thought about Rube Holly and Luck, fooling around under their blankets, blissfully undeterred by the fact that Eben had never been more than a stone's throw away. Eben had a young man's strong desires, but of that sort of thing he was not capable.

"I-I just thought ..." He stumbled over the words. "After what your father's done to you and all ..."

"Help me forget," she said, and kissed him, a lingering kiss. Eben's deeply ingrained caution was swept away by a rising ride of passion. She pulled him down to the ground, on top of her. Her fingers worked feverishly at the fastenings of his buckskins. Eben forgot about everything else—

the guards, Don Carlos, Remo, Silas, California, everything. A moment later they lay flesh to burning flesh, heart to racing heart, and she locked her arms and legs tightly around him, holding him a willing captive inside her, and her soft cries were sweet music to his ears.

Later, their passion spent, they lay beneath the trees, curled up together, lying on their sides, back to front. Eben's strong arms were wrapped around her, and his face nestled in her still-wet hair. He felt a contentment more complete than he had ever experienced.

"I love you more than I can say, Eben," she whispered dreamily. "We must never be parted. I think I would die."

Eben felt desire stirring in his loins again, and she laughed with gentle delight, but then they heard Rube Holly, just beyond the trees, calling Eben's name, and reality came crashing down upon them. Dawn traced the eastern horizon with pale yellow highlights. The brigade was breaking camp.

They dressed in a hurry and made their way through the trees, meeting Rube Holly on the other side. The concern on the old trapper's grizzled features drained away, replaced by relief, then by amusement, as he recognized the look on Sombra's radiant face.

"Now just what have you two younkers been up to back in them there bushes?" he asked, smiling.

Wearing a foolish grin that said it all, Eben just shook his head and walked on by, hand in hand with Sombra.

The beating Silas Nall had suffered at the hands of Don Carlos Chagres's *vaqueros* had been designed to mold him through physical intimidation into a more malleable traitor to his own kind. It had also done Don Carlos some good to watch an American suffer so, even if it wasn't Eben Nall. The *vaqueros* had enjoyed taking their frustrations out on the Yankee because their *patrón* had been giving them hell every day since Sombra's disappearance.

But the exercise had failed to work its painful magic on Silas—it just served to make him more determined to doublecross Don Carlos. Somehow, some way. Because Silas Nall was not without his ego, and ego's handmaiden, pride. He had been thinking along the lines of turning the tables on Chagres—until he had witnessed the murder of Padre Pico.

That had scared him. As Don Carlos methodically turned the priest's skull into a bloody pulp, the resolve drained out of Silas, leaving him an empty, trembling shell of a man. Never in his life had he seen anything so coldblooded, so brutal, so . . . so inhuman. From that moment he was terrified of Don Carlos and willing to do anything Chagres asked of him, if it meant escaping, even if only temporarily, the fate of the priest.

Silas became only gradually aware of the effect the murder of Padre Pico had on the men who rode for Chagres. The *vaqueros* who had, like Silas, been stunned witnesses to the deed, spread the word among their *companeros*. They were fiercely loyal to their *patrón*, but to the man they were also good Catholics, if not always devout ones. They had done bad things at the bidding of Don Carlos; they had burned, looted, brutalized, and terrorized. Some of them had even raped and killed in the name of their *patrón*, and with his blessing. But they agreed among themselves that they had never done anything so evil as to kill a priest. That was something Gaviota might have done, without compunction, but none of them had liked Gaviota anyway, as most men naturally hate what they most fear. Gaviota had been without a soul. The *vaqueros* believed that they had souls, and every one among them would have balked at killing a priest, even if the *patrón* had demanded it, for fear of what would happen to their everlasting souls should they commit such an unspeakable act. To their way of thinking a man could kill anyone but a priest and be absolved of the crime in God's eyes.

And so, on the following day, when six *vaqueros* rode out of Monterey behind Don Carlos, accompanied by Silas Nall, they found their loyalty to Chagres challenged for the first time in their lives. If Don Carlos sensed that something was wrong he did not reveal it.

In fact, Don Carlos was so consumed by his obsession for Sombra, and his rage at all Americans—Eben Nall in particular—that he failed to notice how unusually grim and subdued his men were on this day. He had no regrets for killing Padre Pico. He had long despised priests and everything they stood for. Had ever since his childhood. Priests, he was firmly convinced, were the most vile and hateful of creatures. They were rapacious, unprincipled predators who victimized the people and cowed their victims with the most powerful weapon at man's disposal—religion. They cloaked their greed and their lust behind a facade of righteousness.

Padre Pico had been a thorn in his side for many years, an outspoken opponent to his scheme to deal California's missions a death blow. Killing a priest, particularly Pico, didn't bother Don Carlos in the least. The nerve of that bastard to rebuke him for what he had done to his own daughter, which was nobody's business in the first place!

No doubt, mused Don Carlos bitterly, Pico had done as much and even worse in his time. Certainly the priest Chagres had known as a child—and who had known Chagres in unnatural ways—had done much, much worse.

Just thinking about Sombra in the arms of that American, Eben Nall, made the *haciendero*'s blood boil. *If Padre Pico had thought for one minute that by marrying Sombra to that Yankee son of a bitch he had somehow thwarted me, he was sadly mistaken,* Don Carlos thought. It would make no difference. Sombra would soon be a widow. She belonged to him, Don Carlos Chagres, and would never belong to anyone else. The image of Sombra's pale, willowy body haunted Don Carlos, made him ache with desire, as it had done for years, even before his wife's demise. In a world where priests raped and robbed their own followers, what could be wrong with a man's passion for his own daughter?

They rode west out of Monterey, to the site of the brigade's old camp, where Don Carlos had been once before, the day after Sombra's disappearance, in the company of Lieutenant Ramirez. The brigade's trail pointed north, but, to the surprise of Silas Nall, Don Carlos continued in an easterly direction, riding hard all day. By sundown men and horses were bottomed out. The next day was no different.

At the end of the second day they met Remo and thirty heavily armed *vaqueros*. Now Silas understood. He had wondered what had happened to Remo. Obviously Don Carlos had dispatched the man some days ago to Hacienda Gavilan, and now he was on his way back with every able-bodied man he had been able to get his hands on. They were a tough-looking bunch, too, thought Silas. All hell was going to break loose when they finally tangled with Falconer's brigade.

Now Don Carlos turned north. The next day they cut the trail of the brigade. Chagres and Remo parlayed for a while. Then the *haciendero* had Silas brought before him.

"How old is this trail?" asked Don Carlos.

"Couple days."

Chagres nodded. "That agrees with what Remo has told me. I am glad you did not lie."

Silas could not meet the man's eyes. The fear that had haunted his every waking moment since the murder of Padre Pico reached up and grabbed him by the throat. He hadn't even thought about lying. But, as he realized what Don Carlos might have done to him if he had, he almost lost control of his bladder.

"You know these men," said Don Carlos. He meant the trappers of the brigade. "You ride with them. You know their tricks. Lead me to them."

"Listen," said Silas, terrified at the prospect of failure. "Hugh Falconer is a legend among the mountain man. He's lived with the Shoshones, for God's sake. He knows more about this kind of thing than I ever will. Hell, I only spent one season in the high country before I came out. You can't expect me to . . ."

"Shut up," said Don Carlos, steely-eyed.

Silas shut up.

"No excuses. Remo will be watching you. Do not try to fool him to save your friends. And do not lose the trail."

Silas glanced at Remo. What was the *haciendero*'s game, anyway? Remo could probably read sign as well, or better, than he. *So why am I here?* It had to be that Don Carlos had something else in mind for him when they caught up with the brigade. But what?

Whatever it was, Silas was sure he wasn't going to like it.

Chapter 38

The next day, about noon, Hugh Falconer called a halt in a stand of trees. The brigade had been pushing hard all morning, heading due north. So far they had seen no sign of pursuit. Not a single Californio had crossed their path. This part of the country appeared untouched by the human hand. But Eben Nall recalled having thought the same thing some weeks ago—just before being waylaid by three cutthroats, rescued by Remo and his companions, and hauled off to the hacienda of Don Carlos Chagres.

That wounded deer I chased all over God's creation sure changed my life, mused Eben, with a fond glance at Sombra.

The terrain itself was not much changed from that found in the vicinity of Don Carlos's feudal empire. Rolling hills, dotted with clumps of trees, golden valleys of wild oats and lush grass, plenty of creeks but no major rivers to cross. Game was plentiful, too, which was sheer torture for men who were short on provisions and under strict orders not to discharge their weapons. Falconer could tell his men were suffering, even though they suffered in stoic silence, as befit mountain men. He dispatched Blue Feather, the Nez Perce warrior, whose bow and arrows were finished, to bag some game. Though he had seen no evidence of it, Falconer was convinced they were being tracked. His instincts, honed by years of surviving by his wits in the mountains, told him so, and he had learned to listen to instinct.

Rufus Fuller, the man who had sustained a bad fall during the crossing of the Sierras, suffering multiple fractures, was slowing them down. Though the travois upon which he had spent a fortnight had been done away with, Fuller was unable to endure the long hours in the saddle required of him. During the noonday stop, Fuller called Falconer over.

"You boys are going to have to get along without me, somehow," said Fuller, trying to make a joke of it. "Don't rightly know how you'll manage it, but those are the facts."

"You sure, Rufus?"

"Just can't keep up the pace, Hugh. I'm sorry."

Falconer was not one to deny the obvious. Fuller was man enough to face the truth. Could he do any less?

"Might be the best thing for you," he said.

Fuller nodded. "I know. I'll just slip off up the next crik we come to. Won't leave no sign. Anybody's after us, they'll keep on after you boys. Then all I got to do is find a good place to lay low for the winter. Come green-up I should be healed enough to make it across the mountains."

Falconer held out a hand. "Reckon I'll be seeing you then."

"It was fun while it lasted," said Fuller, as he shook Falconer's hand.

"Best of luck to you."

The rest of the brigade filed past Fuller to say their so longs. Every man present donated something, some dried venison, powder and shot, a bit of tobacco, a blanket.

As they tightened up their saddle cinches in preparation to ride on, Gus Jenkins watched Falconer without seeming to. He could tell that leaving Rufus Fuller was weighing heavily on Falconer.

"No booshway likes to quit on one of his men," said Jenkins, speaking from experience. "But in this case we're all better off. Especially Rufus. Hell, he may be the only one of us to get shed of California. If he plays his cards right and keeps his head down till spring, I'd say his chances are pretty good."

Falconer nodded. "It's the logical thing to do. I realize that. But it still cuts against the grain with me."

"You let Bearclaw Johnson go without a fuss."

"That was different. There was no stopping Bearclaw. We never really counted on him going the whole way with the brigade anyway, did we? He's been known to strike out on his own whenever it suits his fancy."

"That's true. Most of the men figured a grizzly finally got the better of him. But my hunch is he'll show up again. Some men are just too all-fired mean to die. Bearclaw is one of those men."

"But Rufus Fuller, that bothers me," confessed Falconer, scowling. "Reminds me of something that happened a long time ago."

Jenkins studied Falconer's grim countenance. "Happened to you, did it?"

Again Falconer nodded. "It was my first season in the high country. I fell in with a bunch of free trappers. Wolf Montooth was booshway."

"Montooth!" Jenkins exclaimed. "Talk about all-fired mean."

"Yeah. But I didn't know any better, until it was too late. We went up into Blackfoot country, to trap along the Judith. Naturally, we ran afoul of the Blackfeet. But Montooth had said it was worth it, that we'd find prime beaver country, and we did. The Blackfeet came down on us like the wrath of God. Had a big scrape. We managed to drive them off, but we knew they'd be back. A man named Dutch Hamblin was bad hurt. No way he was going to live, but he was strong and stubborn and slow to die. There were only five of us left then, not counting Dutch. Rest were thrown cold. Montooth and the other three decided to leave Dutch. They wanted to pack up what plews they could carry and get the hell south of the Musselshell before the Blackfeet came back."

"And you weren't having any of it," surmised Jenkins.

"No. I stayed with Dutch. I wouldn't say he was a friend of mine. Wasn't like that at all. But we were a brigade, and I figured a brigade ought to stick together, no matter what. You know what the Blackfoot would have done to Dutch had they found him still alive."

"Yeah." Jenkins knew how adept the Blackfeet were at making death a real bad experience.

"Montooth figured I was good as dead," continued Falconer bleakly. "So he stole my plews and rode off with the others."

"Son of a bitch. Did the Blackfeet come back?"

"Sure they did. But Dutch died the night before. The Blackfeet showed up at dawn the following day. I got shed of them by the skin of my teeth."

Jenkins knew that if Dutch had still been alive that morning, Hugh Falconer would have gone down fighting at his side. Falconer was just made that way.

"Well," he said, "I can see now why you feel the way you do about leaving Rufus. But it ain't the same thing at all, Hugh, you can see that, can't you?"

"I reckon."

Jenkins swung aboard his horse. "Whatever

happened to ol' Wolf Montooth, anyway? He just kind of disappeared about ten years ago."

"No," said Falconer grimly. "Not exactly. I killed him."

"That's when you went off on your own."

"I wasn't going to rely on anybody else but myself, ever again. Lived by that rule for fifteen years." Climbing into the saddle strapped to the back of his shaggy mountain mustang, Falconer scanned the rest of the company as they wearily made ready to move on.

"But here you are," said Jenkins. "With a whole brigade relying on you."

"What's left of a brigade," corrected Falconer. He had lost three men to the Digger Indians, six to the soldiers. Add Doc Maguire, Silas Nall, Bearclaw Johnson, Sixkiller, and now Rufus Fuller, and of the twenty-nine men who had followed him away from the Green River rendezvous last summer, there were only fifteen still with him, along with a trio of squaws.

"Nobody thought we'd all come back alive," said Jenkins. "We didn't ask for no guarantee or anything."

"Was it worth it, Gus?"

"Oh, hell, yes, Hugh. I've had a grand old time." Jenkins grinned. "I wouldn't have missed it for anything. Now I've got something worthwhile to tell my kids, something that beats all I've ever seen or done."

"You haven't got any kids, Gus."

"I'm going to work on that as soon as I get back."

Falconer smiled. "Come on. Let's ride. We don't want to keep the little lady—whoever she is—waiting."

Remo was the first to notice that the horses they were tracking traveled with empty saddles. They

were a couple of miles from the creek when the
vaquero suddenly called a halt. He jumped down
off his horse and knelt to give the tracks a closer
inspection. Then he gave Don Carlos his assessment, and Chagres looked at Silas, and Silas knew
immediately that something was very wrong.

"It is a trick," said Don Carlos, in English for
Silas's benefit. "Most of the horses we are following carry no riders."

Silas felt a chill travel down his spine to his
scrotum. He was on the verge of death at that
moment; the Grim Reaper was breathing down
his neck.

"You did not know, did you?" asked Don
Carlos.

"No. I swear on my mother's grave, I didn't."

Don Carlos grunted, pretending skepticism. He
could tell the American was telling him the truth.
Silas was too afraid not to. But Chagres wanted
to keep him guessing. That way the American
would be inclined to continue telling him the
truth.

The *haciendero* turned back to Remo. "How
long ago?"

"Yesterday."

Don Carlos nodded. The mountain men—and
Sombra—were only a day or so ahead of them
now. Thanks to Remo's sharp eyes they would not
increase their lead by this subterfuge.

"They must have stayed in the creek," said
Remo.

"Upstream?"

"Yes, *patrón.* They are running to the north, up
through the big valley. It is their only hope." The
vaquero turned and scanned the distant blue line
of snowcapped peaks to the east. "I know of no
way across the Sierras this late in the year."

"Neither do I." In a way, mused Don Carlos, it

was a shame. Had the mountain men really gone east they would soon be trapped in the western foothills unable to cross the Sierras because of the winter snow. The valley of the Sacramento would give them a clear and relatively easy passage to the Oregon Territory. In a fortnight they could be out of California.

Not that boundaries would protect them. Don Carlos did not care how long it took, or where the trail led him. He would chase Hugh Falconer and his men to the ends of the earth, to the end of time, if need be.

He didn't think it would take that long though. *In a few days, at most, I will run them into the ground,* he thought. *I have almost forty men, against half that number. The Americans are doomed. They will all perish. I will take their heads to display in the streets of Monterey, and the people will know that I, Don Carlos Chagres, have protected them from the Yankee barbarians. Something the current governor-general proved unable to do.*

Don Carlos smiled. The arrival of Falconer and his brigade would work in his favor, demonstrating to the people that they would soon confront a grave risk. The arrogant, avaricious Americans were coming. They would covet California. Who wouldn't? The people needed a strong leader, a man made of sterner stuff than Don Luis, to keep the Americans at bay. *A man like me.* Certainly not Don Luis, who had greeted the mountain men with open arms. The fact that he, Don Carlos, had introduced Falconer to the governor-general was of little consequence. Don Luis had welcomed the Americans to Monterey, and look at the result. Worse, Hugh Falconer had committed murder while in the governor-general's custody—in the governor-general's very presence, in fact! Don Carlos could see himself occupying that house of yellow sandstone on Monterey's great plaza. It would happen soon.

"Good work, Remo," he said. "I can always rely on you, can't I?"

He reined his horse around sharply and headed back for the creek, followed by Silas Nall and the *vaqueros*.

Remo took his time remounting, letting the others go on ahead. His features were inscrutable, as always. But his thoughts were racing.

Don Carlos had made a huge mistake in killing the priest.

For one thing, it had altered irrevocably the *patrón*'s relationship with his *vaqueros*. Many of them were having second thoughts now about how far they would follow Don Carlos.

Don Carlos was consumed by arrogance, so he could not see the truth lurking in the eyes of his men. He wasn't even looking. He just assumed they were still loyal to the death. And he could not see that all of California would turn against him now. Especially the *campesinos*, the poor laborers. Almost to a man they took their religion very seriously. And why not? It offered them a far better life in heaven than they were enduring here on earth. You just did not kill one of their priests. Remo was aware of his *patrón*'s political aspirations. They were finished now. Don Carlos would never be governor-general. The people would not stand for a priest-killer holding the highest office in the land.

And Don Luis would use the death of Padre Pico to eliminate his chief rival—of that Remo was certain. Don Carlos would answer for his crime, and all his money and influence would not save him from a death sentence. He had lost everything in a moment of rage, and, best of all, he was too blind to see it.

So the hacienda was there for the taking. *At last,* thought Remo. All that must be done was to get Sombra back from the Americans. Sombra, of course, was the key. *I will have her,* thought Remo. *She will have no say in the matter. And, once she is mine, Hacienda Gavilan will be mine, as well.*

That his *patrón* was doomed did not bother Remo, not in the least. When the time came he would not lift a hand to help Don Carlos. *I can always rely on you, can't I?* Remo almost smiled. Almost, but not quite. Don Carlos was such a fool, really. He misunderstood Remo's loyalty. Remo was loyal to himself only. Not like most of the other *vaqueros*, who thought of Don Carlos as a kind of god—or had until the death of the priest. For fifteen years Remo's best interests had been served by doing everything Don Carlos had asked of him, without question. All the while, Remo had planned one day to ask Don Carlos for Sombra's hand in marriage. He had become like a son to the *haciendero*, the son Don Carlos had never had, and Remo had been fairly certain that when the time came for him to ask, Don Carlos would approve the match.

But then Remo had discovered his *patrón*'s dirty little secret—that he was visiting Sombra's bed. Consuela had told him, careless in her desperation, hoping Remo might do something to save her beloved Sombra from this horror of horrors. Consuela, too, had misjudged him. At that moment Don Carlos had become Remo's rival, and Remo had despised him for taking a liberty he himself had long wished to take. Worse, Remo had realized that Don Carlos would never let Sombra marry. She belonged to him, and he would not part with her while he lived. But Remo had been too clever to take issue with Don Carlos, knowing that it was a confrontation he was bound to lose. And he had never let on that he knew the secret.

Now, finally, after all these years of waiting and scheming, the moment was almost upon him, and Remo could foresee that all his dreams were going to come to fruition. All his desires would at long last be satisfied. Thanks to the Americans. They had been the catalyst, after all.

Remo spurred his horse into a gallop. He had trained himself never to show emotion, never to let anyone know what he was thinking unless it was to his benefit to do so. The other *vaqueros* were looking to him for guidance, because the killing of the priest had brought them to the very brink of turning against their *patrón*. But they would not go over the edge without him. He had not given them a clear signal, yet—and would not until the time was right.

If anyone had looked closely at Remo at that moment, they would have seen him gloating, in spite of his best efforts to appear impassive.

Chapter 39

Five days after Falconer rejoined the brigade, and almost two hundred miles north-northwest of Monterey, they saw soldiers for the first time.

The soldiers were not coming up behind them from the south, as they had expected, but appeared to the north, athwart their escape route, a detail riding from west to east, across the breadth of the Sacramento valley. There were only seven men in the detail. When they spotted the mountain men they turned their ponies west and hightailed it.

Falconer was clear about what had happened. Don Luis, the governor-general, was no fool. He had alerted units garrisoned in the north by hard-riding couriers, and the soldiers were patrolling the valley in hopes of spotting the fleeing Americans. They had concluded that the only really viable escape route for the brigade was to the north— the same direction Jedediah Smith had taken in his flight from the authorities some years ago.

"When they show up again," said Taggart, "they'll have a lot more of their friends with them. Maybe we ought to go after 'em, Hugh. Run 'em down and kill 'em, before they can spread the word."

Falconer shook his head. He had already considered and discarded that option. "We'd have to run our horses into the ground to catch up with them. And if that patrol doesn't report back when and where they're supposed to, they'd know it was us."

"So what do we do?" asked Gus Jenkins.

"Keep moving."

The next morning, though, a larger detachment appeared. Falconer had chosen the site for the brigade's night camp with all due care and consideration for the lay of the land—a bosquet of trees on a hill, with open ground for hundreds of yards in every direction, and a creek running along the base of the eastern slope. A strong defensive position.

"Must be fifty, sixty of them," remarked Jenkins, standing alongside Falconer as the latter surveyed the approaching column. "Guess this means our horses get a rest today," he added, in a paltry attempt at lightheartedness.

Falconer was grimly silent. They had good cover, and water available, and still plenty of powder and shot. But how long could they hold off the soldiers? And even if they managed to keep this detachment at bay, how many more were just over the horizon?

Clearly, this was the end of the road.

The column halted two hundred yards from the trees, guidons flapping in the warm breeze, snapping like gunshots. An officer rode forward alone, checking his horse half the distance to the wooded hill.

"Looks like he wants to palaver," said Jenkins. He experienced a strong sense of déjà vu. This was exactly how it had happened before, with Lieutenant Ramirez, and he figured it would play out no differently this time around. That officer yonder would request their surrender. What would be Hugh Falconer's response? Jenkins was pretty certain of that. Falconer was not going back to that iron cage in the Monterey presidio. Hell would freeze over before that happened. So the soldiers would attack, and many would die. Jenkins began to take a long, slow look at the countryside, thinking that this was as good a place as any to die.

The officer sat his horse, ramrod straight, patient as Job.

"Reckon I'd better go hear him out," sighed Falconer. "Have the men spread out and take cover, Gus. Watch all sides."

Astride his mountain mustang, Falconer rode out to the officer. The Californio wore a dragoon's helmet with a scarlet horsehair plume and a brass chain-link chin strap.

"Señor Falconer?"

"That's right."

"I am Captain Cuellar, at your service."

"Cut to the quick, Captain. We don't aim to go back with you."

"Is Sombra Chagres with you?"

"She is with her husband, Eben Nall."

Cuellar's lean brown face registered surprise. "I was not aware . . ."

"You speak English damned well, Captain."

"The governor-general sent me here for that reason."

Falconer figured that wasn't the only reason. Cuellar looked like a fighter. "You're from Monterey, then."

Cuellar nodded. "I knew Lieutenant Ramirez."

"He was a good man. A shame he had to die."

"I have seen many good men die, señor. It is a soldier's duty to die for his country, if called upon to do so. Ramirez and I talked the night before he led his troops into battle against your men. You should know that his heart wasn't in it. He admired you and your men. Did you know that?"

"The feeling was mutual."

"But you say Sombra Chagres is married to one of your men?"

"Ask Padre Pico, at the Carmel Mission. He performed the ceremony."

"Padre Pico is dead."

Now it was Falconer's turn to be surprised. "When did that happen?"

"Five days ago. Don Carlos Chagres killed him. That is what the other priests at the mission have said."

Falconer shook his head. "Another good man dead. How many more, Captain? How did it come to this? We didn't ride all this way to start a war."

"Why *did* you come to California, señor?"

"Hard to explain. Because we wanted to see what was on the other side of those mountains. That was part of it, anyway. And because the kind of life we know is just about done for. Pretty soon there won't be a place for our kind anymore."

Cuellar peeled the gauntlet off one hand, reached under his tunic, and brandished a rolled sheet of heavy vellum secured with a seal of scarlet wax. This he offered to Falconer.

"What is this?" asked the mountain man.

"Safe passage for you and all your men. It bears the signature and seal of the governor-general himself."

Astonished, Falconer took the document. "I don't understand . . ."

"The charges against you have been dropped."

"But why?"

Cuellar shrugged. "I am only a soldier, señor."

"But you have a pretty good idea."

The dragoon officer suppressed a smile. "If I had to guess, I would say you have Don Carlos Chagres to thank."

"I see."

"The murder of the priest puts everything in a new light. Your man, the one who killed the prostitute, paid for his crime. Now Don Carlos must pay for his. Before, the people sympathized with Don Carlos and feared you and your men. They believed him when he said his daughter had been kidnapped. I know I did. But now I wonder, what kind of man is he, that he could kill the priest? Perhaps Sombra Chagres ran away from him and for good reason. Now the people fear Don Carlos more than they fear you. The governor-general, of course, is aware of this..." Cuellar shrugged.

Falconer nodded. It all made perfect sense.

"As for the death of our brave soldiers, and of your men, that is regrettable," continued the dragoon captain. "Don Luis concedes that it was all a big mistake, as you would say. He is convinced that your motives for coming to California were good. While it is true that one of your men killed that woman, Don Luis believes it would be unjust to punish all of you for one man's misdeeds."

So everything, thought Falconer—Doc Maguire's murder of the prostitute, Eben Nall's helping Sombra escape her father, the death of Padre Pico—all of it was overshadowed by the power struggle taking place between the governor-general and Don Carlos Chagres. Don Luis had ordered Lieutenant Ramirez to capture the brigade because, at the time, his rival had held all the cards. Don Carlos would have used the governor-general's unwillingness to deal with the mountain man "threat" to his own advantage. Knowing this, Don Luis had been pressured into making an ill-advised decision, one Falconer had begged him not to make, one that had cost the lives of many men—Lieutenant Ramirez among them.

By killing Padre Pico, Don Carlos had given all

the cards to Don Luis. The governor-general now held the winning hand and could afford to let the brigade go in peace. Falconer felt like laughing out loud, so great was his relief.

"You are not—how do you way?—out of the woods just yet, Señor Falconer," warned Captain Cuellar.

"You're right. Don Carlos and his *vaqueros*."

"My orders are to arrest Don Carlos and return him to Monterey for trial."

"You can expect a stiff fight from the men who ride with him."

"Perhaps." Cuellar glanced over his shoulder at the column of dragoons a hundred yards behind him. "But these are the finest troops in California."

"I reckon you'll find Chagres back there somewhere," said Falconer, inclining his head to the south.

"Hot on your trail, I suspect." Cuellar saluted him. "*Buenos dias, señor. Vaya con Dios.*"

"Good luck, Captain."

Cuellar rejoined his dragoons. Falconer rode back to the trees.

"We're free to go on our way," he told Jenkins.

Jenkins was sure he hadn't heard right. But then he saw the dragoons on the move, swinging wide around the tree-cloaked hill and heading south. He watched them go with slack-jawed amazement. While Falconer had been parlaying with the officer, he'd been thinking about all the things he'd never gotten around to doing in his life and now, since he was about to die, never would do. He felt like a man condemned to the gallows who had just received a last-minute reprieve.

Falconer relayed the good news to Eben Nall. Eben was settled in behind a log with Rube Holly, rifle ready, powder horn and shot pouch laid out.

Eben ran to find Sombra who, with Luck and the other two squaws, was holding the horses in the middle of the bosquet.

"We're free, Sombra!" exclaimed Eben. "We're going to live through this. Those dragoons are out here to find your father. He's going to be arrested for the murder of Padre Pico."

Sombra was aghast. "Padre Pico! Dead?" The priest was part of her earliest childhood memories.

Eben nodded, his elation tempered with sorrow. "Our good friend is dead. But don't you see, Sombra? You don't have to leave California now, if you don't want to."

"I-I do not know. My father is very powerful..."

"He killed a priest. All his money and influence will avail him nothing."

"But what do you want to do, Eben?"

"Whatever you want, my darling. I will be at your side loving you until the day I die."

Sombra melted into his arms. "Can it be true? Are we really free?"

Eben nodded. It was as though he had finally awakened from a long nightmare.

Chapter 40

When he saw the dragoons coming, Remo could scarcely keep a smile from his face. He watched Don Carlos closely. The *haciendero* appeared blissfully unconcerned. *He is a fool*, decided Remo. *The moment I have been waiting for all these years is finally at hand*.

Captain Cuellar gave Don Carlos a brisk salute and spared the forty Gavilan *vaqueros* a wary glance. It was a well-known fact that the men who rode for Chagres were exceedingly loyal to their *patrón*. They recognized only his word as law, and Cuellar was wondering how they would react to what he was about to do.

Not that it mattered what they did. He had his orders, and he would carry them out.

"Have you seen the Americans, Captain?" asked Don Carlos, peremptorily.

"I have. This morning."

It was mid-afternoon. Don Carlos felt the blood quicken in his veins. They were closing on their prey. But wait. There was something amiss. These dragoons had not been in a fight—Don Carlos could tell as much with a glance.

"And you let them go in peace?"

"I did," replied Cuellar. "After giving them a letter of safe passage bearing the seal of the governor-general."

Don Carlos blanched. "The fool!" he cried. "He doesn't know what he has done!"

"The governor-general knows exactly what he is doing, señor," said Cuellar curtly.

The *haciendero*'s eyes narrowed. "Be careful of your tone, Captain."

Cuellar nodded at Silas Nall. "Who is this man?"

"His brother kidnapped my daughter, Sombra."

"The safe passage applies to him as well."

"I intend to use him, to exchange him for Sombra."

"You will release him immediately."

"I will do no such thing. How dare you dictate to me."

"Don Carlos Chagres, you are under arrest. I have written orders to that effect, if you would care to see them."

Remo couldn't resist any longer. He smiled.

Don Carlos, rendered momentarily speechless, stared at the dragoon captain.

"The charge against you is murder," continued Cuellar. "The murder of Padre Pico."

Don Carlos laughed harshly. "Get out of my way," he snarled, and raked his horse with his silver spurs.

Cuellar grabbed the concho-studded cheekstrap of the bridle on the *haciendero*'s horse. Don Carlos responded to this outrage by lashing out with his quirt of braided rawhide. The dragoon was ready for it; he clutched the quirt and pulled. The quirt was looped around the *haciendero*'s wrist by a rawhide thong, and Cuellar was as strong as he was quick. Don Carlos found himself lurching forward out of his saddle. He hit the ground, bounced to his feet with an incoherent cry of rage, and launched himself at the mounted officer. Cuellar had already freed his booted foot from the stirrup and now planted it in the *haciendero*'s chest, propelling him backward. Don Carlos lost his balance and struck the ground a second time.

The *vaqueros* had never seen their *patrón* treated in such a manner. To a man they put their hands on their pistols.

"Remo!" shouted Chagres.

Cuellar's pistol was drawn and pointed at Remo. "Do not interfere," warned the dragoon.

Remo scanned the grim, weathered features of the *vaqueros*. Most of them were watching him. They were all stunned by this turn of events. Waiting for his signal, as they had done for years. Always before, when Don Carlos had spoken the law, Remo had instructed them on the means of carrying out that law. No one questioned Remo's authority to do this. *I have always been the* patrón's *trusted lieutenant. Always—until now.*

"We will not interfere," Remo told Cuellar.

Cuellar was surprised. This was not at all the response he had expected from the men of Don Carlos Chagres.

But he was no more surprised than Don Carlos himself. Sitting on the ground, Chagres gaped at Remo, slow to accept the fact that he had been betrayed.

"You should not have killed that priest," Remo told him, his tone cold and matter-of-fact and lacking respect.

Cuellar's curt gesture brought a pair of dismounted dragoons forward. They stood over Don Carlos. Chagres got to his feet. The soldiers took him by the arms and relieved him of the handsome matching pistols in his belt. He tried to shake them off, but they held on.

"Put him on his horse," said Cuellar. "Out of respect, Don Carlos, we will not place you in irons. But if you try to escape, I will shoot you myself. I would like your word of honor that you will not put up any resistance."

"You have it." Don Carlos glowered at Remo. "Traitor. *Ladron.* Do you think Hacienda Gavilan will be yours? Do you think you can be rid of me so easily? No court in California would dare convict me. You will answer someday for your treachery. I promise you that."

He still cannot accept the truth, mused Remo, unconcerned by these threats. *He is a dead man. He would be better off trying to escape, so that the captain can kill him. It would save him much humiliation, and he is a very vain and proud man.*

"Señor," said Cuellar, addressing Remo, "you will release the American and return to Hacienda Gavilan at once." He turned to Silas, switching to English. "You are free to go. Your friends are a half day's ride to the north."

A moment later the dragoons were riding west, with Don Carlos Chagres as their prisoner.

"What do we do now, Remo?" asked one of the *vaqueros.*

Remo knew the question was foremost on everyone's mind. These men were like children, in a way. They had never had to take the initiative. Their thinking had always been done for them.

"My loyalty now rests with Sombra Chagres," he said, careful to keep any trace of the smug satisfaction he felt from revealing itself on his stern countenance. "We must rescue her from the Americans."

"But the Americans have been given safe passage by the governor-general himself," said another *vaquero.*

"I ride for Sombra Chagres," snapped Remo. "Who goes with me? Those who do not choose to, may go their own way. Make up your minds! Quickly!"

Only eight of the Gavilan *vaqueros* turned their horses and rode away. That didn't bother Remo. He had expected a few defections.

"Reckon I'll be going, too," said Silas Nall.

In the next instant he was staring down the barrel of Remo's pistol.

"You will come with me."

"But the man said I was free to go."

"The dragoons are gone. You will come with me."

Silas shook his head. "Eben won't trade that girl for me."

"How can you be so sure?"

"Because I wouldn't, were I in his moccasins."

"We will find out," said Remo. "Tomorrow."

Silas knew he had one more day to live.

With the governor-general's guarantee of safe passage in hand, Hugh Falconer permitted the brigade to remain on the tree-cloaked hill the rest of the day. Men and horses all needed rest. Tomorrow would be soon enough to continue north—at a much more leisurely pace. He did not intend to linger long in California even though, with the arrest of Don Carlos Chagres imminent, they were no longer in danger. It was time to go home. Falconer missed the mountains and the high plains. The high country had lost its allure for him with the death of Touches the Moon. But that was no longer the case. He was homesick.

For the first time in over a week the mountain men built fires, cooked venison steaks over the crackling flames, and brewed up some coffee. They were short on such staples as coffee and tobacco, but Oregon Territory was only a fortnight away, and with luck—and some sharp bartering—they would be able to replenish their supplies by trading with the Hudson's Bay people. The trappers of the Hudson's Bay Company had been their keen rivals for many years, but after what they had been through, the mountain men weren't worried about that.

"We're not carrying any traps," said Jenkins, as he and Falconer and Rube Holly sat around a campfire with night closing in around them. They were discussing the kind of welcome they could expect from the Britishers up north. "It ought to be clear as mother's milk to them that we're not trying to horn in on their fixin's."

Falconer agreed. "And remember, they gave Jed Smith a helping hand."

"Well, I for one don't trust them damned limeys," growled Rube Holly.

Jenkins chuckled. "You don't trust anybody, old-timer."

"No, I don't. That's the gospel truth. How d'you reckon I've gotten so long in the tooth and kept my topknot?"

"Pure spite," answered Jenkins.

Early the next morning, as the camp stirred in the pearly hue of dawn, Falconer found Eben Nall sitting against a tree with his leather-bound journal open across his knees.

"Occurs to me," said Falconer, "that your wife stands to inherit a lot of land here in California. Does she want to stay, now that she has nothing more to fear from her father?"

"She's still afraid of him. I told her it was all the same to me if we stayed. Whatever she wants to do. But it's a hard decision for her, and it will take some time."

Falconer had his pipe packed and lit. Sitting on his heels, he puffed and pondered for a while. "You should know, Eben, that pretty soon there'll be a war fought for this country."

"A war?"

"The people here are wary of Americans, and with good reason, if you ask me. We took Texas away from Mexico, and folks here figure we'll try to do likewise with California. And they're probably right. We will. Our people are coming west, like they've done since the first one of them set foot on the eastern shore. They're not going to stop at the mountains. Mountains never stopped them before. Nothing will, until they get to the ocean. They see this land and they'll want it."

He recalled his conversation with Benjamin Bonneville back at the Green River rendezvous. Bonneville had believed that it was the destiny of the United States to possess California, and Falconer had a strong hunch that there were a lot of people who agreed with him.

Eben nodded. "I hadn't thought about that."

"Maybe you should. You're an American, and being married to Sombra and living in that big, fancy hacienda won't change it. When war comes you'll be caught smack-dab in the middle."

"So you think Sombra and I would be better off leaving."

Falconer shrugged.

"I was giving some thought to what you said about raising horses," said Eben. "But the way I see it, the mare is rightfully yours. When I gave you that money pouch it was shy about a hundred dollars in gold, and unless you intend to go all the way to Connecticut to collect from Shagrue, you'll never see it again. So the mare is yours."

"My Shoshone cayuse isn't much to look at," said Falconer, "but I'm right fond of him. You keep the mare."

"But that means you're out a lot of money on my account. I can't accept that."

"I don't care about the money. Got no use for

it, really. Tell you what. If it makes you feel better, I'll take the first foal out of that mare."

"Sure," said Eben, unconvinced. "You won't take it. Everything you've done for me, a whole string of horses wouldn't begin to repay . . ."

But Falconer was no longer listening. Staring south, he rose slowly to his full height and removed the clay pipe from between his clenched teeth.

Eben looked south too—and saw a black clot of riders coming toward them across the amber sea of sunlit grass.

"I can't make them out," he said.

"The *vaqueros*."

"But I thought . . ."

"So did I. But I guess it's not over quite yet."

Chapter 41

Remo called a halt several hundred yards shy of the wooded hill. He could see the mountain men moving among the trees. The smoke of their morning cookfires plumed into the powder-blue sky. How many of them were left? No more than twenty. Remo was aware of the damage ten of the Americans had done to the soldiers in the battle on the outskirts of Monterey. But he did not particularly care how many of his *vaqueros* had to die as long as he got Sombra back. He had no intension of getting himself killed. Not that he wasn't a brave man. But he had too much to live for now.

He turned to Silas Nall. "Get down."

"What are you going to do?" Now that the moment he had been dreading for days was upon him, Silas felt his courage disintegrating.

A pistol materialized in Remo's hand. He aimed it at a spot between the American's eyes.

Silas Nall dismounted.

"Now," said Remo, "walk out in front of us. Go ten paces. Eleven, and I will shoot you. Call out to your brother."

"I'm telling you, Eben won't . . ."

"Do as I tell you."

Silas looked into Remo's dead black eyes and waded through the tall grass ten paces toward the brigade's camp. Cupping his hands around his mouth, he shouted his brother's name.

"Wagh!" exclaimed Rube Holly, standing along-side Eben Nall. "That's yore no-account brother, Eben!"

Eben nodded bleakly. He had not recognized Silas at first. His brother wore the clothes of a poor laborer in place of his buckskins. Eben scanned the mounted men sitting their horses behind Silas. Don Carlos Chagres was not among them.

"I don't see Don Carlos," he told Falconer.

"He's not there."

"What in tarnation is goin' on?" queried Rube Holly, exasperated.

"It's Remo," muttered Eben. "It's got to be."

"Spell it out," said Falconer.

"Remo wants the hacienda for himself," said Eben. "He wants Sombra, too. With Don Carlos out of the way, it's all his for the taking. But there's just one little problem. Without Sombra he can't do it."

"My Gawd," said Rube Holly. "You mean he wants to trade."

Eben studiously avoided the old-timer's one-eye sympathetic gaze.

Guts churning, he knew that at this moment he faced the most difficult decision of his life. He had little doubt what fate lay in store for Silas if he refused to give Sombra up. And, of course, he could not do that. He remembered the dream he'd had, populated by Don Carlos and Sombra and Remo, the latter with a pistol to the head of a kneeling man. In the dream the kneeling man had been him. In reality it was his brother with Remo's pistol to his head. *My own kin*, thought Eben. *My own flesh and blood.* The dream had become a terrible reality.

"I'm going out there," he said.

"What for?" asked Rube. "You know what he wants, and *I* know you ain't gonna do it."

"I've got to try to save my brother's life."

The old-timer grabbed him by the sleeve as he started to turn away. "This time yule get yoreself kilt, sure as shootin'. I cain't let you do it, Eben."

"You can't stop me."

Rube Holly was hurt. "Dammit, Eben. You've been like a son to me . . ."

Eben instantly regretted his tone of voice. "I'm sorry, Rube. But, don't you see, I have to *try*. I know he's not much good, but Silas is still my brother, for better or worse, and I'd have a tough time living with myself if I didn't do everything in my power to save his life."

"Then I'm going with you."

"Rube, stand by Sombra. Please."

Reluctantly, Rube said he would.

Eben collected the Appaloosa mare. He was checking the loads in his pistol and Kentucky rifle when Sombra came to him.

"I've got to go," he said, anticipating her words.

But he had misjudged her. Again. As he had the night he'd gone into Monterey to try to free Hugh Falconer from the presidio.

"I know," she said softly, maintaining a brave front. "That is why I love you, Eben Nall."

He took her in his arms and kissed her. It was a mistake. His resolve began to melt away. He hastily pulled back, climbed into the saddle, and did not look around at her as he rode down to the edge of the woods.

Falconer joined him there, astride his mean-spirited mountain mustang.

"I'm riding with you."

"No. He's my brother . . ."

"He's part of this brigade. That makes him my responsibility."

Eben considered that a weak argument. Silas

had been the one man Falconer had not selected at the rendezvous.

"I've turned my back on a couple of men," continued Falconer, "and it doesn't suit me. I won't do it again."

"I'm not going out there to talk."

Falconer nodded. "Talk would be pointless."

Eben started to tell him that, in his studied opinion, there wasn't a chance in hell of their coming back alive.

But one look at Falconer's expression informed Eben that it wouldn't do any good. Falconer could calculate the odds as well as he, and he was still going to come along.

Stirrup to stirrup they rode out of the trees and across the sun-drenched valley toward the Gavilan *vaqueros*.

"Damned fool," muttered Silas, watching in disbelief as Falconer and his brother came on.

"You see?" asked Remo. "Your brother is not going to let you die, after all."

You don't understand, thought Silas. *Eben is not coming out to rescue me, but to die with me.*

"That makes him a better man than you, doesn't it?" said Remo.

"Yes," said Silas flatly. "He *is* a better man."

Of course, I knew that all along. That's why I envied him so . . .

He started running.

"Eben! Go back!"

Muttering a curse, Remo aimed his pistol at the fleeing American.

Eben kicked the Appaloosa into a leaping gallop. "Silas! Get down!"

Falconer pulled his pistol and fired. The range was still too great for any kind of accuracy, but his bullet struck Remo in the shoulder and ruined his aim. Remo's pistol discharged, but the shot went wide, missing Silas completely.

As Eben reached Silas he leaned in the saddle, reaching out a hand, intending to swing his brother up on the mare behind him.

Falconer steered his mustang in such a way that he placed himself between the Gavilan *vaqueros* and the Nall brothers—just as a dozen of Remo's men fired. Several bullets struck the mustang. Two hit Falconer, one gouging a bloody chunk out of his thigh before plowing into the leather of his saddle. The second hit him squarely in the left arm, inches below the shoulder point, tearing muscle and flesh but missing bone.

Eben had Silas up on the mare and was turning the Appaloosa as Falconer and the mountain mustang went down. Rifles began to speak from the wooded hill. The mountain men, marksmen all, plucked a few *vaqueros* out of their saddles. The rest of the Californios kept shooting from the decks of pivoting, snorting horses. A bullet struck Silas in the back. He slumped forward, his chin striking Eben's shoulder a painful blow, then began to slide sideways off the Appaloosa. Eben tried to reach back and catch him, but it was no use. Silas toppled limply into the tall grass.

Some of the *vaqueros* were swarming around Falconer now. He was their nearest and most vulnerable enemy. But Falconer wasn't nearly as vulnerable as they thought. He came up out of the grass with his rifle spitting flame and death. At this close range the bullet's impact lifted a *vaquero* completely out of his saddle. The man's horse ran out from under him. He hit the ground dead. Another *vaquero* was swept off his horse as Falconer used the empty rifle like a club. The rifle's stock shattered and so did the man's skull. Dropping the rifle, Falconer launched himself at the man's horse as it swept past him. But a third Californio came out of his saddle, the blade of his big bel- duque flashing in the sun. They collided in midair, went down in a tangle. Falconer plunged his Green River knife into the man's chest with such force that he could hear the rib cage crack like brittle twigs. A bullet fired at close range tugged at Falconer's buckskin hunting shirt. He whirled, flipped the bloodied knife, and hurled it at the Gavilan man who had just tried to shoot him in the back. The *vaquero* clutched at the knife, buried to the hilt just below his sternum. Falconer lunged forward with a snarl like a panther's, dragging the dying man off his horse with one hand while clutching the saddle's horn with the other. The horse was on the run, and Falconer had a mo- ment's difficulty as he tried to haul himself into the saddle with one wounded arm. By a supreme effort he got aboard.

Eben checked and turned the Appaloosa as his brother fell. Ignoring the bullets burning the air around him, he bent down in the saddle until his shoulder touched the horn, reaching for Silas, shouting his brother's name above the din of bat- tle. Silas lifted a hand, but he was too weak to lift himself off the ground. His body felt numb and cold. His world was turning black. Before he could come to terms with the fact that he was dying he breathed his last ragged breath.

At that instant Remo's horse plowed into the Appaloosa. The impact almost jarred Eben out of the saddle. As he straightened, Remo lashed out with a knife that looked as long as a cavalry saber from Eben's perspective. It wasn't that long, of course—but it was long enough to slash Eben's chest. The cut wasn't deep, but it hurt like hell. Eben felt rivulets of hot blood on his belly. The only weapon left to him was his own knife. He groped for it, managed somehow to parry Remo's next stroke. The blades clashed. The horses themselves seemed to be locked in mortal combat. The Appaloosa bared her big blunt teeth and drew first blood. The *vaquero's* horse reared suddenly.

Remo had been born around horses, had known how to ride before he could walk, but this time he was caught by surprise. For an instant he had to focus on staying in the saddle, and in that instant he left himself open. Eben drove his knife to the hilt into Remo's side. Remo came out of the saddle then, flipped backward off his pony's haunches, and hit the ground hard, landing on the knife. The tip of the blade ruptured his heart. In one blessedly brief explosion of indescribable pain, Remo died.

Indian war whoops caught Eben's attention. He looked up to see the brigade charging across the valley, rifles and pistols spewing flame and trailing powder smoke. It was the most beautiful sight he had ever seen. Realizing he was in the crossfire, Eben ducked low in the saddle. But the Gavilar *vaqueros* were finished. Remo was dead, along with a dozen of their companions. The devil with the tawny beard had killed four of their friends in a minute's time. The charge of the other mountain men was the last straw.

They turned and ran.

Epilogue

Summer 1839. (Eighteen months later.)

When Eben Nall emerged from the soddy he cast his eyes first in the direction of the corrals. The Appaloosa mare came to the pole gate and whickered at him. There were a dozen other horses in the corrals, as well as a colt, but Eben always sought out the mare first, and the mare always seemed to be watching the soddy in the mornings, waiting for Eben to appear.

After counting the horses, Eben swung his gaze to a black speck moving across the sun-browned plains, way off on the other side of the Platte River. The morning sun turned the river's shallows into ribbons of sparkling silver. It was going to be a hot summer day. A dry breeze made the gray-green limbs of the cottonwood trees along the river and over by the corrals flicker and dance.

Eben stepped back inside and fetched his Sharps rifle from the pegs over the hearth. He tried to get away with it without Sombra noticing, not wanting to alarm her unduly, but she saw him, and her eyes asked a silent question.

"Rider coming." He said it casually, as though he expected no trouble to come of it. But out here on the lonesome, windswept vastness of the high plains you just never could be sure. A man had to be careful.

The baby in the crib was stirring, making cooing

sounds that never failed to tug at Eben's heart-strings. He smiled. *I'll be right glad when my son is old enough to help me take care of this place, look after things, and look after his mother most of all.*

Eben stepped back outside and watched the rider coming on. There was something familiar about the man. Eben decided he knew the rider, even before the man was close enough to identify.

When the horseman was, finally, close enough to recognize, Eben Nall grinned ear to ear, leaned his Sharps against the wall of the soddy, and went out to meet him. He waited on the southern bank of the Platte as Hugh Falconer guided his mustang across the shallows.

"I'm glad to see you're still above snakes, Hugh," said Eben, reaching up a hand.

Falconer shook the proffered hand. Eben noticed his grip was still like a steel vise. The man hadn't changed. Same tawny beard, same lean, whiplash frame encased in fringed and beaded buckskin, same steely gaze. Some things, decided Eben, like the mountains and the sky and Hugh Falconer, always stayed the same.

"How's Sombra?" asked Falconer.

"She's fine. I've got somebody else I'd like for you to meet."

Eben took him inside and introduced him to his son. "We named him Reuben."

Falconer smiled as he picked the gurgling infant boy up to hold him aloft. Eben thought he saw a twinge of sadness on the mountain man's face. He didn't think it was because Rube Holly was dead, but rather a deep-seated regret on Falconer's part that he and Touches the Moon had never had children.

"Rube would be right proud," said Falconer.

"Heard anything about Luck?"

Falconer shook his head. "I checked at Fort

Bridger, but nobody there has seen her. And she's not back with her own people, either."

Eben sighed. He was worried about Luck and disappointed that Falconer had not found a trace of her. If Hugh Falconer couldn't find her, nobody could. Rube Holly had died in his sleep six months ago, and his death had hit Luck really hard. It seemed that she had disappeared off the face of the earth, and Eben was afraid, that having lost the will to live, she had wandered off to die alone.

They went out to the corrals, and Eben pointed to the spindly-legged colt nuzzling the Appaloosa mare.

"There's your horse," he said.

Falconer declared the colt a fine-looking animal. "Had any trouble with Indians?"

"They've tried to steal my ponies a time or two," said Eben. "A couple of 'em are buried behind that hill yonder. Pawnees, I think."

"But nothing you can't handle."

Eben smiled. "No." He looked at the horses again. "In a couple of years I'll start selling off a few head."

"They'll fetch a handsome price," predicted Falconer. "Whatever happened to that journal you were writing, Eben?"

"I sold it."

"Sold it? To who?"

"One day a man showed up at my door. Said he was from a publishing house back east. Wanted to publish my journal. Offered me a lot of money and, well, I needed funds. I had Sombra to think of, and she had just told me she was pregnant with little Reuben."

"Now I wonder how this easterner found out about your journal."

"Captain Bonneville, of course. He talked to just

about every last one of us who came back from California. I didn't tell him about the journal, but I reckon somebody else did."

Falconer nodded. "He must have guessed you weren't about to sell it to him. But he wanted to know what was in it. Anything of use to him concerning California."

"Sorry, Hugh."

"Don't worry about it. In the long run it won't change anything."

Eben agreed, and took some consolation in knowing that, journal or no, Bonneville and men like him were committed to seizing California and would make an attempt to do so sooner or later.

Falconer stayed for the noontime meal. Afterward, he packed his clay pipe with honeydew tobacco as he and Eben stood in a ribbon of shade against the soddy's front wall. Eben invited him to stay for a few days, but Falconer declined. He did not offer any information regarding where he had been or where he was going. Eben desperately wanted to know these things, but knew better than to ask. Every few months Hugh Falconer swung by to check on him and Sombra, stayed a few hours, then moved on. Eben was grateful for that. Falconer wasn't the only one—last spring Gus Jenkins and Taggart had showed up at his door. Like Falconer, they seemed to be drifting aimlessly now that the fur trade was dead, looking for something, a purpose in life beyond just living, perhaps. Eben felt fortunate indeed to have a home, a family, and a dream.

They stood there in the shade for a long spell, not talking much, and finally Falconer stirred himself, knocking the spent tobacco out of the pipe bowl and grinding it into the dust beneath his heel.

"I'll be back next spring for the colt," he told Eben.

"You'd better. I like to pay my debts."

Falconer climbed aboard the mustang. The horse, mused Eben, looked every inch as mean as the one Falconer had ridden on the expedition to California. It also looked like it could run all week and then twice on Sunday.

"You don't owe me anything," said Falconer. "Fact is, I owe you."

"How do you figure?" asked Eben.

"Before we went to California I'd decided I couldn't trust another living soul. You and Gus and Rube and Taggart and all the rest proved me wrong."

Eben saw the opening he had been waiting for. "But you're still searching for something, aren't you?"

"Sure." Falconer took a long look around, at the soddy, the corrals, the murmuring river. "A reason to put down roots, and a place like this to do it."

"You'll find a reason. Because you deserve it."

Falconer smiled pensively. "Well, a man can dream, can't he?"

He turned the mustang sharply, splashed across the shallows, and was soon just a black dot in the vastness of the plains. Eben Nall watched him until he was out of sight. Sombra came out of the soddy, the baby in her arms. Eben put his arm around her and thanked his lucky stars, like he did every morning when he woke up with her by his side.

Falconer never once looked back. Eben hadn't expected him to. Hugh Falconer wasn't that kind.

Read all of
Jason Manning's
Historical novels of the
American frontier!

High Country

Zach Hannah was a raw youth when he left the hill country of Tennessee to seek his fortune in the West. In the year 1825, the distant Rockies offered all the wealth a man could want. The mad demand for beaver pelts spawned a booming fur trade that sent men to battle against the fury of nature, hostile Indian tribes, and even each other in an adventure that only the strongest could survive. Zach Hannah took the challenge . . . to learn the ways of the wild and those who lived in it . . . to discover that white treachery could be as deadly as Blackfoot terror . . . to find passionate love with a beautiful Indian woman—and to fight to the death to protect her . . .

Green River Rendezvous

Zach Hannah was a legend of courage, skill, and strength, even among his fellow mountain men. To the Crow Indians he was a favored friend, to the Blackfeet he was a hated foe, to former friend Sean Devlin he was a rival to be destroyed, and to the American Fur Company he stood tall in the way of its scheme to rob the Rockies of their fabulous wealth in pelts. With his beloved wife, Morning Sky, at his side, a hard-bitten team under his command, a Hawken rifle and a hunting knife in his hands, and treacherous enemies shadowing his every move, Zach Hannah faced the most deadly native tribe in the West and the most brutal brigade of trappers ever to make the high country a killing ground . . .

Battle of the Teton Basin

All Zach Hannah wanted was to be left alone, high in the mountains, with his Indian bride. But as long as Sean Michael Devlin lived, Zach could find no peace. Now, Zach had to track down this man—the former friend who stole his wife and left him to die at the hands of the Blackfeet. It was an odyssey of vengeance that led him from the Yellowstone to St. Louis along the Santa Fe Trail, then back to the high country—where the mountains echoed with the gunfire and blood cries of a cataclysmic war. As mountain men and Blackfoot braves clashed in an epic battle that would change the course of history in the American West, Zach and Devlin squared off in a final reckoning that only one of them would survive.

Flintlock

In 1806, the ambitious and charismatic Aaron Burr was plotting treason against the United States. Ruined as a politician, he devised a scandalous plan to carve his own private empire out of the heart of the young republic and detach the western states from the Union.

President Thomas Jefferson suspected Burr, but he needed evidence. Surrounded by political enemies, he turned to Nathaniel "Flintlock" Jones, a legendary Kentucky frontiersman and peerless marksman. Enlisting the help of young naval officer Lieutenant Jonathan Groves, Jones embarked on a suicide mission of epic proportions as he pursued Burr and his army of ruffians across the dark and bloody ground of Kentucky and down the deadly Natchez Trace. But before the two patriots could stop Burr, Flintlock had to face a ghost from his past whose personal mission was to destroy the United States.

The Border Captains

The fledgling United States had survived the Revolutionary War. And with the turn of the new century, settlers were poised to continue their westward thrust through the dark and bloody killing grounds of Kentucky. But in their path stood the might of the British military, as well as an even more menacing and worthy foe—the brilliant, brave, and legendary Native American chief Tecumseh.

The War of 1812 was about to begin. And in the hands of such American heroes as "Mad Anthony" Wayne, William Henry Harrison, Henry Clay, and Daniel Boone ... with the trigger fingers of a buckskin-clad army ... and in the courage, daring, and determination of frontiersman Flintlock Jones ... history was to be made, a wilderness was to be won, and a spellbinding saga of the American past was to be brought to unforgettable, pulse-pounding life ...

Gone to Texas

In 1834, when President Andrew Jackson decided it was time for Texas to gain its independence from Mexico, he called upon Flintlock Jones and his grandson Christopher Groves. The pair couldn't wait to get into the action, but they got more than they bargained for when kidnappers, river pirates, cutthroats, and bounty hunters lay in wait for them on a blood-soaked trail from Kentucky to hostile Texas territory. It was grizzled old Flintlock's most dangerous mission, as revolutionaries and their enemies fought each other with a passion that blazed hotter than the Texas sun.

Gone to Texas is the gripping conclusion to the epic Flintlock trilogy.

① SIGNET

SAGAS OF THE AMERICAN WEST
BY JASON MANNING

☐ **GONE TO TEXAS** When Flintlock Jones and his grandson Christoph Groves come to the aid of President Andrew Jackson to aid Texas gaining its independence from Mexico, the pair get more than th bargained for as kidnappers, river pirates, cutthroats, and bounty hun ers lay in wait for them on a blood-soaked trail from Kentucky to host Texas territory. (185005—$4.5

☐ **GREEN RIVER RENDEZVOUS** Zach Hannah was a legend of courage, ski and strength ... Now he faces the most deadly native tribe in the we and the most brutal brigade of trappers ever to make the high count a killing ground. (177142—$4.5

☐ **BATTLE OF THE TETON BASIN** Zach Hannah wants to be left alone, hi in the mountains, with his Indian bride. But as long as Sean Micha Devlin lives, Zach can find no peace. Zach must track down this man the former friend who stole his wife and left him to die at the han of the Blackfeet. Zach and Devlin square off in a final reckoning . that only one of them will survive. (178297—$4.5

*Prices slightly higher in Canada

Buy them at your local bookstore or use this convenient coupon for ordering.

PENGUIN USA
P.O. Box 999 — Dept. #17109
Bergenfield, New Jersey 07621

Please send me the books I have checked above.
I am enclosing $_____ (please add $2.00 to cover postage and handling). S check or money order (no cash or C.O.D.'s) or charge by Mastercard or VISA (with a $15 minimum). Prices and numbers are subject to change without notice.

Card #_____ Exp. Date _____
Signature_____
Name_____
Address_____
City _____ State _____ Zip Code _____

For faster service when ordering by credit card call **1-800-253-6476**

Allow a minimum of 4-6 weeks for delivery. This offer is subject to change without notice.

SIGNET   ⬤ ONYX   (0451)

RIVETING AMERICAN SAGAS

TRUE GRIT by Charles Portis. On the trail of a stone-cold killer, deep in Indian territory, a cantankerous kid bent on revenge, a bounty-hunting Texas Ranger, and the legendary, one-eyed U.S. marshal Rooster J. Cogburn, follows a fugitive into a place where the only survivors will be those with true grit.   (185455—$5.50)

CONQUERING HORSE by Frederick Manfred. A magnificent saga of the West—before the white man came. "Offers deep insight into the mind of the Indian . . . as exciting and rewarding and dramatic as the country it describes."—*Chicago Tribune*   (087399—$4.50)

FRANKLIN'S CROSSING by Clay Reynolds. This is the searing and sweeping epic of America's historic passage west. "Gritty realism on the 1870s Texas frontier . . . expertly crafted, very moving . . . this is the way it must have been . . . lingers in the memory long after the last page has been turned."—*Dallas Morning News*
                                         (175549—$5.99)

Price slightly higher in Canada

Buy them at your local bookstore or use this convenient coupon for ordering.

PENGUIN USA
P.O. Box 999 — Dept. #17109
Bergenfield, New Jersey 07621

Please send me the books I have checked above.
I am enclosing $_____ (please add $2.00 to cover postage and handling). Send check or money order (no cash or C.O.D.'s) or charge by Mastercard or VISA (with a $15.00 minimum). Prices and numbers are subject to change without notice.

Card #_____ Exp. Date _____
Signature_____
Name_____
Address_____
City _____ State _____ Zip Code _____

For faster service when ordering by credit card call **1-800-253-6476**

Allow a minimum of 4-6 weeks for delivery. This offer is subject to change without notice.

TRINITY STRIKE
BY SUZANN LEDBETTER

From the heart of Ireland comes the irrepressible Meg
O'Malley, whose own spirit mirrors that of the untam
frontier. With nothing to her name but fierce determi
tion, Megan defies convention and sets out to strike it ri
taking any job—from elevator operator to camp cook–
get out west and become a prospector. In a few sh
months, she has her very own stake in the Trinity min
and the attention of more than a few gun-slinging band
But shrewd, unscrupulous enemies are lurking, waiting
steal her land—and any kind of courtship must wait. .

from Signet

Prices slightly higher in Canada.   (0-451-18644-3—$

Buy them at your local bookstore or use this convenient coupon for ordering.

PENGUIN USA
P.O. Box 999 — Dept. #17109
Bergenfield, New Jersey 07621

Please send me the books I have checked above.
I am enclosing $_____ (please add $2.00 to cover postage and handling).
check or money order (no cash or C.O.D.'s) or charge by Mastercard or VISA (with a $
minimum). Prices and numbers are subject to change without notice.

Card #_____ Exp. Date _____
Signature_____
Name_____
Address_____
City _____ State _____ Zip Code _____

For faster service when ordering by credit card call 1-800-253-6476
Allow a minimum of 4-6 weeks for delivery. This offer is subject to change without notice.

DESERT HAWKS
BY FRANK BURLESON

 e year was 1846—and the great American Southwest was the prize
 an epic conflict. The U.S. Army and the army of Mexico met in a
 ttle that would shape the course of history, while the legendary
 ache warrior chief Mangus Coloradas looked on, determined to defend
 s ancestral lands and age-old tribal traditions against either of the
 vaders or both. On this bloody battlefield young Lieutenant Nathanial
 rrington faced his first great test of manhood . . . as he began a
 reer that would take him to the heart of the conflict sweeping over the
 st from Texas to New Mexico . . . and plunge him into passion that would
 ce him to choose between two very different frontier beauties. This en-
 ralling first novel of *The Apache Wars* trilogy captures the drama and
 al history of a struggle in which no side wanted to surrender . . . in a
 ries alive with all the excitement, adventure of brave men and women—
 ite and Native American—who decided the future of America.

from **SIGNET**

Prices slightly higher in Canada.   (0-451-18089-5—$4.50)

Buy them at your local bookstore or use this convenient coupon for ordering.

PENGUIN USA
P.O. Box 999 — Dept. #17109
Bergenfield, New Jersey 07621

Please send me the books I have checked above.
I am enclosing $_____ (please add $2.00 to cover postage and handling). Send
check or money order (no cash or C.O.D.'s) or charge by Mastercard or VISA (with a $15.00
minimum). Prices and numbers are subject to change without notice.

Card #_____ Exp. Date _____
Signature_____
Name_____
Address_____
City _____ State _____ Zip Code _____

For faster service when ordering by credit card call **1-800-253-6476**

Allow a minimum of 4-6 weeks for delivery. This offer is subject to change without notice.

COYOTE RUN
BY DON BENDELL

On one side stood the legendary Chief of Scouts, Chris Colt, wi
his hair-trigger tempered, half brother Joshua, and the pro
young Indian brave, Man Killer. On the other side was a mini
company that would do anything and kill anyone to take ov
Coyote Run, the ranch that the Colts had carved out of t
Sangre Cristo Mountains, with their sweat and their blood. Th
battle would flame amid the thunder of a cattle drive, the tum
of a dramatic courtroom trial, the howling of a lynch mob, a
a struggle for an entire town. And as the savagery mounted, t
stakes rose higher and higher, and every weapon from gun a
knife to a brave lawyer's eloquent tongue and the strength a
spirit of two beautiful women came into powerful play.

from SIGNET

Prices slightly higher in Canada.   (0-451-18143-3—$4.

Buy them at your local bookstore or use this convenient coupon for ordering.

PENGUIN USA
P.O. Box 999 — Dept. #17109
Bergenfield, New Jersey 07621

Please send me the books I have checked above.
I am enclosing $_____ (please add $2.00 to cover postage and handling). S
check or money order (no cash or C.O.D.'s) or charge by Mastercard or VISA (with a $1
minimum). Prices and numbers are subject to change without notice.

Card #_____ Exp. Date _____
Signature_____
Name_____
Address_____
City _____ State _____ Zip Code _____

For faster service when ordering by credit card call **1-800-253-6476**

Allow a minimum of 4-6 weeks for delivery. This offer is subject to change without notice.